To my mother, Alice Gordon Cooke,
for all the stories she read to me.

The Sanctuary

LORIN

THE TARNSEA

CHELM

Khymer

ISHAR

Laenar

CAERLIN

MAER
CUNIN

AHN

CAVERNON
CITY

Erinon

Cavernon
Bay

SYRYN

THE KINGDOMS

Chapter One _____

"**I**'M very sorry, sir," said the liveried servant boy, barring the entrance to the royal chambers. He looked for aid toward the two impassive S'tari guardsmen who stood ignoring him on either side of the richly curtained archway. "The Earl of Laenar has commanded that he is not to be disturbed. By anyone."

"He can damn well make an exception." Kyellan shouldered the slight youngster aside and stalked into the luxurious anteroom. One of the guards, whom Kyellan had trained, stepped out to prevent the servant from following him. The boy protested loudly. He must be new at his post, Kyellan thought. Most of the denizens of the Tiranon palace knew him at least by sight: a tall, black-haired man with gold-flecked eyes and a right arm that hung useless in a leather sling. If they knew nothing else, they knew not to cross him. His temper was uncertain at the best of times, and today had not been pleasant.

"Tobas!" he called. "Where are you?" A monkey screeched at him from a filigree wooden stand. The room was hung with rich curtains and strewn with cushions that overflowed from soft couches. Bright, new tapestries glowed in alcoves, replacing the ancient heirlooms of the Ardavan line that had been destroyed by the wizards. It smelled overwhelmingly of the young Queen's perfume. Probably to mask the scent of monkey, Kyellan thought sourly. "Tobas!" he shouted.

The royal suite was built around an open courtyard. Kyellan pushed open a door and stepped outside. Colored fountains splashed mists of blue and purple spray into the air of a garden so artfully trimmed and arranged it did not look real. The riot of flowers that had covered the pathways was gone now that it was autumn, leaving a uniform muted green. Yet there was a cluster of bright colors left.

Three of Valahtia's highborn maidens sat together on a bench working halfheartedly at embroidery. Their sheer veils proclaimed them to be virgins seeking marriage, and their purple headscarves showed they were under the Queen's protection, and members of her household.

"Have you seen the Royal Consort?" Kyellan asked. They looked up, pretending to be startled, though they had certainly heard him shouting in the outer room.

"He's in the map room with Senomar and Istam," said the boldest of the three. "Those filthy old men. He said not to bother him. Are you coming to the feast tonight, Captain Kyellan? Her Majesty said there would be games and dancing."

"Perhaps. Excuse me, ladies." He made a sketchy bow and left them to their boredom. Tobas had apparently forgotten that he had asked Kyellan to report to him this afternoon. Tobas had a poor memory lately. For six months now he had ignored Kyellan and Gwydion's continual requests for permission to leave Caerlin for the North. He kept thinking of new reasons why he could not spare them yet. He was behaving more like a tyrant than an old friend, and Kyellan was weary of it.

The map room had been a gardeners' storeroom when Chaeris Ardavan was King. Queen Valahtia had given it to her consort as a place where he could meet with his informal group of advisors. Kyellan knocked on the door with his left hand. "Go away!" a young voice called from within. Kyellan turned the latch clumsily. He was learning to fight well enough with a left-handed sword, but his fingers were still awkward at tasks like counting out coins and lacing his boots.

Tobas rose from his chair in the small room, knocking a chart to the floor from the table. "I thought I said . . . oh, it's you, Kyellan. That's right. I sent orders for you to report to me personally once the questioning was over. Did the Redeemer spy have anything to say?" He ran a hand through his short, curly hair, and a ruby ring Valahtia had given him glinted against the brown.

The two white-bearded advisors looked up curiously. Kyellan nodded to them and glared at Tobas. "Nothing of any use. I spent the afternoon smelling sweat and fear and listening to the man's screams, and all I learned is that Valahtia's brother Arel is trying to hire more mercenaries. I could have heard that in any wineshop in Rahan Quarter."

"Nothing about the new fortress Arel is building on Syryn?" Tobas said worriedly. "The Prince is sure to move against us. But when?"

"He can't have enough men yet," Senomar said. The gaunt-framed old man was a battle engineer and expert on siege machines, who was helping with the repairs to the fortifications of Cavernon City. "Captain Kyellan has convinced most of the mercenaries to enlist in the Caerlin army."

"And the other Kingdoms are still working to heal themselves after the wizards' occupation," Istam said. "Even if their rulers support Prince Arel's claim, they can spare no one to send to his aid." One of his dark eyes peered at them from a fold of flesh. The corpulent advisor had been a Nyesin priest until his sun-god had failed him by refusing to appear to fight the wizards. He was an astronomer and a poet, and Tobas valued him for his insight.

"Many of their soldiers fought under my command against the wizards," Tobas said. "They might refuse to attack me. Kyellan, we should send spies to find out the mood of the armies of Parahn and Keris and Ryasa. Find some good men for me."

"Find them yourself," Kyellan said quietly. "I've done enough. The S'tari treaty troops are trained, the mercenaries are hired. I've briefed and equipped and questioned spies. All of that could have been done by any competent officer."

"There aren't any other Caer officers left," Tobas said. "We need you."

"I've spoken to Gwydion. We've agreed you'll get no

more help from either of us. You've delayed our journey too long, Tobas.''

"Even if I wanted to let you go, Valahtia would still refuse," the young Earl said in frustration. "Arel's spies know by now that she's five months pregnant. She's afraid he'll attack soon, to prevent our son from being born.''

"He doesn't have the men," Kyellan said.

"You're needed here," Tobas repeated. "Not wandering around Garith searching for something you aren't even sure is there.''

"There is nothing for me here," Kyellan said. He thought of the priestess who carried his child, who hid from the world in guarded seclusion in two high tower rooms of the palace. Briana would not reply to his messages, would not acknowledge his existence. "Nothing, Tobas." He turned without a bow or a word of courtesy and strode from the royal chambers.

The throne room was decorated for the feast with tall wooden trees of candles that reached nearly to the high-beamed ceiling. The jewel inlays of Valahtia's huge throne and the ornaments of her courtiers sparkled gaily in the warm light. Kyellan glowered from a corner at the bright young Queen. Her raven hair was caught in elaborate sweeps at either side of her face, framing its animation as she chattered with Tobas in the smaller throne to her left. A russet velvet gown, simply cut, showed her round abdomen, but her body was still breathtaking. Kyellan had once been willing to grant her anything she wished. He had long since tired of that. She had turned twenty years old a month before, and still she sometimes behaved like a spoiled child. She trusted Kyellan to protect her. So she had given orders that no ship's master was to accept him as a passenger, and he was forbidden to leave Caerlin. Gwydion was included in those orders. She valued the young wizard's advice, although Gwydion was intensely disliked by her court.

"You're supposed to be enjoying yourself," a woman's voice said in the accent of the poorest underclasses of Cavernon City. Kyellan looked behind him. Alaira moved out of a pool of shadow into the candlelight. She wore a dress of fitted red brocade, and clear jewels glowed at her ears and around her neck. Her short, straight black hair swung across her thin face, partly obscuring the long scar that ran from her nose to her jawline.

"I don't like these affairs any more than you do," he said. "And I'm not very good at pretending."

Alaira grinned up at him. "We're both as out of place here as your pretty Queen would be on the Thieves' Highroad of Rahan."

"She isn't my Queen," Kyellan muttered.

"No? I thought you boasted to me once that she'd granted you more favors than just a medal for heroism." Her sharp dark eyes were mocking. She was his oldest friend, and they had often been lovers. He could not keep anything from her.

"That was before she was Queen," Kyellan said grudgingly.

"And before you met Briana. I know." Her voice was low, and would not carry in the crowded hall, but still the priestess's name startled him.

"Don't say that where anyone can hear. She's going to be First Priestess." He had never been so foolish about a woman before. It had been more than six months since he had last seen Briana. At their last meeting, she had said it would be best if they never saw one another again. It was likely they never would, yet he could not forget her. She was a priestess of the Temple of the Goddess, and would soon be head of her Order. She was Alaira's age, twenty-one years old, and she too was a dancer, with thick auburn hair and sea-green eyes. She had said she loved him, but she was not willing to give up the Goddess and her priestesshood to be with him.

"Don't worry. I'll keep your secret." She laughed.

"Have you seen Gwydion and Chela? They were supposed to be here tonight. I didn't see them at the tables."

"They're in the garden." Alaira waved toward an arched portal with drawn curtains that led to one of the Tiranon's public gardens. "Chela wanted to dance, but Gwydion doesn't like parties much."

Kyellan nodded. The young landless nobles of Valahtia's court were especially hostile toward the wizard. Gwydion had been insulted to his face at the last gathering like this. Valahtia continued to invite him to her parties to show the court her regard for him, and he had no choice but to accept. Gwydion had fought with the alliance against the invaders, but the people of Caerlin made no distinctions in their hatred of all wizards.

A consort of lutes and viols began a lively dance tune from a platform near the throne. The gathering separated into fluid groups of dancers, merrymakers, and intriguers. Nobles and ladies, ambassadors and officials eddied through the room. Candlelight glinted on embroidered surcoats and headdresses. A large party of young noblemen in pastel costumes escorted a few of Valahtia's veiled maidens out the archways into the garden. From the sound, they were very drunk. The Queen stepped down from the throne on the arm of her handsome consort to join the dance.

"If you were waiting to talk to her," Alaira said, "you'll have to wait until she's tired."

He had meant to approach her again about the journey. "Come." He took Alaira's arm. "Let's escape this noise and find our friends."

A cool night breeze rustled the curtains as they passed into the garden. A half moon glowed behind thin clouds, and veiled lamps hung from the branches of the trees and reflected in the little stone-lined pools. The towers and minarets of Cavernon City were darker shadows against the clouds, but the streets of Rahan Quarter were far out of sight to the southeast.

"It's almost winter." Alaira shivered a little. Kyellan put his arm around her and found a marble bench where they could sit beside one of the pools. The laughter and shouting of the young courtiers faded ahead of them on the cobbled path. "If we don't leave on this great journey of yours soon, we won't be able to go until spring."

"Do you still want to go? After living here in the Tiranon? Half the voyage we'll be cramped on shipboard, and from the Garithian coast it's still nearly two weeks journey overland to Akesh. We don't even know if the Wizards' College will still be there. The wizards might have destroyed it before beginning their invasion."

"And if it is there, you can't be sure of finding out how to heal your arm." Alaira reached across his chest to touch the leather sling. "I know. You've said it before."

Kyellan looked down at her coarse black hair as she leaned her head on his shoulder. He had tried to explain to Alaira what he wanted to find at Akesh, but she did not really understand. She had the vague idea that he had learned some magic from Gwydion, and that if he learned more he might be able to heal his useless right arm. It would take more than healing magic. The muscles and nerves in his shoulder had been severed with the blow that had almost killed him in the final battle against the Shape-Changer Onedon.

He did not remember that time very clearly. He had learned that Onedon was his father, and that he was also a Shape-Changer and a wizard. He had almost joined with Onedon against his friends. The wizard part of him was ambitious, power-seeking, dangerous. Briana had brought him back to himself. Her love had been strong enough to bring him back. He never wanted to allow the Shape-Changer to gain control of him again. But if he intended to regain the use of his sword arm, he would have to learn to control his wizard Power.

The Shape-Changer was deeply buried now. The only traces of it were the flecks of gold in his dark brown eyes, and the hope that somewhere in the ancient libraries of the Wizards' College he could find a way to control the thing. Turn it to his own purposes, without succumbing to it.

"You don't have to go," he said again.

"I won't be any trouble." She looked up at him, wide-eyed. "Please don't leave me behind, Ky. What could I do here? I want to go with you."

"Valahtia would find you a job in the palace."

She shook her head, her black hair falling across her eyes. "I'm getting tired of all this luxury."

"So am I." He smiled. "We'll go together, then. If the Queen ever relents."

A high scream shrilled through the peaceful garden, followed by shouts and cries of anger. The music from inside the palace danced on gracefully. Kyellan leaped to his feet, his hand going reflexively to his sword hilt. It was not there. He had gone unarmed to the feast, except for the slim, jeweled dagger with which he had eaten. He drew that.

"What is it?" Alaira ran after him down the path.

"I don't know." The lamplight made the stones seem to

glow, white and polished and slippery to run on. The shouts
led them up a slope, past an artificial waterfall, toward the
tracery of branches at the edge of a grove of leafless trees.

"Stop it!" a young voice shrieked. It was Chela's, Kyellan
realized as he drew near. "You've hurt him!"

"Coward!" a slurred and drunken falsetto yelled. "I lost a
brother to cursed wizards' fire on the Cavernon City walls.
Don't you have any magic? Defend yourself, or I'll kill
you!"

In the center of the manicured lawn within the grove,
Gwydion stood white-faced in a circle of drunken youths. The
wizard's golden hair caught the lamplight, and his slit-pupilled
cat's eyes glowed in the night. One of his thin, gloved hands
clutched the silk of his right sleeve, which was slowly seep-
ing blood. Five pastel noblemen had drawn daggers to press
in on him, while two others held Chela to keep her from
interfering. The Garithian girl twisted wildly in their arms,
still shouting. Her long red hair had come loose from its
upswept court style. Five of Valahtia's maidens and ten more
young nobles stood watching in uneasy fascination.

"Don't be foolish," Gwydion said in a low, strained voice.
"I have no quarrel with you. You're drunk, or you'd realize
that."

"Your wizard friend isn't very experienced in barroom
fights," Alaira said at Kyellan's elbow. "That's the quickest
way to anger an opponent."

"Drunk, am I?" shrilled the youth who had spoken before.
He had long, wavy black hair, and was surely younger than
Gwydion's eighteen years. "I'll show you how drunk I am!"
He lunged inward with his knife hand. Gwydion twisted away
from the blade, but another courtier moved in and he scarcely
avoided a cut across the ribs.

Kyellan caught the jeweled collar of one of the five circling
youths. He jerked him backward and threw him to the ground
with a force that knocked the breath from him. "Bring the
guards!" he shouted to Alaira. She turned and ran back
toward the throne room.

The other four youths paused to look in his direction.
Gwydion edged away slowly. The leader of the circle waved

the others back toward the wizard and shouted at Kyellan, "Keep out of this! It has nothing to do with you!"

He wore a sky-blue tunic with the device of one of Cavernon City's oldest families worked across the chest in red. Kyellan measured his skill at a glance. The boy was undoubtedly fast; he had probably picked up some street fighting in the taverns of Rahan. But even if he had not been drunk, he would have posed no challenge to a one-armed captain of the Royal Guard.

"Stop them, Kyellan, they're going to kill him," Chela said fiercely. The slim fourteen-year-old began a soft chant in some wizards' language. Kyellan hoped she was devising a spell of protection for Gwydion. The wizard had lost his own Power before the last battle in the war, and he had apparently lost his dagger tonight. Three of the pastel youths still darted in and out with their knives, trying to draw blood. Gwydion had no defense.

The blue-clad youth facing him seemed to recognize his name even in his drunken state. The glitter of his slim blade wavered as the hand holding it began to shake. With a soft laugh, Kyellan swept his own dagger in an arc under the boy's guard. The point split a thin line across the embroidered family crest, not touching skin. The youth leaped backward, afraid but still stubborn. They circled each other warily. Kyellan turned to where he could see Gwydion.

Bright green sparks suddenly flared around the wizard, as if the blaze of his golden hair had ignited. One of his tormentors was flung backward with the force of his lunge toward Gwydion's ribs. The youth landed unconscious beneath a tree. Lamplight shone down on his slack face. The other two pastel nobles turned and ran with cries of horror from this display of the feared wizard magic. The young men holding Chela let her go and faded back into the awestruck crowd.

"Don't hurt him!" Gwydion called.

Kyellan shrugged and smiled at his opponent. The youth stood his ground with drunken bravado. Kyellan kicked out savagely at the boy's dagger hand and sent the knife spinning away through the air. He closed his fist around his own dagger and smashed it hiltfirst into the boy's jaw. The sky-

blue youth fell, and sat there unhappily with blood dripping
from a cut on his ear.

There was a clatter of steel being drawn, and six S'tari
guardsmen followed Alaira into the circle with their scimitars
held ready. Their dark faces were set in fierce lines, but when
they saw what had happened they sheathed their weapons.
Their leader saluted Kyellan, and spoke in S'tari. "I see you
didn't need our help, Captain. Shall we clear away this
refuse?"

Kyellan nodded. "The ones on the ground are the ones you
want." The S'tari picked up the three downed youths and
pinioned their arms behind them. The boy who had been hit
by the magical defensive field still glowed faintly green. That
was the color of Chela's magic, though the nobles probably
thought it had been Gwydion's doing.

Alaira laughed up at Kyellan. "That didn't take you long.
The courtiers will be disappointed. Half of them followed us
to see a wizard get killed." Kyellan could hear that she was
right; a lively, chattering crowd was spilling down the pathways toward the grove.

Chela pulled up Gwydion's sleeve to examine the slash on
his forearm. "I'm all right," Gwydion said shakily. "No
harm done."

"No harm?" The Queen strode into the circle with two
more S'tari guards beside her and Tobas at her heels. "A
guest attacked in my garden? For no reason?"

"He's a Goddess-forsaken wizard," said the blue-clad youth,
struggling in the grip of his guards. "That's reason enough.
They've already killed them everywhere else."

"It's time we were free of them, indeed," an old man said
from the press behind the Queen.

"Take them away for questioning," Valahtia said furiously. "They may be Redeemer spies, sent by Arel to kill
one of my most trusted advisors."

The leader managed to straighten as he was dragged from
the circle. "Your Majesty, we are no spies! We are true and
loyal Caer noblemen. My father was the Cavernon City overlord before the wizards came! I'm of the House of the City.
You can't do this!"

Valahtia deliberately turned her back on him. The guards

pulled the three youths down an avenue that opened in the crowd, which seemed delighted by the scandal. "Is he who he says he is?" Valahtia said when the prisoners were gone.

Tobas nodded. "I believe so. And he's caused trouble before."

"How deep is that cut?" Kyellan asked at Gwydion's side. "We should try to find the blade."

"It doesn't seem to be poisoned, if that's what you're afraid of," Chela said, pulling the edges of the wound apart to examine it more closely.

Gwydion put his unhurt arm around her. "That wouldn't have mattered if the last blow had landed. Luckily Chela was able to shield me." He ran a hand through her piled red hair, mussing it further. "There'll be a backlash, love. You'd better go lie down."

"I'm all right," she insisted, though her face was unusually pale. "Just a little faint."

Now that it was over, Kyellan felt angry. He turned to Gwydion. "If you don't have the Power to defend yourself, you're foolish to go out unarmed."

"I had a dagger. I dropped it when I got this cut. Besides, I didn't think I'd have to be ready for a battle at a feast." He bowed to the Queen and Tobas. "Your Majesty, Royal Consort, if you'll excuse me, I'm going to get Chela to bed." They walked slowly away, headed for the distant wing of the palace where their quarters were.

"He didn't even thank you for rescuing him," Alaira said indignantly. She was flushed from the exertion of her run.

"He doesn't like to feel helpless," Kyellan said. "But he is, and he will be until we get to Akesh and find a way to get his Power back."

Valahtia shook her head firmly. "You aren't going."

Kyellan met her dark eyes wearily. "Your Majesty, this isn't the first time Gwydion has been harassed. Your subjects aren't very happy with your amnesty orders for the remaining wizards in Caerlin. Gwydion is a convenient focus for their hate."

Tobas moved to the Queen's side and spoke in a barely audible voice. "And rumors are spreading, Val. People say you and I are puppets of the evil wizard we keep at our court." They had agreed not to argue in public, and Kyellan was surprised to see Tobas taking his side.

"That isn't true," she said petulantly, looking from one to the other. "Gwydion is my friend, and I value his advice."

"It's time we let them go," Tobas murmured. "There's a ship in Laenar harbor that leaves in three days for a trading voyage north. The *Jester,* under Soren, a loyal man."

"I'd like to be on it," Kyellan said.

The beautiful young woman looked at him, hurt. "If you want to leave me so badly, then go. Tobas says you've refused to help us if we make you stay. Even though you know Arel will attack."

"What difference could one man make?"

"None," she said. "No difference. I was foolish to think otherwise."

"Are we really going?" Alaira whispered to Kyellan.

Valahtia sighed and reached a hand up to straighten the simple silver crown she wore in preference to her father's jeweled headpiece. She spoke ruefully. "Yes, you're going. I'm sorry, Ky. It hasn't been right to keep you here, and Tobas told me so often enough. I'll have my scribe Mirrem draw up a safe-conduct letter for the four of you, with my seal. For what good it will do. None of the other Kingdoms recognize my right to my throne." She turned and walked away. Pregnancy had not yet robbed her of her grace, Kyellan thought as he watched her.

Tobas did not follow her. His boyish face was troubled. "Ky . . ."

"Is it true what she said?" Kyellan asked quietly. "You've been arguing for us?"

"I couldn't tell you how I felt," Tobas said in a rush of words. "I'm her consort; I have to support everything she does, believe in her . . . usually I don't mind it, but with this . . . I had to watch you start hating me." He swallowed hard.

"I was angry," Kyellan admitted. "But I couldn't hate you, Tobas. You ought to know that." He reached out his good hand to Tobas's shoulder and drew him close.

The younger man hugged him fiercely, and stood back. "We've been together for a long time," he said. "I wish I could go with you now. And I hope you find whatever it is you seek."

The flagstone floor was cold on Briana's bare feet as she paced back and forth in the inner room of her tower suite. The window beside the three narrow beds was open, and a breeze from the walled garden far below filled the curtains like sails. A scroll in its leather case rolled a few inches across the small table where Briana did her work. A plump, young S'tari woman sat on the marble window seat, grinding dried herbs for tea. She did not seem to have felt it.

"What happened down there?" Briana muttered. "Someone was using Power. Even the child was aware of it." The unborn babe was restless within her. He was only six months grown, but she felt the stirrings of Power within him as surely as she felt his small kicks and movements. There was no question he would be another Shape-Changer, like his father, Kyellan.

"Tapeth will be back soon," Yalna said. "She'll know." The woman of the desert tribes was nineteen, two years younger than Briana. She was training to be a midwife. Her aunt Tapeth had brought her along when she had come to serve Briana, driven by visions. Yalna wore no veil in the inner room. Her tightly curled black hair fell to her shoulders over jingling earrings of strung coins, and her robe was white against her red-brown skin, in contrast to the black priestess robe Briana wore.

"Could it have been Tapeth?" Briana asked curiously. The older S'tari was a priestess of a different Order from Briana's. Those S'tari women with Power chose to worship the immortal spirit Va'shindi, She-Who-Guides, whom Briana knew as her Goddess's messenger. Tapeth claimed that Va'shindi had come to her in a dream to tell her she should go to Cavernon and attend the Candidate for First Priestess.

Yalna sifted the coarser parts of the herbs through a sieve into a small clay bowl. She shook her head thoughtfully. "Those who follow She-Who-Guides have some sensitivity to past and future, and the visions sent by their Mistress, but not the sort of Power you mean."

Briana had only begun to learn about the S'tari religion,

and she found it fascinating. The women vowed fealty to Va'shindi, but that was their only vow. They had no Temples, no rituals or secret languages. They acknowledged the existence of the Three-Fold Goddess, but thought Her requirements for Her priestesses too harsh. Tapeth had left a husband and a son in the desert. She was not horrified by Briana's pregnancy, as another priestess of the Goddess would be.

All Briana's life she had served Wiolai, the Maiden aspect of the Goddess. Then she had fallen in love with Kyellan and learned that her love was part of an ancient and secret ritual, known only to the First Priestess and her chosen successor. To become First Priestess, Briana was required to serve the Goddess in all Her aspects. She had called upon Rahshaiya the Death-Bringer to kill men in battle. Now she had to bear a child, to serve Cianya, the Mother. When her son was born, she had to send him away to be fostered, and return to the life of a cloistered priestess.

A knock sounded on the door of the outer room. Yalna set down her bowl and slipped through the heavy draped curtains that separated the two rooms. Briana heard the latch lift and the stone door swing inward, and Tapeth entered breathing heavily from the climb up the long tower stairs. There was a moment while Yalna helped her aunt remove the heavy veil and cloak she wore in public, and then the two of them pushed the curtains aside and came back into the inner room of the suite.

"Did you speak to the Queen?" Briana asked.

"She was preoccupied," Tapeth said. She was forty years old, and her face was weathered into gaunt lines with sun and wind. Yalna pulled out one of the straight-backed chairs from the small table for her aunt to sit down. "There was an incident at the feast. A group of young ruffians attacked the wizard Gwydion, and he defended himself with green fire."

"That must have been Chela," Briana said. "I hope they're both all right."

"The wizard was cut, but not seriously," Tapeth said. "You'll be pleased to hear that this finally convinced the Queen to allow Gwydion and Kyellan to leave for the North."

"Maybe you should ask them to look for survivors at the

Sanctuary," Yalna suggested. That had been the purpose of Tapeth's attempt to speak to the Queen. Briana wanted to know if any of her sisters in the Garithian stronghold had survived the wizards' army.

"Did you see him?" Briana whispered, ashamed of her need to know.

The older S'tari shrugged. "I saw a grim man in black, looking older than his twenty-three years. But he smiled after the Queen relented, and then I saw in him what you must have seen when you chose him for your service to the Goddess."

"Is he very handsome?" Yalna asked brightly.

Briana had not answered any of his messages, had refused to see him, hoping she could begin to forget. But the child that filled her only reminded her of the void Kyellan had left. Her skin still burned in memory of his touch. If she had not been chosen First Priestess . . . But she had. The Goddess trusted her to carry on Her work. "I'm glad Valahtia has given them leave to go," she said. "Yes, I'll write a letter asking them to stop at the Sanctuary. Kyellan has been there before. He could find it again."

"Did you love him very much?" Yalna said, undaunted that Briana had not answered her first question.

After a moment Briana nodded. "I still do. But it must be as the Goddess wills."

Chapter Two _____

"**I**'VE never been on a boat before," said Alaira nervously. "And I can't swim. What if it sinks?"

Kyellan looked at her and laughed. She sat stiffly on the central plank of the rowboat with the cloth of her dark traveling skirt bunched up in one hand. "Calm weather for this late in the fall," he said. "Wait until we hit a storm."

"If you fell out now, you could probably stand up in the bay," Chela said, sitting with Gwydion across from them. She seemed to have recovered from the backlash of her spell, and was more eager than any of them to reach the ship and begin the journey. Gwydion was cloaked and hooded beside her, his face shadowed in dark wool, his hands gloved. He seemed to be dressed for a blizzard in Garith instead of a cool autumn afternoon in the harbor of Laenar. He had not wanted to attract attention.

Six oarsmen sculled them quietly toward the harbor mouth. Except for small craft, the bay was deserted. The sea wall and the stone wharves of Laenar had been blasted into rubble by the wizards and lay treacherously under the shallow surface. No ship could enter until the harbor was dredged and the piers reconstructed, and that work would require more money and effort than the weary people of Laenar were willing to provide.

"It's deeper out by the ship," Alaira said.

"I've never seen you afraid of anything before," Kyellan

said lightly. She had insisted on going with him, and all she had done since they got into the boat was complain.

She glared at him. "I'm not afraid. I just don't like the way the boat moves. Or the smell of fish."

"You've lived near the sea all your life."

"But I've never been out on it. The closest I've come is sailors' tales." She looked uneasily at the waves that had begun to swell gently around the skiff, and crossed her arms over her stomach. Kyellan sighed. If she was so determined to be ill, she certainly would be.

Soon the skiff bumped against the hull of the *Jester*, a large two-masted merchant ship that rode at sea anchor just past the watchtowers at the harbor mouth. The rowers steadied the boat, hooking metal grapples into a web of taut ropes that stretched over the closed cargo bay door. The merchant vessel smelled of fresh pitch and new canvas and rope. A sturdy plank ladder was bolted to the side of the ship next to the cargo bay, and two bearded sailors above them began to remove the portion of the ship's railing by the ladder.

"Captain Kyellan, is it?" A small, dark, whip-thin man leaned over the side of the ship. "At last. I was beginning to wonder. I'm the ship's master, Soren. Your baggage is in your cabins, and your horses are stabled in the smaller hold. They'll bunk with my men." He laughed. His face was like a wrinkled map, but Kyellan could not guess his age, and his Caer accent was too slight to place his origin. Tobas had said Soren was loyal to Valahtia, and he had agreed to carry a wizard as a passenger, yet Kyellan was not certain he should trust him.

The boat secured, Chela was the first up the ladder. She held her skirt up above her knees with one hand. Gwydion followed, careful not to betray his disguise. Alaira blanched at the strip of dark water between the boat and the hull, but she swallowed hard and climbed very quickly, not looking down. Kyellan fumbled in his belt pouch for coin to pay the oarsmen, then made his way slowly up the ladder, careful of his balance with only one hand to steady him. The oarsmen called out good wishes and detached their boat hooks as soon as he was on deck.

"Welcome," Soren said. "Nemir will show you to your cabins. They're small, I fear. This isn't a ship built for passengers."

"As long as you can get us to Garith, I don't care where we have to sleep," Chela said with a smile.

"We'll speak later," Soren said to Kyellan. Then the ship's master hurried away to order the sea anchor winched aboard. A slight youth with brown hair and a cheerful, unhandsome face waved them to follow him aft.

Kyellan glanced toward the bow first. The *Jester*'s two-story forecastle was stained in a dull pattern of red and black diamonds, and it flew a flag of motley below the Tiger of Caerlin on the foremast. Near the stairs to the foredeck was a small access hatch for the main cargo hold, which would be loaded and unloaded in port by the huge door in the hull. Kyellan turned and followed the others past the mainmast, a barrel-thick trunk that towered over the ship, carrying a huge square mainsail, a small topsail, and a fighting top big enough for two men.

Past the center of the ship, a hatch large enough to lower a horse through was propped open to air out the crew's quarters. That would be an open space of at least two levels, with the crew's hammocks strung over a narrow half deck of planking beside the horse stalls, and with a drop of eight or ten feet from the half deck to the ballast rocks and the skeleton of the keel below.

The young sailor Nemir led them around neat piles of rope and over a deck that was freshly sanded and scrubbed with strong-smelling lye. The twenty men of the crew were mostly in the rigging, setting sail. A few of them were pulling in the sea anchor under Soren's supervision. The sterncastle was unpainted, set behind the ship's wheel. A ladder led up to a railed deck that stretched over the end of the hull. Three doors were set into the wall beneath the deck. One probably led to the master's cabin, on one side of the ladder. The other two were close together on the inner side.

"You and your lady have the inner cabin, sir," said the youth to Gwydion. He opened the door for them. "And you two, the outer."

Alaira turned the handle of the outer door and walked in. Kyellan ducked his head under the low frame and nearly struck it on a hanging lantern that swung from the ceiling. A porthole let in dusky light through thick, flawed glass. Two shelflike bunks were hinged to the walls, nearly meeting in the center of the tiny room. A sea chest stood open behind the bunks, with their packs on the floor next to it. A short metal brazier on tripod legs had stained the corner by the door with soot. They would cook their meals there. A fresh pile of kindling was provided.

"I'll unpack our things," Alaira said. The ship rocked a little as the sea anchor came aboard, and she sat down and grabbed the edge of the bunk as if to still the motion. "You'd better check on the horses." She managed a wan smile.

"They probably have more room than we do," Kyellan said. "I won't be long." He stepped back out and pulled the door nearly shut, to leave Alaira some air.

Alaira sat very still on the bunk for a moment, trying to will away her sickness. This was a calm sea, she knew, and the ship had just left anchor and was not going very fast. How would she feel if there was a storm? She had never really wanted to leave dry land. Maybe she should have let Kyellan ask the Queen to find her a place in the palace.

She laughed softly, bitterly. What place could she have in the beautiful Tiranon? A laundress, perhaps, or a kitchen girl. Someplace where she would not be seen. In the endless months they had lived at the palace she had gone to only a few parties. Every time it was the same. People stared at her scarred face, or they did not look at her at all, no matter how beautiful a dress she wore or how gracefully she danced with Kyellan or Tobas.

There were three men who could look at her without flinching. Gwydion, because he had Chela and did not really see other women. Tobas, because he was courteous and kind, and because he remembered her from the old days when he and Kyellan were guardsmen and she had been Kyellan's lover. And Kyellan, who seemed not to notice that she was any different than she was before. He was different, though. He loved Briana, who had cast him aside as a lady of the

Tiranon might a once-worn dress. Alaira still hoped to win his heart again. But she feared that if he came close enough he would see how ugly she was, and start looking at her as other men did. That she could not bear.

"Alaira? Can I come in?" Chela peered around the door. "Gwydion is busy padding his jars and vials in the sea chest so they won't break no matter how much the ship rolls." She came to sit beside her.

Alaira did not want to think of the ship moving any more than it already was. She swallowed hard and nodded toward the chest. "I told Kyellan I'd get our things unpacked. I haven't started yet."

"I'll help," Chela offered. She crawled over the bunks to tug at the lacing on the smaller pack. Alaira followed her carefully. "This cabin is just like ours, except we don't have a porthole. And we're going to have to stay in ours a lot more than you do. Gwydion says this ship will stop at almost every port, and whenever it does he'll have to stay hidden. They're killing wizards in a lot of places."

"How can you be sure they aren't killing them in Garith?" Alaira pulled out a gown of fine blue silk. She would probably never wear it, but she could not bear to leave it behind. She had never had such nice things before.

"We aren't sure," Chela said with a frown. "But Garith has never bothered the Wizards' College, and no one has heard any stories about it like the tales coming out of Keris and Ryasa."

Alaira nodded, feeling dizzy. She blinked her eyes. The walls narrowed in on her like a dark tunnel as she folded the blue gown and set it in the sea chest. Suddenly she began to topple over, and she fell onto her side on the end of the bunk.

A thin hand clad in a black leather glove touched her shoulder, and Gwydion's voice asked, "Alaira, are you all right?" She shivered and closed her eyes against the dizziness. She did not want to look at Gwydion. He was Kyellan's friend, but he looked very much like the wizard Hirwen, who had ruled Cavernon City with icy cruelty. Hirwen had given her to his guardsmen as a plaything, as casually as a man might give away a ring. That was where she had gotten the scar on her face, but she had worse memories than that. She wondered if she would ever be able to trust Gwydion.

"She's seasick, I guess," Chela said uncertainly.

"We'll put some water on to boil, and I'll make her a drink to settle her stomach," Gwydion said. "Go dip up a panful of water from the barrel by the mainmast. I'll find the necessary herbs."

Chela bent down over Alaira, who opened her eyes again briefly. The red-haired girl had eyes the color of the silk dress. How odd. "Any better?" Chela asked.

Alaira nodded, trying to convince herself the room was not spinning. Chela smiled at her and followed Gwydion out of the cabin.

"They weren't easy to get in here," Nemir said in a respectful tone, looking at the four S'tari horses in their box stalls.

"I can believe that." Kyellan glanced back up at the ladder that led down from the open hatch into the crew's hold. It would have been simpler to walk the horses into the larger hold, but that was reserved for the *Jester*'s varied cargo of silks and spices and grain.

The stalls were aft of the rows of crew hammocks. They were big enough for the horses to turn around in, with rope-slung feed troughs that would level themselves instead of spilling with the ship's motion. The S'tari horses were compact and fiery animals, bred in the desert for speed and endurance but not patience. They moved restlessly, half afraid and half angry. Kyellan spoke softly to each one, in S'tari, and gave them handfuls of oats from the feed sacks.

"They're pretty things," Nemir said as they walked carefully along the edge of the half deck, back to the ladder. The drop below ended ten feet down on jagged ballast rocks that looked like rubble from the Laenar wharves. "But aren't they kind of small? I wouldn't want to try to use one for any heavy work. We had bigger horses on my father's farm."

"These will go all day on a handful of grain," Kyellan said, following the young sailor back out onto the deck. "But you're right, they wouldn't be very good at plowing."

"Ah, Captain Kyellan." The ship's master was with the helmsman at the wheel. Kyellan joined them as Nemir hurried away to his duties. The sailor at the wheel was the oldest man

of the crew that Kyellan had seen, a stocky, heavily muscled
sixty-year-old with a balding fringe of hair that was still black.

"A fine ship," Kyellan said by way of greeting.

"She'll do," Soren said cheerfully. "And I've already been
assured a profit on this voyage with what the Queen's people
paid me. Double for the wizard's passage because of the
danger of having him aboard, and a fair price for my time to
wait for two weeks in some Garithian bay." He looked at
Kyellan expectantly. "Maybe you can explain that."

"After you set us ashore, we'll be headed to the priestesses' old Sanctuary to see if anyone survived there." Kyellan
had received the letter, written in Briana's own hand, the day
before in Laenar. She had said nothing beyond her request
that he go to the Sanctuary, but he felt better than he had in
months. At least she had not forgotten he existed. "If we find
anybody, we'll bring them back for you to take to Caerlin.
The First Priestess will pay for their passage when they arrive
in Cavernon City. If we don't come back within two weeks,
you can assume we found no one there."

"Orders of the new First Priestess, eh?" Soren said with a
thoughtful look on his thin, wrinkled face. "They say she
was a hero of the war. And that she's a young one. She seems
likely to be popular, even if I did hear some grumbling in
Laenar about the new taxes to rebuild the Temples."

Kyellan smiled slightly. "In Cavernon City the people are
being hit twice: once for the Temple, once for the walls. I
suppose it's necessary."

Soren nodded. "The wizards made a shambles of Cavernon.
But that wasn't as bad as what they did to Dallynd. I haven't
seen it, but they say all six walls were destroyed, and the city
with them."

"I was there," Kyellan said quietly.

"I heard about that, sir," said the helmsman. "Didn't you
lead the city's defenses?"

"I'm not very proud of that." He still smelled the charnel
stench of the burning city when he thought of Dallynd.

"But you also killed a wizard there, and stole a galley full
of prisoners," the old sailor said. "Alone, they say."

"Not alone," Kyellan said. Erlin had been with him, the
stocky young archer who had survived the massacre of the

Royal Guard. The boy had more courage and more sense than
Kyellan remembered having at seventeen. The last Kyellan
had seen of him he was broken and bloody in a litter after the
wizards' torture, and the strange immortal spirit Va'shindi
had promised to take care of him. That was nearly seven
months ago. He wondered if Erlin was still alive.

"You have quite a name as a swordsman," Soren said.
"And I see you're wearing a rapier, though your right arm
can't wield it. How are you with your left?"

Kyellan's hand touched the hilt of the left-handed sword
General Diveshi of Parahn had given him after the last battle
with the wizards. "Good," he said with a slow smile, remembering his endless bouts with Tobas in the practice yards of
the palace. "Not quite as fast as I was, but effective."

Soren spoke quickly. "I was hoping . . . well, I have a
store of weapons for my crew, but few of them have any
training. Not a soldier in the lot. And since the wizards
destroyed most of the warships that used to patrol the coast,
there has been a new danger of piracy along the Tarnsea routes."

"You want me to teach your men swordplay?"

"Enough to defend themselves," Soren said with an apolo-
getic air. "And I have a store of bows as well. If a few of
them could learn to shoot, we'd stand up well against the
more inexperienced pirates."

"It will be a long voyage." Kyellan looked up at the
sailors in the rigging. "And your men aren't out of shape.
They could learn something by the time we reach Garith."
He grinned at Soren. "I'll be glad to have something to do."

"Good!" The smaller man clapped him on the back. "If
the weather stays fair, my men will have lots of time to
practice. You can start tomorrow."

Kyellan promised to be on the railed stern deck when the
first shift went off duty the next day. Then he excused
himself to Soren and the helmsman, and went back to his
cabin. He was surprised to find Alaira lying on her bunk pale
and sick, sipping a hot drink from a tin cup.

"I got seasick," she said, embarrassed. "Gwydion fixed
me this."

Kyellan leaned over to sniff the aroma of the drink. It had
the heavy, sleepy smell of a drug made of flowers, which was

popular among the idle old men of Rahan Quarter. "You
won't be awake much longer."

"A fine way to start my first journey," she muttered,
gulping the rest of the milky tea. Kyellan helped her pull off
her boots and her outer clothes, and she crawled under the
blankets in her shift. She smiled weakly at him. "I wanted to
see every land we passed, and have you tell me all about them."

He sat on the edge of the bunk. "Right now if you were
leaning over the port railing, you'd see a line of rock formations far off on the shore of Keris." He spoke softly as her
eyes closed. "That's the smallest mainland Kingdom. Mostly
farmers. The Crown Prince of Keris, Werlinen, is the one
who was betrothed to Valahtia, and he's part of the reason
why she's the Queen of Caerlin now. . . ."

"The Second Rank priestesses?" Briana looked up from
her breakfast. The shutters were open, and morning sunlight
brightened the austere room. "They're early."

"I could tell them to go away and come back later," Yalna
said, braiding one of her strings of pierced coins into her hair.
"But they seem upset."

They usually were. Briana was still confused by the politics
of the Cavernon City Temple. It had little to do with serving
the Goddess, and much to do with preserving the positions of
the handful of priestesses who had been running the Temple
as their private domain. They were used to no interference
from the First Priestess far away in the Sanctuary in Garith;
now they had a First Priestess in Cavernon, one yet to be confirmed, but who was already insisting upon changes and reforms.
Briana understood their hostility, but she had grown weary of it.

"I'll speak to them." She pulled her chair up to the
curtains that blocked the view of the inner room. Yalna
hurried to the outer door with a jingle of half-fastened
coins, and Tapeth moved three chairs into a row facing the
curtains behind which Briana would sit. Briana lowered
herself awkwardly into the chair. She was as big already
at six months as most women would be at eight. And if
other candidates for First Priestess had hidden their preg-
nancies in the past, they could not have needed to take
the precautions she did.

Whenever another priestess was near, Briana shielded herself with mental defenses as strong as those she had used in battle. She could not trust her unborn child to keep quiet. When he was restless, his unformed Power roved in vague probes around the tower suite. Without shielding, he might betray his presence. He might betray that he was the next Shape-Changer. He was getting stronger, and Briana feared that soon her own mental walls would not contain him.

"Yalna will let them in," Tapeth's dry voice said from the other side of the curtains. "I'll stand guard here against any attempted siege."

The door unlatched and swung open with a slight grating sound, and the three Second Rank priestesses walked angrily into the outer room. They took their places in the comfortless chairs without a word, but Briana could sense their mood.

"Good morning, Rithia, Ocasta, and Wynna," she said mildly. "I'm pleased you have come."

Protocol required they wait to be recognized before speaking. Now an imperious voice demanded, "What do you mean by this latest proclamation, Briana?" Rithia was a middle-aged priestess whose undisciplined Power usually gave Briana a headache. She was the Mistress of Ritual in the Cavernon Temple, and was used to being obeyed. "The people will not stand for it."

"I feel the move was unwise," said Ocasta calmly. Her peaceful voice was clear and compelling despite her old age. Briana knew she was devout, but she was also the most stubborn and inflexible woman Briana had ever met. She was the Guide of the Temple, its head in the absence of the First Priestess, and she seemed to be certain she knew the Goddess's will in all things.

"You're speaking of my decision to widen the testing for the novitiate? You must agree that after the persecution by the wizards our numbers are far too low."

"The nobility won't have it, I fear. They thought their daughters were safe after their regular testing at age seven." Wynna was the Mistress of Records, and Briana had been sending Tapeth almost daily to her office to cajole a few more of the scrolls of Temple history.

"Why test girls twice that age?" Rithia said. "They obviously have no Power."

"If you alienate the noble families, they'll stop donating toward rebuilding the Temple," Wynna said.

"They donated enough in past years to keep their daughters free for marriage," Briana said wearily. "The Cavernon Temple seemed to overlook such girls. I would guess none of you are nobly born."

"We had no lack of willing and talented novices," Ocasta said. "The Temple prospered, both in Power and in the means to minister to the people."

"But now we are too few. We have promoted every girl we could to Fourth Ranking to replace those who died, and still there are not enough priestesses to perform the Great Rituals. There are girls, even grown women, who may have the Power to join us. We need them now. Any who are willing. I believe there will be many who would as soon become a priestess as marry some stranger chosen by their father."

"Untrained, and without the Goddess's grace," Ocasta said, "these women you speak of have lost whatever Power they may have had."

"They'd be dry as stones," Rithia said scornfully.

"I've spoken to you of Chela. She has the Power to equal a wizard's, and was never trained in the Goddess's service."

"Then her Power comes from the Darkness the wizards serve," Wynna said. "If she does not call upon the Goddess then her strength must come from evil."

"I fought with her, linked to the Goddess's Seat." Briana tried to keep her irritation from her voice. "She is not evil."

"I do not trust her," Ocasta said. "Or her lover Gwydion."

"The Queen should never have allowed them to leave. Who knows what plots they may set in motion in the North?" Rithia said.

"It's well you'll be at the Sanctuary to keep an eye on them once you're confirmed First Priestess." Wynna sounded complacent.

Briana smiled behind the curtains. "I'll be here. The Sanctuary will be abandoned, sisters. Anyone who survives there will come here."

"What?" Rithia gasped. "You're mad, Briana. The First

Priestess must live at the Sanctuary. It's the holiest place in the Kingdoms.''

"The Seat of the Goddess is here in Caerlin," Briana reminded them. "The work has begun to study it and learn its Power. It is the strongest force we have yet known."

"The Hidden Temple," Ocasta said thoughtfully. "Even the Temple at Khymer does not know where it is, though five of their Second Rank priestesses have gone there to work with the Seat. Why such secrecy, Briana?"

"The Seat could be very dangerous if it fell into evil hands." Briana shivered, remembering the wizards Belaric and Onedon who had almost gained control of its awesome Power. "The Sanctuary is too far away. I will not be cut off from the world as my predecessors were. My place is here, working to heal the wounds of the land and the people."

"Your predecessors worked within a thousand years of tradition," Rithia shouted. Her chair scraped backward on the stone floor as she got to her feet. "But you sit here in this self-imposed seclusion and think of ways to change that tradition. If you continue thus, Briana, you will find yourself opposed."

"I am the chosen successor of the late First Priestess," Briana said. "You cannot oppose me." She wished she could step through the curtains and shake some sense into them.

"You were alone with the First Priestess when she died," Wynna said, rising in her turn.

"We have accepted your word that she named you her heir," Ocasta said. "And we have not questioned the months of contemplation you have undertaken before being confirmed. But if you show your intentions to be contrary to the Goddess's will, we will know that you are not the First Priestess."

"How can you claim to know the Goddess's will?" Briana felt her child move in response to her anger, and she quickly reinforced her shields.

"Already you question the ancient ways," Ocasta said coldly. "You ventured perilously close to heresy in using Rahshaiya's aid against the wizards. You propose to accept as priestesses any women who wish to join us, without regard for the proper order." She got slowly to her feet. "Would you make yourself another Hailema, the Unholy One who was imposed upon the Temples by a profane king?''

"I did not seek to be First Priestess," Briana said furiously. "I was chosen. Nothing you say can change that."

"We will see," Ocasta said. "Come, sisters." They strode to the door and swept through it in a rustling of woolen robes. The door shut behind them, and Briana heard the latch fall into place.

"They are such fools!" she exploded. "How dare they threaten me?"

Tapeth opened the curtains and looked down at her in sympathy. "They know you are the Goddess's Chosen. No one with Power could deny that. But they are used to their comfortable ways. Their authority."

"They're afraid they'll have to work harder under your rule," Yalna said with a wry smile. She came forward and reached out both hands to help Briana get to her feet.

"I won't accomplish anything unless they work with me." She smoothed her robe over her huge abdomen and walked over to the window seat to stare out at the Queen's private garden. Perhaps the Goddess was testing her will and resolve through these women. She would not give in to their complaints.

Ocasta had accused her of heresy on little evidence. If the old woman knew everything Briana had done in the war, she would have been horrified. Briana had called upon Rahshaiya, when the third aspect of the Goddess was usually shunned. She had used her Power without prayer or ritual when there had been no time for such things. She had killed men without remorse. She had fallen in love with Kyellan, and had made love with him knowing he was the Shape-Changer and their child would be a wizard. Did that make her morally unfit for her post? Perhaps, by the usual reckoning. But it seemed the Goddess did not care. Briana was Her chosen servant. She could not have escaped that if she tried.

Chapter Three ─────────────

"BUT why? Why can't we even try to use it?" Gemon said in frustration. She sat curled up in a slim ball at the entrance flap of the hide tent, just outside the circle of the other five women who made up the Hidden Temple. They were all old Second Rank priestesses from Khymer. The canyon of the Goddess's Seat loomed around them like a silent city, teeming with force and life and Power. And these fools would waste it.

"No, Gemon," Iona said calmly. Her lined face scarcely moved when she spoke. "The First Priestess sent us here to study the Power of the Goddess's Seat, to learn to understand its wonders. That is all." The others nodded sagely, like four aged marionettes on the same string.

"The First Priestess didn't send me," Gemon said. "The Goddess's messenger, Va'shindi herself, brought me here. I can't believe she meant for me to sit meekly before the Seat and do mental exercises." That was all anyone did. They went into quiet trances, seeking the Goddess in dreams, and they kept immaculate records of their attempts to measure the various ways the Seat heightened their abilities.

"Perhaps that is exactly what she meant for you to do," said Niketa gently. She was the oldest of them, as small as a child. "You have a great deal of Power, Gemon, but it is undisciplined and your thoughts are often chaotic. If you are to be promoted to Fourth Ranking and take your vows in the spring, you must learn more patience.''

"Work diligently at the tasks you are set," Iona said, "and I will have no doubts when I recommend you as a priestess.''

"I fought in the battles against the wizards while you were hiding in people's cellars in Khymer," the novice said furiously. "I traveled with Briana and the old First Priestess from the Sanctuary, and saw the wizards' army murder my sisters." She got to her feet. "I know better than you what Darkness is still abroad in the world. The Seat of the Goddess should be used to cleanse the Kingdoms, not kept here polished like a statue in a museum.''

"You are the youngest and the lowest ranking here," Iona began.

"And the most powerful," Gemon countered.

"That may be. Yet you will obey your superiors.''

"Even if they ignore the will of the Goddess?" Gemon said scornfully. She ducked under the tent flap and stalked out into the rocky canyon. The Goddess's Seat rose to fill her vision, a huge, rough-hewn throne that seemed to have grown of its own accord out of the canyon wall. She had been linked with it once before, briefly, until the Shape-Changer Onedon had blasted her into near death with a glance. Gemon was sure she could link with it again.

Va'shindi had healed her not only of her injuries from the battle, but of the old weakness of her lungs that had made her ill most of her life. She was strong now. Far stronger than those old women. Gemon climbed onto a low step before the throne and knelt with her hands pressed flat to the stones. She could feel its Power pulsing eagerly within.

The Seat was a tool that could be used for any purpose. Gemon would use it to convince the timorous priestesses that they must attack their enemies, the enemies of the Goddess. She would make them believe it was the Goddess's will. And it was, Gemon thought angrily. It had to be. Why else had she been brought here?

"Your sword isn't a hoe," Kyellan said in amusement as he deflected Nemir's awkward chopping blow. "Look. A two-handed stroke from above is probably the easiest move to block. When you raise your arms like that it's obvious what you're doing. And you leave yourself open to a quick lunge from underneath.'' He demonstrated, waving his curved rapier tip an inch from the young sailor's throat. ''Which is what you should be trying to do to your opponent.''

''But I can't get anywhere near you from underneath. You won't let me,'' Nemir protested.

''The boy has a point,'' Gwydion said from his perch on the railing of the sterncastle deck. ''If he ever has to use that sword, it won't be against the finest duelist in Cavernon.'' His bushy golden hair shone in the sunlight; his hood and cloak were packed away until the next village port on the southern coast of Ryasa. They had been voyaging a week now, and the *Jester*'s crew had begun to get used to the wizard's presence. A few still scowled at the sound of his voice.

''I could let them practice against each other,'' Kyellan said. ''But what if they run into a pirate who knows what he's doing?''

''Then nothing you can teach them in a few weeks will be any help.'' Gwydion jumped down from the railing. The watching sailors parted warily before him. ''Isn't that enough for today? You've been at it for hours, and these men are on duty tonight.''

Kyellan shrugged. ''All right.'' He sheathed his sword and wiped sweat from his face with the back of his hand. ''Tomorrow is the second watch's turn, men. Look down from the rigging and you might learn something.'' The crewmen laughed wearily and moved to pile their swords back into the weapons box, a heavy, caulked crate, bolted to the deck. Gwydion followed Kyellan down the ladder and across the main deck to the water barrel by the mast.

''I know you wanted something to do,'' the young wizard said, ''but this is getting monotonous. They aren't even improving.''

Kyellan splashed a dipperful of water across his face, then drew another to drink. On a trading voyage like this, the ship put into harbor almost every day. The supplies of food and water were always fresh. ''They're getting comfortable with their weapons,'' he said. ''They'll know which end of the sword to point at pirates, and they'll have some idea of how to keep from getting killed at the first pass." He looked sidelong at his friend. "If you'd join us, you wouldn't be so bored. As I recall, you're pretty fair with a sword, for a wizard."

Gwydion held out his hands. Kyellan had long since stopped noticing the supple leather gloves that covered them. Gwydion never took them off, since the flesh had been burned from his hands by a demon the wizard had been powerless to control. Kyellan had never seen Gwydion's injuries, but he could envision them.

"No grip," Gwydion said after a moment. "The first blow from another sword would knock mine out of my hands. That's what happened to my dagger in the garden."

"Sorry," Kyellan muttered. "I didn't think."

"I'm not worried. If we're attacked by pirates I'm sure you'll protect me." He did not smile. "Chela and Alaira are cooking some of that fresh beef you bought in the last village, if you're hungry." He turned and walked back toward their cabins, under the sterncastle deck where the weapons practices were held.

This voyage was getting uncomfortable, Kyellan thought as he followed Gwydion. It would be another week before they reached Chelm, then a few days there, and a few more days before they reached the first navigable Garithian bay. By that time he hoped his friends' moods would improve. It was not only Gwydion. Chela was restless and irritable, and even Alaira was behaving strangely. Sometimes she seemed afraid of him. She was barely courteous to Gwydion. Kyellan knew she had been badly treated by the wizards, but she should have recovered from that in six months. He supposed they would all be more cheerful when they finally left the confines of the ship.

Morning fog nestled clammy and chilling over the secluded little bay. The clear stream that flowed into the Tarnsea soaked the hem of Erlin's rough woolen robe, though he had it belted up over his knees. He bent to pull up another fish trap, shivering. The trap was a weighted funnel Pima had woven of strong reeds, with strips that slanted inward to allow a fish to swim inside but prevent him from getting back out. A large trout had bloodied itself with the effort of trying to escape. Erlin unlatched the back of the trap and shook the fish into his bag to join four others the night had brought. He felt sorry for the creatures. He and Pima were equally trapped, though they were in a more pleasant place than the fish had been.

The messenger of the Goddess, Va'shindi, had brought them here shortly after the battle for the Goddess's Seat. Erlin had been unconscious at first, then delirious, and it had only been within the last month that he had been able to walk far. He did not know for certain where they were. He guessed they were northeast of Laenar on the Tarnsea coast, several days ride south of the Seat and probably no more than a few miles from the edge of the S'tari desert. He had wakened to find himself in an old stone cottage on a low hill, with a view of high, barren ridges inland and grassy meadows rolling down to the tiny bay.

Erlin latched the trap again and set it firmly in the rocks in the deep part of the stream. He was grateful to Va'shindi for healing him after the wizards' torture, and for helping Pima through her pregnancy, now eight months advanced. But he had the feeling the Goddess's messenger was using them for some purpose of her own. He had never been so lonely before. He loved Pima, but he had grown up in a large family in the biggest city of the Kingdoms, and after he had left his parents his family had been the Royal Guard. He longed for people. Even the thin-faced novice Gemon would have been welcome company. He wished Va'shindi had brought her here with them.

"Did you get fish?" Pima called down from the top of the path.

"Five of them!" He splashed out of the water, mud squishing under the soles of his heavy leather shoes. His feet ached most of the time. Their bones had been too crushed and misshapen to knit back together properly even given Va'shindi's skill at healing.

Pima waited for him to climb the hill. Erlin smiled up at her. He did not regret stealing her from the priestesses. The former novice was prettier than ever with her pregnancy, round-faced, her soft brown hair thick and shiny. She was huge with child, but she was sturdily built. She should bear with little difficulty.

He was breathing heavily by the time he reached the top. Pima kissed his cheek and took the bag of wriggling fish from him. "Maybe later, when you're rested, we can go to the high meadow and find some greens to cook with them. You'll have to pick them. I think if I bend down I'll fall over." She laughed.

"Just point out what you want." He linked an arm in hers as they walked back toward the cottage. The bag of fish bumped against his leg, and he thought of the trap. "Is she coming today?"

"She said she would."

"Good. I have something to say to her."

"Don't make her angry, Erlin. What if she left us here? What if she never came back?"

"Left us here? She's keeping us here like pets, and I'm tired of it," he said irritably.

"Do you want to leave?" Va'shindi said quietly. Erlin turned. She sat on a mossy rock in the meadow by the cottage. The colors of her filmy gown were grey and mottled this time, and her eyes were moss green. Her night-black hair was caught behind her neck. Her uncanny beauty was muted, and she looked tired. Erlin did not think it was possible for an immortal spirit to get tired.

"Of course not," Pima answered for him. "Don't mind him, Mistress. His feet hurt." She walked over to the rock and lowered her heavy body to sit on the ground beside Va'shindi.

"I want to leave," Erlin said. "As soon as the baby is born and Pima is well enough to travel. We should have gone a month ago. I was well then, and Pima wasn't so far along."

"But I detained you, is that what you believe?" Va'shindi said with a lift of her delicate eyebrows. She seemed human enough, Erlin thought, except when you met her deep, ageless eyes.

"You asked us to stay," Pima said, pulling at Erlin's hand until he sat down beside her.

"I have told you that I am forbidden to interfere with human destiny. I would not have forced you to stay here, if you had truly wished to go." She smiled at Erlin. "Are you so unhappy?"

He looked down at the autumn-yellowed grass. "It's beautiful here. But there's nothing to do. I feel useless."

"What if I gave you a reason to stay?" Va'shindi said intently. "An important task, something only you can accomplish, and only here in this valley? For such was my purpose in bringing you here."

"A task for the Goddess?" Pima said, awed.

"For Her First Priestess. I have told you that Briana is with child, and by the Shape-Changer. Her son will be born soon after your daughter. The child will be a wizard, and given the current mood of the Kingdoms he will be in danger. He must be protected. He must be kept safe."

"Here?" Erlin was startled.

"My S'tari women know of this valley, but no others do. Briana's son could live here as a brother to your child. If you and Pima would agree to be his foster parents. Briana would be far happier if she knew the child was with someone she trusted." The black-haired woman reached out with both hands and touched their cheeks with cool fingers. "You may have time to decide. If you agree, Briana will leave the city and journey here before her pregnancy advances too far. The child will be born here, secret from the world." She began to fade, an eerie but familiar sight, dissolving into the air like a heat-mirage. "I will return tomorrow."

As soon as Va'shindi was gone, Pima turned to Erlin. "I want to do it."

"She gave us time to consider," Erlin said. "We should take it. I'd like to return something of what I owe to Va'shindi for saving my life . . . but if we agree to this we'll never be able to leave this valley."

"Maybe we could. In a few years, maybe people will forget to hate the wizards, and Briana's son will be safe anywhere."

"We can't be sure of that."

"It doesn't matter," Pima said impatiently. "Erlin, don't

you see? This is a way for me to serve the Goddess again. To repay Her for what I did when I left the Temple to be with you. We have to do it.''

He could see the determination on her round face. Erlin sighed and stood up to help Pima to her feet. "We'll talk about it again. Come. Let's have some breakfast."

Alaira looked down from the foredeck of the *Jester*, where she stood with Chela while the ship was towed into the harbor of Chelm. They had been voyaging for two weeks, moving in and out of village bays, never staying anywhere long enough for Alaira to spend time ashore. Now they would be in a real city for three whole days. She could not wait.

Chelm did not possess a good natural harbor. Such were rare on the Tarnsea coast. The shoals at the mouth of the river Is'nai just north of the city made it too dangerous for ships. So the ancient builders of Chelm had extended the land they had, creating massive sea walls that curved in two concentric circles to enclose the docking bay and the complex of piers and jetties and warehouses. Small fishing boats and tugs were moored in the inner circle, which had a shallow, narrow outlet. Larger freight ships and the occasional warship were drawn through a deep passage in the outer circle by teams of sturdy rowboats. The harbor had gates that could be closed, and ballistae and catapults mounted on the seaward walls for defense. As a result, Chelm was the safest port in the North. Soren had said that he was willing to pay the high tariffs for its use.

It was a prosperous-looking place, Alaira thought. The piers were crowded with ships. At either side of the outer circle were dry docks built along the sea wall, where new ships rose like tattered skeletons and old ones were being refitted. "Didn't the wizards attack them?" she asked Chela. "I don't see any battle damage."

"They were one of the first cities to fall," Chela said. "The wizards took them from within. When we were trying to go south last spring, we were going to get a ship here. But the city had already fallen, and we didn't even get to see the port. Oh, look. That must be the harbormaster waiting for us on the pier, to inspect the cargo and get his fees from Soren.''

A richly dressed Ryasan stood at the end of their assigned docking pier. He was a stout man, wearing a fur hat and cloak though the autumn wind was not chill. A little knot of clerks surrounded him, bearing account books and wearing belts studded with feather quills. A grey-robed priestess of the Goddess waited a short distance away. Her hood was pulled up to shadow her face.

"Why a priestess?" Alaira wondered aloud.

"Maybe to bless the cargo." Chela chuckled. "People in Chelm take their religion seriously, Gwydion says."

"Three days." Alaira sighed blissfully. "I want to find a bazaar or a craft street and spend some of the money Queen Valahtia gave us. It may be our last chance."

"We can try to get Kyellan to take us ashore," Chela said. "Since neither of us speaks Ryasan and he does."

The rowboats detached their tug lines as the ship rocked against the pier, and workers threw massive mooring cables aboard for the sailors to attach to rings at the prow. The two young women leaned over the foredeck rail to watch. Some of the dock workers noticed them and called out; they could not understand the words, but they could guess. Chela giggled and waved. Alaira allowed herself to feel flattered, though she knew they would not look at her so admiringly if they could see her scar.

The gangplank was lowered for the harbormaster's party to come aboard. "Let's go down and listen," Chela said, heading for the forecastle stairs.

"If we can understand what they say." Alaira followed her down.

"They'll speak Caer. Gwydion says that's the language of trade," the fourteen-year-old said with an assurance that sometimes set Alaira's teeth on edge.

"I don't see Kyellan," Alaira said in a whisper. "He's probably in the cabin with Gwydion."

"With a drawn sword in his lap," Chela said. "In case the clerks decide to inspect in there."

Soren and the harbormaster began to go over the accounting of the ship's goods while the clerks wrote in their leather-bound books with quiet pen scratching. The priestess was more interesting. She had brought a smoking censer with her that smelled of sweet incense. Now she set it down on the deck and knelt beside it, pushing back her hood to breathe in the fumes.

She was strong-featured, in her early thirties, with bright blue eyes and the pale hair of an Altimari. Alaira watched curiously as she raised her hands and moved them in slow gestures through the smoke, chanting softly to an atonal melody. "What's she doing?" Alaira leaned against the rope wrappings at the bottom of the mainmast.

"I don't know," Chela whispered nervously. "A ritual. An invocation, maybe. . . . I don't like it."

The priestess's voice began to get louder. Soren looked in her direction. "Forgive me, Borodin," he said to the stout harbormaster. "What's the purpose of this? I've never seen such a thing before in the harbor of Chelm. Or in any harbor, for that matter."

Borodin scratched his head under his fur hat. "Ah. Yes, this is new. The Temple is wary of danger from incoming vessels. Some unscrupulous seamen will do anything for a price. Even transport a cursed wizard. Not that I'd expect that of you, Soren," he said courteously. "Even though you do fly Caerlin's colors, and the usurper Queen has been misguided enough to grant amnesty to wizards. Rumor has it she keeps a wizard at her own court. . . . Well, that's what is said. I'm not sure I believe it of a daughter of Chaeris Ardavan."

"Then you're searching for wizards?" Soren said off-handedly.

"The good women who serve the Goddess seek out the presence of Power. They've already found two hidden wizards for us."

"What did you do when you found them?"

"Killed them, of course. And impounded the ships that harbored them." Borodin frowned. "The ships' masters and crews were allowed to leave Chelm, if they could find anyone to take them."

Chela went pale beneath her sunburn. "Gwydion has no Power for her to find," she said in a bare whisper. "If that's her method, he may be safe."

Alaira suddenly felt a weird pressure inside her mind, as if someone was fingering over her thoughts like cloth in a market stall. She fought revulsion. She had felt such a touch before, at the age of seven, when the Cavernon priestesses had tested her. They had not wanted her, even though she had shown some slight talent.

Beside her, Chela stiffened and said two unfamiliar words that stung Alaira's ears. The grey-robed priestess got to her feet and looked at them with a predatory expression.

"My lord," she said in Caer, "I have something."

"A wizard?" Borodin looked startled. "On this ship?"

She shook her head impatiently. "No. I sensed Power from only two minds aboard. Hers, and hers." She pointed at Chela and Alaira. "It is my right under the new laws to take them for the Goddess."

"What?" Alaira said in disbelief.

"Dear me," Borodin said. "That business of retesting girls for novices? Are you quite sure?"

"Completely," the priestess said. "They have Power. They should be priestesses, according to Briana's proclamation. No matter who they are." She walked over to the mainmast and looked scornfully at Alaira. "How much did your father pay to keep you from the Temple? Hmm? And you!" She turned to Chela. "What possessed your Temple to let you go? Do you know how strongly you reek of Power?"

"Alaira and I are not children," Chela said. "We can't be forced to be priestesses."

Soren nodded agreement. "These women are paying passengers, under the protection of Queen Valahtia."

"Are they married?" the priestess asked. "No. Then they must come with me."

The ship's master smiled slightly. "Surely there is another way, my lady. A donation to the Temple, perhaps?"

The blue-eyed priestess looked at him coldly. "You could be arrested for trying to bribe me."

"She is within her rights to demand them," Borodin said unhappily. "The priestess Briana . . ."

"Would never force anyone to join the Temple," Chela said.

"The Temple at Chelm was almost destroyed," said the priestess. "We had only fourteen Ranking women left. We were compelled to interpret the Candidate's proclamation more strictly than others might. The law of Chelm gives me the authority to take you."

"How can the law of Chelm apply to us?" Alaira demanded.

Borodin shook his head. "It does. Part of the harbor compact. Any ship entering here is subject to every law of the city."

"We never agreed to any compact," Chela said fiercely.

"It doesn't matter," said the harbormaster. "You're bound by it. My sincere apologies." He turned to Soren. "Don't resist this, my friend. If they go peacefully, we'll consider the matter ended. If we have to take them by force, we'll impound a large proportion of the *Jester*'s cargo as a fine, and rescind its docking rights. Is that what you want?"

"I don't want trouble," the ship's master said quietly. "Let me speak with my passengers in private for a moment."

Chela and Alaira followed him into the space under the forecastle, out of hearing. "What about the Queen's safe conduct?" Alaira asked.

"It may mean something to the city overlord," Soren said. "And the higher priestesses of the Temple may be less likely to turn down a donation. I'll do my best to get you out, my lady. You can be sure of that."

"Then you want us to go with her?" Chela whispered, making an effort to keep her voice calm.

"For now. What choice do we have? They'd send soldiers after you next, and as good as your Captain Kyellan is with a sword, he couldn't keep them from taking you. He'd get himself killed in the attempt, and half my crew with him." Soren's dark eyes were intent on them both.

"And Gwydion would be discovered," Chela said fearfully.

"I don't want to go," Alaira said. "Those priestesses frighten me. What if they spellbind our minds, as the wizards did to their soldiers, so we don't want to leave?" She shuddered.

Chela shook her head. "They won't have the Power to do that to us. I'll shield us both if I have to. And Soren can probably get us out by tomorrow. If he doesn't succeed with the overlord or the priestesses, we can somehow manage to escape."

The ship's master looked somber. "I hope you don't have to. If you do, you can't make the attempt before the last day the *Jester* is here. You'd be found and taken back. You would have to get here just before we sail, at sunset on the third day. We won't be able to wait for you if you're late. Another ship will be ready to take our place. Do you understand?"

"We'll be there," Chela said. "If you can't get us free."

"Getting you free will be easy compared to explaining this to Kyellan," Soren said dryly. "He'll be furious."

Chela smiled thinly, and took Alaira's hand. "When we get back, we'll tell him it wasn't your fault."

"I'll see to it you never command a Caer ship again," Kyellan said bitterly, sitting at the table in the master's cabin with Gwydion at his side. "Chela and Alaira were under the Queen's safe conduct, and you betrayed them."

Soren did not even look at him as he searched through a sheaf of papers to find Valahtia's letter. "I'm going to do all I can to get them back, Captain."

Gwydion did not seem very upset. "We have money to offer the priestesses. Maybe enough."

"I'll see what I can do first," the ship's master said. "Stay on the ship, both of you. We don't need any more trouble." He shut the door on them, and they heard his quick footsteps across the deck.

Kyellan pushed back his chair and stood up, nearly hitting his head on the low ceiling of the cabin. "I can't believe this. Abducting women to make them priestesses. And by Briana's orders!"

"Maybe not," Gwydion said. "There have been corrupt Temples before."

"We should have gotten a safe-conduct letter from Briana as well."

The young wizard leaned his elbows on the master's table. "It's Chela's own fault that priestess detected her Power," he said ruefully. "She was careless. She should have been shielded."

Kyellan scowled. "The war's over. There shouldn't be anything to shield against. Damn it, Gwydion, how can we just sit here?"

"Soren will get them back. If he doesn't, we'll go after them. It won't hurt Chela or Alaira to be novice priestesses for a few days. Who knows?" Gwydion smiled. "They might even learn something."

Chapter Four ─────────────

P AST the well-kept docks and piers of the harbor circles,
the city was a warren of tenements and alleys. Alaira and
Chela followed the priestess down a wide, cobbled street that
cut through the squalor, lined with wineshops and sailors'
inns. The street opened out into a broad square. A thick wall
surrounded the newly rebuilt Temple of Chelm, a compound
of peak-roofed buildings that stood some distance away from
the wall at the front but crowded against it at the back. Alaira
could see that the edges of the roofs nearly touched tenements
on the other side.

The wall had one high iron gate, guarded by four city
militiamen. Alaira looked measuringly at the gate guards as
they passed. She liked soldiers generally. Maybe she could
contrive to make friends with them to help their escape. But
she was no longer pretty, and she did not speak Ryasan. Oh,
well.

In the muddy yard of the compound, a few grey-robed
women were supervising novices of varying ages. The white-
robed novices were weaving on great looms, laying out herbs
to dry, washing soiled robes in large tubs. It looked like hard
work.

Alaira remembered hearing that priestesses could read minds.
She tried thinking obscene thoughts, but no one seemed to
notice. The priestess who had taken them from the ship led

them into the largest building and down an arched stone corridor with walls as blank and cheerless as a dungeon's. There were no paintings or tapestries to warm the cold stone. Alaira shivered. The priestess stopped and opened a door.

"The robing room," she said. "Remove your clothing here, and you will be given new garments."

The door closed behind them and a latch turned into place. The robing room was a bare cubicle that still smelled of fresh mortar. There was a bench hewn from the rock on one side, and a deep basin of cloudy water on the floor for bathing. Alaira reached down and tested the water with a finger. It was freezing. "What a gloomy place," she muttered.

"We'd better do as she said," Chela said as she undid the lacings on her tunic. She slid out of the garment and started working on her heavy skirt. "We want them to think we're going to cooperate."

"I can't pretend I want to be here," Alaira said.

"Then try not to say anything."

The door opened again and a short, plump priestess stepped in with an armful of white wool. She smiled at them in a motherly way and laid the clothes on the stone bench. There was a novice robe for each of them, with lengths of rope for belts, and rough leather sandals. "We're so glad to have you here at last," said the woman, in slow Caer. "Everyone is eager to meet you. We all knew what you looked like, of course, but it's different seeing you in person."

"Wait." Chela scowled. "What do you mean, you already knew what we looked like? Were you expecting us?"

"The priestess who took us probably sent word ahead," Alaira said. She undressed quickly and pulled one of the white robes over her head. It fell shapelessly to her feet.

"No, dears." The priestess shook her head. "I'd have thought Falla would have told you. We've been waiting for you for two days. Ever since the Goddess's messenger herself came to us in our dreams and told us you were coming. Falla would have recognized you easily, even if she hadn't sensed your potential Power. We're very glad you're here."

"The Goddess's messenger? Va'shindi?" Chela looked puzzled.

"You are favored of the Goddess," said the woman complacently. "It is time you serve Her as She desires. When you have finished dressing, Falla will take you to your cell." She went out and latched the door again.

Alaira belted her robe with one of the ropes. It bunched unflatteringly against her slim body. "Who is this Va'shindi?"

Chela pulled off her boots and tied sandals to her feet. "She's a very powerful, very ancient spirit who serves the priestesses' Goddess. I think she was human once. But why would she want us to be priestesses? I don't understand."

"If they think we're that important, if may not be easy to escape." What if they could not find a way to leave? Alaira did not think she could stand such a life. She was no virgin maid to live cloistered and quiet. She smiled suddenly. Perhaps that was her answer. She could get them to kick her out. She could tell the other novices tales of her life in Rahan Quarter, about the giddy times when she had been briefly rich from some great theft, about the nights she had danced in the taverns for the wild young noblemen from the Tiranon.

The blue-eyed Altimari priestess returned, and they followed her down the barren corridor. She took them to a small cell with two cots, an unlit brazier, and a hook on the wall for hanging robes on. "Here we are," Falla said briskly. "Eventually you'll sleep in the dormitory with the other novices, but you'll have this room to yourselves while you make the adjustment. You'll be expected at dinner tonight. I'll come to escort you. Your lessons will begin tomorrow."

"You can't keep us here against our will," Alaira said.

"The Goddess sent you to us," said Falla. "You cannot deny that. You are in turmoil, fighting what cannot be changed. Try to find peace, sister. The Goddess will welcome you into Her heart." She smiled and shut the door. Alaira heard the bolt slide into place.

Chela tested one of the cots, then flung herself full length on it. "At least we're on dry land for a few days. Isn't that what you wanted?"

Alaira looked for something to throw at her, but there was nothing. She kicked over the brazier instead.

"A message from the Hidden Temple?" Briana took the leather pouch from Tapeth. "Good. Their report was overdue. I've been wondering what they've learned about the Seat of the Goddess.''

"The courier came with the latest caravan," Tapeth said. "They sent it up when they remembered it.''

Briana cleared a space on the table, pushing scrolls and books aside, and pulled the oil lamp closer. It was a cool evening, and she wore a shawl over the shoulders of her black robe. Yalna had gone into the city with one of the young S'tari guardsmen, and she and Tapeth were alone in the tower rooms.

She unfolded the paper and read it aloud. "The priestesses Gemon, Iona, and company greet their esteemed superior, Briana, Candidate for First Priestess. Our research is proceeding well. The Seat of the Goddess is indeed a most powerful tool for Light in the world. As we direct and focus its Power for the Goddess's purposes, we are certain that we will soon eradicate the Darkness that yet remains in the land. With your blessing on our endeavor, we are certain to succeed. May the Goddess smile upon you in Cavernon City, as She is with us in this hidden place of Her Power.''

"What do they mean, they will eradicate the Darkness?" Tapeth said, frowning. "What Darkness?"

"I don't know." Briana reread the letter. "It sounds as if they're using the Seat. Using its Power against someone. And what is Gemon's name doing first? She's only a novice. This is in her hand, too.''

"Perhaps you should plan to visit the Hidden Temple after you go to the messenger's valley to have your baby. It's not far from there.''

Briana nodded after a moment. "I will. I need to find out what this means. I told them only to study the Seat, not to try to use it.'' What was going on in that shielded canyon by the Tarnsea? Something foolish, she feared. And possibly very dangerous.

"We may be gifts from the Goddess," Chela said sleepily from her cot on the evening of their second day in Chelm, "but they don't know what to do with us.''

The cell was cold and damp. It had been raining outside all day. Alaira huddled under the thin blankets, still wearing her white robe for warmth. "They put me in a class with seven-year-olds," she muttered. "Seven-year-olds! They say I can't read."

"You can't." Chela laughed.

"That isn't what I mean. They're trying to teach me to read Ryasan, and I can't even understand them when they speak it. The little girls laugh at me." She had never been so frustrated.

"Well, I'm doing no better in the higher classes. They can find no evidence of the Power Falla sensed in me. They couldn't even teach me to raise the Goddess's Flame. They don't know to check for the presence of shields."

"I don't want to wait here another day," Alaira said rebelliously.

"We'll escape tomorrow afternoon. You can manage that long."

"If I don't strangle someone first."

"That's the Temple, Captain," Soren said, pointing to the other side of the square where he and Kyellan stood on the third day in Chelm. "Home of the haughtiest female I ever met. They call her the Guide. She laughed when I tried to bribe her. And the city overlord was no friendlier. I hope you're right that your girls can escape."

Kyellan studied the newly built compound and the listless Ryasan soldiers who lounged at the iron gate. If he had had such men in his command in the Royal Guard, the S'tari would rule Caerlin today. "Alaira was in and out of noble houses better guarded than that when she was ten years old."

If Chela and Alaira did manage to escape, they would have help. It would be almost impossible for them to make it to the docks unnoticed wearing novice robes. Soren had stationed pairs of his men along the streets and alleys that led toward the harbor; each pair carried a bag of sailors' clothes to disguise the women if they found them. If they did not escape, Kyellan was going in after them. He had no plan beyond that much.

"I don't blame you for worrying about that lady of yours," the ship's master commented to pass the time. "She's a pretty

thing. I could find it in me to envy you. Nice figure, nice way
of moving. Pity about her face, though.''

"The scar is wizards' work," Kyellan said. "She was
captured during the occupation of Cavernon City." Soren
naturally assumed he and Alaira were lovers. He wished they
were. He still loved Briana, but he could not live like a dead
man because of it. He and Alaira knew each other so well and
had been friends for so long that it was awkward and strange
to be sleeping with her without making love. Yet he feared to
approach her. She had been badly hurt by the wizards' soldiers. He knew she was afraid, and he had promised they
could simply be friends on this journey. It was a promise he
regretted more and more.

"No, I can't see that girl of yours as a priestess," Soren
went on. "Nor the other one, the red-haired one. Too wild.
Your wizard's a lucky man." The wiry man waved to a
young sailor who was running toward them from the northern
side of the square. It was Nemir. "Wonder what he wants?
He was supposed to be guarding the back of the Temple with
Merabo.''

The lean youth was breathless when he reached them, and
his eyes were wide. "Sir! Sir, I can't find Merabo. I can't
find him anywhere. I went to check on some noise in an
alley, but it was just a dog fight, and when I came back he
was gone. He left this.'' He held up one of the bundles of old
sailors' clothes.

"He probably just took some unauthorized shore leave,"
Soren said casually. "Try the wineshops, lad.''

Merabo was one of the older men of the *Jester*'s crew, a
hard worker but quiet. Kyellan had never spoken with him.
He had joined in the weapons training, but had already been a
fair hand with a sword, so Kyellan had paid him little attention.

"That isn't all, sir," Nemir said unhappily. He glanced at
Kyellan. "He was talking about the wizard. Merabo was.
About how he heard there was a reward in Chelm for anyone
who turned one in. He wanted me to go with him to tell the
soldiers. I wouldn't, though. Now he's gone.''

"How long ago?" Kyellan demanded. "Where did you
lose him?''

"Show him, Nemir," Soren said grimly. "I'll get back to

the ship, and gather my men from the streets. If you find Merabo, bring him back quietly. Nothing to attract the attention of the city guards, understand? If they learn there's a wizard aboard the *Jester*, we won't have a pauper's chance to get out the harbor gates. And your yellow-haired friend will be as good as dead.'' He hurried away.

What about Chela and Alaira? They could not leave without them. But they might have to, to save Gwydion's life. Kyellan gripped his sword hilt and followed Nemir. "You were waiting in an alley, you said. Behind the Temple. I haven't seen Merabo approaching the soldiers guarding the gate. He must have gone another way.''

''I never thought he'd really do it, sir,'' Nemir said. ''None of us liked the idea of serving on a ship with a wizard aboard, but your friend didn't cause any trouble. Soren said we had to protect him like any other passenger. I never thought Merabo would do it.''

''It was inevitable, I suppose.'' Kyellan was not really surprised. Now they would need a miracle to get out of this city. And they could not pray to Briana's Goddess for aid. It seemed that this time She was on their enemies' side.

Alaira felt the shield Chela extended her wrap her mind with warmth like a soft blanket. For a moment she had to struggle to think clearly through it. Chela took her hand, steadying her, and whispered in a voice thin with the effort of her spell, ''All right? Let's go. Lead the way.''

Alaira nodded. The priestesses had just finished their last meal of the day, and some of them were stealing a few more moments to gossip while others hurried to their tasks and lessons. Chela had said that no one would notice them, and it seemed to be true. A few women smiled at them as they passed, but no one remembered that they were the new novices, unwilling converts who were supposed to be watched.

The yard was muddy from the latest rain, and in places it had sunk to reveal bits of the old foundations of the Temple the wizards had destroyed. Chela had said there was a lingering smell of death to the place, and Alaira was glad she did not have the sensitivity to sense it. With Chela close behind, she hurried through the yard toward the back of the priestesses' compound. She had managed to locate a narrow flight of stairs in one of the buildings that stood against the rear wall. If luck was with them, and with the patronage of Shilemat, the Rahan god of thieves, the stairway would lead to the peaked roof. It would be no Thieves' Highroad, but it would have to do.

Alaira glanced back at Chela. The younger girl's face was pale and beaded with sweat. "We've scarcely begun," Alaira said. "You look tired already. Are you going to make it?"

Chela looked at her impatiently. "Of course. Here, this is the door."

The tall stone structure had a few small rooms on the first floor and the cells of the black-robed Second Rank priestesses on the second and third levels. Alaira feared the women who wore black. They were old and white-skinned, and were rarely seen during the day. They performed secret rituals after moonset. The door was unlocked. Alaira opened it and paused on the threshold, eyeing the stairway suspiciously. It looked as dark and empty as it had yesterday. "Surely they'll know we're here."

"We'll move like shadows through their dreams," Chela said. Her blue eyes shone unnaturally in the dimness. "Go on."

Alaira shut her eyes for a moment, remembering that she was a night-dweller of Rahan, and she had lived through things that were far worse than anything these priestesses could do. She walked over to the stairs and began to climb. Her bare feet were noiseless on the fresh-laid, unworn stone. Chela made no more sound than a wraith behind her.

The narrow way opened out into a landing where two tiny lamps burned in wall niches, smelling of scented oil. Chela stopped Alaira with a hand on her arm. "There's someone up there. On the next landing."

Alaira heard the soft chink of glass set back into place, and quiet footsteps from above. Probably an early-rising Second Rank priestess, lighting the lamps for her sisters to see in the dark. "She'll know we're here," she whispered.

"I'll strengthen our shields." Chela breathed deeply for a long moment, then lifted her hands and pressed her palms to

Alaira's cheeks. A fog enclosed Alaira's mind, a heavy mist, weighing her down, making her sleepy. "There," Chela murmured. "Now go on."

There was silence from above them. The priestess had moved on down the corridor. Alaira padded up the steps, feeling light-headed, and peered cautiously around the corner of the stairwell into the third-story hall. An old black-robed woman had her back to the landing. She was busy with the ritual of the Goddess's Flame, which Alaira had seen a few times at the Temple. The old priestess waved her hands in the air above a brazier at one end of the hall, and soon a tall white flame sprang up without being lighted, an eerie pale fire that wavered in its own breeze.

Chela nudged Alaira forward. A ladder was set under the eaves of the roof. It led up into a closed hatch. Alaira pulled her novice robe through its belt until its hem cleared her knees, then climbed the ladder, keeping one eye on the oblivious priestess in the hallway. The hatch was secured by a leather thong. Her fingers remembered their old skills. She untied it and lifted the hatch noiselessly.

A cold breeze damp with threatened rain ruffled her short black hair. Alaira put her palms against the rough shingles of the roof and pulled herself through. She crawled aside for Chela to follow. They shut the hatch again and paused to look around.

The roofs were steeper than they had looked from below. They would have to crawl to keep their balance. Alaira sighed. Roofs in Cavernon City were much more civilized, flat and smooth, as easy to walk upon as an uncrowded street.

"I can't hold the shields for both of us much longer," Chela said. Her eyes were glassy in the evening light. "We'd better be far from here when they fail."

As nervous as a little child on her first time out with a master thief, Alaira started across the roof. She imagined the priestess below listening to the scrambling noises from the eaves. Surely they would be discovered. She wished that Kyellan was with her, urging her on with taunts and dares as he had when they were children, yet always willing to come back and help her if she got into trouble. He would expect her to make it. He would be waiting for her.

The wall rose almost to the edge of the roof, and it was a short leap from the wall to the slope of a lower roof on the other side. Alaira was grateful to discover that she had not lost her agility in the months of soft living in the palace. She cleared the jump with ease, landing on feet and hands like a cat. Chela followed. She slipped on the rain-wet roof, but recovered. They were out of the Temple compound at last. A chaotic maze of houses and alleys and close-set rooftops awaited them in the approaching dusk.

The sailor Merabo had vanished. Kyellan and Nemir searched the streets and shops around where he had disappeared, with no luck. Foreboding was growing in Kyellan, and he paused to make certain that Nemir loosed the retaining thong from his sword hilt and loosened the short weapon in its sheath.

The boy looked at him in dismay. "Do you think I'll really have to use it?"

"I hope not. But if it comes to fighting, stay close to my right side. And don't try anything fancy. You shouldn't need much skill against these Chelm soldiers, unless they're far better than they look."

"What now? We'll never find Merabo."

"We'll head back to the ship. But we'll keep to the alleys, and go carefully. No sense in inviting trouble."

They passed behind the Temple compound where the wall was unpainted. The house and shops here were old and ragged, leaning together like hard-of-hearing gossips. The alleys and muddy streets smelled like the Rahan Quarter of Kyellan's childhood. It was not a memory that made him feel nostalgic. Women sat on doorsteps or hung out clothing over their windowsills on upper floors. A few called to the men as they passed. Nemir blushed at their language, but Kyellan laughed and shot back friendly insults. The women giggled and waved at him, commenting to one another on his handsome face and sharp tongue.

From the air above him as he passed a dingy crack of an alley, Kyellan heard a familiar tune whistled in a breathy voice. He stopped so suddenly that Nemir stumbled into him from behind, and glanced to either side to be sure they were not watched. Then he slipped into the narrow space. Nemir followed him.

"Did you sing that song to the priestesses?" Kyellan called softly upward. "A good thing they probably didn't understand Caer." It was a tavern song of Rahan. Some of the later verses were too obscene even for most night-dwellers' tastes.

A white-clad figure with bare legs swung from the edge of the slanted roof six feet above Kyellan's head. She let go and rolled at his feet. Kyellan reached down to help Alaira rise as she rubbed a scrape on her arm. He hugged her and kissed her lightly on the lips. The startled look in her dark eyes as he released her made him remember he should not have done that. Well, he was glad to see her.

Chela dropped more awkwardly, forgetting to collapse when she hit the ground. She swore softly in Garithian and sat in the garbage of the alley holding her left ankle.

"It isn't broken, is it?" Alaira bent over her in concern. "I should have looked harder for a ladder."

Chela tried to smile. "I'm not very good at this sort of thing. But it's only twisted. I'll make it to the ship."

"Here." Nemir held out the bundle he carried. "Master Soren said for you to wear these."

Alaira untied the package and shook out the old, worn sailors' garb. "I suppose Chela and I are skinny enough to pass for boys. If no one looks too closely. All right. Just watch the ends of the alley for us, will you?"

Nemir turned around immediately, red-faced. Kyellan grinned at Alaira and walked slowly to the other end of the narrow space between the houses. He found himself looking out on the main street that led to the harbor. In the distance, coming from the direction of the square, marched a large squadron of soldiers in an almost disciplined formation. He heard shouting. People of the city were running alongside them. "Come on, ladies," he said, turning back toward the alley. "There's no time."

They had been quick. Both were stamping their feet into overlarge boots. Chela's face was grim with pain. They wore rough tunics and wide-legged trousers, tight-fitting woolen caps and belt knives. "Will we pass?" Alaira asked. "What's wrong, Ky?"

"They know about Gwydion." He and Nemir each took one of Chela's arms to help her walk. They started off at a fast stride down the middle of the cobbled street. "One of the sailors betrayed us. We have to reach the *Jester* before they do." The soldiers were only a few blocks behind.

"They'll close the harbor gates," Nemir said. "We'll be trapped."

"There are a lot of people back there," Chela said weakly. Kyellan could feel the heat of her skin where he gripped her arm. She was feverish. What had happened in that Temple? Alaira seemed to be all right. "I can feel their hatred. I'm sure I can do something. Frighten them, delay them . . ."

"Save it," Kyellan said. "We may need your Power to help get the *Jester* away." He tightened his grip on her as she stumbled and almost lost her balance.

Workers on the docks, clerks and officials, all looked past them without noticing them, wondering at the soldiers behind them. No doubt it was a familiar sight, sailors hurrying at the end of their shore leave to reach their ship before it sailed. Chela's disability added a touch of realism. Her eyes were glazed, and she stumbled as if drunk.

The rowboats were in place before the *Jester*, with their tug lines attached. The gangplank was still down. They crossed the pier almost at a run and hurried up the steep ramp onto the main deck. "Take Chela to her cabin," Kyellan told Alaira. With Nemir's help, the two women headed aft.

Soren's men were all on deck. Some were in the rigging awaiting orders. Others were unloading the weapons box on the sterncastle. There were two men at the helm, and the rest waited in a nervous group on the main deck. The ship's master shoved his way past them to Kyellan. Soren was sweating so heavily he looked as if he had been caught in the rain.

"They're behind us," Kyellan said. "Cast off as quickly as you can."

The squadron of Ryasan soldiers stormed past the warehouses and jetties, the din of their boots shaking the piers. The people who swarmed after them were calling for wizard blood. As they rushed closer, Kyellan saw that they carried long, hooked boarding ladders with weighted ends. They marched with a strong easterly wind that was laden with rain.

"It's your choice, Soren," Kyellan said quietly. "You can give them Gwydion, or you can fight."

The smaller man looked up at him with narrowed eyes. "It's too late for a choice, Captain. If they find the wizard they'll take my ship." He raised his voice. "Cut the tug lines and raise sail! Second watch, arm yourselves! The Goddess damn you, move! We have the wind with us!"

Chapter Five ————————————

THE sailors pulled in the gangplank and cast off the mooring lines, but the Chelm soldiers reached the end of the pier with their boarding ladders and flung them toward the ship. The *Jester* rocked as the ladders fell and hooked on its railing. Soldiers climbed up.

"Raise sail!" Soren shouted again, running to the mainmast to call up to his men in the rigging. In the prow below the forecastle, two sailors leaned over to cut the lines that tied the ship to the slow rowboats that would have tugged it out of the harbor. The men of the second watch swarmed down the sterncastle ladder with their bared swords.

Kyellan drew his left-handed rapier and ran to the ladder as the first Ryasan soldier reached the railing. The lean young man dodged his first blow and leaped to the deck, drawing his own sword. Their weapons clashed high and they both sprang back to check the expected downward blow. Kyellan grinned and crouched in a more careful defensive stance. His opponent was no beginner. They were of an age, of a height, well matched.

More soldiers clambered onto the ship. The armed sailors ran to engage them. Kyellan was pleased at how eagerly they sought the fight. They were tired of practice bouts.

Kyellan lunged at his soldier and nearly lost his balance. He recovered quickly, but it sobered him. His right arm hung

64

useless when it should have been helping him counterbalance his moves. It was a weakness Tobas had been quick to exploit when they had practiced in the Tiranon yards. Kyellan would have to compensate as he had not needed to while teaching apprentice swordsmen.

The Ryasan closed with him in a flurry of elegant strokes. Kyellan's defense was reflexive. He mirrored his opponent's steps and anticipated his blows until the soldier tired and stepped back again, already breathing heavily. The lax discipline of the Chelm city troops, Kyellan thought. This swordsman had not been forced to stay in top condition. Kyellan had been working out for two weeks in endless sessions with Soren's sailors. He moved forward to press his advantage.

The heavy whack of canvas unrolling against the mainmast sounded over the cries of the frantic sailors who fought to hold their ropes as the sail bellied in the wind. They would either get out of the harbor or they would capsize from too much canvas too soon. A few crewmen spread the small triangular sail on the foremast, and two high in the fighting top bent over the railing to drop the roll of the topsail. Flying its flag of motley red and black, the *Jester* seemed to mock the city and its angry soldiers as it heaved away from the pier with the easterly wind. The boarding ladders were dragged off the docks. Soldiers fell into the water.

Kyellan wounded his opponent with a slashing cut to the side as he twisted to avoid another sailor's attack. The young Ryasan cried out and staggered back. Around the two of them, a small-scale battle raged. Perhaps fifteen soldiers had made it aboard before the ladders became useless. Ten of Soren's men, all the second watch, were ranged clumsily against them. But as the sails were set, men of the first watch scurried down the rigging to join in the fight. The Chelm soldiers would be outnumbered.

Kyellan looked toward the harbor mouth. Men were running along the top of the sea wall toward the silent, menacing outlines of the defensive ballistae and catapults. They could probably be turned inward, in case any enemy ship breached the gate. One good-sized stone thrown from a ballista onto the *Jester*'s main deck would probably go straight through the hull.

He saw a sailor go down under a death blow from a hand axe. Nearby, young Nemir looked to be in trouble. He faced two soldiers with his back against the mainmast. Kyellan ran to help him.

The ship listed deeply with the wind, scarcely under control. Alaira stumbled and nearly fell as she helped Chela into Gwydion's cabin. The wizard took the girl from her and sat her on the bunk. Chela leaned against him weakly. "Is she wounded?" Gwydion asked Alaira.

"No. She's sick," Alaira said. "She has a fever. She shielded us to get us out of the Temple, and she twisted her ankle." Outside the half-open door, one of the older sailors fell to his knees with a sword buried in his stomach. Bright blood spurted onto the scrubbed deck. "Why are you still hiding in here?" Alaira demanded. "They know you're here. That's why they've come. You should be out there fighting with Kyellan and the sailors."

"I can't," he said quietly. "My hands won't hold a sword. I don't even have any Power. What can I do?"

Chela took a shaky breath and spoke. "We have to keep them from closing the harbor gates. If they do, we'll never get out." Her small hands clutched his shoulders. "I have Power, Gwydion, but you have the knowledge. Tell me what to do. I don't know how to keep them from closing the gates."

"You're too weak," Gwydion protested as she got to her feet. "Chela, you can't!"

"Have to," she said unsteadily. "Or we'll never get out. And they'll kill you." She was near tears. "They'll kill you, Gwydion."

"Could she really do anything?" Alaira asked.

"We can try," Gwydion said with sudden resolve. "Up on the stern deck where we can see the gates. Come, Chela. I'll help you." He put a strong arm around her waist, and they hurried out the door and up the ladder to the deck above the cabins. Alaira followed them, drawing the belt knife that had come with her sailor costume, with the vague hope of protecting them if any soldier tried to stop them.

The deck of the sterncastle was the only part of the ship

that was not swarming with fighting men. Alaira leaned on the uprights of the ladder and looked for Kyellan. She saw him near the starboard railing, just as he ran a soldier through and shoved the man over the side. There were fewer Ryasans now, but there were also fewer of the ship's crew. The ship sounded with cries of the wounded and shouts of those still fighting. The wind was growing stronger, and it had begun to rain in earnest, making the planks of the deck slippery and treacherous.

"They're closing the gate," Gwydion said. His bushy golden hair blew around his face and into his eyes. "Chela, they're closing it already."

"Then I'll open it. Hold me, and tell me what to do," she commanded.

Alaira clutched the top of the ladder as the ship swayed again. She blinked against the rain and strained her eyes to see the harbor gate. The thick stone slabs sent up ripples of forced waves as teams of men worked winches on the walls to close the only exit from Chelm port. The crewmen still in the *Jester*'s rigging saw it too, and cried out in fear.

Gwydion held Chela tightly around the waist and began to speak words of Power. Though they had no strength behind them, his voice was harsh and strange, and Alaira shuddered. Chela repeated the words after him. Her girlish voice was distorted by them, and her face beneath her red hair looked as fierce and confident as a seasoned warrior's. Alaira could feel the magic growing. She felt a tingling in her bones, until her body seemed to burn from the inside. She wished she was not standing so close.

A glow of green light rose around the ship. Only the tops of the masts were free of it. Like a fog, it hung before the faces of the combatants and rolled along the decks. Men screamed, though it did not touch them. The helmsman, who had been fighting to stay at the wheel, now stood frozen with fear as the *Jester* steered an unerring course for the gates, under full sail with a driving wind.

"We're going to hit!" someone shrieked. Alaira braced herself and closed her eyes. The impact rattled the ship and made the foremast creak, but there was no sound of splintering wood. She looked. The green light had taken the brunt, crashing into the gate with the force of ten battering rams, carrying the ship along in its protective embrace. The stones of the gate quivered and burst apart, as if their mortar suddenly would not hold. The ship heaved through the narrow passage, scraping its portside hull lightly against the sea wall.

Ballistae rained stones, and catapults long fiery arrows, but the missiles bounced off the shield and fell harmlessly into the water. Some of the sailors cheered. The remaining soldiers bunched together in the center of the ship, frightened. Most of them appeared to be wounded, as were most of the crewmen. Alaira counted eight soldiers and twelve sailors on their feet. The odds were not overwhelming, but when Soren challenged them the soldiers surrendered. They were disarmed and thrown through the green fog into the rainswept sea, to swim back to the wall if they could.

The four sailors who were unwounded climbed back into the rigging to lash the sails firm for the open sea. When they were out of range of the siege machines, Gwydion spoke softly, and Chela repeated his words in a hoarse crow's whisper. The *Jester*'s eerie glow vanished, and the red-haired girl collapsed in the wizard's arms.

Alaira sheathed her belt knife and helped Gwydion pick Chela up to carry her. "Will she be all right?" she asked softly.

"She's strong," Gwydion said. They started slowly and carefully down the ladder, Alaira half-supporting Chela from above, until they reached the deck and Gwydion took her again. "There has to be a huge backlash to a spell so powerful. Don't worry." Yet his face was drawn with fear.

"She was weak already," Alaira muttered. "And sick."

Kyellan and Soren joined them at the door to Gwydion's cabin. Both men were exhausted and streaked with blood that did not seem to be their own. Kyellan put his arm around Alaira's shoulders and looked worriedly at Chela lying limp in Gwydion's arms. "How is she?"

"Gwydion says it's just the backlash to her spell. She's only unconscious," Alaira said quietly.

The ship's master looked up into Gwydion's tense face. "You and your lady saved my ship, wizard. I don't know how you did it, but I thank you."

"If it hadn't been for me, no one would have attacked your ship. And Chela wouldn't have been hurt." Gwydion moved past them into his cabin, laid Chela on a bunk, and closed the door.

Soren turned back toward the main deck of his ship. It stank of blood and death. Bodies lay scattered, and the wounded slumped against bulkheads. "Here I thought the war was over," he said. "I don't think the *Jester* will ever dock in Chelm again."

Kyellan spoke wearily. "The Queen will reward you for protecting us. Most would have given Gwydion to them."

Soren looked at them narrowly. "It might have saved a lot of bloodshed." He walked away across the stained decks, calling out to his men to throw the dead overboard, friend and enemy alike.

"Come, Alaira," Kyellan said. "Most of the crewmen are wounded. Gwydion will be busy with Chela, so we'll have to try to tend them. There are bandages and salves in my pack."

"I can find them." She reached up on tiptoe and kissed him impulsively. "You fought well."

"Thank you." He smiled slightly. "I'd have fought better if I'd known that would be the reward."

The rain continued into the night as the *Jester* glided quietly beside the wooded Garithian coast, wary of pursuit. Twelve of Soren's men lived. Of them, five were slightly wounded, and three others were not expected to survive until morning. They lay in their hammocks in the lower hold, their wounds stitched and bandaged. There was little else that could be done for them.

Kyellan stood with Soren on the stern deck near midnight, gazing out into the blackness of the ocean and the forest. Rain ran cold down his face, and his clothes were soaked. He was exhausted, but he could not sleep. There was no sign of any other ships. Yet it seemed impossible that Chelm should let them go.

"Did you expect trouble, Captain?" Soren asked softly, not looking at him. His voice was weary and defeated.

Kyellan shook his head. "No. Not like this. I'm sorry."

Soren's dark eyes squinted in folds against the driving rain.

"It was my own man betrayed us. Merabo. He had no more reason than most to hate the wizards. I think he lost a sister to wizards' raiders." He laughed harshly. "At least my men fought well. That I owe to you."

"They're good men. They were overmatched, but they did what they had to. Give them two weeks rest in Garith while you wait for our return, and they should be able to sail the *Jester* home."

"Look there," Soren said abruptly, pointing into the dark clouds. "A flash of white. Did you see it?"

Kyellan saw nothing but black rain. He shrugged. "A sail?"

"Staying just below the horizon." Soren frowned. "Waiting for us to stop to rest. I wish I knew for sure."

"Send someone up into the fighting top to look."

"I don't know if any of my men could make it up there and back down again, in the shape they're in. The younger sailors were the most reckless in the fight, and every one of them is wounded. My older men are too stiff and slow for safety in the highest rigging. And too heavy."

"I'd go," Kyellan said, "but I can't climb very well with only one arm."

"I have to know what's following us," Soren muttered. "What about your lady? She's unhurt, and light enough. Has she done any climbing?"

Alaira took off her boots and replaced them with a pair of the cork-soled shoes the sailors used for climbing wet rigging. She tied the hood of her cloak securely and hurried back out onto the rain-swept deck where Kyellan and Soren waited by the mainmast. The web of rope that led past the huge mainsail and the smaller topsail looked likely to break under her weight. She hated the ship, she hated the way it moved, the dark water that surrounded it, the fitful wind that blew the rain into the sails. The wooden basket of the fighting top swayed like the leaf crown of a sapling. Still, this could not be that different from other climbing she had done. Easier, even. The ship's rigging was meant to be climbed, while she had scaled walls so smooth they were like polished glass.

"I'm not commanding you to do this, my lady," said Soren. "You're free to refuse."

Alaira smiled at him. "I'm glad there's something I can do." She still wore the sailors' clothes in which she had escaped from Chelm, which would make it easier still.

"If you don't see the sail at first," Kyellan said, "stay up there as long as you can in case it appears. But if you start to get too cold, come down right away. Before your hands are too numb to grip the ropes. Understand?"

"I'll be all right." She held up a pair of leather gloves. "I'll put these on as soon as I reach the top." She stuck the gloves back in her belt, looked up, and jumped to catch the lowest cross-ropes of the mainsail rigging.

The rope was thick. Her clasped hands barely reached around it. It felt harsh and stickery, though it was soaking wet. Alaira took a deep breath and pulled herself up. She hooked her trouser-clad legs around the rope and reached for the ladder of rigging that led to the lower spar of the mainmast. The spar was lashed into place to catch the prevailing wind, but still the ropes swayed and stretched as she climbed up them. Alaira revised her initial thoughts. She would take a sturdy, polished stone wall any day before these insubstantial ropes. And the rocking motion of the ship in the choppy sea was much worse up here. She tried hard not to think about being sick.

Rain soon had soaked her hood so that it clung to her head like cloth made of seaweed. She pulled it back impatiently, preferring wet hair to the heavy, sharp-smelling wool. Rain washed into her eyes and down her neck. She blinked furiously to see as she climbed.

Her strong, slim fingers hooked into the ropes lashed around the lower spar, and she squirmed onto the beam. It was flat on top, wide enough for her two feet to stand together, but it shook and swayed alarmingly beneath her weight. She tried to imagine she was walking along a rooftree. The wind filled the huge sail that pulled against the spar. Alaira shivered and tried not to look down as she eased along the length of wood to the knotted web of rope that would take her higher.

Though the rigging was frightening and dangerous, Alaira had meant it when she told Soren she was glad to climb it.

She had tried to sleep, but could not. She was worried about Chela. She could not help thinking it was partly her fault. If the younger girl had not had to shield Alaira too in the escape from Chelm, she would not have been nearly so weakened. Gwydion insisted she would be all right, that it was only the backlash from the spell. But Alaira had looked in on Chela an hour ago. The thick mass of red hair spread over her pillow was the only color about the girl. Her face was thin and ghostly pale, beaded with sweat, the only part of her that was visible over a mound of blankets and cloaks. She looked worse off than the three dying sailors in the hold.

"See anything yet?" a faint call came from below in Soren's voice. Alaira glanced down. The deck looked narrow and dark, between the vast stretches of black water. If she fell, she could not be sure of falling onto the ship. She did not want to think about falling into the sea.

She hooked her legs tightly in the web and freed one hand to shade her eyes against the rain. For a long moment she looked back the way they had come. Nothing but clouds and ocean and rain. "No!" she shouted. The wind seemed to steal her voice away, driving it into the sails along with the rain. But the ship's master had heard her. He waved a hand at her to go on.

Alaira climbed steadily, carefully, never releasing one hand or foot unless all three of the others had firm holds. The ropes were soggy in her grasp and smelled of wet hemp. She thought longingly of the warm sunshine of Cavernon City. But it seemed only a short time before she was balancing on the upper spar above the mainsail and climbing past the topsail, and then her hands gripped the ring of bent wood just beneath the fighting top, and she scaled the wooden basket and swung inside.

Her heart beat loud and fast, and her hands and face were sweating even though she was shivering with cold. Her legs felt quivery and weak. She crouched down inside the basket, out of the wind, and pulled her gloves on, then retied her hood and buckled her cloak tightly. The fighting top had room for two men standing close together. The sides were the height of Alaira's chest. The tapered pole of the topmast rose through the center of the platform, and the entire structure waved back and forth in a sweeping arc with the wind and the rocking of the ship.

Alaira stood up and gripped the edge of the basket tightly, then looked down. The choppy waves rose almost the height of the *Jester*'s deck railing, but from here the sea looked almost calm. It did not feel that way. She swallowed hard, refusing to be sick. The mainsail below her blocked the view of Soren and Kyellan standing underneath. She wondered how they could possibly hear her even if she had something to tell them.

"No," Chela murmured in her sleep, or her delirium. Gwydion was not certain which it was. "No, you can't, I won't let you. . . ." Her blue eyes flickered open briefly, and for a moment they focused on Gwydion's face hovering close over hers. "Do you feel it? They're coming . . . have to stop them. . . ." Then she shuddered weakly and her head lolled to one side in unconsciousness.

"Who's coming, Chela?" he whispered urgently, gripping her thin shoulders through the blankets. "What is it?"

She did not answer. Gwydion smoothed back a strand of wiry red hair from her forehead. She was hot, as if she had been lying in the sun. There were precise circles of red on her cheeks, like rouge against the pale skin. He did not know what to do. He had seen violent results of spells before. He himself had slept for days after destroying a sea monster in the harbor of Keor last spring. This was different. It was as if Chela was still trying to use the Power she had expended, and the effort was burning her up from within.

If this was the backlash to the spell he had given her to protect the ship, she should be completely drained and sleeping deeply to recover her strength. Something within her would not grant her that release. Gwydion wished fervently that he had his Power back, to reach into her mind and calm whatever frightened her so.

He got up from the bunk and went to the sea chest to rummage through his vials of medicines and herbs. Perhaps if he burned some of the stupefying flower drug over the cabin's small brazier, it might numb Chela's thoughts and send her to sleep. He could not get her to drink it in the form of tea while she was unconscious. He began to prepare a pan for the dried flower petals, though it seemed as useless as bandaging a man's death wound.

Alaira had been shivering in the fighting top for almost an hour before she saw the flash of white against the darkness behind them. It appeared only briefly, and did not seem very far away. It did not look like a sail. More like a broad band of lightning. If it was a sail, there was no moon to reflect off it and make it glow that way. But she could not be sure.

"There's something out there!" she yelled as strongly as she could. Cries from below told her the others had seen it as well. She leaned as far as she dared over the edge of the wooden basket. Figures were climbing up onto the sterncastle. The four unwounded sailors, Soren, and Kyellan, all pressed against the railing to stare into the darkness behind the *Jester*.

The night was blacker, somehow, and the rain clouds overhead were thicker and lower. A sudden strong wind tore at Alaira's hood and pulled it back off her face. Her chin-length black hair blew out behind her, tugging at her scalp. The topsail just beneath her snapped out with the gust, and the fighting top swayed. Alaira clutched at the central pole to keep her balance. As suddenly as it had come, the wind stopped, and the sails quivered and hung slack in the stillness.

The rain stopped too. Alaira looked down. Even the dark ocean was quiet, and the ship moved gently in place like a cradle. She did not like it. She had not liked the rain or the wind or the choppy waves, but she liked this far less. High up on the top of the mast, beneath the black clouds, she felt alone and vulnerable, like a target.

Alaira heard a hissing noise above her and felt the skin prickle all over her body. She looked up to see a globe of fierce white light hovering over her like a hanging lantern, no more than two feet above her head. It had no smell, but it crackled like fire. She shrank back against the pole. The ball of light leaped as if thrown to balance briefly on the very top of the tapered mast. Alaira stepped away from it, clutching the edge of the wooden basket, unable to breathe. With the speed of running water, the fire-globe rolled down the mast in a shower of sparks and vanished through the bottom of the platform.

Alaira heard men cry out in terror below. What was happening? A roaring filled her ears as the wind returned with the fury of a gale. The sails strained forward and the fighting top arced with them. The black clouds burst in a flood of driven rain. Thunder crashed through the sky like an avalanche, and the *Jester* was caught in the teeth of the storm.

Gwydion stumbled backward into the wall of the cabin with the listing of the ship. The brazier toppled, scattering burning coals across the floor toward him. The pan of aromatic flowers rolled, as the cabin tilted like an overturning wagon. Chela tumbled from her bunk among the coals. She cried out weakly.

The ship righted itself for a moment before it began to tilt the other way. Gwydion kept his balance with difficulty. He picked Chela up in his arms and put her back on the bunk. She had fallen wrapped in blankets, which smoldered in places. She did not seem to be burned. The ship lurched drunkenly. Gwydion swore as he bumped his shin against the wooden frame of the bunk. A thin sheet of water began to seep in under the door. Now he could hear the thunder and the howling of the wind.

He took a rope from the sea chest and tied Chela securely to the bunk. Then he went to the door and forced it open. Spray drenched him. The *Jester* rode low in a trough of giant waves that rose nearly the height of the ship's mast. The deck was awash with rain and broken waves. The men who had been on watch were running to the rigging and swinging themselves up into it while Soren and Kyellan opened the crew hatch to shout for the rest of the crew to come on deck. The mainmast swayed and creaked with the violent movements of the ship, and high in its fighting top Gwydion could see Alaira clinging, a small and terrified figure.

He braced himself against the doorframe as the *Jester* was swept by a crashing wave. Water swirled past him knee-high. The foresail ripped from its lashings to flap like a tattered flag.

"They've come!" Chela shouted from inside the cabin. Her voice was high and frightened. "They've found us!"

Gwydion realized what she meant as he looked out over the huge, mountainous waves. At the top of each one, hovering like a scrap of sea-foam caught before its fall, burned a fierce, white flame. Streaks of white fire wrapped around the mainmast, not burning it. This was no natural storm. Some- one had caused it. Someone with more Power than Gwydion could have wielded at the height of his strength. And there was nothing either he or Chela could do to fight it.

Chapter Six ────────────────

ALAIRA had feared a storm since the beginning of the voyage. Now that it had come, she was too frightened to be seasick. The mast swayed so far that she was nearly dipped into the waves. She wrapped arms and legs around the slim pole of the mast top and closed her eyes as the spray washed over her. She heard a man's shriek, and looked down. One of the sailors who had climbed into the rigging had been swept from the upper spar where he had been furling the mainsail. Alaira saw him vanish into the black water.

The sail fought against its ropes like a great trapped bird trying to spread its wings. The remaining sailors clung like leeches to the rigging, cursing faintly over the fury of the wind. Slowly, the vast canvas of the mainsail rolled within its ropes up toward the upper spar, until it was lashed firmly to the wooden beam. Then two of the three crewmen climbed up toward the topsail.

They were two of the older men, more experienced fighters who had not been wounded in the battle; heavyset and slow, they still were surefooted on the rain-drenched ropes. They called up to Alaira, but the wind stole their voices. After a moment she realized they were asking her to climb down to help them from the top of the smaller sail.

"Oh, gods," she whispered, unable to hear herself. She supposed she had to start down sometime. The *Jester* rolled

heavily into another trench between high waves. Alaira stripped
off her wet gloves and put them in her belt again, then inched
over the side of the fighting top. She was suspended over the
waves. The shrill wind tried to pluck her off, but she lowered
herself to the bentwood ring at the base of the platform,
hooked her knees inside it, and let go her hands to grasp the
rail beside her legs.

Now she could reach the upper spar of the topsail. She
wound the ropes around their cleats as the sailors released the
sail from beneath. The canvas rolled obediently up toward
her. She tied as strong a knot as she could with the slick,
heavy lines, then started down the rigging. The sailors descended just below her, watching her carefully. She wondered
if they thought they could catch her if she fell. Alaira gripped
the ropes so hard that her fingers hurt as heavy waves broke
over the ship. It was harder going down than going up, she
realized, even in fair weather. Her feet had to search for the
next lines in the rope web. She could scarcely see where she
was going in the fury of the storm.

At last she was creeping along the lowest spar of the furled
mainsail, and then she swung down from the bottom of the
rigging and dropped to the deck. Kyellan had been waiting
for her there. He caught her around the waist with his good
arm as she fell, to keep her from slipping in the river of water
that swept across the deck.

Alaira shivered against him, burying her face in his chest. It
was foolish to think she was safe on this storm-tossed ship
just because she was out of the rigging, but somehow when
Kyellan held her she thought it impossible anything bad could
happen.

Kyellan hooked his fingers into Alaira's belt as the ship
lurched violently, and waves foamed around their knees to
dash them back against the mainmast. "I'll get you back to
our cabin," he shouted to be heard over the wind. "You'll be
drier there, at least." She looked up at him, and he had to
smile at her bedraggled appearance. Her cloak was heavy and
dripping, and her sailors' clothes clung to her slim body. Her
black hair was plastered to her head.

"What are you going to do?" she asked loudly.

"I have to go below and see to the horses. They'll be terrified. We can't afford to lose them. We won't get to Akesh without them."

One of the three unwounded sailors who had just come down from furling the sails now staggered across the deck, pulling a rope behind him. The rope was attached to the forecastle bulkhead at chest height. He wrapped it around a cleat on the mainmast, attached another rope, and struck out aft.

"What's that for?" Alaira shouted.

"So we can cross the deck without being washed overboard. Come on." Kyellan pulled her to the rope and kept a grip on her as she clung to it and walked toward the sterncastle. The deck had been almost deserted at the beginning of the storm. Now all the crewmen who could walk were struggling to winch down the ship's longboat onto the deck. The helmsman had lashed himself to the wheel, and clung there grimly as he and Soren fought to keep the vessel upright and headed before the wind. Kyellan strained his eyes to see through the blackness of night and towering waves. There was a slope of darkness near them on the port side. The coast of Garith? If it was, then they were too close.

"I want to stay with you," Alaira said as they reached the crew hatch. "I'll just get seasick if I wait in the cabin. Maybe I can help you with the horses."

"If you want." Kyellan lifted the hinged hatch cover. Water poured into the lower hold, down the ladder. "Quickly, Alaira."

She held her breath to descend the ladder into the hold. The seawater swept over her. Kyellan followed her and closed the hatch, stopping the torrent. The sound of the storm was lessened here, and now he could hear the horses' screams. The four animals battered themselves against their stalls and kicked at the doors, their heads flung back, their ears flat to their wet skulls. In the dim light of lanterns swinging over the crew's hammocks, Kyellan could see that two of the horses had bloody scrapes across their chests and sides.

The three dying crewmen lay tied to their hammocks, still and silent. Perhaps they were already dead. There was a shallow sea in the hull. Water had come through the hatch

when it was opened, but not enough to cover the jagged
ballast rocks and rise nearly to the half deck of planking.
Kyellan's hopes lessened as he watched the pool sloshing
with waves created by the ship's motion. If the *Jester* was
carrying this much water, there might be damage he could not
see. Holes in the caulking of the planks, or boards loosened
by the impact of the waves—the longboat might well be
necessary. He did not think the ship would ride out the storm.

He and Alaira moved across the creaking half deck, clinging to the ropes of hammocks. The ship shuddered heavily,
almost knocking them from their narrow path. Alaira cried
out as her feet left the planks, but her grip was sure on a rope
and she regained her footing. Kyellan let go of his own
handhold to steady her. She looked up at him miserably.
"Did you see the white fire?" Her voice was thin and
frightened.

"I saw it. Gwydion says this storm is being created and
controlled by magic. There are flames on top of all the
waves. But whoever it is has only attacked with the weather."

"Isn't that enough?" she said shakily. "This storm is
terrible. Look how frightened the horses are. . . . How can
we calm them down? How can we even get near them?"

Kyellan moved carefully past her to the first box stall. The
grain in the feed-trough was sodden, lumped into a gluey
mass. The horse's saddle and bridle still hung on the wall,
though the lighter currycombs and brushes had fallen to be
trampled underfoot. The nearest horse was a slim, fiery mare
who screamed and flailed her forelegs, mad with fear. She
was likely to go down with the ship, Kyellan thought. Perhaps she knew it. It would be impossible to pull a horse up
through the hatch in a sling in such a storm. There was no
other way for her to get out. "We have to tie them," he said
grimly. "Give them less room to move, so they can't hurt
themselves. They won't like the idea."

A rope hung on the outside of the stall. Kyellan made a
clumsy loop of one end and climbed up to stand on a cross-
piece of the stall door. He leaned forward precariously. The
mare bared her teeth at him and lunged. At the same moment,
the *Jester* heaved forward and leaned almost onto its starboard side. The mare lost her footing and fell against the

slats. Kyellan threw the loop over her head as she staggered back onto her hooves. "Alaira!" he shouted. "Help me tie her down."

The black-haired girl was behind him quickly. She took a firm hold on the rope. They looped it over the post at one end of the stall and wound it tightly, until the horse was forced to stand still with its head caught. "Look," Alaira panted. "The others have quieted down to watch us. It ought to be easier. . . ."

There was a sudden burst of white fire on the hatch ladder, lighting up the dark hold. Kyellan and Alaira both whirled to see a globe of silent flame break apart and fall in floating strands into the seawater that filled the lower hull. Ball lightning, Kyellan thought, not magic. He had heard sailors speak of the eerie way it could travel through a ship. But wasn't ball lightning usually found during a dry storm, when the sky crackled with life but no rain came?

Alaira bent close to the edge of the walkway, looking out into the water that glowed with streaks of white flame. Then, with a speed that overwhelmed her, a huge wave rose from the pool. She screamed. Capped by white light, the swell crashed down on her and swept her into the water. Kyellan stood frozen for an instant as he saw Alaira choke and go under, borne downward as if clutched by a giant hand.

The water in the hold churned savagely, as violent as the waves in the storm outside, and an impossible wind howled past his ears. If she hit against the rocks at the bottom . . . Kyellan leaped in after her. The water closed cold and salt over his head. It glittered like black curtains threaded with silver, and it was alive with Power. Kyellan could feel it as he kicked to the surface for a deeper breath. It pressed in on his shields, wakening the trapped Shape-Changer spirit inside him. Gwydion was right. The storm was the work of some powerful enemy.

He dove as deeply as he could toward the bottom of the hold. The flame-tinged water forced its way into his mouth and nose, burning him; but he ignored it. Where was Alaira? He could not see a finger's length past his face. He reached out blindly with his good arm and caught a handful of woolen cloak, heavy and welcome. Farther down he touched Alaira's limp form, facedown between two ballast rocks. White fire outlined her body at his approach. He reached his arm around her slim waist and kicked upward. She seemed much heavier than she should be. The water bore down on them both like leaden weights, and tugged at them from below. He began to think he could not reach the surface. It should not be so far. The water could be no more than ten feet deep.

The *Jester* shuddered and ground to a halt, sending a shock wave through the water in the hold that propelled Kyellan and Alaira to the surface. Kyellan gasped hoarsely for air and dragged the limp girl to the edge of the deck planking. He shoved her up onto it and pulled himself out after her before he looked to see what had happened.

The hull was stoved in. Water roared through a gaping hole in the side of the ship opposite the half deck and the horse stalls. They had run aground, on one of the shallow rock formations that made ships' masters plot courses well away from this part of the Garithian coast. The *Jester* shook again from the impact of the storm waves, and rolled in a crippled lurch away from the rocks. The ocean forced its way into the lower hold. Soon the water would swamp the half deck.

Kyellan turned Alaira's scarred face upward. She choked and coughed, but she was breathing. "We have to get out of here, old friend. No time to rest now." He braced his feet against a deck cleat and pulled her upright. She leaned against him, half-conscious.

The bow of the ship had begun to go under, and the pool in the lower hull tilted little by little. The end of the deck where the ladder led upward was already flooded. The three sailors who had been lashed to their hammocks were drowned, if they had not already died of their wounds. Kyellan looked at the jagged hole in the planks opposite him. It was big enough for a horse to swim through. It would be madness to try, but it was certain death to stay here.

"What—what are we going to do?" Alaira asked, struggling in his grasp to look wild-eyed at the submerged hammocks and the two rungs of the ladder that still remained above water. "Ky, look at the ladder . . . you can't get to it without swimming, and I can't swim."

"Hold onto the post here." He set her beside the first stall. "We're going out on the horses. Through that hole."

She began to laugh weakly, clinging with both hands to the post they had wrapped the mare's lead rope around. "Oh, gods, Ky . . . I can't ride either. I—I never told you, because I thought you might leave me behind."

"You don't have to ride. Just stay on." He drew his belt knife and cut the mare's rope. The animal stood still, frightened beyond rearing or screaming at the way the floor of its stall kept tilting beneath its hooves. The whites showed bloodshot around its dark brown eyes. Kyellan unlatched the door of its stall and threw it open. The horse looked in terror at the foaming water that washed in over the planks. It did not move. "You'll have to swim sometime," Kyellan told it. "Better now while you can still get out."

"This is crazy!" Alaira shouted.

"We aren't far from the coast," Kyellan said grimly, unlatching the other stall doors. The three geldings, two bays and a grey, stared at him dully. "Horses are stronger swimmers than any man. They'll make it to shore. All we have to do is stay with them." He pushed past the heavy flank of one of the bays and took its simple S'tari bridle from the wall. The knotted length of rope went over the horse's lower jaw, with a long single rein to the left side. Kyellan took a halter rope and wound it securely around the horse's thick neck. "This one is yours."

Alaira inched over to him, looking like a waif in her ill-fitting sailor garb. "We'll never make it," she protested as he boosted her onto the horse's bare back.

"Wrap your hands through the ropes, one on each side of the neck. Lean down. That's it." He looped the end of the rein around one of her arms so it would not tangle the horse's legs in the water. "If your knees lose their grip or a wave pulls you off, don't panic. The horse will drag you along until you can regain its back." He reached up and kissed her lightly on the forehead. She looked down at him miserably, her eyes still unfocused from the blow on her head she had gotten from the ballast rocks. There was a bloody knot on her scalp, and her hands were raw from climbing the rigging.

Kyellan turned away from her and splashed through the

white-threaded water into the next stall. He bridled the other bay for himself, mounted, and twisted the rein around his left hand and wrist. Then he shouted a S'tari battle cry and dug his bootheels into the tender flanks of his mount. Terrified beyond endurance, the bay leaped from its stall and sank immediately over its head in the black water.

Kyellan felt the shock of the cold and the sense of waiting Power again, but this time the animal beneath him churned its four legs and began swimming strongly. They broke the surface. Kyellan saw the dark shapes of the other three horses in the water. They had followed their fellow's lead, as he had expected. Alaira was a small shadow bent over the largest horse's neck. "Hold on!" he shouted to her as she bobbed underneath momentarily and emerged shaking her black hair and sputtering.

It was impossible to guide the animals, but as they swam frantically around the rapidly rising pool in the hold they soon found the splintered opening where the rocks had plunged into the hull. Kyellan's horse ducked its head and fought its way through the rushing water until it was kicking with powerful strides through the waves outside the ship. The rocky coastline looked farther away than Kyellan had guessed, but he could still see its dark outline in the night.

For a moment, Alaira's horse was beside his, but then they were swept apart. The brown mare and the grey gelding struggled in the ocean nearby. Kyellan looked behind him to see the *Jester*, with its sterncastle high in the storm-tossed sea, slowly and inexorably sinking under the waves. The mainmast had almost vanished. Only the fighting top still waved near the water's surface. Kyellan could not watch long. Half-drowned by each new swell, blind and numb from the sting of salt spray, he clung to his horse's back. They made slow progress toward the shore.

Briana fought against the hand that smothered her screams. She opened her eyes to the blurry outline of a dark face, and struggled to wake from her nightmare. An angry knot of Power churned in her womb, sending sparks of agony into her mind. Oh, Goddess, what was happening? She had been lost in a dream of drowning, in a sea of rolling white waves. She could still hear the screams of horses, the protesting creak of straining canvas and rope, the cries of men.

"Shh, my lady, be quiet," Tapeth murmured fearfully, holding her shoulders. Yalna knelt beside her cot in the greyness of dawn, her hands over Briana's mouth. "What is wrong? Is it the babe coming before its time? Lady, you must not scream so, they will hear you in the palace."

Briana focused her gaze on Tapeth's familiar, worried face and forced her cramped body to relax. After a moment, Yalna released her and reached gently to probe her swollen stomach, pressing with her fingers through the black woolen robe. "It is not the babe," the young midwife said in relief. "Are you all right, Briana?"

She tried to slow her gasping breath. She was no longer trapped by what she felt. Her unborn child was restless in his unconscious Power, but his terror no longer gripped her. She did not know if the dream had been her own or her son's. But why would a babe in the womb dream of a storm at sea? Kyellan was at sea, she remembered. With the thought came the certainty that he was in danger. Briana wanted to clutch at her memory of him and try to reach over hundreds of miles to keep him safe. That would take more Power than even she had, and she was the strongest priestess of the Goddess.

"It was . . . only a dream," she finally whispered. "I am sorry it disturbed you."

"An unpleasant dream," Tapeth said dryly. "Either you or the Shape-Changer was angry enough to overturn my cot with Power during it."

Briana wiped sweat from her forehead and sat up slowly. "After I leave for the seacoast maybe you'll be able to sleep in peace."

"You should leave soon, my lady," Yalna said seriously. "You shouldn't travel in your eighth month. And you seem to have less and less control over the child. Suppose something like this happens when you are talking to the Second Rank priestesses through the curtains?"

Briana looked past the kneeling girl to the window. Grey dawn light was filtering through the closed shutters. They might as well rise, since none of them was likely to get any more sleep. "We'll leave tomorrow, Yalna," she decided.

"Arrange for horses and peasant clothing, and make certain the S'tari Guard knows not to hinder us."

Yalna smiled in relief. "We'll leave Tapeth here to keep the door, and pretend the Priestess Briana has gone into even deeper seclusion."

"It will be a pleasure to turn those old women away," Tapeth said, walking over to open the shutters and breathe in the cool morning air. "You need not fear that anyone will learn you are gone."

"I'll leave you with a few proclamations to send out at intervals. And some blank papers with my seal, in case something happens I should respond to. Yalna is right. I must get out of the city before my child does something to betray himself."

The babe was rarely quiet now as it began its seventh month. She tried to remain vigilant and well shielded, but such constant use of her Power drained her strength lower daily. She felt sometimes like a vessel filled with storm, as the active and inquisitive mind of her unborn wizard son reached out and battered against the limits in which she had enclosed it. Occasionally a sharp probe of unfocused Power escaped her barriers, and though it usually had no object, once it had created a whirlwind of the ancient papers she was studying. This time had been the worst yet.

Alaira had once told her Kyellan's mother had hated him. Briana did not remember precisely what the girl had said, but Alaira had thought it was because the birth of a child had ruined the woman's chances for a good marriage. Briana suspected a different reason. An untrained woman with no sensitivity, no control, would have been terrified by the seemingly random, unexplainable events that would have surrounded her pregnancy.

Kyellan's mother had been horrified by the child she carried. She had transmitted that fear to her son. The Shape-Changer, sensing danger if he was born a wizard, had altered his form to his mother's desperate wishes. He emerged a human child. Still, his mother would not have been able to completely forget her fears. She could never have loved her son.

Briana was determined not to be frightened by her child.

She had the Power and the knowledge to cope with him, if anyone did. Perhaps the Goddess was testing her through this, testing her endurance and her calm. She would not fail.

As if to refute her sleepy thoughts, the child within her gave a few innocent kicks. She felt like a drum beating from within. She rubbed her taut stomach as she rose from her cot. As Yalna and Tapeth began to fold the bedding on the cots, she went over to the small brazier in the back corner of the room. Briana calmed her mind with a ritual she had learned when she was seven, and began to whisper her morning invocation of the Goddess. As her hands gestured in lingering motions through the air, the Goddess's Flame rose brilliantly white to burn two handspans high and one broad above the unlit coals.

Gwydion sat cross-legged beside the sputtering campfire in the light rain. The storm had ended as suddenly as it had begun. The Tarnsea beyond the forest slope was quiet and unthreatening, dappled by raindrops in the rosy dawn. The hulk of the *Jester* was sprawled over the rocky shallows in several places. The battered longboat on the shore was all that remained intact.

He had managed to get Chela, his baggage and Kyellan's safely to land. Now the slim, red-haired girl lay asleep in restless fever between the piled packs, a tent of blankets sheltering her from the rain. Eight variously wounded and exhausted sailors lay curled upon the ground near the fire. Soon it would be Nemir's turn to take a watch. Soren lay prone on his back, but Gwydion knew his eyes were open, still squinting up into the drizzle.

He wondered if he should have tried so hard to escape the wreck. What did it matter? He was somewhere on the southern coast of Garith, with no horses. Even if Chela could walk, it would take months to get to Akesh by foot. Kyellan and Alaira had not made it to the longboat. Gwydion had opened the hatch of the water-filled hold to search for them just before the ship went down, but all he had seen was black ocean and floating timbers. Whoever had attacked the *Jester* had done their job thoroughly.

*   *   *

The sun lightened the top of the high cliff walls, and the nearby surf pounded in with the tide onto jagged, rocky shores. Yet the canyon of the Goddess's Seat seemed out of time, not a part of the chill autumn morning. Gemon felt the Power slip away from her, ebbing. It left her as weak as she had been during the worst of her illness, but she was exhilarated. They had done it. She might still only be a novice, but now these old and powerless Second Rank priestesses were listening to her. Following her.

The circle was still on the first steps of the gigantic throne. "Well done," Gemon said. "We have not killed him, but we have delayed his journey and punished those who helped him. Well done, sisters."

Iona's eyelids fluttered open in her wrinkled face. "Still you have not proven to me that this Kyellan is a wizard. Even if he is, I am not certain he is a danger. His Power seems to be mostly unconscious, and surely he cannot control it well enough to use it effectively. If he intends to use it for evil at all."

"He is the Shape-Changer," Gemon said with weary patience. "The same evil spirit that almost killed me, that would have killed me if it had not been for the healing aid of Va'shindi. The same evil spirit, only in a different body."

"You have convinced us to work against Darkness," said Niketa. Her child-sized form was drawn up with pain and exhaustion. "We had thought to turn the two women you told us of to the Goddess, but we failed. I am not sure it was right to invoke Va'shindi's voice and form in any case. I did not see that the women were evil. And as for this Kyellan, even if he is what you say, he fought with Va'shindi's blessing to defend the Goddess's Seat from the wizards. He has the favor of the First Priestess."

Her favor? Gemon scowled. She suspected Kyellan and Briana of being lovers, though she would not accuse the First Priestess of such heresy until she had proof. Kyellan could not be forgiven that. At the Sanctuary, it had been said that the penalty for such seduction was death. "The wizard Gwydion also fought against his kindred, but that does not mean he follows the Light. Kyellan is going to Akesh to achieve control over his Power. If he succeeds, no one will be safe from the evil ambitions of the Shape-Changer.''

Iona looked at her dully. ''What do you propose we do? Beyond raising storms at sea and risking the wrath of the Goddess's messenger by using her form to invade the dreams of the Chelm priestesses?''

Gemon managed to rise to her feet on the stone step. She looked down at them. ''We have to stop him before he reaches Akesh. We have to attack him directly. He will try to defend himself by becoming the Shape-Changer. Then you'll know I'm right. And then we must kill him.''

''But to summon Rahshaiya . . .'' Niketa said in an awed voice.

''No, no. Don't be foolish. We have no need for Rahshaiya. We will not follow Briana's lead and invoke the Death-Bringer. The Seat of the Goddess will provide all the Power we need. It is a weapon, sisters. A weapon to be used against Darkness. If we do not use it so, we will have failed in our duty to the Goddess.'' She smiled thinly as the older priestesses nodded in agreement. She was learning to control them with words alone. She no longer had to use her link with the Goddess's Seat.

''Your vision leads us, Gemon,'' Iona said. ''We will do as you say. But I must see that this Kyellan is a wizard before I will add my Power to any attempt to kill him.''

''I will prove it to you,'' Gemon promised. ''And then we will destroy him.'' There would be no doubts left. And together they would make the Hidden Temple a force to be feared and respected in the world.

Chapter Seven ———————

F OG wrapped the Garithian coast as Kyellan and Alaira trudged southwest from the point where they had come ashore. Kyellan led his dark bay gelding, and the other three S'tari horses trailed with lowered heads. They had been bred for endurance, but they stumbled over stones on the hillsides and blew out their breath in short gusts. Their long manes were tangled with seaweed and branches, their tails were hopelessly snarled, their hides matted with mud. The tender parts inside their hooves were caked with dirt and crusted sand; they would soon go lame if they were ridden in that condition.

"Are you sure this is the right way?" Alaira muttered for the third time in the last hour. Her sailors' clothes, like Kyellan's, were ragged and filthy, and the cut on her scalp had bled to mingle with mud in her hair. "How do we know where the *Jester* went down? Or if the storm carried us above or below the place?"

"If we don't find any signs of it by midday, we'll turn around and go the other direction," he said wearily. They descended a pine-clad slope into a valley between two low hills. The Tarnsea was still and mild off the shore to their left, but piles of driftwood and the beached bodies of sea creatures attested to the storm the night before. Sharp-smelling pine needles crunched underfoot as they walked, and the fog beaded with sweat on their skin. Kyellan ached all over. Even his lifeless arm seemed to throb, though he knew he had no feeling in it. He found it difficult to believe that he was still alive. He supposed the horse he rode from the ship's hold had struggled in the water for an hour or more before staggering up a rocky embankment to stand shuddering in the wind. Kyellan had fallen off its back then, and he had wakened at dawn to find the other horses and Alaira sleeping just out of the shallow water of a sheltered cove.

"Look up there," Alaira said some time later, squinting her salt-reddened eyes toward the crest of the next hill. "I don't think that's fog."

Kyellan could not tell what she meant at first. Then he saw a long tendril of darker stuff than the silvery mist rising through the dense pines at the top of the hill. "Smoke?" he said uncertainly.

"And there's something out beyond the rocks, in the ocean."

A piece of the ship's hull jutted up like an angular rock formation, perhaps a hundred feet from the shore. "Maybe we've found them." He tugged at the rein of the horse he was leading. The others followed at a quicker pace. Alaira trotted to keep up with Kyellan's lengthened stride, breathing in heavy rasps. Now he could hear the crackle of the campfire on the ridge, an alien sound in the silence of the forest and the gentle surf.

Halfway up the hill, a slim young man leaped out to challenge them. "Who's there?" Nemir cried, waving his drawn short sword. When he recognized them he gaped at them like a fish.

Kyellan grinned. The salt-dried skin of his face seemed to crack with the effort. "Glad to see you, lad."

"Master Soren! Gwydion!" the sailor shouted, running ahead of them to the sputtering campfire. The ship's master stood up from his seat by the flames, and Gwydion came to meet them, relief briefly erasing some of the lines of worry in his angular face.

"I thought you both were dead," the young wizard said quietly. "And the horses lost, of course. How did you do it, Ky?" He gripped Kyellan's shoulders lightly with his gloved hands and pulled him into a quick embrace.

"The horses saved us," Alaira said, giving Gwydion a hug in her turn, to Kyellan's surprise. "Is Chela all right?"

"She's still sick. Come up to the fire. Have you had any breakfast? All the bread stored in the longboat was ruined in the storm, but there's salt pork and fresh water."

"That sounds like a feast." Kyellan allowed Nemir to take his horse's rein and lead the animal to a tree where it could be tied. Other sailors got to their feet and took the other horses. They would need to be rubbed down and fed, but for now just standing still was what they needed. Kyellan sat down beside Soren at the fireside. Alaira sighed contentedly as she joined him, holding her hands out to the flames.

"Gwydion even rescued our baggage," she said. "Look."

"I want to get to Akesh," Gwydion said, putting pieces of pork in a skillet to fry for them. "And no magician's storm is going to stop me."

Kyellan looked up at the still, foggy air. "Do you have any idea who it might have been? I wonder if it was even directed at us. Maybe someone was just practicing controlling the weather."

"Practicing?" Soren shook his head. "I'd say they knew what they were doing. If the wizard is right and the storm was someone's fault. I'm not sure I believe that. The Garithian coast is always treacherous this time of year."

"The white flames were someone's doing," Gwydion said. "The storm may have been natural, but it was enhanced by Power. Chela felt it coming."

"What bothers me is the flames," Kyellan said thoughtfully. "They're a symbol of the Goddess, aren't they? It might have been the Chelm priestesses."

Alaira shook her head. "Chela said none of them had much Power. They never suspected what we were doing when we escaped. They couldn't have handled anything that big."

"Then someone used the Goddess's Flame who had no right to." Kyellan frowned and stared at the flames. The meat in the skillet crackled in its own grease, but he was too tired to be very hungry.

Gwydion glanced uncomfortably at Kyellan, looked away, then finally spoke his thoughts. "It may have been someone who had every right to the flames. I've been thinking about this. No one individual has the Power to call up a storm that way, and control it after it has formed. It had to have been a group. I think it might have been the priestesses who control the Goddess's Seat. That thing has enough Power to affect us even at this distance.''

"The Goddess's Seat?" Kyellan's voice went cold. "That would mean Briana. Briana would never attack us. That's insane, Gwydion."

"Probably. I wish Chela would get better. She may have some idea who it was."

It could not be the Goddess's Seat. Briana would have no reason to try to prevent them from going to Akesh. To try to kill them. She had asked them to go to the Sanctuary for her. Gwydion had to be wrong. He had to be.

Briana tried to ignore her discomfort. She rode on a padded saddle with a pillow beneath her heavy stomach, and her horse had been chosen for its ambling gait, yet already her back ached. Her senses were overwhelmed by the smells and sounds of the crowd, after six months in the peaceful seclusion of the tower rooms. The women all seemed shrill, the men ill-tempered, the animals filthy. She could not wait for the silence of the desert.

With two nondescript horses loaded with haphazard-seeming bundles hanging from saddle straps and piled on the back, Briana and Yalna passed unnoticed in the throngs that crowded the Caravan Road around the outside of the city walls toward the northeastern gate. The streets that led to the gate from within the city were quiet and shaded, lined with the townhouses of aristocratic families and court officials. Travelers were forbidden to go that way.

Briana had dulled her dark auburn hair into a muddy brown with herbal dye, and darkened her pale skin with a solution of charcoal and water that made her sneeze. Yalna had found her the simple clothing of a northern Caer peasant, a full skirt and tunic with a headcloth and a heavy veil. She could not disguise her sea-green eyes, but she did not think anyone would look closely enough at her to notice.

"How are you feeling, my lady?" Yalna leaned over from her saddle to ask. The plump S'tari girl handled her slow-

moving horse expertly, weaving past erratic farm wagons and
scurrying children. Briana followed her as best she could. She
had learned to ride a horse out of necessity in the past year,
but she did not really understand the animals.

"I'll be glad to get out of this press," Briana said, trying
to look cheerful.

"They'll be with us for a few days at least. That mule
caravan ahead of us is probably headed for Khymer; we'll
turn off the road before it does."

Briana shaded her eyes against the slanting morning sun to
see the long string of laden mules, driven by a few youths
with whips, and guarded by a patrol of mercenaries from the
Cavernon City forces. "Why do they need guards?"

Yalna laughed behind her veil. "There are rumors of brigands in the desert. Some of my people still think of Caerlin as
the enemy. They don't believe the treaty will last, so why
should they abandon their ancient ways?"

"Because that is the only way to achieve peace."

Yalna looked at her sidelong. "We S'tari are not used to
peace, my lady. Perhaps we will learn."

Kyellan stepped back from the brown mare and looked
ruefully at the makeshift rig he had fashioned. If only he had
been able to bring the goat-fleece saddles with him from the
wreck of the *Jester*, he would not have had to tie blankets to
the horses' backs with lengths of rope. He had padded the
rope around the horses' bellies with cloth, but it was still
likely to chafe. The ropes that lashed the baggage on would
cause more problems.

Gwydion half-carried Chela over to the mare and lifted her
onto its back. Kyellan reached up his hand to help steady her
as the wizard began to tie her carefully to the baggage packs
behind her. Chela's fever had broken during the past night,
but she was still weak and scarcely aware of her surround-
ings. At first Gwydion had not wanted to move her, but then
he had decided she would be no worse off on the journey
overland than in the rough camp on the hilltop.

"Maybe you should tie me on, too," Alaira said. She had
managed to mount the smaller bay gelding with the help of
the young sailor Nemir. Now she sat awkwardly on the horse

with her hands clenched at the front of the layered blankets
that served as a saddle.

Kyellan grinned at her. "Sit up straight and get your
elbows down. You'll stay on. We won't be going very fast."

Gwydion tied a last knot and turned from Chela's mare to
mount the grey gelding that stood patiently waiting. "We're
ready," he said.

The morning was clear and cool. The sun had risen an hour
before, and the Tarnsea sparkled below the pine-covered
hills. Most of the sailors had returned to the warmth of the
campfire after helping with the horses. Nemir stood holding
Alaira's horse still, and Soren waited for Kyellan beside his
tall bay gelding.

"You'll wait for two weeks before you start down the
coast?" Kyellan asked, grasping a handful of mane and leap-
ing up astride the big horse. The bay fit his long legs better
than most of the S'tari breed, but his feet still dangled a little
past its flanks.

"We'll wait," the master of the wrecked ship assured him.
"If you come back with any priestesses, we'll take them with
us."

"Are you sure you want to risk going to Chelm?" Gwydion
said as he wrapped the lead rope for Chela's mare around one
gloved hand.

Soren's wrinkled face smiled. "I'm not planning to an-
nounce myself as the master of the *Jester*. Chelm is a large
enough city for nine ragged men to go unnoticed. We'll split
up, find berths on vessels headed for Caerlin, and work our
way home. If you bring us priestesses, we'll leave them at the
Temple there until their people can send for them."

"I'm sure the Queen will reimburse your losses if you
explain what's happened," Kyellan said. It would depend on
Valahtia's mood, but there was a chance she might.

"If she won't, there are plenty of ship owners in Caerlin
who would trust me to run their trading. I won't starve."

"You're a good man, Soren," Kyellan said. "If I ever get
a chance to repay you . . ."

"It's as the Goddess wills. We may meet again." Soren
stepped back from Kyellan's horse, and he turned its head
downslope. "Until then, may She go with you."

''Farewell!'' Nemir called, releasing Alaira's horse. She reined it awkwardly after Kyellan. Gwydion followed, leading Chela's mount. They made their way slowly down the spongy slope. Kyellan was not sure where on the ship's coastal charts they were, but he knew that if they headed directly north they would eventually intercept the Sanctuary road. All they would have to do then would be to follow the road east until they reached the high plateau where he had first met Briana.

Kyellan did not think they would find any priestesses at the Sanctuary. The armies of the wizards' invasion, the first wave of the Kharad, had marched down from their hidden training ground in the mountains through the broken lands where the Sanctuary stood. The ancient refuge of the priestesses had to have been destroyed. The wizards could not risk having it at their backs. But at least he could send word to Briana of what had happened there.

They traveled at a pace slow enough for Chela's led horse to avoid rocks and boggy ground. It was two days and half a third before they intercepted the dusty track of the Sanctuary road. Then, on the morning of the fourth day, they topped a rise in the road and saw the flat-topped hill in the distance, surrounded by weird formations of rose-colored stone and twisted, barren hills. The filtered sunlight of the cold and cloudy sky glimmered off a hint of white stone on the top of the huge plateau; the walls of the priestesses' Sanctuary itself.

''How far?'' Alaira wondered aloud, as Kyellan brought them all to a halt and peered out over the broken plains.

''Ten miles to the base, I'd guess,'' he said after a moment. ''We can be there by this afternoon.'' He glanced back toward Chela, and shook his head. She did not look good. ''We'll have to camp before trying the climb. The last time I was here it took the caravan most of a day to make the top.'' Chela did not look capable of making it to the base. She rode without seeing her path, staying upright only with the aid of the ropes that bound her onto her horse. Her hands dangled limp and pale against her thighs. Every now and then her head would nod, and she would begin to drift as if to sleep, but with her blue eyes wide open. When they stopped at night she lay the same way, not sleeping.

Their pace increased as they descended into the rocky valley. Silence fell again. The road led them around great boulders the size of houses and along the edges of jagged rifts and rockfalls. The sky was dark grey, heavy, constantly threatening, but thus far it had been a dry journey. The horses' hooves plodded with dull thuds in the dust. A chilling wind blew on an unchanging hollow note, swirling dust around them to add new layers to their already thick coats.

Chela had been born in this country. Her village of Poavra was a few days distant to the northwest. It had been utterly destroyed by the wizards. Chela was its only survivor. Kyellan knew she still had nightmares about the massacre, but surely it should please her to be riding through her homeland again. If she was aware of it at all. She made no response to attempts at conversation. Her illness had made them all mute, as if in a sickroom.

They stopped for an hour at midday to rest and eat. Dried meat and withered apples from the ship's stores, hardtack from the supplies they had packed in Caerlin, the last skin of water from a stream they had crossed two days before. Kyellan ate his ration slowly, watching Gwydion's attempts to get Chela to eat. The girl's skin was taut over her cheekbones, pale and grey now that it was not flushed with fever. She looked tired and old, far older than fourteen years.

Alaira ate quickly and got up to stretch her legs along the road. She was learning to ride fairly well, but it was obvious she did not enjoy it. She walked stiffly, wincing with each stride. They were all sore, more so than should have been necessary. It was the lack of proper saddles. Kyellan wished now that he had risked a few more minutes in the hold to bundle the goat fleeces and leather straps onto the back of one of the horses.

"Hasn't anyone ever been on this road before?" Alaira called as she wandered back to the group. "There aren't any tracks at all."

"The wizard's army marched here eight months ago," Kyellan said. "And just before that the royal caravan crossed it in both directions. The wind blows the dust over the tracks in a few days.''

"So no one will know we were ever here," she said in a small voice. "What a desolate place."

He smiled wryly, remembering his own reaction to the highlands of Garith at his first sight of them. He had seen no beauty in rocks and dust and scrub-brush gullies. Now he did find beauty here. It was a remote and distant sort of beauty, though, which had nothing to do with men and had no interest in their reactions. "It isn't so bad in the North," he said. "Or so Gwydion has told me. Around Akesh there are huge forests of masthead pines. And the College is near the shore of the Small Sea."

"It will all be covered with snow soon after we arrive," Gwydion said, finally giving up with Chela. She had eaten only a few bits of meat and hardtack. "But it's beautiful in the winter, with the Small Sea frozen hundreds of feet out from the shoreline, and the trees bent with snow. You'll like it, Alaira.''

"Maybe. It's a lot farther away than I expected," she said. "What's so important about it, that you have to go there and no place else? There are other wizards still on Barelin, aren't there? Some of the ones the Queen gave amnesty to went there.''

"They fought with the Kharad, and I fought against it," Gwydion said quietly. "They would not welcome me on that island.''

"What makes you think they'll welcome you at Akesh?" Her voice was challenging.

"They'll tolerate me," he said. "All I want to do is study in the libraries. Find out how to regain my Power, and teach Chela things she can never learn without the books of lore. The Masters of the College are all dead. All the most powerful wizards went south with the invasion. The only people left at Akesh would be the oldest and the youngest, those who have used up their Power and those who still haven't gained theirs. I don't think any of them will be angry enough with me to care whether I stay or go.''

The sky muttered fitfully. Kyellan looked up at it as he repacked their food stores. The clouds were black over the

Sanctuary plateau. It might storm before they reached the top. He did not think it was cold enough for snow, but it was the beginning of winter in Garith; it might be possible. "We'd better go on," he said. "We may need shelter tonight. There are supposed to be caves around the base of the plateau, where the priestesses stored their carts and their grain. Maybe we can find them."

"Caves?" Alaira said distastefully. "Maybe a rift or an overhang in the rocks would be enough."

"It will be a cold night," Gwydion said. "Chela will need warmth, and rest. Maybe she can sleep if we're out of the open."

They got Chela back onto her horse and well secured; it was becoming a familiar task. When their riders mounted again, the S'tari horses plodded forward wearily. The Garithian highlands had quickly taken the spirit from the desert animals. They disliked the wind and cold, and they bore heavier loads than they were accustomed to. Still, they would keep going as long as their riders asked them to.

The clouds dipped lower and the wind sharpened. Kyellan pulled up his hood and fastened his cloak, hoping that whatever the weather had planned would wait until they had found a place for the night. It did not pay any attention to his hopes. Within a half hour, a light sleet began to fall, drizzling down to cling in icy crystals on the rim of his hood. They stopped to wrap Chela more securely in shawls and blankets, and went on at a faster pace toward the dark slopes of the Sanctuary plateau.

They rode in the chilling sleet for hours more, unable to escape the cold. By the time they reached the first rise of the huge flat-topped hill, the sun had gone down, taking with it the meager warmth it had provided through the clouds. The sleet blew heavier, in whirling gusts that sent stinging bits of ice into their faces and numbed their hands on the reins. The horses walked with their heads hung low and their ears flat, breath puffing from their nostrils in thin white bursts.

After almost an hour of searching on the leeward side of the plateau, Alaira found a stone-arched passageway in a narrow cleft. Kyellan lit the end of a piece of firewood from his horse's pack and held it up as a makeshift torch to lead them under the archway into the dark hole beyond. He hated enclosed places. He always had. The air seemed to press in on him like hands, half-smothering. Alaira walked behind him, leading both their horses. Gwydion followed her, leading his mount and Chela's, with Chela still swaying on her horse's back.

The chamber they entered had apparently been used for grain storage. A fine layer of wheat dust shifted under their feet, and a few stalks of hay remained in a corner. The wizard army had probably taken its cache for provisions. The ceiling was low and rough, but the hollowed-out cave was dry, and large enough to hold four people and four horses for a night out of the storm.

Kyellan and Alaira cleared a space beneath a rocky outcropping, brushing away the dust, and built a low fire that soon filled the room with thin smoke despite their efforts to keep it contained. Gwydion set Chela close to the blaze. She coughed harshly as he wrapped her in blankets and went to rummage in his pack.

"Her fever is gone," Gwydion said. "But I don't like that cough. I'll brew her some more of the flower tea, for what good it will do."

"It seems to quiet her." Alaira helped the wizard set a metal rack over the low-burning fire for his water pot.

"It should put her to sleep. I've been making it strong enough. But she won't sleep at all. I need Power to find out what's wrong with her, and to heal her properly." He bent over his bag of herbs.

"We could leave the two of you down here out of the weather tomorrow," Kyellan suggested, sitting back against the stone wall away from the fire. "Alaira and I can go up and take a look at the Sanctuary."

Gwydion considered for a moment. "No. We should stay together. Chela will make it to the top. We're sure to find shelter there for tomorrow night, even if it's among ruins."

"Whatever you think." Kyellan shrugged.

Alaira sat down close to him and shivered suddenly. "This is such a strange place. It feels . . . awake." She put the palm of a hand against the wall. "The air, the stones, everything."

"The entire mountain is a place of Power," Gwydion said as he crouched over the fire to fix Chela's tea. The orange light shadowed his face under his thick golden hair, and glinted off his slit-pupilled eyes. "And it was the same way before the priestesses took it for their Sanctuary."

"They call it a holy place," Alaira said. "A place where the Goddess is closer to them."

"It's a place of Power," Gwydion repeated. "For anyone who knows how to seek it out and use what they find. If the priestesses abandon it, who knows what it might become?"

"It is so cold," Chela said clearly. They all turned to look at her, startled. Her blue eyes remained unfocused, and she did not speak again. Gwydion got up and put another blanket around her shoulders, then knelt beside her and stroked her thick red hair.

"I wish you could tell me what's wrong," he muttered.

"Do you think they'll all be dead?" Alaira asked Kyellan quietly. "All the priestesses?"

He put his arm around her and drew her closer. "We know the wizards came this way."

"Will the . . . the bodies still be there?" Her scarred face turned up toward his.

"After eight months?" He shook his head. "A few bones, if the wizards didn't burn them."

"There's a chance a few might have escaped," Gwydion said. "It's unlikely they stayed here, though."

"Maybe you should stay down here tomorrow," Kyellan said. "You've never seen what war can do, not on a large scale. It isn't pleasant."

"I don't need you to protect me from it," Alaira said with a flash of anger. "I've seen worse things than bones, and I've seen what the wizards could do."

"I know," he said softly. "And I wish I could have protected you from that, Alaira."

"I learned to take care of myself," she said, pulling away from him. "I had to. When I needed you, you weren't there." She walked over to tend the fire.

Kyellan stared after her. She had never accused him of anything before. He had not known it mattered that much to her. No, he told himself, that was not true. He knew. He had always known; he had just found it convenient to ignore Alaira's feelings for him. "I'm sorry," he muttered.

He gazed at the flickering fire-shadows on the cavern walls, remembering his first night in the priestesses' Sanctuary. He had climbed the walls on a foolish mission to sleep with Valahtia, who had been a princess then. He had walked through low corridors that seemed to lie in wait for him, past doorless holes like gaping mouths, and he had seen lights and heard voices. He had dismissed it all as his imagination. Now he knew it had been more than that. His unconscious shields had blinded him, the shields that had also hidden his Shape-Changer half from him.

The Sanctuary had allowed him to escape its walls. Yet in the end it had trapped him. Trapped him in sea-green eyes and a wary smile, in the quiet courage of the priestess Briana. Perhaps in the end it would kill him for his crime, for coming uninvited inside its chaste walls. Kyellan stared at the fire, letting gloom wrap around him like his stiff, wet cloak, as the storm began to howl around the plateau outside the smoky cave.

Chapter Eight ——————

"**I** don't think there's anyone here," Alaira said. A scarf she had wrapped up to her eyes against the icy wind scratched her nose with wool fibers, and she tried not to sneeze. The sleet chased around the high white walls of the Sanctuary as if seeking entrance, eddying back at the four riders. The great stone slabs of the gate had been thrown down by some powerful force. They lay blackened on the frozen earth of the entrance. Beyond them, the ancient buildings of the compound stood quiet and apparently undamaged except for their doors, which had been torn from the hinges.

They had climbed the plateau road for eight twisting, exhausted hours. The road had been washed out to the bedrock wherever it had not been half-choked by rock slides. The cultivated fields at the top of the huge hill had been planted but never harvested. Wind and rain had matted down the crop of mountain wheat, and birds or small animals had dug up the potatoes. The paths were overgrown with weeds that were now muddy and slick with ice. It was obvious that no one had cared for the place since the spring.

"We need to be sure," Kyellan said. "Let's have a look inside."

"Wait," Gwydion said from his grey horse. "Men aren't supposed to enter the Sanctuary uninvited. We shouldn't anger anyone who might still be here."

"The wizards profaned the place," Kyellan said as he dismounted. "I don't think our walking around in there will make a difference."

"It might frighten them," Alaira said, sliding awkwardly from the back of her bay. "If there is anyone here but ghosts." She peered uneasily into the sleet-fogged yard. The tall stone buildings cast no shadows in the storm. "I'll go in first, if you want."

"You don't have to," Kyellan said.

"I'm not afraid." She met his gaze challengingly, and he looked away. They were uncomfortable with each other after last night. She had not meant to say what she did, but it was done. It was an old anger. She had felt abandoned at age fourteen, when Kyellan had gone away to join the Royal Guards and left her to make her way as best she could in Rahan Quarter. She had always loved him. He never meant to hurt her, but somehow every time it happened that way.

"Don't explore too deeply," Gwydion cautioned her.

She stepped up onto one of the heavy stone slabs that blocked the gate. It rocked slightly underfoot. She walked carefully across the length of its blackened surface and jumped down into the Sanctuary yard. Patches of yellow grass had cracked and broken the stone paving. She passed a well with a broken cover, and a toppled weaving loom that still held a half-finished length of rotted white cloth.

The first building she came to was a tall, domed structure of cracked and weathered rock that had once been smoothly polished. The carved wooden door lay in an icy puddle at the foot of the steps. Alaira went inside. A long expanse of arches and pillars showed this to be a Temple of the Goddess. It was probably where the women had worshipped, in long rows on their knees, as the priestesses had in Chelm. Broken windows on the eastern side let in the dim grey light of afternoon, along with fitful spurts of sleet. The flagstone floor was damp.

Alaira went on to the next building. It was flat and without decoration. Rows of cots stood orderly along the walls of the single huge room, but dust and weeds had blown in to pile in the corners. She guessed it had been the novices' dormitory. She left it for the next structure, which seemed to be a collection of classrooms. Its door had shattered into a stack of kindling.

"Anyone here?" she called within. A faint whispering echoed her as if in mocking reply. She felt once more the strangeness she had sensed last night in the cave. This place still lived, even if its inhabitants did not.

The huge central edifice glowered at her, its tall doors gaping like broken teeth. Alaira stood on the threshold, her heart pounding loud and frightened. The silence within seemed to suck away the whistling of the storm.

"If there's anyone here, come out," she called weakly. "Don't be afraid. Briana sent us to find you." She backed away from the building, half convinced its gap-toothed mouth would answer her.

The place was empty. Alaira walked quickly back toward the main gate, chiding herself for her fear. Then she felt the ground shifting beneath her feet, as if something was waking after a long sleep. She felt a twitching, a vibration. Her breath caught, and she ran back over the gate slabs to stand panting beside the horses in the sleet.

"Are you all right?" Gwydion asked in concern. Alaira nodded.

"You didn't find anyone," Kyellan said.

"Nothing. Not even bones." She forced her voice to be calm. "As if they all escaped, or vanished."

"Maybe they had some warning," Gwydion said. "Maybe they sensed the danger in time and found a place of safety."

Kyellan shrugged. "Well, there's no one to mind if we seek shelter now. Did you see a good place for us to spend the night, Alaira?"

"In there?" Her fear returned. "Couldn't we just camp by the walls on the other side, out of the wind?"

"Chela needs more warmth than that." Gwydion led the sick girl's horse up over the stone gates into the yard. "It may snow by morning."

"I don't like it in there," Alaira called after him. She turned to Kyellan, who was gathering the reins of the other horses to lead them inside. "There's something wrong about it. We should stay away from it."

"You may be right." He pulled the horses past her. "But

I'm willing to risk it for a warm fire under a roof. Are you coming?''

Alaira wished she knew more about Power. She wished she had more of it. All she had was a sensitivity to people, to places, to the feel of things. The Sanctuary did not feel right. Yet she did not know enough to convince the others. They would not listen to her. She bent her head against the driving sleet and followed Kyellan toward the domed Temple.

Kyellan woke in a fog to the sound of his name being whispered all around him. For a moment he did not move. He was not dreaming. He could feel the hard, cold stones of the Temple floor under his thin blanket, and his neck was cramped from lying curled up inside his cloak. He could smell the nearness of the horses, their warmth and musky odor, and hear their soft snuffling noises and their restless movements as they slept. The mist settled on his face as he sat up. He could not see very well. He rubbed his eyes.

The fire still burned low and steady, and Alaira had fallen asleep from tending it. She looked soft and vulnerable as she slept. Her cropped black hair fell back from her thin, scarred face, and her cloak was in disarray around her. Her arms and throat were uncovered in the chill. Kyellan picked up his blanket to put it on top of her, but he could not reach her. The fog wrapped him in enveloping arms and whispered his name in a voice he knew. Briana's voice.

"Kyellan . . . Kyellan . . . come with me. . . ." He was not certain he heard it aloud, but it was real. It was Briana. He was sure of that.

Gwydion slept near the wall, oblivious. Chela lay under a mound of blankets with her blue eyes open, watching him. For a moment it looked as if she was trying to say something. Then the dark mist closed in and cut off Kyellan's view of the others, leaving only an opening like a narrow corridor that led down the aisle of the Temple to the doorway.

"Briana?" he said uncertainly. He heard the voice laugh, fading ahead of him down the tunnel of fog. Curious and still half asleep, he followed. His boots made no sound on the flagstone floor.

*   *   *

Briana opened her eyes suddenly, disoriented, thinking someone had called to her. The night sky was clear overhead, brilliant with stars. A cool wind off the barren desert rocks stirred the sand around the shallow, silted well of the little-used oasis. The horses were still at their picket line, and Yalna slept deeply, curled up in a depression in the sand. She had not spoken, then. Strange.

Briana felt light-headed and nauseated, as she often had in the first months of her pregnancy. Her back ached fiercely, worse than it had when she had dismounted at sunset. They were five days out on the Caravan Road, near the point where they would turn off to the northwest toward Va'shindi's valley. Six miles behind them was the large, spring-fed hollow of Green Camp, crowded with mules and wagons and drivers. They had passed its comforts, preferring to keep to themselves.

There was no one near, only wind and stars. Briana closed her eyes again and willed herself back to sleep, trying to ignore her discomfort. It had only been a vivid dream, she thought. She needed her rest. Tomorrow would be another hard day's ride.

The cold bit into Kyellan when he reached the open doorway and walked down the stone steps into the courtyard of the Sanctuary. He pulled his hood forward, holding a fold up in front of his mouth and nose to block the frigid air from his lungs. The broken stones of the yard were slippery with a thin layer of snow. Kyellan's breath filtered over the cloth in a thin, pale mist against the darker fog that compelled him on.

"Kyellan . . ." Briana's voice whispered gently.

He went on. It was magic, that much he knew even in his disoriented state. Briana was not here. She was far away in the Tiranon palace, waiting to have her baby so she could become First Priestess, and then he would have lost her forever. Yet, she was calling him. The Sanctuary had been one of the priestesses' holiest places; maybe Briana could somehow project her Power to speak to him here. But why? He could not guess. If she had that ability, she could have found out for herself what had happened here, without sending Kyellan days out of his way on his journey to Akesh.

The dark mist parted before him and closed behind him as
he entered the tall doorway of the Great House for the third
time in his life. The first time he had entered as a trespasser,
uninvited, unwelcome. The second time he had come with
Prince Arel to see the ceremony in which the Prince had
received the Goddess's blessing. He had seen Briana dance
that night, he remembered. This time he was certainly in-
vited. The low corridors flowed together before him, not
seeming to branch or turn at all, until he reached the silent
flagstone courtyard under the dark, clouded sky. This is
where she had been. The moon had smiled down on her that
night. Kyellan could almost smell the cloyingly sweet incense
and hear the soft drumming of Briana's bare feet against the
stones as she whirled and leaped.

The Great House rose on all sides of the inner yard.
Kyellan looked around uneasily. The fog had formed itself
into black-robed figures, hooded and cloaked. He could not
see them clearly. They led him to a low door on the other side
of the courtyard, the only unbroken door he had seen in the
Sanctuary. He reached out with his left hand and turned the
latch. Behind the door a steep, narrow stairway without a
handrail sank into a black shaft underground.

For a moment he paused. He did not like to be enclosed,
with the weight of earth above him. He remembered his
imprisonment far below the wizard Belaric's palace in Khymer.
But Briana's voice led him on, and though he could not see
the faces of the black-robed wraiths around him, they seemed
to smile in encouragement. He did not want to appear afraid.
He started slowly down the worn rock steps.

The stairway seemed to have been chiseled out of the
bedrock of the plateau. His shoulders nearly touched the
rough stone of the narrow walls on either side. The black-
robed women descended with him. He wished he knew who
they were. It was cold. Perhaps the earth here was frozen,
though winter had scarcely begun. Perhaps it had never thawed.

"Where are you taking me?" he asked after trying to speak
for a long time.

"Here," said a voice that was not Briana's. "Here. The
Temple of the Altar."

Black robes swept around him, faintly rustling. A door

opened before him, and he stepped into a room where white flames burned upon seven stone pillars. Shadows of the ghostly women filled the room. Was it some ritual, or the memory of a ritual that had been performed here for centuries and repeated itself even though the priestesses were gone? Kyellan realized he was afraid. He did not belong here. Alaira was right; they should never have come inside the walls.

The ceiling was so low he could touch it, and it was rough and jagged, hung with small points like the roof of a cave. The floor was bare, smooth rock, not joined stones. Kyellan moved farther into the room. In the center of the circle of flame-topped pillars stood a squat, black rock shaped into a crude cube the height of Kyellan's waist. It drew his eyes. He suddenly sensed its Power as the trapped Shape-Changer spirit within him writhed against its bonds. It felt the danger.

"The Altar," said the new voice. It seemed familiar. One of the black-robed forms turned to face him at last, and he recognized the thin face and narrow eyes of the novice Gemon. How could she be here? They had left her half dead beside the Tarnsea, to be cared for by Va'shindi. "It is a piece of the Goddess's Seat," Gemon said, laying her hand on the top of the black altar stone. The stone was real but her hand was not. She was no more substantial than sea-foam.

"How did it get here?" Kyellan asked warily. Four other women had turned toward him now. He did not know them. They were small and wrinkled and old, and looked at him with somber expressions.

"It has been here for a thousand years," Gemon said. "Not even the First Priestesses knew it was a part of the Goddess's Seat. But we are studying the Seat now and learning its secrets. This stone is its heart, one of the sources of its Power. That is the reason we were able to bring ourselves here to greet you."

Kyellan tried to force his mind to waken fully. The black wraiths were moving back away from him, leaving him in the center of the room near the altar stone. "The Goddess's Seat?" he repeated. "Did Briana send you, Gemon?"

The young novice looked at him thoughtfully. After a moment she nodded. "Yes. Yes, Briana sent us here. She is with us in spirit. She sent us here, armed with the greatest

Power of Light in the world, to destroy the greatest evil left in the world.''

Kyellan staggered back under a sledgehammer blow of force from the dark stone. It dashed him against the wall with the strength of a vast wave. The wraith-priestesses began a wailing chant, and webs of white fire sprang up from the flaming pillars to reach out for him. He tried to move, to throw himself back through the open door, but the Power of the stone kept him pinned.

The net of flame enmeshed him from above, trapping his good arm so he could not draw his sword, burning through his clothes to his skin. He cried out in pain, struggling against the fiery web. This was how Briana had killed a wizard once, by burning him with the Goddess's Flame. Now she sent it here to kill him. She had asked him to go to the Sanctuary, knowing it was a place where she could easily channel the Power of the Goddess's Seat to destroy him. Kyellan writhed in the enfolding ropes of fire. The high voices of the chanting priestesses pierced him, and suddenly he was being pulled like a trussed animal toward the altar stone. He could feel it waiting to suck the life from him.

"Die, Shape-Changer," Gemon hissed nearby. "Die knowing you were betrayed.''

Betrayed? Yes, Briana had betrayed his love. He owed her nothing. He did not have to submit to this. He was no weak, defenseless being to be crushed like an insect. Gemon had said it; he was the Shape-Changer. He would die if he did not summon that Power, if he did not let down his barriers against it. The pain . . . the pain was too great. He could no longer think beyond it. The web of fire dragged him to the altar to kill him, and he felt himself begin to change.

A wave of horror swept through Kyellan, and he made a weak attempt to stop himself. But the Shape-Changer spirit took him like a snake emerging from a discarded skin. Kyellan felt himself shrinking, falling away from the fiery pain, smothered, until he was no more than a restless spark in the alien mind of the wizard. He was lost.

The pains began abruptly in the darkness before dawn. Briana woke from a dream in which she had been searching

through dark stone tunnels with a lamp lit by the Goddess's
white flame, but she could not find Kyellan. Her face was
wet with tears of loss and grief, her Caer peasant clothes
drenched with sweat. She heard thin, distant screams, and
shock and agony tore through her body like a lance. It was
her baby screaming in the womb, and the pain that rippled
across her belly was like nothing she had felt before. She
whispered Kyellan's name again, still half in her dream, until
the next contraction doubled her over and she understood.

"Oh, Goddess, not yet," she whispered. "It's only been
seven months. Oh, please, Cianya, no . . ." She tried to keep
her voice low. She tried not to cry out. She knew sound
would carry over the desert, and she did not know how far.
They might hear her in Green Camp. They might hear her at
the Hidden Temple.

The low fire had gone out, and Briana had tossed her
blankets aside in her nightmares. She reached out to gather
them up again, shivering in the wind, but another prolonged
burst of pain made her gasp and curl into a tight ball over her
distended stomach. She rocked back and forth with her teeth
clenched.

"What?" Yalna murmured, sitting up slowly and rubbing
her eyes beneath her sand-encrusted veil. Then she scrambled
over to Briana and grasped her shoulders fiercely. "You
should have waked me! How long has it been like this?"

Briana shook her head as the pain subsided for a moment.
"Not . . . not very long. I just woke up. I was dreaming.
Something has happened to Kyellan, something terrible. . . .
He's gone, Yalna, I can't find him anywhere. . . ."

"To Kyellan!" The young midwife put a hand on either
side of Briana's abdomen and leaned her ear against it. "To
you, I'd say. Those are no false pains. That baby is ready to be
born."

Another wave swept over Briana, and now she felt her
child's Power fluttering against her shields in confused protest.
"It's too soon!" she cried, unable to keep her voice low.
"Only seven months. Yalna, isn't there a way to make it
stop? A way to make him wait?"

The S'tari girl shook her head. "Once begun, you have no
choice. You're big enough, even if it's only been seven

months. Perhaps the child will be strong enough to survive. But what caused this? I've never seen it happen without some terrible shock, some injury to the mother or the unborn babe.''

"Something has happened to Kyellan," Briana repeated. The empty feeling of her dream and the fury of the small entity within her seemed intertwined, bound together.

"Whatever the cause, we'll manage," Yalna said briskly. "I'll make a drink that will relax you and ease your pain. In the meantime you must unbraid your hair and undo every fastening in your clothing, and I will loose the horses. They will not wander far. Nothing must be bound or tied.''

As Yalna hurried away, Briana began to fumble obediently with the knotted thongs that secured her thick braids. She had never seen a child born. She had known to expect pain, but not that it would be like this. Yet women bore children every day. It was normal. Perhaps it was also normal for her to be tortured by fears for the child's absent father, and to long for him to be with her. Perhaps that was all her dream meant. Oh, Goddess, she prayed, let Kyellan be all right. He was so far away.

The Shape-Changer thrust aside the bonds of fire as if bursting frayed ropes. Strength coursed through him. His right arm broke its leather sling as his body assumed its true form, much like Kyellan's but subtly different, better. He knew that his short hair was now a brilliant gold, his eyes yellow, his cheekbones higher, his skin paler. He was the strongest wizard alive, in the prime of his youth, and at last he had won the battle for control. He was free. The one who had subjugated him was now trapped himself, like a fluttering moth in a corner of his mind. He laughed and got to his feet.

The sendings of the five priestesses grouped together somberly to face him, still assured of the Power that they drew from the vast well of the Goddess's Seat. He was amused to realize that they wanted to face him in this form. They wanted the triumph of having killed the Shape-Changer. Why they hated him he did not know. All that he had done, in the brief moments when he had used his Power before, had been for the benefit of their distant Goddess.

The form he had worn, the form that had somehow taken

over as if a suit of clothes could compel its wearer, Kyellan,
had loved one of them. Briana, the one who would be First
Priestess. Now she was ranged against him. Or was she?
They had told him so, but the Shape-Changer could not find
her with them even in spirit. In fact, he sensed that they had
done this without her knowledge. He laughed at the spark of
Kyellan in his mind. Poor little creature, to despair of his
great love when it had all been a lie. The Shape-Changer did
not regret it. If Kyellan had not thought himself betrayed, he
would never have relinquished his control. Now it was too
late.

The priestesses attacked in concert, singing in flame-tongued
voices, chanting prayers against Darkness. The Shape-Changer
set up reflexive defenses, and searched his ancient memory
for a way to combat them. He did not remember much.
Usually he had to relearn the skills of a wizard in each new
incarnation. He had not yet had the opportunity to do so in
this life.

The priestesses were strong, five determined women with
the Seat and its heart-stone behind them. He was sore pressed,
but he saw that they had made one foolish mistake. They had
chosen to attack him in spirit form, leaving their bodies
behind untenanted. The silver threads of their soul-lines
stretched almost invisible to the heart-stone, and from there
he imagined they were connected to the Seat and thus to their
bodies. But no wizard apprentice would make himself so
vulnerable.

The Shape-Changer erected a screen of black flame, to
confirm their belief that he worshipped some mythical Darkness. He left his strong new wizard body standing there, and
catapulted his own soul along the line of the priestesses'
Power back to the canyon of the Hidden Temple. They had
constructed a strong road; he traveled along it easily. The
furious entity within him that was Kyellan took the opportunity to fight, but he battered it down with little difficulty and
caged it deep inside his own spirit.

The priestesses' uninhabited bodies sat in a handfast circle
on a broad step at the foot of the Goddess's Seat. The
Shape-Changer was amused to see that it was raining on
them. He shouted a challenge down the soul-road and at-

tacked the bodies, knowing the priestesses would fly back to
defend themselves. He inflicted a few major injuries and
killed one of the older bodies with his black flames, then he
slipped back along the thread of his soul-line to the dark cave
under the Sanctuary.

He found his body exhausted when he rejoined it. With a
last effort of will, he wrenched control of the heart-stone from
the priestesses, preventing them from returning to fight him
again. Three of them were badly injured, and one would die
soon, since no soul could live long in this world without its
housing. He felt, on the whole, that he had done very well, but
it was unaccustomed exercise. He was as weary as if he had run
twenty miles in an overweight form. And now he discovered that
the building around him was shaking apart, its ancient stones
stressed beyond endurance by the battle within its foundations.

Rocks spilled from cracks in the low ceiling. He heard a
rumbling on the stairs. Abandoning the heart-stone, which he
had thought he might take with him, he erected a shield of
deflection around himself and rushed through the doorway
and up the narrow stairs. Great slabs of stone sheared off
from the walls. Shaken, he ran faster as the stairs crumbled
beneath his feet and the shifting earth threatened to smother
him. One thing, oddly, he shared with Kyellan: a fear of deep
places. If the stones trapped him in his weakened state, he
would take a very long time to die. But eventually he would.

The Shape-Changer emerged covered in dust, his clothes in
tatters. But he was out. The Great House fell into smoldering
rubble around him. The sky was still black though it was
dawn, and a fierce snow pierced his shield. He discarded the
exhausting protection, keeping only a rudimentary mental
defense against magical attack, and pulled the remnants of his
cloak up around his chilled face. Then he started across the
ruins to greet Kyellan's three friends.

The cup in Briana's hand spilled hot liquid over Yalna as
her body jerked with the new contraction. Briana arched her
head back with a strangled scream, dimly aware of the midwife's pain, her mind a whirling maelstrom of agony and
wordless Power that combined her own and her son's. Her
shields had broken at the last onslaught. They lay in shards

throughout her mind. The infant Shape-Changer battling from her womb had forced her to untie that last knot, loose that last bond. He was free now to emerge.

Oh, Goddess, it was time. Briana felt she was being torn apart. She had drunk enough of Yalna's numbing tea to put a horse to sleep, but still she feared she would go mad with the pain. Her mind was emptied of everything she knew but the names of the Goddess. She repeated them over and over, not so much as a prayer but as a way to hold on to something familiar. Wiolai, Cianya, Rahshaiya. Wiolai, Cianya, Rahshaiya.

"Now, Briana," Yalna said fiercely. Her voice seemed far away. "It's up to you. Almost done. Almost over. Just a little more."

Briana cried out as her torn and stretched muscles tried to push down on the hard mass inside her. The tearing went on and on, and then it seemed her bones cracked apart as the child emerged into Yalna's waiting hands. Briana collapsed, awash in pain and relief.

The cry of the Shape-Changer at his first breath rang out over the desert like a challenge. He was unshielded, Briana thought in a panic. His confused, angry Power would carry farther than his voice. "Give him . . . to me," she said hoarsely, reaching up with arms that seemed sheathed in lead. "Must have . . . shields."

After a few moments Yalna lay the naked, slippery infant in Briana's arms. The young priestess looked at her child in wonder. He seemed to blaze with light. He had a short fringe of hair like polished gold, and his eyes glowed through squinted golden lashes. Even his skin had a tawny hue.

Briana found a last reserve of Power deep in her mind, and drew it out to raise shields from the baby's vast aura of wizard strength. His brilliance faded. Briana did not have the Power to force him to change into a human-looking child, however. He would have to stay well hidden the rest of the way to the valley.

"Cian," she whispered, drawing the Sign of the Goddess on the baby's forehead. "Your name is Cian, for the Mother of us All, Cianya, in whose service you were born." The blind mouth searched for her breast, but she knew she had no milk. Her body had not expected the birth so soon.

Yalna reached down and took the child away. "I'll boil down some goat's milk cheese to feed him. He seems strong, and he's as large as any full-term babe. He won't suffer if we wait here a few days for you to recover. You've lost blood, my lady."

Briana shook her head weakly. Her body cramped again with the afterbirth, but finally Yalna's tea numbed her against the pain. "No," she said. "We can't risk Cian being noticed. We'll leave today. Just let me rest a little while . . ." Her voice trailed off vaguely. She felt Yalna draw warm blankets over her, and she slept.

Chapter Nine ───────────

GEMON lay as cold as ice at the foot of the silent Seat of the Goddess. A vast exhaustion weighed on her. She was utterly drained, but she did not think she was hurt. Her body refused to obey her command to sit up, as if it had forgotten her in her absence. She drew upon the last vestige of her link with the Seat to infuse her limbs with enough strength to rise. Even then she moved as slowly as her thoughts. Hot needles pressed into her with the pain of returning circulation. She forced herself to her knees and looked around, eyes burning with the effort.

They lay sprawled, as she had been, toppled like broken glass figurines. The smallest of them was dead. Niketa's body was horribly burned, her eyes open and still in their sunken nests. The helpless stench of death hung like a curtain before the impassive stones of the Seat. Rosy dawn light began to color the topmost rocks of the canyon rim. Gemon rose to her feet.

The others were beginning to stir. Iona moaned and coughed blood, and tried to sit up. Gemon hurried to assist her. She was sorry for the priestesses' injuries, but this was war, as much as the defense of the Kingdoms had been. Now the course of the Hidden Temple was plain. They had to continue to work for the destruction of the creature of Darkness who had been Kyellan. It would take time to regain their strength,

and they might be forced to move to a new location now
that the Shape-Changer knew where they were. They would
find other methods than direct attack. They were not defeated.

"The Shape Changer," Iona whispered as she rolled painfully to her hands and knees. "I feel him still, raging at us.
He does not seem so far away." Gemon supported her as she
rose, and tried to follow what the old woman meant.

It was true. She felt it as she held onto Iona's thin arms.
The fury of the Shape-Changer, distant but certainly not as far
as Garith. It was a dim disturbance in the atmosphere of the
canyon. A wordless anger, chaotic, childlike. Unmistakably
their enemy, yet somehow different. Gemon listened to it
until it suddenly ended, and she began to suspect what it
might mean.

The horses stamped their hooves on the broken stones of
the yard and jerked against the ropes Alaira held, terrified by
the thunder of shaking earth where the Great House had been.
Dust and bits of rock swirled in choking clouds from the
demolished building. Alaira fought to hold the four picket
ropes, bracing her feet against the edge of the Temple steps.
Gwydion had waked her at the first rumbling from underground, and he had carried Chela outside while Alaira got the
horses.

Alaira looked at the settling ruins in the center of the
compound. "He was in there, wasn't he?" she finally managed to ask over the tightness in her throat. "Is he dead?"

Gwydion smoothed back Chela's red hair and did not look
at Alaira. "No human could have survived that, but he may
have changed. It would be better if he had died. I would
rather have to grieve for Kyellan than deal with the Shape-
Changer in all his Power."

Alaira did not begin to understand what Gwydion meant
until the golden-haired wizard strode from the rubble to speak
to her in Kyellan's voice. "Good morning," he said cheerfully. She knew the low timbre of that voice, its slight Rahan
accent like her own. She knew the lines of the face, the way
the lean body moved, but the hair and eyes were golden.
Alien. "Come, Alaira," he chided. "Don't look so sur-

prised. You must have guessed there was something more to your foolish soldier friend.''

"Who are you?" she breathed. "What have you done with Kyellan?"

He regarded her in amusement and turned to speak to Gwydion. "Your guess was right, wizard. It was the priest-esses of the Goddess's Seat. But I was stronger."

"They attacked Kyellan," Gwydion said. "And he had to summon you to defend himself. But you've taken him over completely. He would never have allowed that to happen."

"I don't need to justify myself to you," said the Shape-Changer. "Your Kyellan was near death when he finally let me through. And he had given up hope, convinced his be-loved Briana was one of those who were trying to kill him."

"Was she?" Alaira asked, feeling numb.

"Of course not. The Hidden Temple acted without her knowledge. They thought they would destroy the Shape-Changer. They were mistaken." He smiled. "Instead they woke a Power to be feared. One that will not sleep again."

"Then you have no intention of giving the control back to Kyellan," Gwydion said coolly.

"He kept me imprisoned for almost twenty-three years, except for a few moments last spring. It's my turn."

"What . . . what are you going to do?" Alaira whispered.

He walked over to her and lay a hand over hers on the horses' ropes. She did not dare pull away, for fear the horses would bolt, but the Shape-Changer spoke a few strange words and the animals quieted and stood calmly. "Nothing very terrible," he said, releasing her hand. "I'll go to Akesh with you, to learn the skills to use my Power to its fullest. From there, who can tell? Come, Gwydion. We'll get the baggage. It's morning. We should be off." He walked with Kyellan's long stride up the steps and into the Temple.

Alaira whirled on Gwydion as he set Chela down and moved to follow. "You can't let him stay like this! You have to stop him. Make him change back."

"I don't have the Power to confront him," Gwydion said quietly. "Not now. When Chela is stronger and I'm myself again, we'll do what we can. Kyellan is still in there. He'll be looking for a chance to take control again. We'll try to give him that opportunity. But there's nothing to be done now.'' He propped Chela against a stair and went inside.

Alaira wanted to scream, to attack the usurper who wore Kyellan's shape, to refuse to go with them to Akesh. She did none of those things. It was too overwhelming. Too incredible. She did not know how to react. The tears that had threatened at first subsided into a sort of bewilderment, and she waited quietly as the horses were loaded, Chela was tied into place, and Gwydion mounted his grey gelding. The Shape-Changer moved to assist her onto her bay, and she flinched away from him and swung up unaided. He smiled mockingly at her and got on his horse to lead them out of the blasted gates of the Sanctuary into the cold grey dawn of the plateau.

By early afternoon they had reached the base of the steep, winding road. By evening they were miles to the northwest of the Sanctuary, making slow progress across broken, hilly wasteland, which continually forced them far out of their way to get around deep rifts and canyons and impassable ridges. Chela was unconscious most of the time. Gwydion was grim and silent, and Alaira had no words. The Shape-Changer led them cheerfully, asking their advice on the direction they should go and then taking his own counsel. He stopped them briefly to eat a midday meal on the way down from the plateau, and again to fill their waterskins from an icy rivulet they crossed on the barren plain.

As the day went on, Alaira began to think that surely this was all a dream. The man she had known all her life could not have suddenly become another person. It was impossible. It could not be believed. As dusk gathered and the snow fell heavier with a freezing wind, they rode into a vale surrounded by exposed ridges of jagged rock. The scrubby pine trees that filled the sheltered little valley had been stripped of greenery and branches. As Alaira stared in horror at the fruit of those trees, she realized with a sense of relief that she was having a nightmare.

They had found the priestesses of the Sanctuary. The bodies, still clad in rotted tatters of grey and black and white robes, dried and preserved by wind and dust, hung from the trees like a field of scarecrows. Gwydion reached out to grasp the reins of Chela's horse and pull it to a stop. Alaira held her restive mount still; its ears and nostrils twitched, though there was no smell of death here.

The Shape-Changer drew back his golden head to gaze up at the long-dead women in distaste. "The wizards found them here," he said. "They did not resist their deaths."

"Afraid that to use violence would offend their Goddess," Gwydion said softly. "I saw that happen in a battle in the forest."

"Some sort of glamour must have been set around the bodies," the taller wizard said thoughtfully. "To keep away scavengers and keep them entire. I felt there was something here, and led us to the source of my feeling, though I didn't know what we'd find. At least now we know what happened to the priestesses."

"You sound sorry," Alaira said, surprised. "I thought you hated the priestesses."

"I have nothing against these wretches here," the Shape-Changer said. "I fought against those who sought my life, but this . . . this was a waste of life. Of Power."

Alaira looked away from the bodies. "It's obscene for them to hang there like that."

"Ride on ahead," said the Shape-Changer. "I'll release them from the spell so they can lie in peace."

"We'll wait for you on the next ridge," Gwydion agreed. "Come, Alaira."

She turned her bay gelding's head to follow Gwydion and Chela, and she did not speak until they were out of the vale and out of sight of the Shape-Changer. "What is he doing?"

"What I would have done if I'd had the Power," Gwydion said. "Putting their trapped souls to rest." His voice was thoughtful. "We have to remember he isn't evil, Alaira. The priestesses say he serves Darkness, and it seems terrible to us that he stole Kyellan's body. But he only serves himself. During the battle for the Goddess's Seat, he helped Kyellan against the wizards. He's as likely to help us as he is to hurt us."

"I think I understand"—Alaira shivered—"but that doesn't mean I have to like him."

Briana swayed oblivious in her saddle, grateful for the plodding, ungraceful gait of her wide-backed mount. They had started again at sunset. Yalna had padded Briana's saddle with blankets and cushions, and she did not ride so much as she lay as if on a couch, her knees drawn up and her body numbed with the flower drug. They had left the Caravan Road now and took an angled path toward the distant ridge of hills beside the Tarnsea. In the darkness the land was featureless and silent, unthreatening. A thin layer of sand covered the bedrock, cushioning the horses' hooves as they landed.

Yalna carried the infant Shape-Changer wrapped in a bundle of cloth. She had dulled his bright fringe of hair by rubbing dirt into it, and put him to sleep with a minute amount of the tea in his goat's milk. Briana did not think he would attract attention if anyone passed them on this desolate trail. Travelers might wonder what had possessed them to take such a tiny baby on a journey, but that would be all.

Yalna had said they would reach the valley where Erlin and Pima waited in two more days of traveling. There, Briana could rest. She wanted nothing more than to lie down and not have to rise again. Her flaccid stomach still gripped her with cramps, as if to make up for the shortness of her labor. She had bled heavily. Yalna had told her it was well she wanted no more children; she would be unlikely to conceive again, much less bear a child to term. If her son had grown to nine months before his birth, it might have killed her. She supposed she should be grateful to the nightmare that had brought on her pains before their time.

But still foremost in her weary thoughts, drowning out concern for her baby or her own suffering, was her fear for Kyellan. Her feeling of loss in her dream had been so real. She trusted her own Power well enough to believe that something terrible had happened.

The campfire flickered brightly beneath the snow-laden branches in the sheltered copse of pine trees. A dark forest stretched out to the north and west, but where they had camped was still near its edge. The Shape-Changer had built the fire, moving through a habitual sequence of steps, striking sparks from worn flint and steel, arranging the wood in a tentlike shape over a mound of kindling. To Alaira it was like watching a murderer performing a skillful imitation of the man he had killed.

"There," the tall wizard said in satisfaction. He squatted back on his heels and looked around the circle. "Now if one of you will start our supper, I'll have a look at Chela. Maybe I can find out what's wrong with her."

"Don't touch her," Alaira said fiercely as he moved toward the prone form of her young friend.

The Shape-Changer looked past her to Gwydion. "She'll die with much more of this. If I can help, I will."

"Anything will be more than I can do. Go ahead," said Gwydion miserably.

Alaira pulled her knees up to her chest and hugged them, glowering at the Shape-Changer as he bent over Chela and pulled the blankets back from her pale face. The girl muttered something about the cold and reached unseeing for the blankets again. The wizard caught her wrists and held them gently, stroking the backs of her hands with his fingers. His face grew calm and distant, and after a moment his yellow cat's eyes were as blank as Chela's blue ones. He knelt like a statue, not even blinking.

"This may take some time." Gwydion rose to his feet. "I'll start a stew." He filled a pot with snow from a nearby drift, and added pine nuts, some pungent dried herbs from his pack, and chopped pieces of salt pork and apples. Alaira watched him sullenly, but he seemed not to care that the Shape-Changer could be doing anything to Chela.

A cold wind blew bits of old snow from tree branches to make the fire sputter. Some melted icily down Alaira's neck. She stood up restlessly and walked away from the fire, down into the hollow out of sight of the camp, where the horses were picketed. The four animals looked at her placidly, unloaded, rested, well fed on warming grain. Alaira remembered she had once been afraid of them. She still was not a very good rider. She fell off at least once a day when her mount lunged to avoid a trickle of falling rock or leaped unexpectedly across a ditch. But now the horses had become familiar, comforting, warm and uncomplicated. Not treacherous like people. She pulled a comb from a saddlebag and went to work on the snarls in the grey gelding's mane.

Chela cried out, a thin, piercing sound. Alaira dropped the comb and ran back over the rise to the camp. Gwydion knelt by Chela on one side with the Shape-Changer on the other. They supported her as she coughed and shook. "That's it," said the Shape-Changer in encouragement. "You're coming back. You have to fight to reach us. That's the way."

"What are you doing to her?" Alaira demanded uncertainly.

Gwydion smiled up at her. "He's bringing her out of it. Look, Alaira. She's back with us." He hugged Chela as her coughing fit subsided. The girl clung to him weakly, her eyes no longer unfocused and staring, but blinking in bewilderment at the Shape-Changer.

The tall wizard's hands shook. He pressed them together in his lap and breathed deeply. "It was her Power, replenishing itself. It was drawing on all her strength, not leaving her anything with which to fight her illness."

"So she's going to be all right?" Alaira asked.

"I don't have any healing knowledge," the Shape-Changer said. "That part is up to her, but she should be able to heal herself. Then after her body is strong again, she can work to rebuild her Power." He went over to the stew and stirred it. "Gods, I'm hungry. This isn't ready yet. You'll have time to finish that job you started on the grey's mane." He grinned at Alaira.

She almost smiled back, but caught herself. Whatever he had done for Chela, it did not make amends for what he had done to Kyellan. Alaira brushed past him to look down at Chela. Gwydion had laid her back onto the blankets, and she was already going to sleep. Really going to sleep, for the first time in a long while. Gwydion's face had begun to relax from the lines of tension it had borne since Chela's illness started. He almost looked eighteen again. Alaira shook her head in disbelief and ducked back through the trees to the horses.

The animals were moving restlessly on their picket ropes in the darkness. They had been calm before. Alaira spoke soothingly to them and picked up her comb again. The gelding greeted her with a nervous whicker, twisting its head around to nuzzle at her shoulder. Alaira stroked its nose and went back to its half-finished mane. The dark pine shadows fell across the horses' backs in thick stripes. Alaira looked up at the sky. The heavy snow clouds hid the moon, but they gave off enough light for her to see her work.

The mare at the far end of the picket line stamped and snorted, swinging its hind end into the horse next to it, its hooves dancing. What was the matter with them? Alaira's gelding suddenly bared its teeth and snapped at shadows. At nothing.

"What is it?" Alaira said in exasperation. Then she turned and saw the creature behind her.

It was man-shaped, a little larger than a man, with oddly pointed shoulders and long teeth that glittered as it opened its mouth and reached for her. Alaira leaped away, scrambling under the nearest branches. The creature made a weird hissing sound and bounded after her. She screamed and glanced back. It had small, leathery wings that unfolded to help it balance as it ran. It was shaggy and long-limbed, and its musky animal odor must have been what had frightened the horses.

Branches whipped at her arms and face; she had run into the densest part of the glade. Alaira felt claws tear the back of her tunic. She twisted to one side. The thing that chased her stumbled and lunged, but she ran past it, back the way she had come. Oh, gods. There were more of them in the space around the horses, foul winged things. Some were no higher than her waist, squat and lumpy as toads; some were lean and tall against the shadowed trees. They had a tangible odor of Power about them. Demons, Alaira realized. She had seen a few at the wizards' court in Cavernon when she had been a captive.

The shaggy one behind her caught her around the waist. Its claws linked with a clashing sound in front of her. Alaira kicked furiously backward and fought to draw her belt knife, but the thing's sinewy arms were in the way. She was pinned by a strength far beyond her skill. The rest of the obscene creatures pressed around her, mouthing wet and grating sounds.

She screamed again, as loudly as she could. The horses were rearing and pulling frantically against their ropes. Surely someone would hear.

The demon lifted her in the air like a child and threw her over its shoulder. It leaped off at a gallop away from the hollow, away from the camp into the thick forest. The others followed in a gibbering procession. Alaira writhed and kicked, but the clawed arm held her like a vise. Her face pressed against the matted fur of the creature's back. The odor was nauseating. The flapping wings fanned her in a cold wind. A nightmare, she thought desperately. Still the same nightmare as before. None of it is real.

The demons ran as swiftly as deer through the dark forest. Even the toadlike ones leaped along at a furious pace. Alaira had thought of demons as smoky, insubstantial creatures, like evil ghosts. These were hard and muscular and smelled of wet fur and sulphurous breath. The one that carried her was oblivious to her scratches and blows and kicks.

There was a crashing noise behind them. Alaira raised her head as far as she could over the bouncing shoulder of the demon. One of the bay horses galloped toward them faster than the demons were running. The Shape-Changer rode it, shouting words she did not understand. His pale hair blew behind him. Probably he had come to join his friends, Alaira thought fearfully.

Light blazed from the wizard, and the creature carrying Alaira suddenly halted in its tracks and dumped her heavily to the ground. She landed on top of a tree root that bruised her ribs and knocked the breath from her. Her eyes watered furiously, and she gasped like a landed fish for a hold on the chill night air. The demon stood over her with its long legs planted wide. The assortment of ill-matched creatures that had run with it gathered together around Alaira, facing the Shape-Changer. They screeched defiance at him.

Alaira could see him through their grotesque legs. He slid off the barebacked horse and spoke in a loud, commanding voice. The words echoed like an avalanche through the trees. A stir of uneasiness went through the demons, and they moved back a step. The Shape-Changer advanced on them, shouting. His short golden hair stood up like an aura, and his eyes blazed.

To Alaira's surprise, the demon creatures suddenly broke away from her and moved abjectly toward the Shape-Changer, waving their clawed arms in horrible parodies of homage and apology. The taller ones bowed, and the squatty ones groveled at his feet. The wizard glared at them, but did not draw his sword. He spoke to them sternly in a tortuous language. The ones that could fly gained the air laboriously and flapped away; the others walked into the trees in small conversational groups, glancing back as if in awe at the Shape-Changer.

Alaira lay still after she regained her breath, and silently drew her belt knife. He would not have her without a fight. It would not be easy, even if he had commanded demons to kidnap her for him. The wizard walked slowly toward her, his boots crunching in the pine needles. She could not see his expression in the darkness, except for his bright yellow eyes. The cat's pupils were dilated. He bent over her and drew a breath to speak, and she lashed out with the knife for his ribs.

The Shape-Changer caught her wrists, his teeth flashing in a startled smile. Alaira struggled to free herself. "I'll kill you!" she shouted. He lifted her to her feet by the wrists and held her at arm's length, looking down at her in apparent amusement.

"If you kill me," he said calmly, "you'll never get your Kyellan back. You'll kill his spirit as well, Alaira. Or had you forgotten?"

The fury drained from her, but she was still frightened enough to hold onto the knife. "What . . . what are you going to do?"

"What do you think? Take you back to the camp for a bowl of stew. If I can trust you not to knife me in the back."

"Then you didn't . . . those weren't your creatures?" she said weakly.

His grip loosened on her wrists, and he chuckled. "They are now. I've commanded them to act as outriders for us and warn me if any more stray, masterless demons cross our path. They didn't know who they were dealing with." He let her go.

Alaira sheathed her knife and rubbed her wrists. They would be bruised, as were her ribs. "What were they?"

"Demons that were conjured up by the wizards of the Kharad for battles or spells," he said. "Their masters were killed before they had a chance to dismiss them, leaving them stuck in this world with no commands, no purpose. They're easy enough to control."

"If you made yourself their master, why don't you dismiss them like you said?"

"They may be useful. I'll keep them from causing trouble. Don't worry." He started back toward the restive horse, and glanced over his shoulder. "Coming?"

"I don't want to see them again," Alaira said with a shudder.

"Maybe now you'll be pleased to have me along." He stroked the bay's neck lightly. It was quivering in reaction; he must have had it under some sort of spell to get it to chase the demons. "Those demons would have attacked you when you stopped here. What could Kyellan have done to rescue you?"

"He would have killed them all," Alaira said. "Not made them into pets." She grabbed a handful of the horse's mane to mount, but the Shape-Changer stopped her with a hand on her shoulder. She turned around indignantly.

His expression was thoughtful in the dim moonlight. "Why do you want Kyellan back so badly, anyway? Think about it, Alaira. He never gave you what you wanted. You said yourself he was never there when you needed him."

"Things would have changed for us," Alaira said angrily. "This journey was going to change him."

"Was it?" His voice was strangely intense. "He loved Briana. He could never give you that. He didn't even think of you when the priestesses were attacking, when he finally gave up and let me take control. All he thought about was Briana. He would never have been yours again. You know that."

"How can you say . . . you have no right . . ."

"I know Kyellan. Better than you or anyone else could. You're better off without him." He stepped back to let her mount.

She wished she had plunged the knife into his heart. She

pulled herself onto the horse's bare back, unable to speak for her anger. The Shape-Changer mounted behind her. His strong arms reached around her to tug on the horse's halter rope and guide it back to the camp.

"Just leave me alone," she said finally.

"It may be too soon," he said softly in her ear. "But consider what I've said, Alaira. Kyellan didn't deserve you. I'm not in love with any priestess. I think you are very beautiful. And no one can keep me from getting what I want."

Chapter Ten ─────────

"AN emissary from my brother?" Valahtia said in uncontrolled surprise, half rising from her father's ruby and emerald throne. She saw Tobas turn sharply in her direction from his conversation with two of the S'tari delegates in a quiet corner of the throne room. She settled back quickly in her seat, pulling up her feet to rest them on the pile of cushions at the base of the overlarge throne. "This is unexpected news, Lord Foerad."

The old man she had appointed her chamberlain bowed slightly in response, but she was sure she saw a fleeting look of scorn in his eyes. She was too young, too inexperienced, too female. Her six months pregnancy only made it worse. As if he was anyone to judge her. Foerad was the youngest brother in a family of country nobility from the farmland around Laenar. He had been overlooked by the wizards. All Valahtia's court was thus, since most of her father's retainers were dead. The very young and the very old, minor relations suddenly granted titles, trying hard to imitate the courtly skills of those who had been born to their positions.

"It is the first time Prince Arel has sent us a messenger openly, Your Majesty," the chamberlain said gravely. "Your response to the gesture will be watched, both by Arel's people on Syryn and by the other Kingdoms. You must be careful not to encourage his pretensions, yet you cannot afford to ignore what he may have to say. I counsel a cautious middle road. . . ."

"I'm well aware of your counsel," Valahtia snapped, drumming her fingers on the polished surface of an armrest. "And I'm weary of being lectured, Lord Foerad. I am Queen here, and I will find my own counsel. Do you understand me?"

The old man flushed, and murmured, "Perhaps it would be well if your Royal Consort were to be consulted." He backed away, stiff with indignation, and turned from the carpeted aisle toward Tobas. Like many others at court, he assumed she was ruled by her lover.

Arel was an enemy to her state and crown, yet he was also her older brother. She had to acknowledge that relationship. Her claim to the throne was based upon it. She could not refuse to see his messenger. She wondered if the emissary had come diplomatically from Prince Arel or arrogantly from the King in exile. She suspected the latter. It was supposed to be Foerad's job to tell her such things, but she would not call him back to ask him.

Tobas smiled at her as he strode toward the throne. Of all of them, Valahtia thought, only he looked the part of a nobleman. He had the bearing of a soldier and the grace of true courtesy. He was not bound by the artifice of her newly born, as yet unwieldly court. She returned his smile.

"Your Majesty." He bowed before her and took her hand, then moved to his seat on the lesser throne beside her. They had learned very quickly that their relationship must be formally correct in public.

"My lord, did Chamberlain Foerad inform you that an emissary has come from my brother in Syryn?" Valahtia said in a voice loud enough to be heard through the crowded audience hall.

Tobas nodded. "I have heard that the Queen has not yet decided whether to receive him."

"I have reason to doubt that my brother wishes me well," she said clearly. "But I must receive his messenger. Therefore, please ask my S'tari Guard to position themselves through the chamber and around my throne to protect me against any treachery. You will send your best men, well armed, to escort Arel's messenger to me."

She was pleased to see Foerad's brow furrow as he realized the insult this would offer Arel and his supporters. Some of the younger nobles loosened their rapiers in their sheaths and made a show of looking fierce, while the highborn maidens registered amusement behind their veils.

Tobas rose and bowed deeply. "At once, my Queen." Over her outstretched hand, he whispered, "How many men for the escort? Too many will seem ridiculous for a harmless messenger."

"Four," she murmured in reply. "Two before and two behind, at a respectful distance." She would not know until later if he approved of her decision. When she was holding court, he deferred to her, though they might argue for hours in private. She knew it was hard for Tobas. In the councils of the generals, his was a leading voice. In the throne room, he had to appear to be only her shadow.

The S'tari guardsmen moved at Tobas's orders. Four of them hurried out the farthest side door, and the others formed a formidable line on either side of the carpeted path in the center of the hall. The nobles and ladies moved back under the arches and against the walls. Valahtia wished her throne room was not so crowded. Few of those present had any petitions to bring her or favors to receive. True suppliants waited outside to be admitted by the chamberlain. Her courtiers liked to practice their manners and conduct their intrigues in the Queen's presence. A few of the older men expected her to consult with them if there was an important decision to be made. It was very tiresome.

"Lord Foerad, the emissary from my brother may be admitted to my presence." Valahtia sat forward as he went to obey her. She was eager for something to happen at last, beyond the tedious work of spying and surmise.

The ivory and gold doors at the entrance were thrust open by silk-clad pages, and two of the S'tari guardsmen stalked in. Behind them walked a little man with his face tightly composed. He was dressed all in black except for the emblazoned Tiger of Caerlin on his surcoat and the ruby pendant around his neck. Valahtia suppressed her initial anger. Her brother had the right to dress his servants in the livery of his house, whether he called himself Prince or King. The other two guardsmen pulled the doors closed behind them and followed the messenger inside.

Arel's emissary walked quickly between the lines of stone-faced warriors toward Valahtia, until the front pair of guardsmen crossed scimitars in front of him ten paces from the throne. "Do you expect me to shout, Your Highness?" he said, using the title she would have if she were still only a princess.

Valahtia was amused. She had affronted him deeply if he had abandoned formal phrasing in his first words. "Your voice carries well enough, and we have no secrets here. I welcome you for my brother's sake. I trust Prince Arel is well."

"As well as any man may be who is in exile from the Kingdom he loves. He has sent me to remind you that his place is here."

"His exile is of his own choosing," Valahtia said. "My brother would be most welcome at my court."

"Rather than return to the court of an usurper, the true King of Caerlin will remain in Syryn with the loyal subjects who have chosen to follow him there." The messenger, it seemed, had remembered his speech. "His Royal Highness the Crown Prince Arel wishes it to be known that he bears no ill will toward his younger sister Valahtia. She bore herself valiantly in the struggle to liberate Caerlin from the wizards' tyranny. It is not to her discredit that she was convinced to proclaim herself Queen on the advice of self-serving barbarian chieftains and over-ambitious generals of the resistance. She is young, and a woman, and therefore easily led."

Valahtia bit back an angry retort. She would hear him out, though the messenger infuriated her by speaking as if she was not present.

"The Prince, heir to the Kingdom of Caerlin through his father's wishes and the blessing of the Goddess, requires that his sister surrender to him his throne. He will be merciful. If she will submit to his will and marry the Crown Prince Werlinen of Keris, as was agreed in Altimar, he will provide her with a full dowry and his blessing."

"And if the Queen does not surrender?" Tobas said fiercely.

"A Council of Royalty will convene within the month in Keris," the man said. "If by that time the pretender Valahtia

has not renounced her claim to his throne, the Prince Arel
will be declared King of Caerlin by his peers, and he will
return here and take his throne and his crown by force. I
await a reply.'' He turned and started to walk away.

"You need not wait," Valahtia said, motioning to her
soldiers to block his path. The emissary whirled to look up at
her. The usual protocol would demand days of deliberation
with her counselors before she answered him. She saw Foerad's
face turning purple where he stood with two other older
nobles.

"Well, Princess?" said the emissary curtly.

"You may inform my brother that he forfeited his right to
the throne of Caerlin by his cowardice during the war. He
refused to ride with the armies that saved this Kingdom. I am
Queen by right, and no one holds authority over me. I bear a
child of the blood of my house and the royal house of the
Earldom of Laenar. When my son is born, the new First
Priestess has promised to grant him the Goddess's blessing to
rule Caerlin.'' She paused, searching for words. "I rule here,
as Queen by acclamation of the citizens of Caerlin, and as
Regent to my unborn son. If Arel chooses to attack me, he
will be an outlaw and a traitor to his father's house. My army
is strong, and my allies the S'tari are brave and loyal. You
may relay those words to your master, sir, and leave my
palace as quickly as you can.'' She nodded to the guards,
who moved forward to escort the messenger from the room.

The audience hall erupted in a vast murmuring. She could
hear some approval and some protest. The young nobles who
worshipped Tobas crowded around him chattering eagerly,
hoping for his opinion on what was likely to happen now.
Valahtia caught her chamberlain's eye and waved him forward. "Lord Foerad, I will hear no more supplicants today.
Dismiss whoever waits outside and tell them to come back
tomorrow. And ask Earl Tobas to attend me.''

"Your Majesty, I wish to beg you to reconsider your
answer," he said intently. "There is still time to call back the
messenger.''

"You may submit a formal protest to me if you wish. Or
petition for redress of grievances, on behalf of my brother's
emissary.'' She glared at him. "But I would recommend

neither." She clapped her hands in dismissal. Courtiers looked up in surprise. The audience session usually lasted three hours, and this one had only gone for an hour and a half.

Foerad hurried through the hall, muttered a few words to Tobas, and went out to dismiss the remaining petitioners. Tobas excused himself to his young admirers and came to bow before the Queen. "May I escort you, Your Majesty?"

She took his hand and descended the throne, feeling light-headed as they walked through the press of bowing nobles and out an archway into one of her private gardens. A servant shut the door after them. A soft breeze blew through the open walkway, a corridor of roofed stone arches shaded by potted trees that would be moved to the other side of the path in the afternoon.

"Regent to my unborn son!" Tobas repeated. "My love, you are incomparable."

She found that her hand was trembling in his. "I should have made him wait. And had Mirrem write me out a speech, with copies for all my advisors to argue over."

"You would have ended up saying much the same thing, but much less directly," Tobas said in a dry voice.

Valahtia giggled unsteadily. "I sounded like a S'tari boasting at his manhood feast. My armies are strong, my allies brave and loyal . . . Arel will laugh."

Tobas shook his head, his boyish face serious. "He won't be amused. It's true. He doesn't have an army to challenge us."

"Not yet. But he will have. Recruiters for his Redeemers are everywhere." She picked up a loose stone from the walkway and threw it hard across the walled garden. "I should have made Kyellan stay, even if I had to let Gwydion go. He could have kept my mercenaries from going with Arel. They trust him. Where is Arel getting the money to buy them away from me? I should send for Kyellan and command him to come back."

"If any message could reach him in Akesh . . ."

"And if one could, he wouldn't come." She sighed. "I know. Did I do the right thing, Tobas?"

"In letting Kyellan leave? I think so."

"No. I mean in there, just now."

He put both hands gently on her shoulders, and his dark eyes trapped hers. "Do you think I'd advise you to marry Werlinen? Yes, you were right. If you'd disguised your answer in flattering phrases your brother might have thought you really were weak. Now he'll know he can't sail back into the harbor and expect you to meekly hand him the crown. He'll have to work to get the other royalty to help him with their armies, which will take time. I'm not even sure he can do it. Some of those generals helped put you on this throne."

"All we need is enough time to establish our claim," Valahtia said. "When our son is born, he'll be King and I'll be Regent. And Briana will be First Priestess soon. She supports me. The people will follow the lead of the Temple."

"And Arel will be defeated." Tobas hugged her.

"Oh, Goddess, I hope so," she whispered, clinging to him. "Because if I resist him and he wins, I don't know what he might do to me. Or to you, Tobas. I really don't know what he'd do."

The demons did not often appear as the travelers continued their journey to Akesh. Alaira would have preferred it if they did not appear at all. But occasionally one of them would lope down from a hilltop or flap over a ridge to report to the Shape-Changer that the way was clear. They were no better looking in the sunlight than they had been at night. Knowing Alaira's distaste for his outriders, the Shape-Changer did not allow them to approach very closely. But still he refused to dismiss them back to the Otherworld where they belonged.

That morning, after the strange wizard had brought Chela back to awareness, the girl had seemed much better. She had insisted she was strong enough to ride without being tied to her brown mare. Now, as evening lowered in heavy clouds over the forest, she was exhausted. Her face was grey, her hands limp on the rein. Alaira rode close beside her, ready to lunge and catch her if she began to topple from the horse.

Gwydion rode with the Shape-Changer in the lead, pointing their way. He had come through this part of Garith when he had left Akesh in the last month of winter, a brash and idealistic boy. Now he was returning, without Power, scarred and weakened. He did not know what welcome he could expect.

Yet he seemed cheerful enough. He and the Shape-Changer had talked easily all day, as if they were old comrades. It made Alaira furious. Why did Gwydion have to be so friendly with him?

The S'tari horses jogged slowly over meadows covered with light snow and beneath the branches of tall masthead pines, seeming tireless. Alaira thought they, too, would be glad when the journey was over. They were bred for endurance, but not to withstand the cold of an early Garithian winter. Whenever the riders stopped to rest, the horses pressed in against each other, shivering and stamping their feet. When they started again, the animals moved stiffly at first.

The ground rose abruptly at the end of a long meadow ahead of them. Gwydion reined in his mount. "How is Chela?" he called back.

"We need to stop," Alaira said. "She's barely staying on."

"The river is just ahead. We'll cross it before we stop for the night. If we don't do it now, we'll have to take time after the crossing in the morning to build a fire and dry ourselves out."

"What does it matter how long we take?" Alaira asked irritably. "Chela is tired, and so am I. There's no one waiting for us at Akesh. One more day won't matter."

The Shape-Changer's golden head turned toward her. "We'll cross the river before nightfall," he said. "We all want to get to Akesh as soon as we can."

"I wish I'd never heard of the place," Alaira muttered.

They could see the river from the top of the rise. It snaked half frozen from the distant mountains to the east, flowing toward the west where it would widen into the Small Sea. The Wizards' College was on the northern shore of that huge freshwater lake. Alaira had seen it on the *Jester*'s charts, and she knew it was still days away. Gods, she was tired.

The horses stopped of themselves at the edge of the slick riverbank. Gwydion urged his grey gelding forward. A thin crust of ice broke under the horse's hooves, and it floundered chest-deep into the sluggish black water. The horse snorted and balked at the cold, but it lunged forward suddenly when Gwydion slapped its rump. It half swam to the opposite bank

fifty feet away, and scrambled up to stand with its head
down, shivering.

"Go on, Alaira." The Shape-Changer moved his horse up
beside her. His leg touched hers, and Alaira flinched. "I'll
lead Chela's mare across. It isn't that deep. Pull your feet up
and you won't even get wet."

How was she supposed to ride the horse with her feet
pulled up? Alaira sighed and kneed her small bay gelding in
the ribs. It pawed the icy crust delicately with a hoof and
drew back. "Sorry," Alaira said to the horse. She brought her
hand down hard behind her in imitation of Gwydion.

The gelding trotted forward into the river, its ears laid back
flat. The freezing river lapped up around Alaira's waist. The
horse held its head high, scarcely clearing the water. She had
forgotten that her mount was much smaller than Gwydion's.
She leaned forward and clasped her arms around her horse's
heaving neck, pulling her legs up into a crouch. The surface
of the river shifted and sank beneath her mount's unsteady
hooves, and then Alaira felt a sickening lurch as the horse lost
contact with the river bottom and began to swim.

The water soaked immediately through her woolen clothes
and forced its way inside her boots. Her cloak floated behind
her with the horse's tail. The darkness, the cold, everything
reminded her of her nightmare ride in the ocean on this same
horse. She had clung to it, though she was nearly drowned
with every wave, and the horse had fought its way to shore,
though it was scarcely in better shape.

Kyellan had been there the next morning, as wet and
exhausted as she was, but his enfolding arms had felt so
warm and safe. Alaira choked back a sob as her mount lunged
to the top of the bank and stopped in the sheltering trees
beyond the river. He was gone. There was nothing left of him
in the golden-eyed stranger who followed her across the river
leading Chela's horse. Nothing left.

The tears she had refused to allow herself for two days
could no longer be denied. She wept in mourning for Kyellan
and for her own dead hopes. She cried herself to sleep that
night in the rough camp near the riverbank. Nothing Chela or
Gwydion could say would comfort her, and the Shape-Changer
did not try. He sat with his long legs stretched out before him

on the opposite side of the fire. The last thing Alaira saw before she slept was the glitter of his yellow eyes reflecting the flames.

Wrapped in white cloth to veil him from the strong late afternoon sun, Cian squalled weakly in Briana's arms. She rocked him gently back and forth with the horse's swaying movements as it walked along the dry streambed. He would not be quiet. "He's hungry, Yalna," Briana called.

Leading her own horse and walking with her eyes fixed on the ground, Yalna did not seem to hear. She was looking for a sharp bend in the dry wash that Tapeth had described to her. It would point their way to the hidden valley. "Yalna!" Briana said again, helpless to soothe her red-faced infant.

The plump S'tari girl glanced back at them. "Give him a little more water. We don't have any more goat's cheese to strain."

"But . . . he's getting weaker," Briana said. A wave of dizziness swept over her, and she blinked rapidly as the streambed blurred and darkened. She pulled Cian closer, afraid she would drop him.

"And so are you," Yalna said sharply. "If I can find the way, we'll reach the valley by nightfall. Can you ride that long?"

"I'll try." Briana fumbled with the cork on the waterskin that hung by her knee on the saddle, and twisted a rag to soak it in the stale, warm water. Then she got a secure hold on the baby and squeezed drops of the water from the rag into his open mouth. He swallowed greedily, then began to cry again when he realized it was not food. "I'm sorry, Cian," Briana murmured.

"Here!" Yalna said moments later. "This must be it." She had reached a notch in the dry bank, a sharp-sided cut that did not appear to have been formed with the rest of the wash. "It points north. That's what Tapeth said. All we have to do is go that direction." She mounted her horse again and urged it up over the bank into the low, stony hills. Briana followed slowly. She rode with her knees hooked together over the pommel of her saddle, and with Cian in her lap; she was sure that she would fall off if the horse so much as trotted.

They kept the setting sun directly to their left as they rode through gravelly notches between the rugged hills. The ground crunched beneath the horses' hooves. Shadows cooled them a little as evening approached and they climbed higher. It was almost dark before Briana felt the sea breeze.

"I recognize that ridge from Tapeth's description," Yalna said, pointing. "There's a trail down somewhere on the other side of it. We should be able to see the valley from the top."

They reached the stony promontory and rode around it. The damp air bathed the cracked and dried skin of Briana's sun-burned face. She breathed in deeply. A soft mist lay below them like a sheer curtain over the land, but she could see sloping meadows and gentle, grassy hills, and a spring-fed stream that ran down to a narrow inlet too shallow and rocky for ships. A thread of smoke rose from the firehole in the small stone cottage on one of the hills.

Erlin and Pima would be there. They had never been far from Briana's thoughts in her months of waiting in the Tiranon. When Tapeth had told her they had agreed to raise her son, a great burden had lifted from her. She had feared leaving Cian with strangers, however well-meaning they might have been. Pima had been trained in the Goddess's service. She would know what to do with a child with Power.

Yalna's horse led the way down the steep, twisting trail, walking slowly and carefully so its hooves did not skid on the loose shale and gravel. Briana held Cian tightly to her as her horse followed gingerly. She did not try to guide it. It could see the shadowed way better than she could in the dusk. The path had been made by S'tari priestesses in Va'shindi's service. They came here sometimes, Tapeth had said. The place had long been sacred to the Goddess's messenger.

The sun set over the black waters of the Tarnsea far below. Only a faint glow was left in the west. The valley slowly lost its green color as Briana and Yalna descended, fading into greys with the approaching night. A feeling of peace, of calm, of healing Power rose from the valley. Briana opened her shields a little to let it wash over her with the cool sea breeze. This place seemed untouched by war or death. It seemed a place where no pain could exist. It was fertile, lush compared to the desert hills that surrounded it; only the Power of the Goddess could have kept it from discovery by Caerlin farmers. The weak and hungry baby in Briana's arms quieted and opened his golden wizard's eyes wide as he, too, felt the calm of the valley. Briana smiled down at him. If she could not have him, she could think of no better place for him.

At last the switchback trail eased out onto a high meadow, where the stream bubbled from a chill spring set in a hollow lined with rocks. Yalna grinned back at Briana. "I knew we could find it!" she shouted. Her voice echoed back at them from the wall of hills.

A door opened in the cottage, and the form of a short, stocky youth was silhouetted in a rectangle of yellow lamplight. Erlin waved. Briana heard the cry of an infant, a strong and healthy sound compared to Cian's thin wails. Pima's child had been born, then. Briana smiled to herself. The novice had been discreet, but if her baby had come at full term, then Pima and Erlin had to have been sleeping together since before the siege of Dallynd. Briana had not suspected them until almost a month later.

Yalna rode ahead of her along the bank of the stream, then turned her horse up on a footpath to the top of the hill where the cottage stood. Erlin hurried to meet them. "My lady Briana!" he cried. "You're here at last. We were worried at the delay."

"We stopped for a day," Yalna said. "We had little choice." She slid down from her horse and walked with Erlin to Briana's mount.

The priestess bent over Cian and pulled the cloth away from his face and head so Erlin could see him. "His name is Cian," she told him softly, looking down into the youth's blurry face. Her vision would not clear. He looked older, she thought, older than his eighteen years. His hair had grown out from its soldier cut, and hung around his neck in wiry black curls.

Yalna reached up and took Cian. "Stop gaping, and help the First Priestess from her horse," she muttered.

Erlin did as he was told. Briana put her arms around his wide shoulders and let him lift her out of the saddle. She tried to stand when he swung her to the ground, but her legs would not bear her weight. Erlin quickly caught her about the waist and held her up. He was a few inches shorter than she was, but he supported her easily. "My lady, are you all right?"

"I'm just . . . tired," she whispered, leaning on him as they walked to the open cottage door.

"It was a difficult birth," Yalna said. "Before her time, and still the baby was too big for her. She has lost blood."

Erlin picked Briana up like a child and lay her on a stone cot covered with a mattress of pulped rushes. It felt as soft as feathers after the hard desert ground. Briana forced her eyes to stay open, and looked around. "Where's Pima?"

"She's asleep," Erlin said quietly. Briana saw the curled-up form of the Kerisian girl beneath thick blankets on another, wider bed at the other side of the small cottage. "Our daughter was born only yesterday," Erlin added. "An easy birth, and Va'shindi was here to help. Pima was able to walk a little today, and she should be much better tomorrow. But by afternoon she was exhausted."

Yalna bent down over a large reed basket on the floor beside Pima's bed. She laid Cian beside the other baby, who was wrapped in a mound of cloth against the chill. All Briana could see of the child was a fringe of coarse black curls at the top of her head.

"What's her name?" Briana asked sleepily.

"Taryn. Va'shindi named her, for the Tarnsea."

"The Goddess bless her," Briana said automatically, before the darkness swirled in on her.

Chapter Eleven _____

"SHALL I wake her?" Yalna's voice reached distantly through Briana's fading dream. "She'll want to greet you, Mistress." Her tone was diffident and respectful, even awed. Briana struggled to bring herself out of her heavy sleep, slowly becoming aware of the dull ache in all her muscles and the deeper pain in her torn womb. Thick blankets covered her, and she lay curled on her side on a soft mattress.

"No, do not hurry her," said a gentle, half-familiar voice. "I will wait."

Briana forced her way to the surface of her mind from the deep place where she had been, and opened her eyes. The fire in the center of the cottage had gone out, and daylight streamed in from the firehole and the open door. Pima sat on the other bed, holding a golden-haired infant to her breast. Beside her, Erlin rocked their small daughter absently in his arms. Pima glanced down and saw Briana's gaze. "She's awake." A smile widened her round face.

"Here. Drink this." A slim hand raised Briana's head, and a cup was set to her lips. Briana drank obediently. A cool, refreshing liquid slipped down her throat, and the smell of mint rose from it to clear her head of its last cobwebs. She looked up.

A face of uncanny pale beauty, wreathed by a storm cloud of black hair; eyes like smoldering coals, deep and ageless.

143

The Goddess's messenger smiled at her. "Good day, First Priestess."

"Va'shindi," Briana said weakly. "Most people never see you once in their lifetime. I am honored to see you again."

"No need for formality," Va'shindi said, sitting down on the edge of the mattress and denting it almost imperceptibly. "I bring no message but my good wishes. How do you feel?"

"Better," Briana said, though she was not certain of that. Yalna had been standing behind the messenger. Now she moved forward to take the cup and put it down by the fire to be washed. The S'tari girl had cleaned the road dust from her skin and hair, and wore a new robe from her baggage, with a half-veil in deference to Erlin's presence. Her hair was dressed in five glossy braids looped above her shoulders. Her eyes darted continually toward Va'shindi and then away, as if she still could not believe this was real.

"I had meant for your child to be born here, in comfort, and I had meant to be here at your side," Va'shindi said in a troubled voice. "I hope you will forgive me. Events have moved away from my influence. The Goddess feels I have interfered far too much with all this. I have leave to come here today and finish what I began, but after this I must return to my other tasks."

"How can She tell you what to do?" Yalna asked indignantly.

"I am Her servant above all," the strange spirit reminded her. "I owe my Power to Her, and my immortality. I am forbidden to interfere with human destiny, and that is precisely what I have been doing." She sighed. "The Goddess would be justified in sending me back to my death and finding a replacement for the position of She-Who-Guides. But She is merciful. I am allowed a few mistakes. This, I fear, was one. I should not have tried to arrange matters so. Evil may come of it."

Briana felt a strengthening warmth of gentle Power as Va'shindi lay a hand on her brow. She looked up into the uncanny dark eyes and spoke soberly. "How can the Goddess be angry? You've saved Erlin's life, and cared for Pima, and now you've found a way to protect my son. We're all very grateful."

"I hope you continue to feel that way." The Goddess's messenger shook her head. "I do not have the foresight of the One we serve. But I have begun this, and now it must be carried through." She glanced up at Yalna. "This valley must be watched and protected, and I can no longer do so. Your aunt Tapeth will know who among the S'tari priestesses can be trusted. Food and other supplies will need to be brought here, and messages carried."

"We will be honored to serve you," Yalna said shyly.

"I will rely upon you. Know that you have my blessing." She turned back to Briana. "You do not need my blessing, First Priestess. The Goddess favors you. But if you will take my advice, you will rest here in this peaceful place for the two months it would have taken you to wait for your child to be born. Regain all your strength and Power before you go back to Cavernon City for your confirmation. You will need it, if my foreboding can be trusted. Farewell." She bent down and kissed Briana's forehead. Her lips felt cool, and yet they burned with Power. She rose lightly from the bed and glided across the room, sunlight shining through her robe of shifting stone-color. Her black hair and her gown blew back as if in a breeze as she went out the door, and then she faded and was gone.

Briana and Yalna stared after her, but Erlin and Pima were used to the messenger's comings and goings. Pima asked eagerly, "Will you do that, Priestess? Stay here two whole months?"

"Tapeth expected us to be gone that long," Yalna said. "And you left her those proclamations so people will think you're still there. I think we should stay."

"I would like to," Briana said slowly. "But, Yalna, there is no need for you to stay with me. Now that my baby is born your duties are over. You could return to Tapeth, or go back to your tribe. I can find my way back to Cavernon City."

"Are you so eager to be rid of me?" Yalna chuckled. "No, I'll stay, and guide you back to the city. There are brigands in the desert, even though we didn't see any of them on our way here. Without me, you might be in danger. But no S'tari will harm anyone who bears the ornaments of a consecrated healer, a midwife. And you'll be safe as my companion."

"I'm not strong enough to argue with you." Briana smiled gratefully at her. "Very well. We will both stay."

On the evening of the third day since they had crossed the river, the Shape-Changer halted the riders just below the hills of Akesh. He looked suspiciously up at the Wizards' College. Jagged buildings carven from heavy wooden logs reared dark on the hilltops against the clouded sky. He knew that he had been here before in previous incarnations, but that was as far as his memory went. The towers of the College were as ominous and threatening as the black waters of the Small Sea behind them.

There was a thin strip of forest between the coast of the huge freshwater lake and the hills of Akesh. A black stretch of denser forest flowed north along the horizon. They had been in and out of it all through their journey these past days. At first they had ridden along the coastline, but the Shape-Changer and Chela both had felt something strange in the water. The Small Sea was sluggish and peat-fogged, the size of the island kingdom of Syryn, stretching from the river in the west across the wastes of northern Garith. Eventually it narrowed again and ran into the great ocean. The Shape-Changer had sensed mindless things in its depths, lake creatures deformed by magic or summonings from the Otherworld. He could not tell which. But he felt it was best to stay some distance from the shore.

"Do you think we should just ride up there?" Alaira said uncertainly, reining in her horse behind him. "The demons you sent ahead as heralds haven't come back."

"They're unlikely to welcome us," he said, scowling up at the towers. "The demons told them who we are. They know Gwydion fought against their Kharad, and if they connect me to Kyellan they know I did the same." He touched his boots to his horse's flanks and trotted forward. "We'll go, but well shielded." He did not have to remember any particular spell to erect a strong wall of Power around the four horses and their riders. It glimmered lightly against the snowy meadow and the grey sky, though only he and Chela could see it.

He could feel Chela's Power beside him, strengthening his shield, though she was not linked to him. The young girl had regained much of her strength over the last several days. At the height of her Power, she more than any other would be justified in challenging the Shape-Changer. Luckily she was as yet mostly untrained, and dependent on Gwydion for her training. The wizard would be an ineffective teacher without Power of his own. Still, eventually he supposed Chela would attack him. He would be ready.

At first the cluster of dark buildings on the hilltops was silent. The Shape-Changer reached a tendril of probing Power out through a minute hole in his shield and sensed the dim collective mind of the wizards who hid inside. They were all in one location, the central tower, ringed by the other hills and standing higher than the other structures. They were pitifully weak. Youths not yet out of their apprenticeship, old men who had wasted their Power in years of futile anger and plotting. He even felt the wild Power of some of the wizard children, harnessed by their elders into the linkage and scarcely under control. That was foolish. The old wizards would spend more energy trying to discipline the children's strength than they would gain from the effort.

"Do they mean to attack us?" Gwydion asked quietly.

"I'm not certain," the Shape-Changer said. "But even in concert they aren't very strong. If we wanted to, Chela and I could easily destroy them."

"Try not to hurt them," Gwydion said. "There are few enough of us left anymore."

"As you wish." They rode on, passing the first hill of Akesh. An empty sentinel tower rose at its crest, and two small misshapen winged things lay crumpled at its foot. The Shape-Changer urged his nervous bay gelding forward, and looked down at the bodies of his demon heralds. The snowy ground where they had fallen was blackened by their blood. There was a glamour set around them that held their forms in this world, where no demon could remain after death. The Shape-Changer spoke a sharp word and they dissipated. It was an inconvenience to lose such useful servants, but he could not be angry at the futile gesture.

"I don't like this place," Alaira said fiercely, holding her smaller bay back as the other three rode forward into a notch between two hills. "I'm not going in there."

The Shape-Changer reached back in irritation and placed a spell of obedience on her horse, forcing it forward. Alaira pulled at the rein, but the S'tari animal could not respond. It fell into place beside Chela and matched her brown mare's gait. The Shape-Changer wished he could put such a spell on Alaira herself. He wanted her, but he wanted her to come to him freely.

"What's that?" Gwydion muttered as they approached a bend in the path. The Shape-Changer turned his attention from Alaira, and heard it too. Growling, a heavy shambling noise, coming toward them. He sent his probe ahead and found that the thing was shielded. He could not tell if it was a summoning or a magically enhanced forest beast. From the sounds he was certain it was large, and angry.

His horse fought the command to go on. It reared and danced backward from the musky smell of the approaching beast. The other horses were equally frightened. Alaira clung precariously to hers as it moved forward in jerks, forced to obey the Shape-Changer's spell. He spoke a soft word to release it. The animal stopped suddenly and stood with its ears pricked forward and its eyes wide as Gwydion and Chela reined in their mounts beside it.

"I don't know if it has Power of its own or if the wizards are shielding it," the Shape-Changer said. "But it may be meant only to frighten us away. Stand firm."

With a challenging roar, the beast rounded the bend in the notch and saw them. It was huge. Taller than the horses and as wide as a team of oxen, the animal looked vaguely like a bear. Its thick black fur, its humped back and shoulders and its powerful long forelegs were bearlike. A heavy, muscled tail with a horny end slashed back and forth behind it as it reared up on hind legs as thick as tree trunks. Scythe claws curved from the fingers of two humanlike hands, and the sharp teeth of a great cat protruded from its massive jaw.

The Shape-Changer extended his shield in front of him. The beast lumbered through it unhindered. It was not an illusion then, no magical sending. The wizard tried a blast of

focused Power, black fire like that he had used against the
Hidden Temple priestesses. The bear-thing roared and focused its small dark eyes furiously on him, but its thick fur
was barely singed. Its shield was strong enough to protect it
from such a direct blow of Power. The Shape-Changer looked
up thoughtfully. He could bring down half the hillside with a
blast to bury the creature, but one of the towers would go
with it. Perhaps a tower with the very book he needed to learn
the lore of his ancestors.

He allowed his horse to back up a few paces as the black
beast shook the ground, lumbering toward him. The Akesh
wizards were more resourceful than he had guessed. They
knew his magical skill far outweighed theirs, so they sent
brute force against him. There was probably a way to deal
with it, but the Shape-Changer's vague memory did not in-
clude any such spell.

"Get away from it!" Alaira cried. He was surprised at her
concern. He would have thought she would cheer on the
beast. But no, she did not want him dead. Then her hopes of
someday regaining Kyellan would die, too.

How would her heroic, foolish soldier face such a monster?
Foolishly, the Shape-Changer answered himself. With a sword.
He drew Kyellan's sword with his right hand. It did not feel
balanced, and he remembered it was a left-handed blade. He
transferred it quickly, hoping his body and his muscles would
remember how to do this as well as they remembered how to
build a fire and ride a horse.

With his lapse in concentration, his hold on his S'tari
mount broke. It reared violently and twisted out of control as
he lunged to one side to try to force the horse in that direction
and fell off. The wet, snow-covered ground hit hard, and the
Shape-Changer rolled to his feet still holding the sword. The
black beast swerved and came toward him. The Shape-Changer
ran to the side of the steep, slippery hill and climbed, his
boots scrabbling for purchase on the rounded stones.

The monster swiped a paw at him. Long, knife-edged
claws caught the calf of his boot, ripping the leather as if it
were gauze. He lunged upward out of the thing's reach, and
looked back at it. It could not jump, or climb the steep

hillside. It was too awkward and heavy. It roared defiantly at
him and then turned its head to seek less elusive prey.

Another horse panicked, and Alaira tumbled to the ground.
Chela held her mount under firm, spellbound control and
leaned down to offer Alaira her hand as Gwydion drew his
short sword. The Shape-Changer knew Gwydion could not
wield the weapon with his fragile hands. The young wizard's
face was deathly pale, but he urged his horse toward the
beast.

The Shape-Changer reached a point on the hillside just
above the monster, and leaped down onto the thick hump that
rose from the beast's neck, swearing at his own folly. His
legs clamped against the layers of winter fat, and he stabbed
downward. His sword sliced easily into the hump, but it only
infuriated the beast. Its head swung back, and it reared onto
its thick hind legs. Its tail slashed gouts of earth from the hills
on either side. The Shape-Changer clung tightly, shaken and
bruised. He jerked his sword loose and stabbed again, seeking
the hollow at the base of the animal's skull. The humanlike
paws flailed, but the beast was not made to scratch its own
back. It threw itself hard against the hillside, trying to dis-
lodge the Shape-Changer. He thrust the sword down at an
angle a third time. The Parahnese steel slipped between verte-
brae and buried itself deep in the beast's minuscule brain.

The huge body shuddered and stiffened. The ground-shaking
roar was suddenly strangled. The Shape-Changer threw himself off onto the hillside as the beast tottered and fell crashing
to the earth. A flurry of powdered snow rose up in a light
cloud. The beast twitched once more and was still.

"Are you all right?" Gwydion called in a shaken voice.

The Shape-Changer rose to his feet and tried to speak
calmly. "I'm unhurt. Just a shredded boot." His calf was
unmarked. Lucky for the Akesh wizards, he thought. If their
beast had harmed him, he would have been less likely to
spare their lives. He slid down from the hillside and climbed
back up onto the carcass to retrieve his sword. He wiped it
clean of the beast's blood on the black fur and sheathed it
again.

When he climbed down again, Alaira stood beside one of
the sprawled forelegs of the monster. She looked up at him

briefly, then looked away and said in a small voice, ''That was bravely done.''

''Thank you,'' he said dryly, conscious that her tone was more reluctant than admiring.

The two bay horses that had bolted to the edge of the forest now trotted lightly back across the snowy meadows, still half-bound by the Shape-Changer's spell. Alaira moved forward to catch her horse and mount it. The Shape-Changer waited for his to come to him. He was not angry with it, he found. He was too pleased with himself. Though in all his vague memories of past lives he had been a powerful sorcerer, he could not recall ever having been this good at swordplay and warfare. That he owed to Kyellan. At least while the soldier had controlled their body he had not wasted it. It was strong and quick, and had great endurance. He guessed that it would recover easily from the most punishing spell backlash, and scarcely tire during the most demanding rituals.

He mounted his horse. ''Help me raise the shield again,'' he said to Chela. Her Power came alongside his own, though still she did not link with him. In a battle, that would be a dangerous weakness. It did not matter that much today. He was in no mood for further fighting. ''Wizards of Akesh!'' he shouted in a clear voice that carried over the hills. ''We come in peace. We wish only to study and learn here at the College. But if you oppose us any longer, we will destroy you as we destroyed the beast you sent against us. Don't be foolish. We're coming in.''

He created a black pillar of flame to hover just ahead of them as they rode up the hill path toward the center of the College. Let the Akesh wizards, too, think he worshipped Darkness. They might fear him more if they thought he served a Power beyond himself.

''They're awfully quiet,'' Alaira said uneasily.

The Shape-Changer could feel his foes' anger and fear, but the wizards made no move. The four companions rode past low outbuildings, thick-walled structures with narrow windows like arrow slits and heavy, iron-reinforced doors. The taller towers in the center stood on a ring of low hills around the central height. The Masters' Tower rose from a foundation of lake-rounded stone. The walls had been layered together from pine logs, planed and joined and carved in ornamental friezes in panels. The windows were shuttered and few; there would be little sunlight inside. The Shape-Changer preferred the airy houses of the South with their courtyards and archways and inner gardens. He supposed he had learned that preference from Kyellan.

The highest hill was flat-topped, with a small yard in front of the tower's door. The Shape-Changer rode up to the portal and raised a thick iron knocker and let it fall. All was silent for a long moment. Then a board slid back near the knocker and a bearded wizard's face appeared at the opening. "Who's there?" the old man demanded.

"You know our names," the Shape-Changer said from horseback. "Our heralds told them to you."

"Heralds?" repeated the wizard. He had enough of a personal shield to cloud the Shape-Changer's probe, but his hostility and fear were apparent.

"Two flying demons under my mastery."

"They were yours? We assumed they were two more of the masterless summonings that have plagued us since the end of the war. We destroyed them as soon as they appeared. They had no time to give us any message."

"You claim not to know who we are?"

"Let us in, Morfan," Gwydion said wearily, dismounting his horse behind the Shape-Changer.

The old wizard did not seem particularly surprised to see him. "I remember young Gwydion, of course, but how were we to know who you were? There have been other visitors who did not even pretend to be friendly. A patrol of soldiers from Atolan, sent to see if any wizards remained at the College—the black beast killed a few of them and frightened the rest away before they had a chance to find out. And the masterless demons, of course. Sometimes they came in force."

"You know Gwydion," the Shape-Changer said impatiently. "This is Chela, and Alaira. I am the Shape-Changer, the son of Onedon. Are you going to let us in, or do we have to burn the place down around your ears?"

"Let you in? Why—why, of course, good master," said

the bearded man. "We're very sorry for the trouble, and the loss of your servants. If we had only known . . ." The board went back across the hole in the door. The Shape-Changer heard frightened whispering. At last a heavy bolt was drawn back, and the door swung inward. "Welcome to the College of Akesh," said the old wizard. He wore a worn and patched robe and cracked boots. His beard and long hair were both unkempt and tangled, and he smelled musty, as if he had been left too long on a shelf.

The Shape-Changer dismounted and spoke firmly. "You will show us clean and spacious chambers, and prepare food and baths. And you will see to it that our horses are properly cared for, and bring our baggage to our rooms." He beckoned the others to follow him.

"Certainly, of course, right away, my lord," muttered the wizard. The Shape-Changer could feel combined hatred and awe in the old man, and he smiled. Morfan would make a most loyal servant.

"A bath!" Alaira sighed with pleasure at the thought. It would take her weeks to get clean. She slid down from her horse's back and followed Gwydion and Chela into the huge, dark tower. The entire lower story was taken up with one large, round hall, from which a spiral staircase led upward. The hall was crowded with old men and children. All were ragged and looked half starved. All were wizards, and all were male. They stood around a fire as ill-fed as they were, staring at the intruders with haunted yellow eyes. Alaira shivered. There were so many of them. She counted fifteen scrawny old men like Morfan, eleven youths between the ages of ten and sixteen, and thirty boy-children from infants to nine-year-olds.

"What has happened here?" Gwydion said in disbelief, looking around at the barren hall.

It must once have been richly furnished, Alaira thought. The dusty parquet floor was discolored where large chairs and long tables must have stood. There were bright rectangles of unworn wood on the walls where tapestries had hung. In places the carved paneling had been ripped down, leaving the inside of the log walls exposed. They had probably burnt it all for firewood, Alaira realized.

"You can have the Masters' rooms," said Morfan wearily, leading them to the huge staircase. Thick banisters curled upward over scallops of carven wood. Patterns of entwined wheat stalks snaked around the worn handrail. "They aren't being used. No one has felt they had the right to take them."

"Until we appeared," said the Shape-Changer. "We're grateful for your hospitality." His tone was sarcastic, and the old man flinched.

"Morfan, how could it come to this?" Gwydion demanded as they began to climb the stairs. "Did the College have to fall apart with the Masters gone?"

"With the Masters dead." The old wizard turned his rheumy yellow eyes to glare at Gwydion. Alaira was suddenly reminded that everyone in this place had Power, even if it was not strong. "With everyone gone, young Gwydion. Everyone with real Power, even the best apprentices. And you yourself had a hand in seeing to it that none of them came back."

"They can't all be dead. I did my best to help destroy the Masters. They made themselves bloody tyrants in the Kingdoms they occupied. But there were so many wizards with the Kharad, Morfan. Some must have escaped the battles."

"None have made it here," said the ragged old man. "The way is too perilous. All the northern Kingdoms have bounties on captured wizards. I have heard that some have made their way to the island of Barelin, where there were no battles. There have always been wizards in the city of Barena. They may still be there. But Akesh is dying, as you see."

"I could understand a loss of Power," Gwydion said quietly, "a loss of morale. But the children down there haven't been eating much. I didn't see any stores of firewood. Winter is coming, Morfan. You should have been hunting the forests, and gathering wood."

They reached the third landing of the long stairway, and the old wizard led them down a curving hall. Rough torches smoldered in wall sconces that had been made to hold oil lamps. The bare floor of the corridor had once been covered by a carpet. Scraps of it were still tacked to the planks. "We tried," Morfan said after a moment. "We sent out foraging parties all through the summer, until we lost half our apprentices.''

"Lost them?'' Chela repeated. "How?''

"The woods are haunted by bands of free-roaming demons, and great deformed beasts like the one we captured to guard the hills. We don't have the Power to compel them to obey us, and we don't have the strength to dismiss them back to the Otherworld. And the lake . . .''

"I sensed something in there,'' said the Shape-Changer with interest. "Or several things. Very large, and very hungry. Summonings, or merely overgrown animals of this world?''

Morfan shrugged. "I do not know, my lord. They were not there until last winter. There were many secret preparations for the Kharad. Who knows how the Masters created them, or why. But they are in the lake now, and those who venture too near the shore are likely to vanish, leaving only trails of slime where the creatures crawled from the lake to devour them. I am surprised you came that way unscathed.'' He looked thoughtfully at the Shape-Changer. "Or perhaps I am not. Old and burnt out as I am, I can recognize a great Power. So, no doubt, can the beasts of the Small Sea.''

"I am very powerful,'' the Shape-Changer said with a smile. "That much is true. But I have only recently gained mastery over myself. If you and your people will serve me and help me learn the skills of a trained wizard, then I promise you I will make your forests safe for you again. And once I learn their nature, I'll deal with the lake beasts as well.''

"Already he can control the lesser demons,'' Gwydion said in reluctant assent. "We can lead hunting parties and gather wood as soon as we are rested from the journey. You'll find we won't be useless.''

"We will be grateful for any aid,'' Morfan said, his face expressionless. "Here are the Masters' rooms.'' He indicated two ornate cedar doors bound with iron filigree, with large keys waiting in the hasps. "We can't offer you much supper. But I'll send boys to bring you water for baths, and we'll take care of your horses. Someone will bring your baggage.''

"Only two rooms?'' Alaira said.

"Gwydion and Chela in one," said the Shape-Changer. "You and I in the other."

"I sleep alone." She turned her eyes from his easy smile. "Is there another place where I can stay?"

"If my lady wishes," Morfan said, looking at the Shape-Changer uneasily. The tall wizard waved a hand in apparent indifference. "Of course, my lady," Morfan went on. "This way."

Chapter Twelve _____

Early morning fog still shrouded the harbor of Cavernon City, blurring the outlines of masts and spars on the ships docked at its endless rows of piers. Valahtia leaned over the parapet of the sea wall on a rise overlooking the wide bay. Here, the wall was the height of two men. New towers had been added on the heights at either side of the bay. But still, in places, the wall was as low as that of her private gardens in the Tiranon, and no better defended.

"How will this stop Arel?" she demanded of Senomar, who had brought her here to inspect his repairs and his new fortifications. "Or did you think he would arrive by the Caravan Road? On a clear day you can almost see his fortress on Syryn from here." Arel was not there now. He was in Keris at the meeting of the Council of Royalty. Two months had passed since his emissary had demanded her surrender. Enough time for Arel to pull together his army. Valahtia was eight months pregnant now, and she was frightened.

The old battle engineer spoke quietly. "The city has always relied on its fleet to guard it from the sea. The sea wall was the most damaged by the wizards' attack, Your Majesty. And it has never been a high wall. Its foundations aren't broad enough to support more height."

"Then broaden the foundations," she said. "Arel's men won't even need scaling ladders to get over this."

"We could tear down buildings for more rock," Senomar said. "Or send more prisoners to the quarries, I suppose. But if you will forgive me for saying so, my Queen, the goodwill of your people is more important than all the siege machines and new towers and reinforced walls I can build you. The highest walls are breached by treachery."

"Your Majesty!" A strong young voice rang out over the clattering of horses' hooves on the cobbled street behind the wall. Valahtia turned. Tobas halted his mount and slid from the saddle. He was cloaked against the chill mist of the winter dawn, but as he ran up the stairway to the parapet his cloak flew behind him. He was wearing a bright blue surcoat with the Boar of Laenar embroidered in gold, which made him look very handsome, but his face was serious under the brown curls.

"What's the matter?" she called. She and Senomar were alone on the walls, with her two S'tari guards waiting a respectful distance away. There was no need for formality.

"A courier," he panted when he reached them. "A courier has come from Ishar in Keris."

"Where the Council of Royalty was meeting?" Senomar said, his gaunt face falling into somber lines.

"Tobas, you could have sent a page for me," the Queen said. "There was no need to ride all this way alone."

He shook his head. "It wasn't an official herald, and I don't want it spread all over the city. We should be receiving some sort of messenger in a few days, but this was one of my men. They've crowned Arel King in exile. He is returning to Syryn to join his army."

Valahtia closed her eyes briefly and clenched her fists over her heavy abdomen. She had hoped it would not happen. An irrational hope, perhaps, but she had clung to it. "Then they mean war," she whispered.

"It will take time. My spy said that Keris and Ryasa are going to recall their ambassadors to the Tiranon and send them to Arel's court at Syryn. There was some talk of blockading the bay, but that would hurt the other Kingdoms' trade more than it would ours." He was trying to sound cheerful, and almost succeeding. "Istam says no one will want to take the first step toward war. The Kingdoms have been at peace with one another for a long time. They united to drive out the wizards. They'll have to convince themselves to break the alliance if they're to move against us.''

"Arel will convince them," Valahtia said bleakly. "They're sure he's on the side of the right. He's the true heir to my father's throne. The Council is bound up in tradition, especially in matters of succession. And they don't like me.''

Senomar hurried to her defense, though a minute before he had been warning her to beware of treachery. "The Temple supports you, at least, my Queen. The people will believe the Goddess is on your side.''

Tobas looked at Valahtia sidelong, and cleared his throat as if he were having difficulty speaking. "Val . . . Briana supports you, I know that. But another thing my courier told me. There were priestesses at the Council in Ishar. They spoke against you, and a few of them even spoke against Briana.''

"Priestesses from Caerlin?" she asked sharply.

"I don't know. He thought there were a few. They were all angry about your leniency toward the wizards here. And you know we suspect the priestesses of the Cavernon Temple of being behind the killings.''

Valahtia shuddered. She had allowed a few wizards to leave unscathed to make their way to Barelin; she had sent Gwydion off with safe passage to Garith. People had protested that, but it seemed she had angered them most by her edict forbidding them to kill wizard babies at their birth. It was a practice that had been traditional in Caerlin up to the invasion last spring, while all the other Kingdoms had denounced it as barbaric. Now the other Kingdoms were vigilant in preventing wizard births, and Caerlin was reviled for passing its first law in centuries against infanticide.

Despite the law, more and more pitiful small bodies were being discovered in the gutters of the city and washed up against the docks. The corpse of a four-year-old boy had been found a week ago, strangled and buried in a garbage cart. There had been traces of black dye in the child's hair, as if his mother had tried to pass him as a normal boy. The one couple who had been tried for killing their wizard son had insisted they acted according to their devout belief in the Goddess. They said a Third Rank priestess had told them it

would be a sin in the Goddess's eyes if they allowed their
infant to live. They had refused to name the priestess.

"What is Briana thinking," Valahtia muttered. "She's the
one who insisted I show mercy to the surviving wizards. She
stays hidden in her tower, purifying herself for her confirmation as First Priestess, while this—this slaughter goes on
unchecked. She has no control over her Temple or the Order.
Why does she stay silent?"

"It would help if she appeared openly in support of your
rule," Tobas said. "She has never said in public that she
intends to give our child the Goddess's blessing to rule. If she
did, many would turn to us. They know Arel was a weak
Prince; how can they expect him to be a good King?"

"All they know is that he is the true King," Senomar said.
He spat over the wall.

Valahtia started down from the wall, and Tobas hurried to
take her elbow at the stairs and help her descend. She was not
supposed to exert herself at all, according to her attendants, but
she had not thought a short ride through the sleepy dawn city
would harm either her or her unborn son. "We'll have to
respond to the Council's action," she said as the S'tari guards
sprang forward with the horses. "I think I'll send Foerad to
Syryn. He knows the traditions of diplomacy. He ought to be
able to deal with Arel. Reason with him." She sighed. "And
if he can't get him to listen to reason, then Foerad can make a
diplomatic protest and return. Oh, Tobas, why did I ever let
them make me Queen?"

"As I recall, my love, it was your own idea." He helped
her into her saddle. Valahtia drew her cloak close around her
and pulled her hood forward to hide her face. She did not
want to attract anyone's notice this morning. Tobas and
Senomar both mounted, and the S'tari guards waited until
they had ridden half a block before mounting to follow them
unobtrusively. Tobas urged his horse close beside the Queen's,
and after a pause he spoke again. "Send assassins after him.
It's the only way."

"The only way *you* can see." He had mentioned this
before. "I can't do that, Tobas."

"Even the Council would have no choice but to confirm
you as Queen if Arel was dead. They'd be angry, but you're

the last of the Ardavan line. As far as we know Arel has no heir.''

"I wanted him dead before," she said softly. "I once asked Kyellan to kill him. I hated him so."

"Then what's stopping you?" her consort asked in frustration.

"My father is dead. I owe it to him not to kill his son. And the people would see me as someone who murdered her brother. They might follow me, but they would never love me. I'd certainly lose Briana's support. No, Tobas. He may deserve it, but Arel will not die at my hand. Not so long as I have a choice."

"It may soon be too late to choose," Senomar muttered from where he rode behind them.

"Isn't anyone else coming?" Alaira asked Gwydion. Her horse and his stood tied to a post, saddled and geared as if for war, with longbows and spears and full quivers of arrows. The chill morning sliced past Alaira's layers of woolen clothes and seeped up through the soles of her boots from the icy ground. They had been at Akesh for two miserable months, and now it was winter in earnest.

"The Shape-Changer is too busy with his research. I decided to let Chela sleep. She exhausted herself last night with another attempt to waken my dormant Power." He untied his horses and shot an irritated glance at her. He always seemed to be angry. Alaira supposed it was because the smallest ragged toddler here had more Power than he did. "The boys are at their lessons, and that leaves you and me. Coming?"

Alaira scowled and mounted without a word. That left the two of them. Two useless, powerless people who had little to do but avoid one another's bad moods. Gwydion spent some of his time with Chela in apparently futile efforts to regain his lost Power, and Alaira occasionally had to fend off the Shape-Changer's advances, but neither occupation was very pleasant. So Gwydion had put himself in charge of the frequent hunting parties, and Alaira usually went along.

The Shape-Changer had bound all the local demons to his control, though he had not attempted to do anything about the lake monsters yet. The forests were fairly safe now. Alaira had learned to shoot passably, and she could throw a spear with enough accuracy to hit a deer or a wild pig and slow them for other hunters to finish them off. She was not nearly as good at it as Chela was, and she did not have the horse-back skills to ride close to a racing animal, as Gwydion did, to bury a spear in it from above. Still, she made a contribution to the College. It did not bring her much pleasure. It was only something to do.

"I wish I had the courage to just ride out of here," she muttered as her horse half-slid down the hillside behind Gwydion's. Spears that were tied loosely to the saddle bounced against her legs.

"Where would you go?" Gwydion had heard her.

Alaira's small horse floundered through the icy crust on the thick snowpack of the meadow. "I'd ride down to Atolan, if I could find the way."

"And once you were there?"

She sighed and turned her face up to look at the sullen grey sky. "I'd find a way to get back to Cavernon City. I don't care how." She would be a ship's whore if she had to.

"You'd have to wait until spring," the young wizard said. "Not many ships come north in the middle of winter. The ocean is too dangerous. No more than two or three couriers will arrive in Atolan over the four worst months. There may be ships in dry dock there, but you wouldn't be able to get home."

That was not encouraging. Alaira scowled and turned her horse to follow him across the white meadows toward the west. They began to sink into the loose snow beneath the first pines of the forest. It was hard to find game in the haunted woods near the Wizards' College. The Shape-Changer's pet demons frightened away the animals. But if the demons saw a deer or a pig, they would herd it toward the hunters. Alaira hated to see a terrified animal running before the obscene creatures, but she knew how important it was to have fresh meat.

As much as she hated the Shape-Changer, she had to admit that the College was much better off under his rule. He had made the forests safe, and he had set the apprentices to work

building new furniture to fill the empty rooms of the halls and
dormitories, and cataloguing books that had lain in haphazard
piles for centuries in the vast libraries. The wizards were
grateful to him. They called him Master, and deferred to him
as if he was the most learned among them. It was true that his
education was improving. He devoured their books of lore
and labored to construct elaborate spells, exercises that as
often as not had no purpose.

The forest closed in about them, snow-laden branches block-
ing out any view of the thick, heavy sky. Alaira soon lost her
sense of direction. She was far from woodswise. How could
she be? She knew the skills needed to survive on her own in
the night streets of Rahan Quarter, but that had been all she
had learned. Gwydion always knew where he was. He had
lost his Power somehow, but he had not lost the other extra
senses that were natural to wizards: stronger hearing, better
eyesight, a cat's sense of balance, and an uncanny feeling
for place and direction. Alaira wished Gwydion would be
satisfied with being so talented in those ways, and not think
of himself as a cripple because he had no Power.

"Hush," the golden-haired youth said suddenly, though
Alaira had not said anything for a quarter of an hour. "There's
something off to the right." He pulled one of his spears loose
and held it poised. Alaira unslung her longbow and notched
an arrow.

They waited. She had learned that hunting was mostly
waiting. In the cold, with snow dripping from branches into
her hair and down her back, and her horse standing unsteadily
in a drift, stamping its feet occasionally from boredom.

Alaira tried to stop her mind from running in circles. None
of her thoughts were new or interesting to her. They ran over
and over like a grumbling litany. They were surface thoughts,
and she supposed she used them to keep herself from thinking
about her deeper grief and helplessness. Damn it, she could
not even mourn Kyellan properly. He was not dead. But she
would never see him again. He was trapped inside an alien
mind that had somehow once been a hidden part of him.

Her head snapped up at a rustling through the branches just
beside her. In a flurry of snow, a tall, white-flecked deer with
flattened antlers like a helmet bounded across her path. She

shot an arrow at close range, but not quickly enough. It embedded its point into the deer's haunch instead of its breast, and the animal scarcely broke its stride. It vanished again into a tangle of close-grown pines and underbrush.

"After it!" Gwydion said eagerly, leaning forward on his horse to duck beneath the stinging branches. Alaira clung tightly as her horse sprang forward to follow. She leaned down to the side of the bay's neck as they plunged through the brush. Snow sifted from swaying branches and powdered up from the horses' hooves as they passed. Alaira began to regret leaving the warm fires of the College, as she always did after a half an hour out in the Garithian winter. Her face was numb, and her fingers were frozen even though she wore thick woolen gloves.

Gwydion cut across an open glade in front of her, and she saw the deer again, racing close enough beside the horse for the wizard to raise his spear and thrust down. The deer squealed and broke off in another direction, limping heavily, the spear haft hanging from its left shoulder. Alaira fought a wash of nausea.

"It's headed for the shore!" Gwydion cried, urging his horse after the faltering animal.

"The Small Sea?" Alaira shouted in alarm. "Wait, Gwydion . . ."

"We'll bring it down before it reaches the lake," he said as their horses came abreast.

The trees were thinning, and the snow was dwindling into a light cover for the marshy ground. Alaira saw the black water glimmering through the branches ahead. A thin rim of ice extended about twenty feet into the lake from the shore, but the Small Sea did not freeze over as the lesser ponds and shallow bogs in the area did. Alaira halted her horse at the edge of the forest. The dark lake stretched out under the grey sky, its opposite shore too far away to appear even as a shadow on the horizon.

The deer had floundered to the very edge of the lakeshore, where dead reeds and matted growths of moss made a soggy carpet below the sharp rise of the bank. Alaira trotted her horse forward to see. The deer lay panting on its side with its head lying on the thin crust of ice, but there was something else moving slightly out farther into the lake on the ice rim. A dark form, smaller than the deer, and it seemed to be bound with reeds from the shore. "Gwydion, what is that?" she breathed.

His slit pupils contracted as he tried to sharpen his vision. He gasped. "A small demon," he said in disbelief. "Tied and left there . . . an offering for the lake beast? But who would do such a thing?"

Alaira was not even certain she could blame the Shape-Changer. She could not think of any reason why he would want to give one of his pets to the monsters of the lake. And though she hated the demons, she was horrified at this one's fate. To lie there, awake and half frozen, waiting for either the cold or the beast to take him . . . it was awful. "We have to help it," she said quietly.

"We could try," Gwydion said after a moment. "I'm not sure the ice is thick enough to support our weight."

"I'm not very heavy." Alaira slid down from her horse and unslung a rope from her saddle. She tied it around her waist. "You can pull me back to shore if I fall through." She started for the bank and was pleased to see that Gwydion followed her without argument.

Her boots slipped on the steep, icy slope, and she caught herself with her gloved hands before she landed facedown in the mat of moss and reeds on the shore. Gwydion kept his balance more easily. He grasped the end of the rope when she handed it to him. "Go as quickly as you can," he said. "Just untie the demon, don't try to get it back to shore yourself. If whoever did this has been leaving regular offerings, the lake beasts may be near."

Alaira nodded and started out onto the ice. It seemed firm beneath her, and it was too windswept and rough to be very slick. The bound form of the small demon lay near the edge of the ice rim, however. She did not know if the ice there would be as strong. But she had to try. For some reason, she felt she had to save the life of this creature. Maybe it was because she had felt useless for so long. Maybe it was because she was sure the Shape-Changer would have chosen to leave the demon there to die, whether or not he had been behind its situation.

The demon's eyes were lidless, like a snake's, a strange purple color ringed by gold. It was one of the squatty toad-like demons with only small balancing wings. Whoever had put it here had not bothered to bind its wings, knowing it could not fly. Now, as Alaira approached, the wings began to flap in agitation as the fearful eyes stared at her. She shivered with revulsion and crept forward. The ice creaked a little beneath her, but it held. The lake was silent, and even the cold wind had fallen away into stillness.

She drew her belt knife and reached out from a kneeling position to cut the demon's frozen reed bindings. From the condition of the strange ropes, the creature had been there for some time. The reeds split before they parted, but at last they fell away. The demon lay stiff for a moment, then began to flex its grotesque limbs and look in fear at the black water just behind him.

The rope at Alaira's waist gave a sharp jerk, and she turned. "Get back!" Gwydion shouted. "Now!"

The demon shrieked, a high, chilling sound, and Alaira followed its lidless gaze to see a wake like a ship's bearing down on them from the depths of the Small Sea. Only there was no ship to cause a wake. She saw a slick hump break the water's surface for an instant. The little demon was too cold and frightened to move. Alaira lunged and grasped it around the middle with both hands, and lifted it in her arms. It was the size of a large child, but she could hold it. She turned and ran, heedless of the protesting ice beneath her increased weight. The demon's small wings fluttered against her. Above Gwydion on the bank, the two S'tari horses reared and fled.

A great head burst through the ice where the demon had been. It was the size of a farmer's cart, dripping dank black water and lengths of stringy peat. It was all mouth and jagged rows of teeth, Alaira saw through a mist of terror. She ran up onto the bank, still holding the demon in her arms. Gwydion took it from her and turned to scramble up the steep side of the shore. Alaira felt her feet sinking in the bog, and for a moment she thought she was caught. Deep, wet reeds tangled around her boots. "Gwydion!" she screamed.

"Keep moving!"

"I can't . . . I . . ." But she found that the moment she

did move, her feet came out of the mat with a sucking noise.
She leaped for the bank. Gwydion's arms grabbed her from
above and pulled her up just as the lake monster lunged
downward with a bubbling shriek and the deer's body vanished into its gaping mouth.

Alaira turned and stared panting as the sluglike creature
sank back into the dark water of the Small Sea. Its tiny eyes
set in nests of deep wrinkles looked up at them briefly, then
vanished beneath the broken ice crust. A hump showed as it
swam out to the deeper waters, and it was gone.

The little demon she had rescued seemed to have recovered
from its shock. It bowed very low to them both and spoke in
a strange, gravelly voice. "Thank you, lord and lady. I must
leave here quickly, before those that caught me find me
again. I have nothing for the lady but my thanks, but for the
wizard I have this: that which you have lost was stolen.
Abarath has it, in the Otherworld." It turned and ran with a
speed surprising for its size and form into the forest.

"What does it mean?" Alaira said weakly, feeling her
knees about to give way. Her ears still rang with the awful
rending sound the beast had made when it fell upon the deer.
She saw spots in front of her eyes, like the pale, diseased-
looking spots on the beast's glossy hide.

Gwydion repeated the odd phrase in wonder. "Abarath has
it, in the Otherworld. . . . My Power, Alaira, it meant my
Power. And if I know where it is I can surely get it back."
He took her arm. "Come! We have to tell Chela. Hurry!"

"Dear Goddess, it's cold," Pima said cheerfully. "Oh,
sorry, Priestess."

Briana chuckled. "That's all right. It is cold, but it feels
good." They had decided to bathe the infants in the shallow,
fast-moving stream that morning. The sun hovered over the
coastline to the east, promising a warm day for winter. There
were only a few slim bands of clouds over the ocean. Erlin
and Yalna had gone to meet a few of the S'tari priestesses at
the high meadows. The women had brought food and new
robes for the four adults and two infants. They did not know
why they had been told by their mistress to care for those in
the valley, but they did not argue. Briana had wanted to see

them, just to speak to someone new, but she did not think it wise they know about Cian if Va'shindi herself had not seen fit to tell them.

She held her son naked in her arms, against her robe, which she had belted up over her knees. The yellow-haired infant was unusually placid this morning. He did not flail or kick or shoot out sparks of Power to test the shields Briana had constructed for him out of his own energies. He lay comfortably against her breast, looking up at her with wide cat's eyes.

Pima waded into the stream at the wide place they had chosen. Her daughter Taryn wiggled in her grasp. The baby's black curls had already grown so that they trailed down between Pima's fingers where she supported the baby's head. Both children were a little more than two months old, and though Cian had been premature they were of a size.

Briana sloshed over to join Pima, feeling the water cold against her bare legs and the mud and rocks beneath her feet. Cian stirred a little, and his unsteady head shifted until he was looking down at the water just below him. He seemed to regard it with somber curiosity. Briana sighed. She still wondered if it would be right to leave him with Pima and Erlin. He had the vague memories of an ancient spirit and the unfocused Power of an adept. She wondered what his first words would be when he spoke. She wished she would be there to hear them.

She had quickly come to love her baby, though he fed at Pima's breast. She had never before been so tempted to leave the Order and the Goddess's service, not even by her deep love for Kyellan. It was an achingly sweet prospect. Slow and quiet days, under the changing skies of the valley's mild seasons, merely living and watching the growth of her extraordinary wizard child.

Voicing her thoughts, Pima said softly, "I wish you could stay here always."

Briana smiled. "Part of me will." She began to splash stream water on Cian's smooth baby skin. "The rest of me has to be First Priestess. Want it or not, I can't escape it."

Cian laughed. It was an unmistakable sound, his toothless mouth split in a gay smile, his small slippery body squirming at the touch of the cold water and Briana's hands. He laughed. Briana stared at him. "Is he supposed to do that yet?"

Pima held Taryn half in the water. The little girl seemed to like it. Pima picked her up again and held her to her shoulder, warming her. "I don't know. Taryn hasn't laughed yet. But I think Cian will always be an older brother to her, though they're the same age. They're both beautiful babies." She cupped a handful of water and poured it over Cian's round stomach. He seemed to laugh again. "He likes the water. Try holding him down in it."

Briana bent down, carefully supporting the baby's head. At the touch of the chill stream, Cian cooed in pleasure. Briana lowered him into it in a seated position, his head out of the water. He kicked his legs and made rowing motions with his tiny arms. "He's trying to swim." Briana giggled at the serious face her baby made, as if he was trying to master a new skill, or a new element.

"What's that?" Pima said a moment later, squinting toward the bay down the length of the stream. "Briana, look. It isn't the tide, is it?"

A rippling band of waves flowed in over the bay, between the tall rocks, with only still water before it and behind it. Briana felt a prickling of fear, and the stream suddenly seemed very cold as she saw the ripple reach the stream's mouth and begin to travel up against the flow of the clear water. It was unnatural. She could feel it approaching her bare legs, her hands that held Cian's small delighted form beneath the surface of the stream. "Get out of the water," she said to Pima. "Get out!" The younger woman hurried toward the bank.

Briana shifted her weight to pick Cian up and carry him as swiftly as she could away from there, and the baby suddenly arched his back like a flopping fish and squirmed out of her hands to wiggle underwater with the current toward the oncoming wave. Pima cried out, and splashed back into the stream. Briana lunged for Cian and landed on her hands and knees in the water, bruising her flesh on rough stones. The stream washed over her face. She saw her baby moving toward the seeking ripples. Cian did not move his arms or legs in any paddling strokes, but jackknifed his entire body at the hips and straightened it again, bobbing through the water with his wobbly head supported by the buoyancy.

Briana stumbled to her feet and waded at a run after the baby. The golden head surfaced for a moment, just before it went down in a flurry of the unnatural countercurrent. A fierce, bright light glowed from the stream at that point for a moment, and then as Briana plunged her hands down into the ripples and touched the slippery form of her baby the light faded and the current went back to its normal course. Briana gripped Cian and lifted him out of the water in a panic. The slit-pupilled eyes blinked sleepily at her, and the round baby face smiled innocently.

"Is he all right?" Pima reached her, holding Taryn firmly at her shoulder. "He must have swallowed a lot of water. You'll have to hold him upside down and shake him. . . ."

Briana shook her head. "He's fine. Not even a scrape or a bruise. Look." Cian waved his tiny fists and curled his toes in a good imitation of a healthy and happy baby. Briana pulled him close to her chest and waded out of the stream, shivering with more than cold. What had that thing been? What had it wanted? It had not tried to hurt Cian, unless he was hurt in a way she could not see.

She sat down cross-legged in the grass on the riverbank and tried to calm her mind. Cian lay in the fold of her skirt, looking up at her. Briana laid her hands on his stomach and forehead and concentrated on the shields she had constructed for him. She visualized them as a soft, resilient wall, like tightly woven tapestry, that would give a little with Cian's bursts of Power but would not let anything out or in. The picture formed before her closed eyes, and she saw where the tapestry was frayed around a hole as if it had been burned. The hole was very small, perfectly circular, bending the fibers of her mental weaving inward. Whatever had been in the stream had pierced through to see Cian for what he was, with all his Power.

Briana forced back her alarm. With a short, silent invocation to the Mother Goddess, for whom Cian was named, she took up the threads in her mind and wove them again with strands of Cian's wizard Power. The infant mind was tired and confused, and did not fight her with its restlessness as it had done before. Soon the shields were in place again, whole and unbroken. Briana sighed and opened her eyes. It would not help much, with the damage already done. The veil of secrecy was broken. Someone knew of the existence of the newborn Shape-Changer.

Chapter Thirteen ━━━━━━━━━

IT took Gwydion and Alaira more than an hour to find their runaway horses, and by the time they rode up the hill path to the Masters' Tower it was midday. The wizard children had been released from their lessons, and the younger boys ran about in the small yard, scooping up balls of dirty snow and throwing it at one another. The students of the College were as ragged as they had been when the four from Cavernon had arrived, though they were better fed. In a normal year, the Masters would have sent a party to Atolan before winter set in to buy cloth and other supplies for them all. This year no one had dared to go. Alaira felt cheered by the thought. Maybe she could convince the Shape-Changer to send her on such a mission. Since she was not a wizard, the Atolani would not suspect her of coming from Akesh. She could go and return with the supplies, and then in the spring when the ships began their southward runs she could offer to go again. That time she would not return.

If she reached Cavernon City again, Alaira had almost decided to go to Briana. According to Gwydion, the priestess had brought Kyellan back to himself the first time he had changed. She might be able to do it again.

"The Master was looking for you," one of the eight-year-olds called out as Alaira dismounted. He ran across the yard to take her horse. She smiled at him, and the boy almost glowed at the notice. She and Chela were the only women in the place, and the only ones most of the boys had ever seen besides the old nurses that had once been kept for the infants that were brought here. The nurses were gone, whether killed or escaped no one seemed to know. It did not matter. No one had brought any wizard babies to the College since the beginning of the Kharad, nor were they likely to.

"I thought he was busy with some new magical exercise," Gwydion said as they left the horses to be cared for by the eager boys and opened the door of the tower. "Chela said he was expending Power at an incredible rate, and she thought he might even have gone briefly out of his body."

Alaira brushed the mud and leaves from her cloak in the entryway. The round hall looked better with its new, simply-made furniture, but there were still no ornaments on the walls or floor. If Alaira had been raised in a noble family, she would have been taught to make bright rugs and tapestries and embroidered cushions. She and Chela both would have welcomed such work to ease their boredom. But Chela was a Garithian peasant, and Alaira was a child of the streets, and neither had ever had a chance for training in the arts of the nobility.

The Shape-Changer wobbled down the spiral staircase, one hand clutching the carven railing, the other holding up a small lamp to light his path. He looked drunk, but Alaira knew by now it was only the backlash to whatever new spell he had discovered. "I found him," the tall, lean wizard muttered in Kyellan's voice. "Alaira!" He saw her and spoke more clearly. "I did it! I knew I could if anyone could, and I did."

"Good for you," she said, amused. He did look proud of himself. And he was harmless in this state. She did not fear to pass him on the stairs. She and Gwydion started up toward the room where Chela was resting.

"Aren't you going to ask me who I found?" the Shape-Changer said, looking at her bleary-eyed. He looked more drained than she had ever seen him before.

"Who?" Gwydion said impatiently, urging Alaira on up the stairs.

"My son, my heir," the wizard said. "I thought I'd sensed his presence briefly just after my battle with the priestesses, but I thought he couldn't have been born yet. But he was. I found him in a stream.''

''Briana's child?'' Gwydion said with sudden concern. ''What interest do you have in him?''

The Shape-Changer glared at him. ''Don't be foolish. He's my heir, another incarnation of my spirit.'' Then he smiled. ''While I was traveling I left orders with the Barena wizards to retrieve him for me.''

''Do you mean steal him?'' Alaira said.

''If they have to.'' The Shape-Changer shrugged. ''Probably the priestess gave him to some poor couple, who will be glad to give him up for a good price. Unless they really want to raise a wizard child.'' He shook his head slowly, as if trying to clear it. ''No, he'll be much safer with me. I can protect him, and teach him all the things I'm learning so late. Have I told you I've figured out how to alter my form, just as all my ancestors could? I can look as human as any man now if I want. If I hear from Barena that they have my son, I can change myself into some human shape and go there to claim him. With no danger, no suspicion at all.''

''I don't like it,'' Gwydion said. ''It's Briana's child you're talking about.''

''She should be glad to know he'll be trained to use his Power. Besides, the child is far more mine than hers.'' He looked at Alaira again with a cunning expression on his half-drunken face. ''Did you hear what I said, pretty one? I can look human now. I can look like the handsomest man you can imagine. Would you like me better that way? You don't seem to like my wizard form. Would some other please you?''

Alaira shuddered. ''Nothing you do would please me,'' she said softly. ''Unless you were Kyellan again.'' She followed Gwydion up toward the third floor landing.

The Shape-Changer's golden eyes squinted up at her. ''Kyellan again? That could be arranged. His form, with my mind inside. It would require only the slightest modifications. Skin tone and hair color, eyes. It would be easy.''

Alaira closed her eyes against the rising pain of her un-healed grief, and did not answer him.

*   *   *

Chela woke slowly at the insistent touch of Gwydion's hand on her shoulder. She felt his excitement pierce through the clouds of her weariness and the backlash of last night's spells. He had no Power to speak to her mind, but she was still sensitive to him. They had often been linked when they both had Power, and a vestige of the link remained.

"What is it?" she murmured, opening her eyes at last. Shadows flickered across her bedclothes from the smoky oil lamps that rested in wall niches. It seemed to be late in the morning, though the luxurious, fur-carpeted room was dark as usual. It had no windows. Her body ached with a fierce and familiar pain, and her eyes were dry and sore from the tears she had shed again after failing to reignite Gwydion's Power.

"How do you feel?" His golden eyes were warm with concern.

She tried to smile through her sadness. "Tired," she admitted. Beyond Gwydion, Alaira sat in an overstuffed chair near the door, looking weary and half-frightened as she had ever since they had arrived at Akesh. "Here, help me sit up. Names of Power, I'm hungry."

"There's porridge from breakfast," Gwydion said, lifting a bowl from the nightstand. "I'll bring you more if you need it. You have to get your strength back, Chela. Something exciting has happened."

"We rescued a demon from the lake monster," Alaira said from her chair. "It told Gwydion where his Power could be found."

Gwydion smiled and handed her a spoon. "It told me my Power had been stolen. That Abarath had it in the Otherworld. That was the demon that attacked us in the desert, on our way to Khymer. The one that killed Melana."

"I remember," Chela said quietly. She took a bite of the cold, lumpy porridge. It slid down her throat in a congealed mass, but her empty stomach welcomed it. She had to replenish what the spell had drained from her, so she ate methodically. "You had just sent your Power over the miles between us and the wizards' captives to strengthen their shields. Then when you came back, you were so drained you couldn't fight the thing. It killed that poor girl we rescued from Hirwen, and then it got a grip on me, and I destroyed it." She could still

feel the rending pain of the claws that had torn her back.
Gwydion's hands had been burned in his efforts to heal her.
He had saved her life, to lose his own Power.

Gwydion shook his head. "You didn't destroy it. You
disincorporated it, sent it back to the Otherworld. I still don't
know where you found the spell to do it. I never taught it to
you." He sighed. "But the demon was being controlled by
Onedon, who we thought was our friend Firelh. Somehow
between the two of them they stole my Power, and Abarath
took it with him back to the Otherworld. That's where we
have to go to get it back."

"Gwydion, how can that be?" she asked incredulously.
"The Otherworld? Is Power something that can be stolen,
like a purse?"

"If anyone could have done it, Onedon could. He had all
the strength of a Shape-Changer, and all the training of a
Master of the College. He could command a major demon as
easily as you might quiet a horse. I think the demon was
telling the truth." He looked at her eagerly. "At least we can
try it."

She could not share his confidence. "I don't have the
strength to call this demon that stole your Power. That means
we have to go into the Otherworld after it. I don't even know
if that is possible. And even if we can, what do we do there?
Ask Abarath politely to give it back?" The demon that had
attacked them in the desert had been a terrifying creature,
huge and dark with great wings, sharklike teeth, and poisoned
claws. It was nothing like the minor demons the Shape-
Changer commanded in the forests of Akesh. It had once
been worshipped as a god in a temple outside Dallynd.

"We have to try," Gwydion said.

She could not argue with him. He wanted his Power back,
and she wanted it as much as he, though for different reasons.
He had been almost impossible to live with since he had lost
it. And it was getting worse. She loved him, and even so
sometimes he made her furious. "All right." Chela felt exhausted at the thought of the Power it would take to make the
attempt. "We'll try it."

She had studied the books of lore as thoroughly as the

Shape-Changer had, searching for ways to waken the Power
she had thought slept deep within Gwydion. She knew a lot
more about ritual and the structures of magic than she had
two months before. She would have to search her memory of
the books she had read. To find a way to go into the Otherworld. Chela wished for a moment that she had never heard
of magic or wizards.

Alaira had gone to the Masters' library on the fourth floor
of the tower to retrieve the book Chela wanted. She had been
afraid the Shape-Changer would see her and ask why she
needed a book of lore; she had been afraid the old men who
studied there would refuse her permission to take the book at
all. They had only smiled at her and gone back to their
reading of the spidery texts that were crammed around the
circular room in racks of scrolls and mounds of books.

The book Chela had wanted was a small one, bound in a
flaking skin of scaly leather with a broken hasp. There were
many more beautiful books of lore, with smooth-grained
bindings inset with jewels or thickly brocaded. Those were
the ones the old men read in their search for wisdom. Now
the small book lay open to a stained brown leaf closely
scrawled with handwriting. Alaira had never learned to read.
Chela had told her the book was a collection of wizards'
legends, and that in wizards' legends as in all tales there was
likely to be some truth.

The story she told was of a wizard named Rashan and a
powerful demon called Draoth. In the tale their roles were
interchanged. Rashan was caught by the demon and called
into the Otherworld, where he was to perform some difficult
task before returning. What the task was, the tale did not say,
and there was no indication that Rashan had ever returned to
the body he had left like an empty sack on his bed at the
College. The lack of an ending to the tale made Chela believe
it related a true incident. Whether Rashan had been summoned by a demon or not, he had gone to the Otherworld.

Chela and Gwydion meant to follow him. Alaira curled up
tighter in her chair, frightened for them and for herself. They
were doing something that as far as they knew had only been
done once before, and with the likelihood that they could

never come back. Alaira was supposed to guard their vacated bodies, and if necessary to distract the Shape-Changer to keep him from finding out what they were doing. Chela had made her promise that if they did not return within a day and a night, she was to burn their bodies to keep any other free spirits from possessing them. The prospect was terrifying. Alaira wished again that she had never followed Kyellan from the city where she belonged. Hunger and pain had been old companions there, but she did not remember knowing such constant fear.

"We're ready," Chela said. She still wore her nightgown. Her thick red hair was unbound, and fell over her shoulders, making her adolescent prettiness into true beauty. "I'm going to use my Power to detach Gwydion's soul from his body. I'll be doing the same thing for myself, but since I have Power and I'm operating the spell, my body will probably keep breathing. Gwydion's may seem to be dead. I'm not sure. If his heart stops, try not to worry. He can start it again when he returns with his Power."

"What if he can't?" Alaira demanded. "Is this worth dying for?"

"I have to chance it, Alaira," Gwydion said. He had taken off his boots and belt and leggings, and wore only a tunic that hung to his knees. He and Chela had placed a ring of candles along the edges of their bed, and now they lay down together within the ring, clasping hands. The candle flames sent jittery shadows across them. The room seemed to grow colder. Alaira pulled her damp cloak around her and watched silently. Chela kissed Gwydion once on the lips, and they began.

Gwydion spoke the words, since Chela was not yet sure of her pronunciation of the wizards' language. They had constructed a spell from the fragments of the legend of Rashan, binding it with safeguards and shields to prevent the demons whose realm they would enter from taking control of their wandering spirits. Alaira understood none of it, but even her trace of sensitivity was enough to feel the rising Power in the room. It was Chela's Power, tinged with green, smelling of summer earth and sweet meadow grass.

The candles around the bed swayed and their flames grew higher, joining with each other until they formed a thin, unbroken ring of fire. It was orange and red and yellow, fire-colored, except here and there where green sparks flickered like the sparks of an oil-treated pinecone tossed into a hearth fire. For the first part of their spell, Chela and Gwydion would make themselves a door into the Otherworld. They had taken elements from the simplest forms of demon-summoning spells, in which the demon called was not powerful enough to break through the world barriers without a portal.

Alaira watched miserably as the ring of flame rose up from the waxy stubs of the candles, hovering and rising in jerks until it wavered just above the handfast couple on the bed. Darkness grew inside the ring, a smoky, cloudy darkness, and Alaira smelled a strange odor that seemed the opposite of the clean earth-scents of Chela's magic. Soon the space within the flame-ring was completely dark, as if a hole in the room looked out onto a starless night sky. Alaira's eyes burned, and she looked down.

Chela's body convulsed, and the girl cried out softly, wordlessly. Gwydion stiffened and choked and opened his eyes wide, and moved as if to pull away from Chela, but their hands did not unclasp. Then his body went limp with a long exhaling sigh, and Alaira knew without need of proof that he had no pulse or breath anymore. Chela arched backward and her mouth opened, and two transparent strands of green-webbed fog rose from her throat.

For a moment the foggy tendrils hovered unmoving above the two motionless forms. Then they drifted upward toward the blackness within the flames, the disc-shaped hole in the fabric of the world. Silver threads stretched between them and their vacated bodies. Chela had told Alaira these silver lines were the only things that connected the wandering souls to their bodies when they went traveling. So Alaira was horrified to see the amorphous soul-fogs fly up through the ring of flame as if sucked into a whirlpool, while the thin silver threads snapped and drifted down to rest coiled and lifeless on the bedclothes between Chela's and Gwydion's faces.

Alaira leaped forward from her chair, dropping her sodden cloak to the floor. She ducked under the foul-smelling door and reached over the unlit ring of candles to touch the shoulders of each of her friends. There was no movement, no breath in either of them. As she stood there, the severed threads that had bound their souls to their bodies faded and vanished. Above her, the Otherworld door quivered and began to shrink, closing in on itself. The flames went out as they met in the center of the air above the bed, and the clouds of darkness dispersed like wind-scattered fog. They were gone. How could they possibly get back? Alaira was too horrified even to weep. They were gone. This must have been what had happened to Rashan in the legend. They were gone, and now what was she going to do?

The sky was black, and shredded as if by a raking of giant claws to show a flickering of blood-color and fire-color through the rents. The ground was porous, or was it his body that was insubstantial enough to drift downward through the moss? Gwydion thought he had been caught in a timeless moment on the shore of the Small Sea, trapped in the reeds awaiting the unhurried arrival of the monster. But Chela was with him, not Alaira; she clasped him tightly with strangely shaped arms and twisted herself around him like thin rope etched with green. Gwydion saw the curious form of a very small demon gliding across the shredded sky, its wingtips fluttering only a little to propel it through the thick air. If he had come here bodily, he thought, he would not have been able to breathe. He remembered what they had attempted.

"We made it," he whispered to Chela. Or did he only think it? He seemed to hear the words, just as he seemed to smell her warm, woman's scent against the heavy odor of the Otherworld.

"You're all right?" The sound, or the feel, of her voice was relieved. "You were so disoriented I was afraid I'd lose you to a passing gust of color."

Bands of separate hues blew themselves through the unfocused landscape, shifting directions on a whim and twisting another way. Gwydion saw blues and purples and yellows, traveling with their own kind, like ribbons torn from a festive cloak. "No greens," he said. "Except for you."

"It's a big place. There might be some. Do you see the way they pick up the smaller demons and absorb them? I haven't decided if they're predators or a mode of transportation, but I haven't seen a demon coming out of one." Her amorphous form shivered a little. "We'd better learn the ways of the place. We may be here a long time. Our soul-lines were severed in the flight through the door."

Gwydion looked down at his shape, no more than a mass of grey fog. There were a few sparks of yellow light, bits of his wizard Power that had clung when the Power had been ripped from him. The silver thread that was supposed to stretch any distance to keep him connected to his body flapped like a short tail at one corner. "There has to be a way back," he said.

"The door has vanished," Chela said, seeming determined to depress him.

"We'll find my Power before we give up," he said. "The way things seem to be here, it ought to be yellow. And I'm sure I'll recognize the demon that took it when I see it."

Chela shivered again. "So will I. I hope it isn't as belliger-ent in its home world as it was in ours. Do you have any idea where to begin?"

"We have to look for something that's as out of place here as we are. Keep all your senses open. This direction seems as good as any." Entwined like climbing vines, they drifted over the deep, unsteady ground of the Otherworld and began their search.

Alaira sat unmoving in her chair, staring at the bed, for a long time before she began to hear the persistent knocking on the door. She jumped up fearfully. "Who—who is it?" Her voice was high-pitched from tension.

"Is that Alaira?" The Shape-Changer's voice was sur-prised. "I'm looking for Gwydion and Chela. Are they in there?"

She looked at the unbreathing bodies clasped on the bed. They were so helpless, so vulnerable. She could not risk the Shape-Changer seeing them. He might take a chance to rid himself of a few potential enemies. Alaira stepped to the door and took a deep breath. "What do you need them for?" she said with a shy smile, opening the door only wide enough to slip through and closing it behind her.

The tall wizard looked at her in astonishment. Alaira met his alien eyes with what she hoped was a rueful and innocent gaze. He could be no worse than any of the clients she had served in her lean months in Rahan.

"I've been thinking," she whispered, reaching up to stroke his shoulders. His body felt like Kyellan's. The hard shoulder muscles were shaped the same way. She remembered what he had said earlier on the stairs. "And I think I've been silly to refuse you all this time. I was angry about Kyellan, but I can see now that nothing will go back to the way it was." She had to give Chela and Gwydion the chance to succeed, if that was possible. She had to give them time.

"Alaira . . ." He was pleased but confused. "I thought you hated me."

"No," she said. "It's only that wizards frighten me. I know it's foolish, but after what happened in Cavernon, and the time I was a prisoner . . ." She lowered her eyes as if embarrassed, hoping fervently that he would not try to read her mind.

"So it isn't really me," he said eagerly. "It's that I'm a wizard. The way I look."

"And then what you said today, that you've learned how to change your looks, look human . . . that made me realize . . ." She ran out of ideas and resorted to her old tricks, the phrases she had used to make her clients feel good. "I've been so lonely, and . . . and scared, and I need someone to take care of me, even if it's just for a little while."

"Oh, Alaira." There was real tenderness in his voice, and in the way he put his arm around her shoulders to lead her toward his room. She almost felt guilty for her deception. He opened his door, and they were in another Master's chamber, almost identical to the one where she had left Chela and Gwydion. "I told you before, I think you're beautiful," he said. "If you can stand to be with me . . ."

"I wouldn't be here if I didn't want to be," she whispered.

He looked at her thoughtfully, his golden brows drawing together. "If you want to imagine that things are back the way they were, I could be Kyellan for you. The look, the words, the way he touched you . . . everything. Just tell me what to do.''

It would be like making love to a ghost, she thought in a sudden panic. But if she could pretend, as he had said, if she could imagine that Kyellan had come back to her, perhaps that would make the afternoon bearable. She nodded slowly. ''I'd like that.''

He turned his back with uncharacteristic modesty and began to change his shape.

Time flowed without meaning in the Otherworld. Gwydion did not know how long they had drifted, first alone, then changing direction to follow a band of slow-moving demons who seemed to be headed toward a distant grouping of spires that suggested a city. The demons noticed them, and avoided them, probably suspecting they were a variant of the colored streamers that hunted along the spongy plain. Gwydion and Chela were careful not to speak or betray their intelligence. They could understand the demons' talk, and had learned that the color-bands were mindless, and dangerous indeed. They swept up the inexperienced and unlucky, and those demons simply vanished.

The creatures in the traveling group were as varied in form and size as the forest demons the Shape-Changer had captured, and they all seemed about the same level of potency. There were no major demons among them, and none of the small stubborn bits of gellike stuff that were used as bottled healing or poisoning agents in the world of the Kingdoms. The demons moved along purposefully, but at the pace of the slowest crawling members of the group.

As the journey continued, Gwydion began to hear some argument among the demons about their reason for going to the city. He got the impression that the structures far ahead were not houses or the guard-towers of a fortress, but some sort of government buildings where the demons sometimes gathered to hear their leaders, and counsel them on important decisions. This time they were to discuss the uses of a strange new weapon against the color predators, a force that could damage them and drive them away; apparently no one had yet learned how to operate it effectively. It was unpredictable, and some in the party argued that it was useless.

He and Chela could not talk, and so all Gwydion could do was drift along and listen and speculate on the nature of the world in which they might be trapped for a long time. He had always been taught that demons were creatures of Power, innately strong with magical force that could be wielded by any who could command them. This did not seem quite right. Chela had Power, which he knew from experience manifested itself in the form of green flame. On this world, she glowed with a fierce green fire. He had once had Power, and he was sure the yellow sparks inside him were what remained. The demons did not glow at all, and he had not seen one of them use Power for a spell or a sending. Their grotesque and varied bodies were as dull as human forms on the earth. They flew, and some crawled through the porous earth, but these talents seemed characteristic of their world.

Yet he had seen demons blazing with fire in battles during the war, and he knew from his wizard training that demons were powerful forces, dangerous to call upon. They did not seem particularly strong or fearsome in their own world. Gwydion wondered why.

"Abarath brought it back," one of the demons grumbled, and the wizard's hearing sharpened. "Let him risk wielding it."

"He wrestled it to the top of the beacon where it could do some good," said another, in apparent defense of Abarath's courage.

"I don't like it." One of the demons Gwydion recognized as a stronger power than most of the others spoke. His voice echoed itself, as if a high and a low voice were speaking just out of unison. It was an uncanny sound. "Abarath was under the call to the Lower World when he did it. He brought it here because a master told him to. Not because it could help us. Because one master wanted to hurt another. I tell you, it has nothing to do with us. It doesn't belong here. We should have nothing to do with it."

Voices clamored in agreement and dissent, and the argument began again, but Gwydion scarcely listened. He drifted along full of wonder and fear. His Power. It had to be his

Power they were talking about, this alien thing Abarath had brought back with him at a wizard's command. A weapon they could use against the color predators. Names of Power! he thought, if they valued it so, how would he ever get it back?

Chapter Fourteen ————————

IT had not been unpleasant, Alaira thought as she lay on the rumpled bed. The Shape-Changer, still in Kyellan's form, stretched lazily by the fire. It was like living in a memory. Her body had responded easily, as long as she imagined herself with Kyellan. The Shape-Changer had been very gentle. At times, his effort at holding himself back had been the spur to jolt her out of her mood. Kyellan had been a lover who was not afraid of roughness. Sometimes their nights had been more like wrestling matches. Alaira felt tears pooling behind her eyes. She blinked them back firmly and smiled at the black-haired man who sat back down on the bed beside her.

He had done his transformation brilliantly. Everything from the slight arch of the eyebrows to the little squinted wrinkles at the corners of the dark brown eyes. The hair had an uneven wave that would broaden into curls if it was allowed to grow longer. Kyellan's face smiled at her scrutiny.

"How do you feel?" he said in the familiar hint of a Rahan accent. He brought up a hand to cup her chin gently, and his finger traced the line of her scar with a feather touch.

"Good," she said quietly.

"I want you to feel cherished," he said, kissing her lightly on the lips. "Needed." Another kiss. "Loved. You're so beautiful, Alaira. Your face is like the work of a brilliant sculptor, a masterwork, except that his chisel slipped a little while he was smoothing your cheek.''

She had to giggle at that. It was so unlike anything Kyellan had ever said to her. And the Shape-Changer was so serious, so intent on her features. After a moment she realized he had said that he loved her. Kyellan had never said that either. She would have given anything to hear it from his lips. This was probably as close as she would ever come to that old dream. She reached up and returned the Shape-Changer's kiss.

A frantic knock sounded on the door. Alaira stiffened, and the face that was so like Kyellan's looked annoyed. ''What is it?'' he called.

''Master!'' Morfan's voice was frightened. ''I'm sorry to disturb you, but I had thought to look in on the Lady Chela to see if she was awake and might want to break her fast, and . . . well, you had better come see for yourself. Some spell gone awry, I shouldn't wonder.''

''Some spell . . .'' Kyellan's voice repeated, and the Shape-Changer drew away from Alaira in sudden fury. ''And you were to keep me occupied and unaware.'' His voice was flat and bitter. He stood up and pulled on a dayrobe that glinted with silver-threaded embroidery around the hem and neck-band. Alaira thought of the falling silver threads of Chela and Gwydion's soul-lines, and she felt sick. ''Put something on,'' snapped the Shape-Changer. ''You're coming with me.''

She hurried to obey, shrugging into the tunic she had worn hunting. It fell halfway down her thighs without its belt, and the Shape-Changer did not give her time to dress further. He grabbed her hand in a cruel grip and pulled her to the door and out into the hall. The bearded old wizard who waited there blinked in surprise at his lord's new features, but he had Power enough to recognize the Shape-Changer.

''This way, Master,'' he said nervously, hurrying the few paces to Gwydion's door.

''I know the way,'' Kyellan's voice growled. ''Go back downstairs, Morfan, and don't come up again until I call you. Tell no one what you saw here. Understand?''

The old wizard nodded once and turned to descend the stairs. The Shape-Changer opened the door and thrust Alaira inside before him. She staggered free of his grip. He slammed the door behind them and stared. The tableau was unchanged. Gwydion and Chela lay with their hands clasped, red hair and golden spread out on the pillows, not moving, not breathing, their hearts still. Dead, Alaira thought, trying to hold back nausea. Dead, and all the magic in the world would not change that.

Kyellan's shape brushed the candles off one side of the bed and bent over the motionless pair to pass a hand between their slack faces. "What did they do? No secrets now, Alaira. Tell me."

She sank down into the chair where she had watched them perform their spell, and hugged herself against tears. "They . . . they made a door and went through it, and their soul-lines snapped when the door closed, and they can't get back."

"A door?" He looked at her as if he did not see her. "Leading where?"

"Into the Otherworld."

"And what did they hope to gain?"

"Gwydion's Power. They think a demon stole it and hid it in the Otherworld," she said dully.

His borrowed face was a tight mask of anger. "And they left you here to guard their bodies. Don't try to deceive me, Alaira. You know they can come back. That's why they involved you in this. You were to bring them back when they called for you."

She shook her head, confused. "What do you mean? I don't know any way to bring them back. I don't have any Power."

He came over to where she sat and put a hand on her forehead. Alaira cried out at the fierceness of the mental probe that rushed through her mind, leaving her more violated than she had been after her rape by the wizards' soldiers. When he took his hand away she sobbed in anger and pain, dry heaving sobs that brought no comfort.

"They attempted it on the strength of a half-told legend?" he said incredulously. "Not knowing even the most basic techniques for such travel? Blind, foolish children . . . and they think they'll be strong enough to wrest Gwydion's Power from a major demon?" He shook his head. "If I thought they'd succeed, I'd leave them there. I'd be a fool to let them return with Gwydion's Power.''

"Do you mean . . . there is a way for them to return?'' Alaira said between sobs.

"I can call them back. But I'm not going to risk it unless I know they haven't recovered what they seek. That means I'll have to go in after them.'' He glared at her. "Stop that wailing. You're going to have to make yourself useful. I'm going after them. You'll call me back when you hear your name. A voice with Power can penetrate the barriers. You'll hear it clearly enough.''

"But . . . I don't have any Power,'' she whispered. "And how is it possible, with the soul-lines cut?''

"It's simple,'' he said impatiently. "Here in our world nothing can enter from the Otherworld unless it has been summoned. That applies to demons and the other creatures that live there. It is also the only way for visitors to get back. They must be summoned. When you hear me say your name, touch me like this.'' He demonstrated, pressing both of his palms flat against her temples. "Then call me. All you need is my name. Even if the soul-line is severed, the mind has sufficient memory of the body to get back on the strength of a name.''

"What about them?'' She looked past him at the two lifeless forms of her friends on the bed.

"If they don't have Gwydion's Power, there is no reason why they should not return. I'll call them back myself. Things will be as they were before,'' he said with a bitter twist of his mouth. "Now be silent and let me work.''

He did not construct an elaborate spell. He lay down on the fur-carpeted floor and closed his eyes, whispering a few growling words that sounded uncanny coming from Kyellan's lips. A door of blackness swirled into existence just above him. Alaira smelled the heavy odor of the Otherworld. Then the Shape-Changer's body convulsed, as Chela's had, and the fog-tendril of his soul rose from his mouth, glowing with yellow flame. There was a mass of dark grey without fire in the center, and two twisted silver threads extended to the limp body on the floor. One was thick and shining, the other much thinner and paler. Alaira realized suddenly that the narrow thread was Kyellan's. His soul was hidden within the Shape-Changer's. It was true, then, that he still lived, imprisoned in the wizard's mind.

The entwined souls were sucked through the black door, which vanished in wisps of smoke. The two soul-lines fell and dissolved. Alaira got up from her chair and knelt beside what seemed Kyellan's dead body. She took his hand and held it against her chest as she wept, rocking back and forth like an injured child alone in the silent tower room.

The demons' city seemed to have been constructed out of the porous, mossy peat of the Otherworld earth. The buildings were soft and spongy. Doors and windows had been formed by pulling away chunks of the strange material. Gwydion supposed sturdy floors and walls were unnecessary to a species that could fly.

He and Chela drifted through an odd-shaped gate into the city, behind the demons they had been following. All of a sudden, the demons burst into a frightened clamor of voices and shrieks. They had ignored the foggy greenish shapes that trailed after them over the plains, since they had not attacked. But now they were drifting under the shadows of the spongy buildings, joining the crowd that pressed inward toward the center of the city. The demons thought Gwydion and Chela were small pieces of one of the color predators. Apparently the streamers rarely appeared when the demons were gathered in such force.

Frozen, batlike faces clustered together at the windows of the towers, staring at the two human souls as they passed. Winged demons fluttered into the thick air at their approach. Toad-things like the one Alaira had rescued scurried from their path. A cacophony of screeches and roars washed ahead of them and around them like a tide. The noise was so great that Gwydion did not think anyone would hear him whisper.

"They said it was in something called the beacon. This weapon of theirs."

"You think it's your Power?" Chela murmured. "I suppose it's possible. I'd guess the beacon is the tallest tower, the one we could see the farthest across the plains. In the center, where they're all headed."

"They're so afraid of us we may be able to just go in and get it without any trouble," he said hopefully.

Small demons, like the ones Gwydion had summoned for practice as a young apprentice, darted in and out toward them, shearing off before they touched. Gwydion and Chela moved forward steadily. The spaces between the strange towers widened and became an open court, a central round theater with rows of seats, perches, and catwalks. A council chamber of sorts, Gwydion thought. It was filling rapidly with more varieties of demons than he had ever known existed.

A dark, armored figure rose before them, standing thrice the size of the demons in the crowd that eddied fearfully around Gwydion and Chela. It had vast, leathery wings and a long, spiked tail that it held up in one claw as if to keep it from getting muddy. Its grotesque arms were crossed, its monstrous head lowered and frowning. Deep magenta eyes peered at them, and it spoke, a thunderous rumbling sound like a small avalanche. "Don't be frightened." The words rang through the amphitheater. "The green is small, the yellow scarcely glows. Our new weapon will deal with these easily."

A thin, spidery creature dared to approach closer to the two human spirits. "Perhaps an immature form?" it suggested, reaching out a long finger as if to touch them.

Chela wrapped herself around Gwydion again and blazed up in green fire, fiercer than the hue of any of the color streamers they had seen. The spidery demon leaped back, its wavery forelimbs singed. Chela moved forward resolutely, taking Gwydion with her. They drifted out over the lower seats of the court as demons ducked and scampered away from them. Even the gigantic demon who had spoken drew back as they passed. It spoke again, a word Gwydion remembered. "Abarath!"

Scaly faces turned upward to look at the tall, slim spire of the central tower. Gwydion followed their gaze. The pinnacle of the spongy structure shone with golden light. It was fierce against the dull crimson and black of the sky behind it, a tracery of fire that moved and swayed as he watched. The minute traces of Power in him sparked in recognition, and a deep void that had once been his well of magical strength ached to be filled again. It was his stolen Power. It had to be.

A tall demon appeared in the upper door of the tower, its wings spread out from its massive torso like black sails, a creature of nightmare that had once been imprisoned in an urn in a ruined temple. The face of a shark, of a mindless predator, glared down into the court. Gwydion's resolve nearly failed, as he remembered the terrifying battle he had had with this thing in the desert near Khymer. The demons on the tiers of seats pressed back, leaving a large empty space around Gwydion and Chela.

Chela's fiery green substance disengaged itself from Gwydion, and she pulled back, leaving him floating alone, an insubstantial grey shape with flecks of yellow. He concentrated on projecting his voice so all could hear. "Abarath! You stole my Power from me in the desert. Now I demand its return."

Astonished that he spoke, the other demons turned back toward him to stare. Abarath took a rasping breath and said, "I was commanded to steal it." Its voice was not a single sound. Echoes bounced back from the thick atmosphere of a chorus of voices, all low and harsh, speaking at almost the same time. The effect was disturbing. "If you were to summon me to your world and command me to return it, perhaps I would be compelled to do so. That is the only way."

Gwydion knew he could never do that, even if it was possible to return to Akesh. Without his Power he would be a suicidal fool to call on the name of a creature like Abarath. "It does not belong here, any more than you belonged in the temple where you were trapped for long centuries. Release it to me, to return it to its rightful place."

The demon laughed, and the derisive sound was picked up by the smaller creatures that clustered in the amphitheater. "It is not a being. It has no independent thought. It has no preferences. It is a tool. A weapon. We will use it against the colors, and against anything else that threatens us."

"Use it against them!" voices cried from the crowd. "Use the weapon!"

"Gwydion. Chela." A quiet, calm voice spoke beside them, where no one stood. The Shape-Changer, Gwydion knew immediately, but where was he? "Come with me quickly. Before you find your deaths here. I can get you back to your bodies. Come!"

"How can there be a way back?" Chela hissed. "Without a soul-line to follow, and with the door vanished?"

Now Gwydion saw him, a fiercely glowing gold-laced shape drifting in an empty street on the other side of the amphitheater. "You will never find it on your own. Only I know the secret." His voice was still beside them. "Enough of this. *Alaira!*" His shout echoed across the tattered sky, as if he spoke a great word of Power. *"Bring me back now!"* More quietly, he said, "You two will follow at my call. You'll have no choice. It is the way of the Otherworld."

Alaira heard the Shape-Changer's words, distant but compelling. It seemed a long time since he had gone. She still sat on the floor of Gwydion and Chela's room, beside the inert form of the body that wore Kyellan's shape. She was too tired to weep any longer. She was tired, and frightened, and the lingering odor from the Otherworld portal that had vanished made her feel nauseated. Vaguely, she thought she should call the Shape-Changer back. He had trusted her to do it. He had shown her how.

She had not said she would. And if he came back, he might not call Gwydion or Chela back to follow him. Only if he thought he could bring them without Gwydion's Power. They might have found it, Alaira thought. What if she called him back, and then he burned Gwydion's and Chela's bodies so they could never return? Then Alaira would be alone at Akesh with him, and if he had said he loved her, it was only because he had not known how much she hated him.

She did not know what to do. So she sat wordlessly, rocking back and forth, ignoring the voice she had heard.

"Alaira!" the Shape-Changer cried when he did not vanish as he had expected. "Do not disobey me!"

"Use the weapon against them," the huge demon near them in the theater said. "Use it against them all."

"Shield yourselves!" the Shape-Changer said. "They may

not have much control, but that won't keep them from destroying us if they can.''

Chela reached out a green tendril to Gwydion, but he shrugged it away. "No," he said. "No shield for me." She moved forward to argue. "No!" he shouted furiously. "Protect yourself. Get away from here."

In a chorus of bass voices, the demon Abarath spoke from the tower. Gwydion recognized the words of a simple battle spell to catapult force like a stone toward an enemy. If the demons did not have the same sort of Power the wizards did, they seemed to have some magical skill.

Chela's fire burned with a more controlled green, as a glassy surface covered her foggy shape. She spoke from within her shield, her voice thin and frightened. "Gwydion, it's no use. We can't get it back. They'll use it against us. Maybe we should go back with the Shape-Changer. He says he knows a way back. I don't care if you don't have Power. I don't care!"

She thought he was seeking death. Perhaps he was, Gwydion thought grimly. But there was a chance. A bare chance for survival, because the Power the demons were attacking with was his. A part of him since his birth. If they simply threw it at him . . . not a shield, he thought. A sponge, like the spongy surface of this uncanny world. He drifted there, deliberately defenseless, as the yellow flames moved slowly from the pinnacle of the tower under Abarath's half-sung commands.

Then, as if the demon lost its grip on the slippery Power it was trying to control, the tower shot up into flame like a beacon indeed. Demons seated near its base screamed and tried to escape it, but flames licked out and charred them as they fled. Panicked, the smaller demons on Gwydion's side of the court flapped and tumbled over one another in their haste to escape. Chela fell back with them, and Gwydion saw the Shape-Changer move within his glassy yellow shield to stand beside her. They waited at the edge of the amphitheater.

The flames sank down to mass at the foot of the tower. Then they flung themselves across the rows of seats and perches toward Gwydion's foggy grey form. Abarath's clamorous voices resumed a pain-filled chant, and the figure of the scorched demon showed at a high window. The flames rolled directly at Gwydion, under more control now as the demon learned how to manage them. Gwydion could feel the heat approaching, and he smelled an acrid odor like that of a lightning strike. Fear gripped him, but he could not flee. The flames were upon him.

Instead of pain he felt a soft warmth suffusing him, spreading, filling all the empty places that the loss of his Power had left. The flames of yellow force attacked him as Abarath commanded, but instead of destruction they brought healing. Fire poured into Gwydion, all the flames compressing and pulling together until they twined in fierce golden light all around and through the amorphous form of his disembodied spirit. He was whole, a wizard again. The fire was his again to control, to use according to his trained will. The feeling was glorious.

The demons wailed their fear and defeat. The Shape-Changer spoke furiously. "You may have your Power, but you have no way of returning. Not without my help. I'll prevent it if I have to destroy your bodies to do it. *Alaira, bring me back!*"

It was the third time. Hours had passed since the last call had sounded from the Otherworld. Alaira had not obeyed it, and she would not obey this one either. She was determined of that. The distant sounds of the day's meals and lessons at Akesh penetrated vaguely into the quiet chamber where she waited; the afternoon had gone, and night was falling. If much more time went by, she feared the three silent bodies that lay in the room would begin to smell of death. The oil lamps were guttering.

She heard her name again. The voice was quavery and indistinct, but she recognized it as Gwydion's. He must have his Power. The Shape-Changer had said that voices with Power could project between the worlds. He had succeeded. Alaira stood up swiftly, and discovered her body was stiff and slow. She hoped the Shape-Changer had told her all she needed to know to summon them back. If she could, she would call Gwydion and Chela. Then together they could call the Shape-Changer back, though he would have left them in the Otherworld if he had returned first.

Alaira leaned over the bed and stretched her hands out to touch them to Gwydion's pale, cool forehead. How could she possibly do this? She was no magician. How could they come back to life now, after so much time had passed? She said Gwydion's name weakly. Her Rahan accent distorted the vowels a little. It probably would not work. Alaira closed her eyes and said his name again, with a heartfelt prayer to any god that might listen. "Gwydion." There could be no magic in the word. She kept her eyes closed and stood there whispering his name for what seemed a very long time, until her outstretched fingers began to feel a dim, spreading warmth.

Her eyes blinked open. She smelled a soft, green, summery scent, like the gardens of the Tiranon; a smell of life, not of decay. A gentle flush appeared in Gwydion's face, moving slowly, bringing color back where there had been none. Alaira stared down at him. If there had been a foggy soul that flew out of the air to reenter the body, she had not seen it. But she could not deny that it had happened. He was back. Alive.

"Oh, Goddess," she whispered as a tired smile split her dry lips. "Thank you." She walked to the other side of the bed and put her hands on Chela's brow to repeat what she had done.

The process of returning to life seemed achingly slow to Alaira, though it only took a quarter of an hour. At last the two young bodies breathed at a normal rate, and their eyes opened, brilliant gold and the blue of deep-dyed silk.

"We did it," Gwydion whispered hoarsely. His hand tightened on Chela's. Their eyes met, and they came together in a fierce, exultant embrace. Alaira turned away, feeling like an intruder.

Her eyes were arrested by the still form that lay on the fur rug at her feet. The Shape-Changer. He was still in the Otherworld. He would not be able to get back unless one of them called him. How long would it be before Kyellan's handsome body would be truly dead, stiff and rotting? Her throat closed up, and she clenched her fists at her sides, refusing to cry.

"Alaira," Chela said weakly. "We did it. We found Gwydion's Power, and he has it back."

"That's good," Alaira managed to say.

Chela swung her bare feet down off the bed and stopped at the sight of the figure on the floor. "Kyellan?" she said in disbelief.

"No. The Shape-Changer. He took that form to . . . impress me, before he went after you."

Gwydion climbed more slowly off the bed and knelt beside the body. "I suppose we should call him back."

"If you found your Power, he wasn't going to bring you back," Alaira said. "He would have left you there." She sat down cross-legged at the other side of Kyellan's pale form. He lay silent on the fur rug in the silken dressing gown. The silver threads of the embroidery reminded Alaira of the strange mingled soul-lines she had seen when the Shape-Changer left his body. Kyellan's soul had been there, trapped but still alive. The thought struck her. She sat unmoving for a moment, wondering if she dared. If it was even possible.

Chela sat back down on the edge of the bed very quickly. Her voice shook. "The backlash is coming sooner than I thought. Gods, I'm dizzy. But I still have some Power. . . . Alaira, what are you planning to do that frightens you so?" Her face was pale, beaded with sweat.

"I . . ." She took a deep breath to continue. "I'm going to try to bring Kyellan back into this body. I'm going to summon him, not the Shape-Changer."

Gwydion met her eyes across the prone figure. Alaira could feel the new strength in him, and the golden color of his gaze was fierce with his renewed Power. "It could work," he said. "Kyellan's soul is in the Otherworld with the Shape-Changer's. Try it, Alaira. With all your heart."

Faced with the test, she felt her own weakness more keenly. "You should do it, Gwydion."

He shook his head. "No. You're more closely tied to him than I could ever be. You're the one who can bring him back. Call him."

She placed her palms side by side on the chill forehead, pushing aside loose curls of black hair. "But . . . what if the

Shape-Changer is the one who comes? And he pretends to be Kyellan?''

"I'm a wizard again. I'll know who it is. Call him."

Alaira closed her eyes and thought of Kyellan. She had known him so long. She knew him better than anyone else could. Gwydion was right about that. She had been no more than five when she met him. He had been seven. A wild thing of the streets in ragged clothes, with tangled black hair. Alaira had been caught stealing a piece of fruit, and Kyellan had distracted the stall vendor long enough for her to get away. After that, they had discovered that survival in Rahan Quarter was easier for two children working together. Alaira remembered the night years later when they had first made love. She remembered when he left her to join the Royal Guard. Tears forced themselves from the corners of her tightly closed eyelids, and she whispered his name.

"*Kyellan*. Kyellan, come back. Come back to me."

Kyellan had been trying to fight his way free for two long, weary months. He had waged a futile battle inside the Shape-Changer's mental cage for the life he had once taken for granted. He had seen through the Shape-Changer's eyes, had felt sore muscles and the backlash of spells, had smelled and tasted and touched everything the Shape-Changer had, but it was all beyond his control. Whether he had been exhausted into passivity, or lost in blind fury, it made no difference to the wizard that had once been locked unsuspected inside him. Their positions were reversed. The Shape-Changer found this endlessly amusing.

But as their souls wavered insubstantial outside the demon city, where they had fled when Chela and Gwydion had vanished, Kyellan felt a trembling in the bonds that held him trapped. Sensing the disturbance, the Shape-Changer wrapped tighter around the thin, dull wisp of soul-stuff that was Kyellan. But Kyellan heard his name again, echoing through the black and crimson sky of the Otherworld. He was summoned. The call was insistent. He twisted furiously to answer it.

There was a tearing pain, and the Shape-Changer's shriek deafened him as he felt the cage burst apart and free him. He sensed a flash of helpless terror as the Shape-Changer realized he would remain caught in the Otherworld. Then he was sucked toward an invisible door, and tossed through it like a piece of weed flung onto a beach with the tide's power. He saw his lifeless body on the floor of the room as he plummeted down and passed through the cold flesh to inhabit it once again.

He felt the deep warmth of the rug beneath him, and his fingers curled very slowly into the pile. His body felt numb, but it was quickly warming, every limb tingling with returning circulation. There was a roaring in his ears, and he thought he still heard the Shape-Changer's screams echoing from the Otherworld. A tearing, painful breath inflated his collapsed lungs. He tried to open his eyes, but the lids seemed weighted.

"It worked," Gwydion's voice said incredulously. "Alaira, it worked."

Kyellan heard Alaira break into sobs, and felt the pressure as she fell across his chest and hugged him. The sound cut through the roaring in his confused mind. Great, deep, shaking sobs, a release of all the fear and grief and anger she had felt for so long. He knew how she had mourned him. He had seen it through the Shape-Changer's eyes. He could not move to put his arms around her and comfort her.

At last he was able to open his eyes. The room was dark. The lamps had gone out. There remained a lingering glow about the heavy beamed ceiling, a trace of the awesome Power that had been expended here today, but even that was fading. Gwydion knelt at one side of him, and Chela sat on the edge of the bed. Both looked exhausted, but their smiles were wide. Kyellan could feel Alaira's weight across his chest, and her tears warm and damp on his shoulder. Wonder flushed through him with returning sensations as he realized that he had returned to a body that looked like his own. It was his own, but healed of old scars and wounds. Even his damaged right arm was healed. He flexed the muscles of that arm slowly. It felt good. It felt strong.

"Welcome back," Gwydion said gruffly.

"Hush, Alaira," Kyellan whispered, struggling to sit up with an arm around her. "Don't cry. There's no reason to cry anymore."

"It really . . . is you," she said indistinctly. "I never thought I'd see you again. . . . Oh, gods, Ky, I missed you so much. . . ."

He held her tightly with both arms, feeling a continuing wonder that he could do so. She clung as if she never wanted to let go. He owed her his freedom from the Shape-Changer. Her loyalty, her love, had called him back. Briana was First Priestess by now, far out of his reach. Alaira was here with him. She had always loved him. Maybe now it was time to give her something in return.

Chapter Fifteen ───────────

W HEN he had fully regained control of his body, Kyellan
let Alaira and Gwydion help him to his feet. Chela reached a
hand toward him from the bed and said, "I missed you too.
I'd come give you a hug if I could get up. But the way the
ceiling is spinning around I don't think I'd better try."

"It's the backlash," Gwydion said, moving to the girl's
side. "You have to sleep. You made the door and took me
along with you to the Otherworld, and that required a huge
amount of Power. You may sleep for days. But you were
wonderful." He kissed her and helped her lie down on the
pillow beneath the canopy. Her eyelids fluttered, but she
embraced Kyellan fiercely when he leaned down over her.

"I want to know what it was like," she said. "To be
trapped inside your own head, and to see things through a
wizard's eyes."

"We'll talk about it when you wake up," Kyellan promised. Chela nodded vaguely, turned her head to one side, and
was immediately so deeply asleep that she did not move as
Gwydion pulled the covers up over her shoulders.

"Will she be all right?" Alaira asked quietly, standing
with an arm around Kyellan. "She won't be sick again, will
she?"

"This time it's only a backlash," Gwydion assured her.

A knock sounded on the heavy door. Kyellan looked at the young wizard, startled. "How are you going to explain me?"

Gwydion laughed and went to open the door, full of the confidence of his regained Power. "What is it, Orda?" he said lightly. A skinny, ragged apprentice of about thirteen stood there with a frightened look on his face.

The boy stared into the room, obviously aware that strong spells had been at work there. His golden eyes met Kyellan's, and he blinked, startled. "I . . . I was sent to find the Shape-Changer, sir. But that isn't him. Where is he?"

"Gone for the moment," Gwydion said. "He can't see anyone."

The boy hunched his head down between his shoulders like a scared rat. "That's what we told her, sir. That he couldn't talk to her, not today. And then she went away. Just vanished. Morfan said she wasn't really there at all, she was only a sending. But she seemed real."

"A sending?" Kyellan said sharply. "Who was she?"

"A priestess," said Orda. "She was wearing a black robe. She wouldn't give her name, but she wanted to see the Shape-Changer."

"Did you tell her he was here?" Kyellan asked, feeling a chill. It might have been Briana, he supposed, wanting to tell him about her ascension to First Priestess. Or another ghost bound to the earth by the wizards, seeking release. But that was unlikely. The priestesses of the Hidden Temple must have regained their strength for another attack. He would be easy prey this time. He had no wizard Power to summon in his defense.

"We said he was the Master of the College," the youth said proudly, "and that we'd tell him she was here. Was that right?"

"That was fine." Gwydion frowned. "Tell Morfan we'll be down to speak with him later. You may go."

There was no question who was Master of the College now, Kyellan thought. Orda left the room at Gwydion's command, and closed the door. The wizard turned back toward them. "You'll have to get out of here, Ky. As quickly as you can. She'll be back. And she'll bring her sisters, and the Power of the Goddess's Seat."

"If she doesn't find me here, she'll look elsewhere."

"But she won't be able to find you. You don't have any aura of Power to attract her. No," Gwydion said, "if you leave here you'll be safe. At least for a while. You could come back in a month or two, when the priestesses would have given up their search."

"We could go back home," Alaira said in a small voice at Kyellan's side.

"There will be no ships from Atolan," Kyellan reminded her. "But I suppose we could go there anyway. We could get supplies for the College. Food and cloth, seed for next spring." He looked over to Gwydion for approval. "Since Alaira and I aren't wizards, no one will suspect we come from Akesh. That is, if you want to stay here and become the Master."

"I hadn't thought of what I'd do when I regained my Power. I'd like to stay, I suppose. Rebuild the College, work with the apprentices, get rid of those lake monsters." He smiled wryly. "Try to repair the damage that was done by the Kharad. Dismiss the demons the Shape-Changer bound back to the Otherworld. What else can I do? There's nowhere else for me to go but Barelin, and the wizards there wouldn't want me."

"Then stay. You and Chela. Alaira and I will come back with supplies, and stay here at least until spring when the ships start running again. We'll leave in the morning, if you think we'll be safe staying here tonight."

"I'll set wards around the tower to warn us if anyone tries to get in. In sending or in person." Gwydion opened the door for them. "Go on, both of you. Get some rest. I've got to go try to explain all this to Morfan and the others."

"We have to go," Yalna said firmly. "It's time you were First Priestess. The S'tari who were here yesterday have heard some strange things lately about the Temple in Cavernon. You have to get back."

Briana knew she was right. It was her duty. She did not look forward to confronting Ocasta and the others again, but she was determined to do what the Goddess required of her. She did not want to leave Cian, especially after the strange encounter yesterday in the stream. But the S'tari had promised to guard the valley, and she had to leave him sometime. She did not have a choice.

The healing atmosphere of the valley had speeded her recovery from the birth. She felt stronger than she had for a long time. In the last month she had begun to exercise her body again, limbering her stiff joints and stretching her muscles. She longed to perform the Great Dances again, and as First Priestess she would command more Power in them than ever.

"We'll leave today," she said at last, standing with Yalna on the hilltop near the cottage, gazing back at the misty ridges that cut the valley off from the desert beyond. "Before I have a chance to convince myself I should stay." Her Power had been muddied and confused during her pregnancy, as she fought to control her baby's wild strength with shields that had kept her from extending the most minimal awareness. Now everything was clear again. Sounds, especially, came to her from distant movements in the desert. A crunch of rocks beneath horses' hooves as the group of S'tari priestesses rode back toward their homes; the shriek of a diving falcon; the trickle of water in an underground rivulet that would become the valley's cold stream. Truly the Goddess was everywhere. Briana could not ignore Her call.

From the ridge trail and the stony desert foothills, Briana and Yalna turned their horses northeast, away from the Caravan Road that would lead them back to the city. Briana had meant to visit the Hidden Temple before, but she had not wanted to leave the valley sooner than she had to. She needed to know what Gemon and the others had meant by their strange message about using the Goddess's Seat.

It took them two days to reach the barren, rocky coastline where Briana had once come as a prisoner of the wizard Emperor Belaric. She expected to feel the call of the Seat once again, the sweet insistent pull that had brought her there before. Her farthest-reaching probes of Power found nothing. The low, rounded hills with their strangely shaped rock outcroppings were full of the distant chittering sounds and slow rhythms of small animal life, undisturbed by the awesome strength of the Goddess's Seat. Briana sent her thoughts on silent wings, and all she found were snakes and gophers cool and sleepy in their holes, and birds nesting in the barren branches of twisted trees.

The Hidden Temple had hidden itself well, she decided. They had created a shield that could not be detected. She knew the way without the call. It was burned in her memory, along with the pain and fear of her captivity. By late afternoon of their second day of riding, she and Yalna found the narrow mouth of the valley Briana remembered. The surf was fierce among the rocks down the slope, not quiet and pleasant as it had been in the sheltered bay where they had left Erlin, Pima, and the children. It was a wild section of shoreline. Briana heard the harsh cries of seabirds as she urged her horse up into the stony valley. Two black-winged gulls flew from the opening of the narrow canyon ahead. That surprised her. She did not remember seeing any birds or animals near the Seat before; in her experience, they stayed away from such places of Power.

Still she felt nothing, though she strained with all her senses. Yalna spoke from behind her as she reined her horse to a stop before the entrance to the canyon. "It seems no different from any other place. Are you sure this is it?"

Briana nodded. She dismounted quickly. "Stay behind for a moment. They'll be wary of strangers." She concentrated on dropping her shields so that the priestesses inside would know who approached. The shields had become so habitual during the war and her pregnancy that they fell only with difficulty, and she felt half naked without them. With her Power projecting before her, searching, Briana stepped over the jumbled rocks in the notch that opened out into the canyon of the Seat.

High, jagged walls towered beside her and before her. She recognized the point of rock where Belaric had stood under her attack until a demon had flown down to lift him out of danger. There were rings of small stones and peg-holes in the ground near the entrance, where S'tari tents had stood, but the Hidden Temple was gone and so was the Seat of the Goddess.

Briana could not believe it. She closed her eyes and sought for a distorting shield, an illusionary spell-wall that might change what the observer saw. There was nothing of the sort. Even if there had been, she should be strong enough to see through it. Seabirds nested on the cliff walls, and the vast throne that had reared from the end of the gorge as if it had grown there had vanished as if it had never existed.

They had somehow harnessed the Power of the Seat to move it to another place. Briana knew the Seat could be moved and its form changed. It had been accomplished once before in ancient times when the Seat had been hidden here in the wilderness of Caerlin. Did Gemon and Iona and four old Second Rank Khymer priestesses have the skill of the mothers of the Order? Even if they did, why would they have felt the need to move the Seat? Perhaps there truly was some danger Briana was unaware of. Perhaps the Darkness their message had mentioned truly threatened. It was possible that the Hidden Temple had sent word to Briana in Cavernon City explaining this, and she had not been there to receive it. Somehow she did not think so.

"Briana?" Yalna climbed warily through the notch, and stopped in surprise to look at the featureless walls of the canyon. "What is it?"

"They're gone, and the Seat with them. We'll rest here a few hours. I want to attempt a Power-tracing ritual to track them." She felt she should do something. But if they had the Power and skill to vanish so completely, she doubted they would have left a trail she could follow. Her anger was growing. She had planned to use the Seat, once the priestesses studying it had learned enough about it. Its Power could have helped with the spring's grain crop, encouraging enough to grow that Caerlin could feed the rest of the Kingdoms. It could have helped rebuild the devastation of such cities as Dallynd. Briana had plans for the Seat when she was First Priestess, and the Hidden Temple might ruin them. What was their reason? She wished she knew.

By evening of the second day of their journey, Kyellan and Alaira had left the forest behind. They traveled slowly. Winter held the land in a cruel grip, and it only seemed to get colder as they traveled eastward toward the great ocean. The maps had shown that the Small Sea narrowed there to a river that could be crossed. The horses had no forage once the tall masthead pines were only a black shadow in the distance. They survived on the last of the grain from the stores of the College. Kyellan and Alaira fared as badly, on small sprouted potatoes and wrinkled onions, and a small amount of dried meat left over from the last successful hunting party.

The first day's journey had exhausted them all so that after caring for the horses Kyellan had not even bothered to set a watch. It was lucky there was no pursuit from the Hidden Temple priestesses. The second day was just as wearying, but now they had begun to get accustomed to the frigid cold and the sliding, stumbling pace of their mounts. The horses often had to flounder through icy crusts of snow that rose past their knees. Kyellan wished he had had more time to plan the journey. He would have fashioned shoes for the animals, after the model of the desert boots the S'tari used for deep sand. High, leather hoof-wrappings would broaden the surface of the hoof and spread the horse's weight more evenly. If he and Alaira returned from Atolan while it was still winter, he would make such shoes for the horses.

They kept a respectful distance from the shore of the Small Sea, which meant they rode across high steppes that rose and fell gently, offering no shelter from the unceasing wind. Kyellan pulled up short on top of a broad slope when he saw a tumbled outcropping of granite boulders ahead. He pulled down the cloth he had wrapped around his face to get a better view. The bitter wind numbed his cheeks in a few moments, but the air was clean and tasted good after breathing through wool all day. The thick grey clouds covered the sky from horizon to horizon, settling down like a blanket at the edges.

"Is this where we turn back toward the Small Sea?" Alaira asked through her thick muffler. Her dark eyes squinted against the snow-glare to look toward the south. The black, half-frozen surface of the huge lake glinted miles away.

Kyellan smiled wearily. She had looked at the map, but Alaira had never been taught to read maps. She had little idea of distances. "Not for three more days, until we reach the coast. I was thinking we could stop for the night among those rocks up there." He pointed.

"I wish we were still in the forest," she muttered. "At

least the trees were some shelter. Three more days before we turn south? Then how far to Atolan, where it will be warm?"

"Maybe four more days at this speed." Kyellan urged his tired S'tari horse forward again. The animal moved stiffly, its head lowered into the wind, picking its hooves up reluctantly and crunching them down again into the snow. The S'tari bred endurance into their horses, but Kyellan was not sure that would be enough. The native Garithian breed was shaggy and thick-bodied, covered in layers of fat against the winter cold. Garithian horses were ill-tempered and slow, but it might have been wiser to find a few of them for the journey.

The sun had seemed powerless to warm them all day, but now that it was setting Kyellan missed it. It would not be really dark. The grey clouds still reflected the brightness of the snow, and a dim half-moon was already rising to glow through a heavy curtain on the horizon. Kyellan and Alaira chose the most sheltered place they could find, a cluster of low, flat-topped boulders on the leeward side of a tall outcropping. At least they would be out of the wind.

Kyellan dismounted and found that the snow around the rocks was almost waist deep. The crust on top was light enough to break through easily. The flat surfaces of the boulders were covered only lightly, though. He decided to build his fire on top of the largest one. The bulk of his and Alaira's baggage was dry wood, since they had known they would not be able to gather any.

Alaira had watched without comment as he floundered in the deep snow. Now she walked her horse forward beside the boulder where Kyellan stood, and slid down from its back onto the rock. The well-trained animal stood calmly while Alaira unsaddled it from the boulder. She piled its saddle and baggage on one end of the rock, rubbed the animal down on one side and got it to turn around so she could get its other side. "I can put its blankets on it," she said quietly. "But it won't do much good if the poor thing has to stand in snow all night."

Kyellan brought his horse over and repeated what Alaira had done. She was right, and it worried him. If the horses failed, he and Alaira were not likely to survive. "Maybe we should have stayed at Akesh, and chanced an attack by the priestesses," he muttered. "Gwydion and the apprentices, Chela, the old men, they might have had enough Power to withstand the Hidden Temple."

"They might not have," Alaira said as she tied her horse's blankets securely on. "And then you might have been killed. I couldn't bear that, not so soon after you came back." She seemed calm enough, but Kyellan could detect the edgy emotion behind her words. She still did not know what to expect from him.

He turned away and pulled wood from his pack to build a fire, large enough to last them through the night unless the lowering clouds dumped more snow on them. The flames rose readily from his sparked flint and steel, driving back a little of the settling night. Alaira swept the light layer of snow from the rest of the boulder, and set out their blanket rolls and the heavy furs they had taken from the floors of the Masters' chambers at Akesh. Kyellan set potatoes and onions at the edge of the flames in the coals that had already charred, and sliced strips of dried meat to roast on the point of his dagger. At last Alaira came to sit beside him.

The horses pressed against the boulder, seeking warmth and companionship. Alaira reached out to pat their noses with her gloved hands. "This is no place for me," she said ruefully. "I belong in the sunshine."

Kyellan pulled her close and wrapped his heavy cloak around them both. "I'll wager you wish you never came on this journey. I'm sorry I dragged you along."

"Dragged me?" She chuckled, but he could feel the tension in her. "I had to throw myself at you to get you to take me, in the end. No, I'm not sorry I came. It was awful for a while, but that's over now. And you found what you were searching for, didn't you? Your arm is healed. Even more than that, you don't have to worry about the Shape-Changer now."

"I wonder. He has a lot of Power still. He may figure out a way to get back from the Otherworld."

"He can't get back unless you call him back. I don't think you'll do that, Ky."

The thought made him uncomfortable. What if he was attacked someday by the Hidden Temple priestesses, bent on vengeance? If he could save his life by summoning the Shape-Changer, would he do it, knowing the price would be his soul? His wizard half would never go back to a vaguely aware existence deep within his mind.

He felt sorry for the Shape-Changer. The wizard was a part of him. If the Shape-Changer could be believed, he was the real Kyellan. The black-haired soldier who sat now on a fire-warmed boulder holding a girl in his arms was no more than a figment of his own imagination. Kyellan shook his head, clearing it of such strange thoughts. He was no philosopher. He was back in control of his own life now, and even if that life turned out to be a short one, he thought it would be worth it.

Alaira shivered and buried her head against his chest in a quick movement. "We'll both be frozen by morning. Neither of us has enough blankets to keep out this cold."

Kyellan smiled slightly. "Maybe we'd be better off to share all the blankets."

There was wariness behind her eyes as she looked up into his. "Do you really want to?"

"What do you think?" he whispered, pulling her face up between his gloved hands to kiss her. Alaira was stiff for a moment, but then she yielded and relaxed into his embrace, as if she had never left it.

Tapeth was waiting in the open doorway of Briana's suite at the Tiranon to greet the two weary travelers. From the abandoned canyon on the Tarnsea coast to Cavernon City had taken Briana and Yalna six days of constant riding. The two horses they had left in the lamplit courtyard were almost spent. Briana unwrapped her dusty peasant headcloth as she climbed the stairs. She smiled at Tapeth's grave, expectant expression.

"Va'shindi told me in a dream that you would be here tonight." The lean, tall S'tari woman kissed Briana on the cheek, then turned and hugged Yalna fiercely. "Is everything well for you both? And for the baby?"

"Cian was fine when I left him," Briana said wistfully, passing Tapeth in the doorway to enter the familiar, austere room.

Tapeth followed her with an arm around Yalna, and closed the door behind them. "He should have been taken from you at birth," she said in sympathy. "With you never allowed to see him. But even then it would have been hard."

Not wanting to think about her guilt at abandoning her son, Briana pulled aside the curtains to go into the next room. Two large wooden tubs stood next to the marble window seat, filled with steaming water. "Oh, Tapeth, that looks wonderful."

The older woman drew the curtains and began to help Briana and Yalna unfasten their layers of soiled wool clothing. "I will send word to the Temple in the morning. The time has come for your confirmation, my lady. And for you to come out of your seclusion and move your quarters to the new Temple compound."

"Is the Temple finished?" Briana shed the last underrobe of her peasant costume.

"Not entirely. The Queen's men claimed a higher priority with stones from the quarry. They've been rebuilding the sea wall from the foundations. Everyone thinks Arel will attack soon, since he's been named King in exile." Tapeth sighed.

"How do the people feel about that?" Briana worked her fingers through her tight braids. Her hair fell into crimped waves. The dye had worn away, and it had returned to its natural dark auburn color.

Tapeth sat at the window. "I'd say few of them are partisans of one side or the other. But there is an undercurrent of sympathy for Arel. They feel that whatever his shortcomings he is the rightful ruler. It is a pity the way he fits into so many folk legends . . . the deposed Prince, the King in exile, a romantic figure with a band of loyal followers. That appeals to something in the people."

"It doesn't appeal to the S'tari," Yalna said. "We know what he'd do if he took the throne. He'd declare the treaty invalid, revoke our independence, and claim our lands again." She slid into her bath, and her somber round face relaxed into comfort.

Briana climbed over the edge of the other tub. The water had barely cooled. Tapeth must have known exactly when they would arrive. The warmth enveloped her as she bent her legs to fit her whole body into the bath. It was difficult to think about political questions when all she wanted to do was sit and soak. "It's awkward for the Temple," she said after a moment. "Arel has the Goddess's blessing to rule. The old First Priestess gave it to him at the Sanctuary. It can't be revoked. But I support Valahtia. I know she'll try to keep the peace. I trust her. The people will follow the Temple's lead."

"If the Temple follows you." Tapeth reached to the window to close the shutters against the night breezes. "I sent out those proclamations you left. The first was well received. It was a good idea to reduce the Temple tax for anyone who could provide a few days' labor. But the priestesses did not like the other at all."

"What was it?" Yalna asked from her bath.

"I set a day when anyone who wished could come forward to be tested for the Temple. What happened, Tapeth?"

"Ocasta tried to get in here to see you, but I turned her away. I'd made certain the people saw the proclamation before the priestesses did, so they couldn't stop it. They had no choice but to test the women who appeared." Tapeth's voice was dry. "There were nearly a hundred of them. Most were poor, or from families who had lost their men to the wizards. The priestesses were not pleased with the selection, and they were less pleased when they found that half the women had the minimum amount of potential Power to become novices. It seems the Cavernon Temple has been overlooking girls in the lower classes, as well as those whose parents are wealthy."

Briana nodded. The warm water was making her sleepy. "I suspected that, from something Alaira once told me. Well, they'll have to take them now."

"You'll have to insist, my lady. The potential novices were told they would be considered for admission into the Temple, but they were sent home to wait until the decisions were made."

"But they knew Briana wanted them to be novices," Yalna said indignantly. "How did they dare disobey her?"

"Did I make any response, Tapeth?" Briana asked.

"I used one of the blank proclamations to tell them to initiate the new novices as soon as possible. They said there was no place to put them, since the dormitories were not yet rebuilt. I decided to leave it at that until your return.''

"They'll have to learn to work with me,'' Briana said. ''I'll go tomorrow to look at the Temple and speak with Ocasta about my confirmation. They'll have to get used to the idea that I'm going to be their new First Priestess.'' She sighed and sank lower in her bath. "You did well, Tapeth. I'm going to miss your counsel. You and Yalna have both served me well. I hope you'll stay long enough to see me confirmed.''

"I wouldn't miss it, my lady,'' said Tapeth. ''It's what we've all been working toward.''

Valahtia heard the outer door of the royal chambers open and close, and heavy footsteps come through the front room. Her monkey chattered loudly. She waited impatiently on a garden bench. A page had told her of a disturbance in the main palace yard, and she had sent the fat old Nyesin priest, Istam, to be her eyes. She grew tired very easily now, late in the eighth month of her pregnancy.

"Well?'' she snapped when Istam reached her, panting and puffing.

"Lord Foerad has returned, Your Majesty,'' he said when he regained his breath. ''His ship arrived this morning from Syryn, without advance notice, and he is in the courtyard now.''

"He should have come to me immediately,'' she said with a frown. ''Did he tell you how Arel reacted to my refusal to acknowledge his Kingship?''

"I only observed that he had arrived, Your Majesty. I did not get close to him. There were many men in his train, in your livery, but . . .'' the old man hesitated. ''I do not think he took so many with him on his voyage.''

"What do you mean, Istam?''

"Perhaps they are emissaries from your brother. His people also wear the colors of your father's house.'' Istam looked relieved at the thought.

"I'm not so sure,'' Valahtia murmured. ''It may be so. It may also be treachery. There is a page with my guards at the door to this suite. Send him to Foerad, and command the lord chamberlain to attend me here. You must find Earl Tobas. Tell him to double the S'tari guards on duty, and to come here at once. Do you understand?''

''The page to Foerad, the lord consort here, more S'tari guards.'' Istam nodded. The action buried his chin in deep folds of fat.

''Go quickly!'' Valahtia called after him. She wished she had a less corpulent messenger. At least she was certain of Istam's loyalty. Probably there was no cause for fear, but she knew what her brother was capable of, and Foerad was a weak old fool.

Chapter Sixteen _____

BRIANA walked through the city alone, conscious that soon she could not expect to go anywhere without being recognized. No one noticed a slim, fast-striding Second Rank priestess in her black robe, except for a few who bowed to her in respect as she passed. It would be different for the First Priestess. Half the city would probably attend the public part of her confirmation.

The palace commanded a low rise in the southeastern part of the city. The city streets that surrounded it were lovely, avenues of trees and hilly parks, with a few rambling buildings that housed minor ministries. The palace wall might as well surround them; they belonged to the royal family. The public was allowed to enjoy the parks, but they were patrolled by a disciplined force of mounted S'tari on matching grey horses and in full desert regalia. They were usually peaceful.

Briana walked on, turning from the wide royal streets into a network of lanes between tall rows of middle-class homes and shops. The people were beginning the day's work. Shutters were thrown back on the street levels of the shops, and tradesmen and apprentices swept the refuse of the night before from the walkways into the gutters. Briana smelled a mingled odor of waste and baking bread. Beauty and squalor close at hand, she thought. That was the character of Cavernon City, the greatest city in the Kingdoms, the place where she intended to base her work.

She saw a grey-robed priestess turn down a side street ahead, driving a covered cart; making the rounds for the Temple rebuilding tax. One-twentieth of the profit each merchant had made the day before. Few complained, and those who did complained more about the taxes to rebuild the city fortifications. The people of Cavernon felt guilty, Briana suspected. They felt they had abandoned the priestesses to the wrath of the wizards. They had not dared to defend the holy women. Some who had been brave enough at first to hide a novice or two in their houses had turned them out of doors at the approach of the wizards' soldiers.

A smooth, polished yard paved with flat stones spread in a half circle before the first building of the Temple compound. There was only a low wall the height of a man around the Cavernon Temple. The five varied structures rose above it in graceful forms, some only half finished. The most impressive one arched upward to a flattened dome inset with marble and pink sandstone in a subtle pattern. That would be the great hall of worship, the part of the Temple open to the public on feast days. The Great House, the Teaching House, the dormitory and the Work House were far more important in the life of the Order.

There was no gatekeeper. Briana walked through the open door of the wall and up the steps of the worship hall. The ground on which the old Temple had fallen and the new one risen was less a place of Power than it was a place of peace. Briana lowered her shields to breathe in the soft warmth of the atmosphere. How could anyone here be concerned with petty matters of prestige and pride? It was a place to lift the heart.

The tall doors of the worship hall stood open to the morning breezes. Briana strolled inside to admire the delicate stonework of the interior walls. Much of the material was still discolored from the wizards' uncanny fire, but the stonemasons had worked the crimson and orange stains into subtle patterns, a pleasing effect against the pale, new quarry stones. Light-colored benches marched up the aisles toward the dais at the far end of the hall.

The only priestess Briana had yet seen in the compound knelt on the flagstone floor before the simple altar, three pillars that would be topped with white flame during public rituals. She wore a grey robe, and the ivory band of Fourth Ranking bound her silver-flecked hair. She was old for Fourth Ranking. She would not have remained at that level unless her childhood promise of Power had proven false.

Everything in the hall was comfortable and familiar to Briana, except for a hinged wooden box with an inlaid lid that stood below the altar. The Fourth Rank priestess was scrubbing around it with a brush dipped in clear water. "Good morning, sister," Briana said.

The woman looked up, startled. She had little Power indeed, not to have sensed Briana's presence. Briana had lowered her shields. "Good morning." She rose and bowed. Her brown face was worn with work and frustration, but it had been pretty. "I am sorry, Priestess, but I cannot recall your name."

"We've never met. I'm Briana, the Candidate for First Priestess. This is the first day I've been out of my seclusion, and I wanted to see the new Temple. It is beautiful."

"You're Briana," the woman said softly. "They said . . . but you seem very nice. So young." She shook her head. "Forgive me, Candidate. I did not think. My name is Lakein. I am the gardener here, but they have yet to rebuild the gardens, so I find other ways to occupy my time. Shall I guide you to Ocasta's rooms? I'm sure she'll want to receive you."

"I would be glad of a guide," Briana said with a smile. "But there's no hurry. I'd like to see what I can first."

"The real Altar is underground, of course," she said as Briana approached the pillars. "Only Second Rank priestesses may go there. Ocasta could send someone to show you."

"Then it was saved from the wizards?" Briana asked, interested. If the heart of the Temple had been discovered and destroyed, it would have required an awesome amount of work to create another. The ancient rituals were recorded in the histories, but Briana had no desire to attempt them.

"They never found it," Lakein assured her. Briana stopped to look at the polished wooden box. "That may interest you, Candidate. They say you fought fiercely against the wizards.

It is a token of our victory, and the people believe it to hold a protective Power, though that of course is foolish superstition.'' She lifted the lid.

Briana frowned. The box was filled with tiny bundles of yellow fibers like dried hay. The miniature sheaves were of different shades, ranging from deep gold to a pale beige. ''What is it? Some sort of harvest symbolism? I've never seen such a thing in a Temple of the Goddess.''

''A harvest in a sense,'' Lakein said, her face somber. ''They are locks of hair taken from the wizards that fell in the final battle. There are many of them, aren't there? A fitting reminder of their defeat.''

''What?'' Briana looked closer, horrified. She touched one of the bundles lightly. It was silky, not at all like straw. ''I can't believe this. . . . Don't you people have any knowledge of magic? Don't you realize what this can mean?''

''Magic, Candidate? The followers of the Goddess use Her Power in prayer and ritual, but we don't perform magic. And what is so horrible about this box? It is gruesome, perhaps, but it is something the people understand.''

''Call it what you will,'' Briana said, closing the lid sharply. ''To preserve something that was a part of a dead man can bind the soul in a ghostly state. It doesn't always happen, but sometimes it does. The contents of this box must be burned. Do you understand? Take them out and burn them until there is nothing but ashes left.''

Lakein's initial friendliness was gone. ''Even if I accept what you have told me, does not the Goddess teach that wizards have no souls? Forgive me, Candidate, but it sounds much like village witchery to me.''

''I'll speak of it to Ocasta,'' Briana said tightly. ''Will you guide me to her now?''

The woman nodded. ''You must understand, Candidate, that I have no authority to decide such matters. Ocasta will know what to do.''

''Fine. Please show me the way to her rooms.''

The page was the first to arrive back in Valahtia's quarters. He was a slim, elegant boy of twelve with long black hair, and he ran into the garden and skidded to a stop before he remembered the proper courtesy. He bowed deeply and held that position, breathing hard, his face flushed with exertion.

"You may speak," the Queen said quickly.

He straightened. "I found Lord Foerad, Your Majesty. He said he would be right here. He has many men with him, and another page told me that groups of them went into the palace by different doors. They are all armed, and it is very strange, but one with Foerad is masked."

"What?" She felt blood drain from her cheeks. "Describe him."

"He wore a mask, as if he was going to a ball. It was strange because he was dressed in servant's livery, not noble clothes."

"You must have noticed something else about him. His height, his build. The color of his hair."

The page frowned. "He was of medium height. Slender. His hair was dark and curled at his shoulders."

"How many men were with Foerad?" Valahtia gripped the edge of the ornate bench, willing herself to stay calm. It was Arel. It had to be. A gate opened from within, Senomar had warned, but she had imagined the traitor as a lowborn Redeemer sympathizer, not one of her court. She had made no plans for such an event as this.

"Ten men with him, Majesty. More than forty had left the courtyard before I arrived. Is—is there something wrong?"

"What is your name, page?" she asked abruptly.

"Oralt, first son of the Earl of Erinon," he said with pride.

"Then I will not risk you further. You are released from my service, Oralt. Go quickly. It would be best if you were not found at my side."

He stared at her, realizing she was serious. "There is danger, my Queen? Don't send me away. I'll defend you."

She saw that he would disobey her if she commanded him to leave. "Very well. Go to the door of my chambers again. Stand with the guards and do not let anyone in until my lord Tobas arrives. Be as formal and correct as you can when Foerad and the others appear. They may be courteous long enough to be taken by surprise."

"You can depend on me, Your Majesty," he said with a

fierceness only a twelve-year-old could muster. He knelt
swiftly and kissed her hand, then sprang up and raced from
the garden. Valahtia watched him go, thinking of the son she
bore. She clasped her hands over her stomach and tried to
breathe slowly. If Arel took the throne, her child would never
grow to be like young Oralt. Likely she would not live long
enough to give birth. Oh, Goddess, where was Tobas? If Arel
had depended on stealth and small numbers, if there were no
reinforcements entering an opened gate somewhere in the
city, then perhaps her brother could be stopped.

Soon after the page closed the outer door, Valahtia heard
shouts and clashing swords, and then a high scream that had to
be the boy's. The Earl of Erinon would not be likely to
support Arel now, whether his son was killed or only wounded.
Valahtia fought back laughter, so frightened she was close to
hysterics. She had to face her death bravely. With the dignity
of a Queen. All would see that she and not Arel had been the
true heir to her father's greatness.

But she would be dead. The young woman sat in her
garden amid the colored fountains and the sculpted hedges,
pale but stiff-backed, her hands folded over her stomach to
emphasize her advanced pregnancy. She felt light movement
from her child. Goddess, she thought, you promised him the
blessing to rule. Do not let him die before he comes into the
world.

Shouting broke through into the first sumptuous room of
the royal chambers, and then a clear, arrogant voice quieted
the others. Valahtia's clasped hands were white. She held her
head high as Lord Foerad entered the garden with a drawn
sword. It was bloody, and it looked horribly incongruous
against the silks and rings the old man wore. Valahtia wondered if he had volunteered for the task of killing her. Then
he sheathed his sword and bowed slightly.

"Greetings from Syryn." His voice was dry and courteous.

"I see that you bring my brother's reply to my message,
my lord chamberlain," she said in a voice that somehow
remained steady. "You swore fealty to me once. Are you so
easily made an oath-breaker?"

"I owe my loyalty to Caerlin," he said stiffly. "And to its
true King. He regrets that he cannot accept exile any longer.

He has already been proclaimed King of Caerlin. The people of his Kingdom will welcome him.'' He turned and bowed with hands crossed over his chest in elaborate deference.

Arel strode in smiling like a young tiger, his sword sheathed, a splash of blood on the front of his red and black tunic. A mask hung on a golden cord around his neck, tangled in his curly hair. Valahtia looked at him steadily. He was older, even a little worn; there were new lines at the corners of his narrow brown eyes, though his face was still handsome at twenty-three. ''Dear sister,'' he said. ''I am glad to see you well.''

''You are not welcome at my court.'' She did not rise.

''So your guards informed me. It's over, Valahtia. My best men came with Foerad, and another ship followed with mercenary troops. They're already in the city, with orders to take over quickly and with as little bloodshed as possible. My supporters were ready for me. Even the priestesses of the Temple sent word that they would welcome me. I have men going to arrest your puppet Briana now.'' When she said nothing, he went on. ''I had no desire to besiege my father's city, Valahtia. It would have been a needless waste of lives. Would you prefer that I had attacked and half your subjects died? This way is cleaner.''

''Foul treachery, cleaner than battle?'' She saw Foerad wince. ''Arel, I have nothing to say to you. Kill me quickly and take your bloodstained throne. May it bring you much joy.''

''Kill you?'' He looked genuinely shocked. ''I have no such intention, sister. You will be far too useful to me alive. And I want my people to love me. No, you need fear nothing worse than marriage. Werlinen will leave Keris to come for you as soon as this is settled. He'll keep you well in hand, and powerless to hurt me or my Kingdom.''

''Werlinen?'' Valahtia remembered the foolish Prince of Keris to whom she had been briefly betrothed during the war. She had hated him even before she had fallen in love with Tobas. ''Nothing you do can make me marry that idiot. I will die first, Arel.''

''We'll see.'' He smiled at her, turned, and strode from the garden. She heard him shouting to his men in the corridor, demanding that they capture Tobas. If he planned to keep her alive, what did he mean to do about her baby? Surely he would not tolerate a potential heir to his throne. And if he meant to marry her to Werlinen, first he would have to eliminate her consort. Valahtia wished Arel had killed her out of hand. To use her brother's own language, it would have been cleaner.

Ocasta's rooms were austere, with no decoration of any kind. Briana remembered the woman thought of herself as truly pious and uncorrupted. Perhaps she was, by Cavernon City standards. Ocasta sat behind a large, plain desk. Rithia was with her, bent over an open leather-bound book. Briana had not seen their faces before. She had only spoken to them from behind the curtains. Ocasta's face was heavily wrinkled but serene, with mild eyes and a gentle expression. Rithia looked tense, nervous, her face bony and full of mobility. They looked up as Lakein bowed in the doorway and Briana stepped in beside her.

"The Candidate Briana wishes to speak with you, Priestess," Lakein said. "I guided her here. Shall I leave you now?"

"Stay, good sister," Ocasta said in her soft voice. "Come in, Briana. We have been expecting you." She wore a black robe with silver embroidery at the edges, and it took Briana a moment to realize why that seemed odd. The two-colored robe was reserved for the First Priestess in the rules of the Order. In the Sanctuary, though, the old First Priestess had contented herself with black.

Briana gave no courteous greeting. "Why is there a collection of wizards' hair in the worship hall? I still cannot believe it."

The old woman blinked. "The Temple of the Goddess destroyed the wizards. It is a sign of our victory. A symbol of our triumph."

"A reminder to keep vigilant against those who follow Darkness," Rithia said with a thin smile.

"It is horrible. I told Lakein, and I will tell you. It must be burned." There was something about them she could not grasp. A blurring of their Power, as if they were shielding something from her. As if they were using much of their strength in something beyond the conversation in this room. It made Briana decidedly uncomfortable. Their easy smiles were the worst of it.

"Why do you say that, Briana?" Ocasta asked. She clasped her gnarled hands on the table before her. They shook slightly.

Lakein glanced at Briana and spoke suddenly. "She said that it was magic. That the pieces of hair might bind the wizards' souls to this world. Is such a thing possible, Priestess? I have never heard of it."

"The wizards' souls?" Rithia repeated, lifting an eyebrow.

"Why do I feel as if I am on trial?" Briana demanded. "Do you mean to trap me in some heresy, Ocasta? You know that box in the hall is an abomination. It takes no talk of magic to realize that." With an effort, she forced her voice to lower. "I did not come here to debate with you. It is time for my confirmation as First Priestess. I should be settled into my new duties by midwinter."

Ocasta's smile vanished. "A date has been set for the confirmation of the First Priestess, Briana. Three days from now. But you need not be concerned with it."

"Ocasta will be the new First Priestess," Rithia said calmly. "And she will support the new King, as the Goddess's blessing obligates the Temple to do. You will be tried for your complicity in putting the usurper Valahtia on the throne. Don't make it worse for yourself. Don't use your Power against the soldiers."

Briana whirled around as Ocasta and Rithia let their extended shields fall. She had not sensed the soldiers' presence in the corridor. Now they filled the doorway, five rough mercenaries in red and black uniforms with the Caerlin Tiger on their surcoats. They had not drawn their swords. They did not have to. They held Yalna and Tapeth struggling between them. The S'tari women's wrists were bound, and their black eyes were furious over their veils. The soldiers must have gone to Briana's rooms in the Tiranon, and found their captives there.

"If you try to escape, your servants will be killed," Rithia said from behind her. "Go with them peacefully, Briana. If you cause no further trouble, the King may be merciful. He may simply marry you off to someone to whom he owes a favor.''

Briana stared in disbelief as the leader of the mercenaries spoke gravely. ''The true King Arel has commanded your arrest, Briana of Garith. Come with us.''

Fury swept through her, and she felt the Goddess's Flame gather within her to strike them all down. But if she did that, she would prove Rithia right. She would show herself to be unfit to be a priestess. The Goddess abhorred violence. She clung to that thought and stepped forward with outward calm as two of the soldiers took her elbows. ''You are mad, Ocasta,'' she said. ''Do you think the Goddess will accept you as Her First Priestess? You cannot force Her choice.''

''She has not interfered to protect you,'' Rithia said. ''You who are so sure of Her favor.''

Briana looked past the tall priestess to the white-haired woman at the desk. Ocasta's face was still serene, but Briana could feel the turmoil of her emotions. She met Ocasta's sunken eyes. ''You know you are wrong. In your heart, you know you are not chosen. If you carry this madness through, you may lead the Temple. But it will be a Temple barren of Power and the Goddess's grace.''

The old woman inclined her head slowly. ''I am willing to take that risk. Farewell, Briana.''

The grey-robed woman, Lakein, watched fearfully as Briana was led from the room. Her thoughts were unshielded, and Briana could sense them easily in the atmosphere of Power. She was frightened by what Briana had said. Frightened that her superiors had taken it upon themselves to defy the Goddess's will. Frightened at what might happen to her and all the others in the Temple if the One they served was angered at what they had done.

Briana was very glad as she was marched down the streets that the people of Cavernon City did not know who she was. They saw a priestess under arrest, and two bound S'tari women with her, and it made them wonder how much clemency they could expect from their new King. Not much, Briana could have told them. Arel would be cruel and capricious, and as soon as he was sure of his position he would probably renew the S'tari war his father had fought. For all that, Briana thought sourly, he might end up in history as a romantic figure, a strong king, a hero.

She did not expect Arel to have her married to keep her quiet. If he had learned anything of her character in the time they had traveled together last spring, he would know that would not work. Married or not, Briana would still be the Goddess's choice for First Priestess. If Ocasta was to be sure of her post, Briana would have to die. Then the Goddess's favor would have to go to someone else, and why not Ocasta? She was powerful, and devout. The Goddess would have to make the best of the situation.

Apparently the Temple had known Arel would take his throne today, however he had done it. Briana could only assume it was by treachery. She wondered if Valahtia and Tobas were dead. She did not think they were; she had been close to them both, and she would have felt something if they were murdered.

"We thought they were from the Queen, my lady," Tapeth said quietly. "They asked where you had gone. We didn't know until after we told them you'd gone to the Temple."

The mercenaries scowled at them, but made no complaint about their talking. "It's all right," Briana said. "How could you have known?"

"They think the lord consort escaped," Yalna whispered. "With some of the S'tari Guard. They haven't found him yet, at least."

"Quiet," said the leader of the soldiers then.

The Earl escaped? Briana felt a glimmer of hope that all might not be lost. Tobas was a resourceful young man. Nearly as good a soldier as Kyellan; perhaps better at strategy and planning. He was more thoughtful, less reckless, though he was younger.

"My lady, look," Tapeth whispered. Among the crowds of the frightened and curious citizens that lined the street, Briana saw the flash of a white robe and headdress. A S'tari warrior, a tall dark youth whose black eyes met hers over the heads in front of him. He was only there an instant, then he melted back into the throng.

"What? What did you see there?" the leader demanded, taking Tapeth's shoulder and whirling her around to face him.

The gaunt woman shrugged. "One of my people."

"Should we pursue, Captain?" asked a stocky mercenary with a heavy beard, one of the two who held Briana's arms.

The leader shook his head quickly. "We have our duty. And the King hasn't yet given us orders to bother the S'tari. We have no authority."

The soldiers hurried their pace until Briana was half running to keep up with them. Yalna glided along indignantly, and Tapeth stalked with strides that matched her captors'. They seemed little hampered by their bound wrists. Briana wondered what would happen to them. They had done nothing wrong. They should be released now that they had played their part in her capture. It was more likely, she thought grimly, that they would be sent to the dungeons and forgotten in the confusion. Dear Goddess, was there no way they could get out of this? It was barely possible she could contrive an escape with her Power. She might create an illusion to frighten the soldiers, or simply attack them with the white flame. But the accusations of Ocasta and Rithia haunted her. They called her heretic, unfit, because she had called upon Rahshaiya, because she had used her Power for killing. The thought of further violence sickened her.

The street widened and sloped upward as they rose from the city level into the royal parkland. The sprawling wall of the Tiranon gleamed in the distance. The same banner flew from its walls that had flown when Briana had left it this morning. To the people of the city, perhaps, little would seem to change. A King instead of a Queen. Mercenaries instead of a S'tari Guard. A different First Priestess; but none of them had known Briana anyway.

A disparate stream of people was walking down the royal road back to the city. Merchants and city officials, the poor and the wronged, carrying scrolls of paper upon which they had had scribes write their petitions to the Queen. The day's supplicants, turned away from their promised audience. Arel would have no time for such duties yet. These people, at least, would be annoyed by the change.

Briana's Power-heightened senses caught a cluster of movement, a flash of white and grey and silver, behind a copse of broad shade trees on a slope just below the road. As the five soldiers approached with their three captives, the trees came alive with wild shouts and the horsemen of the park's S'tari Guard spurred around the copse to charge up to the road. Others ran with them on foot, and Briana thought she saw the young man who had met her eyes along the street. The moment was too swift to be sure.

The mercenaries in Arel's livery swore loudly and let go their captives' arms to draw their swords. The riders swept up at them with drawn scimitars, each young S'tari warrior in his flowing robes like a part of his grey horse. Horror-struck, Briana stumbled back away from the soldiers who had held her as they were brutally cut down, overwhelmed by the superior numbers and speed of their opponents. Yalna and Tapeth ran out of the way of the horsemen, but they cried out fierce S'tari words of encouragement. The five soldiers were down, wounded or dead, in a matter of moments.

"Briana, quickly now," a crisp young voice said from above her. She looked up, sick to her stomach, and saw Tobas's boyish face framed by a white S'tari headcloth. His arm reached down for her. She stared at it, not comprehending. The smell of blood and the overwhelming sensation of death had a terrible strength that confused her senses and her Power. She had forgotten how horrible the war had been, in the months she had spent creating a new life. It was as if she was back in the midst of a battlefield. "Priestess, take my hand! They saw this from the walls."

In the distance, the gates of the Tiranon had opened for a squadron of liveried soldiers to pour out. Some were mounted. Briana swallowed hard against her nausea and took Tobas's hand. She jumped up as he pulled her, and managed to scramble onto the back of his grey horse. Yalna and Tapeth, their bonds cut, rode behind two of the fierce S'tari guardsmen. The men on foot had run off, and some of the riders were galloping in close formation up the road toward the enemy forces.

"A delaying action," Tobas said. "So we can get away." He reined his horse around and urged it into a run, followed by the S'tari who carried Yalna and Tapeth, and five other riders. They plunged down the road in a phalanx, scattering petitioners and citizens to the edges, by the Goddess's grace not running anyone down. The moment they were out of the park, they turned sharply into a side street. They were headed for the wall, the eastern wall, Briana realized. There was a southeastern gate out of the city. "We're lucky that boy saw you on the street," Tobas said cheerfully as Briana clung to him and they hurtled through the narrow ways of Cavernon City's merchant quarter. "Once you were inside the Tiranon we couldn't have gotten you out. Not today, at least."

"Why . . . why did you have to kill them?" Briana said dully. The rust-stained scimitar that hung from Tobas's belt brushed against her leg as they rode. If she stopped to think, she thought she would be sick.

"We could have asked them politely to hand you over," Tobas said dryly. "Sorry you were upset, Priestess, but if you mean to work to stop Ocasta and overthrow Arel, you wouldn't have been able to do it from a dungeon."

Briana stared at the buildings that jolted past on their way to the gate. Was that what she meant to do? She had not thought that far ahead. Yet despite her anguish, despite her confusion, it sounded right. To stop Ocasta, to overthrow Arel. If the Goddess was still with her, then that was what she was meant to do.

Chapter Seventeen ─────

THEY took Valahtia up to the tower rooms where Briana had lived. There was only one door from the suite, which could be guarded from the stairway. The window was too high for Valahtia to think of escaping to the gardens below. Besides, she was too large and easily fatigued from her pregnancy. She would not have attempted escape even if she had been left in her old quarters, but it was no use telling them that. They left her there and closed the door, and she heard a bolt fall into place.

She was briefly curious about the prison they had given her. She had seen the outer room before, when she had come to speak to Briana at the beginning of the priestess's seclusion. Now she drew back the curtains and found that the inner room was as plain and barren as the outer. There were three narrow beds, a table, chairs, books, and that was all. Not even a cushion on the window seat, or a rug on the flagstone floor.

How long would she have to stay here? Until her unwanted husband Werlinen came for her? He would not want a pregnant bride. He would wait until after her child was born. Valahtia sat down heavily on the window seat. No doubt Arel would marry very quickly, too, probably one of Valahtia's maidens. He would begin to work to produce a child of his own. Until that child was born, he might let his sister's son live as the only heir to the Ardavan line. It was barely possible that he might.

Valahtia finally began to weep. Tears ran quietly down her cheeks. She did not sob or moan, as she would have done if there had been anyone in the room from whom she wanted sympathy. Valahtia had long known the value of dramatic tears, though she rarely cried when she was alone. There had not often been reason to before. Now she feared for her unborn baby, and she feared for Tobas, and she feared what it would do to her to lose them both.

She was not allowed the luxury of being alone long. Arel opened her door, paused at the threshold a moment, then stepped inside. "Are you comfortable, my dear?" he asked coolly. "The priestess must have lived simply in here. It is just as well. This will remind you that you are not a Queen, only a foolish girl who stole a place that was never hers." He smiled, and his eyes flicked over her tear-wet face, and away again. "Still, it's more comfortable than the place where I've put your lover."

"Tobas?" She bit her lip fiercely. "You've captured him?"

"Of course." Her brother leaned against the wall in a pose of nonchalance. "For the moment, he is unhurt. Understand me, Valahtia. I know you. I know that all of this was your own idea. But I am going to blame it on your advisors, because otherwise I'd have to try you for treason. Then I'd lose a valuable alliance with Keris."

"I don't care what you do," she said quietly. "I won't marry Werlinen. Tobas is my consort."

"You are no longer a Queen, and ordinary women do not have consorts."

"I'll have no other man but Tobas."

Arel laughed. "When did you become so discriminating? The girl I knew sought lovers from the court and from the streets, and even from the lowest class of soldiers. That brat you carry could just as well be the son of Kyellan as of the foolish young Earl of Laenar."

"He is Tobas's son," she said venomously. "And lacking any other, Arel, he is the heir to your throne."

He scowled. "If you're still counting on the Goddess's blessing for him, you can think again. Briana won't be there to give it to him. I've had her arrested, and she'll be tried along with Tobas. They'll be the first to be executed.''

"Executed?'' The word shocked her, though she had guessed from the first that was what Arel intended. "I thought you said no bloodshed.''

"Not to gain me my rightful throne. But after a fair trial by the nobles of the court, in which all traitors except you will be revealed, no one will think me a tyrant for ordering death for the criminals.''

"You can't, Arel,'' she whispered. "Tobas only acted out of love for me, and Briana . . . she serves the Goddess, not the throne.''

"That has already been decided,'' Arel said. "Her Temple wants her dead. But the question of Tobas's fate remains open. You can save his life, Valahtia. Agree to marry Werlinen.''

She looked up into his narrow brown eyes and felt very cold. "Do you mean if I marry him you'll let Tobas go?''

Arel hesitated a moment before he answered. He took a few steps forward to gaze out the high tower window. "No. But he won't be killed. Imprisoned, yes. Somewhere that he'll be no threat. The winter palace in Khymer, perhaps. He'd be well treated.''

"What about my baby?'' she said dully.

"Werlinen might agree to raise him. To adopt him, though not as an heir. He'd lose his claim on my throne then,'' Arel said lightly.

"Do you think he'd agree to that?'' Valahtia could scarcely believe it. Werlinen knew she was no virgin bride; he would be marrying her for her dowry and for an alliance with Arel. But even so, he could hardly be expected to take a child that was not his. A child that was a threat to Arel by his very existence. It would not matter what name her son bore, Valahtia knew. Some day he would be raised as a pretender to the throne of Caerlin by some dissatisfied group or other. Arel had to know that. Werlinen would know it.

"He'll agree.'' Her brother bowed cheerfully and headed out of the room. "I'll give him no choice. I'm glad you can be reasonable, sister. And Tobas will be grateful to you for giving him his life.'' He closed the door and was gone.

She did not remember agreeing to go along with his plan. But he left her little choice. She did not want Tobas killed. Grateful? Tobas would curse her as a traitor to their love. Arel was probably headed for the dungeons now to tell him of her betrayal.

"It's beautiful!" Alaira shouted into the wind. Her horse pricked up its ears at the sound of her voice, and pranced a little as if catching her excitement. Kyellan laughed, gazing over the icy fields to the cluster of wooden shacks and sod huts that crowded together around the edges of Atolan as if to cuddle against the city walls for warmth. The harbor was nearly empty. Only a few fishing boats were out. There were two ships in dry dock for the winter. No sane man would travel the Northern reaches of the great ocean until the stormlock of midwinter broke.

"It should at least be warm," he conceded, "if we stay inside the inn."

"Let's go. I want to sit by a hearthfire for about a week."

They rode into the city, past the shacks outside the walls. The people who lived in the huts were wrapped heavily against the bitter cold, but those Kyellan saw did not look Garithian. Their hair was brown or sandy, not red, and their skin was slightly darker than the Northern type. Refugees from Dallynd, he guessed. They had managed to return to the mainland from the wartime camps on Altimar, but they had no city to live in. Far out of sight across the rivermouth bay to the south, Dallynd could be no more than a burned-out husk.

Kyellan had been to Atolan once before, briefly, when the Royal Guard had disembarked there on its way to the Sanctuary. That had been in the last month of winter, and the sleet and fog that had seemed so miserable then would have been welcome warmth today. Few people were out on the muddy streets between the dark houses. Those who had business outside their homes moved quickly from shelter to shelter, breathing rapidly through their mufflers in filtered white clouds. Theirs were the only horses on the street.

Atolan was not a large city. The sober houses and rows of covered, windowless shops served working people, tradesmen and their families, sailors and farmers who had other jobs during the winter. There was no court life. The King and Queen of Garith lived in a fortress a day's ride to the north-east. Kyellan was afraid Alaira would find it very boring.

The inn that took up one side of the central city square would be the most expensive in Atolan, but it would be warm and comfortable. It was a large three-story building with additions and extensions that rambled through a walled court-yard, with rooms built even over the stables. All the windows were tightly shuttered. The only sign of life was the smoke that rose from the many chimneys. Kyellan swung down from his horse, his boots crunching on the icy mud of the ground, and pushed open the arched gates of the inn's courtyard wall. There was no gatekeeper, and no stabler to take their horses. They would have to see to the animals themselves.

"If the innkeeper speaks Caer, I'll get us a room," Alaira said as she handed him her horse's reins. "And a meal." She hurried away from him up onto the inn's heavy wooden porch, turned a handle, and opened the door to go inside.

Kyellan watched the door shut behind her. He smiled and led the horses to the stables. Alaira had never been shy, or worried about propriety. No lady of the court, or even a merchant's wife, would think of going alone into the common room of an inn. To Alaira, as to Kyellan, taverns were more homelike than anywhere else. In Rahan Quarter, you were doing well if you could afford an upper room in a cheap inn.

The stables were warm and musty-smelling, with a low roof and twenty large stalls. Two shaggy, fat Garithian ponies nickered a welcome as Kyellan led his S'tari horses past them. He would have to find out about buying ponies, he remembered, to carry the supplies for the College on the trip back, a month from now.

Kyellan unloaded his horses, rubbed them down and fed them grain and straw from the innkeeper's stock. He hung their saddles and gear on hooks on the thick log walls and shut the horses into two of the central stalls. His and Alaira's packs were much lightened after their nine-day journey, and he slung one over his shoulder and carried the other under an arm to go into the inn.

The common room was half full of locals in furry jackets

and hide trousers, burly, pale, red-haired men, who turned to stare as Kyellan entered. The innkeeper was a skinny, balding man with a round face like a child's. He smiled and spoke in halting Caer. "You'd be the other traveler from the South? Your lady went on up to start a fire in your room. She asked me to have a meal sent there for you."

Kyellan frowned. Why would Alaira want to eat in their room? The common room would be warmer and more comfortable. Its rough tables and benches were clustered around a huge central fireplace where pots of stew hung over the flames, and mugs of ale were set on the hearth to be warmed. "We'll be staying a few weeks," he said in Garithian. "And we have two horses in the stables."

"I have a boy who can take care of them," said the innkeeper. "Or you can pay me for their feed and care for them yourselves, if you'd prefer. Your room is up the stairs, the fourth door to the left." He turned away to wait on his midday customers.

Kyellan found Alaira laying a fire in the hearth of a large, well-furnished room that boasted two stuffed chairs and an oaken bed with feather coverlets. She had taken off her mufflers and shawl, but she still wore her cloak. "Don't you want to go downstairs?" he asked, setting their packs beside the bed. "Give this room a chance to warm up?"

"I thought we could eat here," she said quietly as she sparked the tinder into flames. She did not look at him, but knelt there holding her hands out to the low fire. Her breath came short and shallow, sending out light puffs of white in the cold.

He shrugged. "At least it's out of the wind." His cloak and gloves were stiff and icy. He hung them on a hook over the mantle to thaw, and sat down on the bed to take off his frozen boots. Alaira still did not look in his direction. What was the matter with the girl? "Did something happen down there? Did someone bother you?" He had never known Alaira to be upset by an indecent remark.

She was quiet for a moment, then she whispered, "They were staring at me."

"They stared at me, too." He laughed. "They aren't used to seeing strangers this time of year."

Alaira shook her head. Her shoulder-length black hair fell across her face as she turned, and Kyellan was startled by the bitterness in her eyes. "It wasn't that. It was this." She touched the jagged scar that bisected her cheek. "I'd . . . I'd almost forgotten. No one at Akesh looked at me like that. Not Gwydion or Chela, not the Shape-Changer. You never have."

"Oh, damn," Kyellan muttered. He could not be angry with the men in the common room. Alaira had been an uncommonly beautiful woman, and she still moved like one, acted like one, when she was unself-conscious. It was startling to find any ugliness about her. It was unsettling. That was what made people stare, not that her face was anything horrible.

"I just have to get used to it again, that's all," she said. "I have to remember what to expect. I'd forgotten." Her voice was calmer. "Maybe tomorrow we can eat in the common room. But . . . but not right now."

Kyellan rose and went over to kiss her upturned face. "If it helps, I think you're beautiful."

She smiled a little. "It helps."

Riding at night and through the day, Briana and the others reached Tobas's ancestral palace at Laenar in the evening of the second day after their escape. The pastel city had had no word yet of what had happened in Cavernon; even if the gate guards knew that Arel was King, it was unlikely they would have turned their Earl away. A squadron of city militiamen now drilled in the orchards below the palace. Briana wondered how long they had before Arel sent troops after them.

She felt a buildup of Power from Cavernon City as the Temple prepared to confirm Ocasta as First Priestess. She knew what they were doing as surely as if she was there. The Second Rank priestesses had been fasting with Ocasta, and the novices and the younger women had been practicing the Great Dances in carefully segmented forms. There were not enough of them to create the most complex patterns, but when they brought what they had rehearsed together tomorrow, there would be enough Power to invoke the Goddess through the dance. Briana could not guess whether the ritual would succeed in making Ocasta First Priestess.

If the old First Priestess had been right, no woman could hold the position until she had borne a child for Cianya. That, Briana was certain, Ocasta had never done. Even the legendary Hailema the Unholy One, who had been forced on the Temple once, had been a noblewoman who had carried children. That had been part of the scandal that surrounded her. But it made her more suited to be First Priestess than Ocasta was.

She had to do something. She had to try to stop the ceremony, or if she could not, at least disrupt it. From her reading of the Temple histories, and from her knowledge of the wizards' techniques, Briana knew it was possible to travel out of her body. This was what she intended to do. She would challenge Ocasta's right to be First Priestess. Of all of them, Ocasta must know Briana was no false Candidate. She would remind her how much she was defying her precious traditions, let her know Briana would not be so easily pushed aside. The Power of their ritual would help her from this end. She could draw upon it. With luck she could frighten them, undermine their belief in Ocasta. More than that was in the Goddess's hands.

She came out of her meditation to find herself once again sitting cross-legged in the middle of a luxurious bedroom of Tobas's family palace. Someone was knocking at her door. "Yes," she called. "Who is it?"

The door opened, and Yalna came inside. The S'tari girl had lost none of her plumpness in all this journeying, from the valley to the canyon to Cavernon City and now to Laenar. Briana was lean and hard, but Yalna still rounded out her white robes with a figure her suitors found very lovely. "Briana?" Yalna had stopped calling her "my lady" sometime during their time at the valley, and Briana was glad of it. They were close in age, and it had always made her uncomfortable.

"What is it, Yalna?" She did not get up.

"Do you need anything else tonight? I've just been talking with the Earl, and he's asked me and Tapeth to do something for him tomorrow, so I want to get to bed early." There was pride in her tone.

"What are you going to do for Tobas?" Briana prompted.

Yalna sat down on the edge of the delicately carved bed, and her hands fidgeted a little at her sides. "Well, you know that the Earl wants to find a way to rescue the Queen, and the men who escaped with us are going to help him, so there's no one else to go. Tapeth and I are going to ride into the desert to warn the tribes to be prepared for war. We're to find Surleien and the Council of Elders, and tell them the Earl is still free and he's on their side." She hesitated. "It isn't that I want to leave you, but this is very important."

"I'll be sorry to see you go," Briana said. "But I'll be fine. It is vital that the S'tari priestesses also know what has happened. They need to know about Ocasta."

Yalna nodded. "And I want to go to the valley where Erlin and Pima are. They're safe enough, but they need to know."

"If there is a war, they may not be safe." Briana rose to her feet. Her exhausted muscles scarcely supported her after the endless ride. "The priestesses watching the valley will have to be prepared to move them if it becomes necessary. Deeper into the desert, away from the fighting. Tell them that, Yalna. Caerlin under Arel's rule will be no place for a wizard child."

"I wish you could go with us," the S'tari girl said quietly. "Could you? Since you aren't going to be First Priestess?"

Briana stared at her. She had not thought of that. She was not going to be First Priestess. With Ocasta as the head of the Temple, she was no longer a priestess at all. She was outcast. There was nothing holding her to the fight. She could give it up, go with Yalna, and be a true mother to her child.

Only if the Goddess had deserted her. Briana could not believe that. She had sworn her life to the Goddess's service. If She was still with her at all, She meant for Briana to be First Priestess someday. Briana shook her head at last. "I'll come to see you off in the morning."

They had been at Atolan three days when the ship arrived, a courier from Dallynd, just to the south. Kyellan and Alaira did not go with most of the townspeople to meet it at the docks. They were warm and comfortable at the inn and saw no reason to leave it. Alaira had once again become used to people's reactions to her scar, though she still did not want to spend much time in the common room. It was a pleasant time, with nothing to do but rest and enjoy each other's company.

Kyellan was in the stables when the inn's boy brought in the four Ryasan horses. They were huge battle chargers, great grey beasts with elaborate trappings in the colors of the Ryasan king's house. Kyellan stopped grooming his S'tari gelding to stare as the boy backed each horse into a stall. He had rarely seen such fine types of the breed. He had ridden such a horse before, a lesser animal, at the siege of Dallynd. What were they doing here? He hurried through the rest of his task and slung his cloak back on for the chill walk across the yard to the inn's porch.

The riders of the warhorses were sitting around a corner table in the common room as the innkeeper hurried to serve them a midday meal of stew and warm bread. Four big men, dressed in black, three brown-haired, one going grey. Alaira had come downstairs to meet Kyellan for dinner, and she sat in the shadows at the other side of the great hearth. A few Garithian laborers ate quietly near the door.

The oldest of the Ryasans turned to look as Kyellan entered bringing a swirl of cold air from outside. Kyellan stared at the man, recognizing him now. The last time he had seen him had been at the generals' council on Altimar before he left for Caerlin during the war. Haval, the sober city commander of Dallynd, who had seen his city go up in flames under the wizards' seige. What was he doing in a tavern in Garith? Kyellan unfastened his cloak and hung it on a rack beside the door, then he turned and grinned at the middle-aged soldier. "Well met, Haval."

"By the gods," Haval said, rising quickly from his chair. "Kyellan! The last man I'd have expected to see here." He came forward to clasp Kyellan's hand and pull him to the table. "I'd heard you were in Caerlin, training guardsmen and organizing the Queen's spies. It's just as well you weren't. Anyway, it's good to see you, lad."

"Alaira?" Kyellan beckoned her over to sit in the last vacant chair beside him. She moved reluctantly to the seat. "Alaira, this is General Haval, the Dallynd city commander.

I've told you about him before. We fought together in the war.''

"Hello," she said with a shy smile.

"My lady," Haval said gravely. "No longer city commander, my friend, since Dallynd is a dead city. King Janorwyn put me in charge of the King's Men, the royal soldiers. Currently we're based in his country palace, ten miles to the east of the old walls. But couriers still land in the bay, and His Majesty thought this news was important enough for me to bring it to the Garithian King personally. I came in on the ship.''

"What news?" Kyellan asked, not liking Haval's tone.

"As I said, it's just as well you're in Atolan. If you'd been in Cavernon City, you'd have been caught up in it." He lowered his voice. "No one here is supposed to know before King Marayn does. But, Arel has taken back his throne.''

"What?" Kyellan fought to keep his voice low. "I didn't think he had gathered enough of an army to attack yet. Do you mean he got through the rebuilt walls?''

Haval shook his head. "It was done by stealth. The King was smuggled into the palace by a noble supporter. There was little bloodshed, apparently. The message I bear announces that Princess Valahtia will soon marry Werlinen of Keris, so she must not have resisted too strongly. There is also an announcement that the new First Priestess will be confirmed on today's date. Some Caer woman named Ocasta. No doubt the King wants to be seen to support the Temple.''

"Ocasta? Who is she? What's happened to Briana?''

"That priestess who was with you at Dallynd?" Haval shook his head. "The statement I carry includes a list of traitors. Arel is requesting no Kingdom grants them asylum. Her name is on it, along with your friend the Earl of Laenar. You'd have been on it if you were there, Kyellan.''

"I hadn't heard anything," he said slowly. "I've been in the North.''

"With your young wizard friend?" Haval said in a quiet voice. "Yes, I knew he passed through Chelm, and they didn't have the sense there to distinguish between enemies and allies. Got their harbor gates blasted for their foolishness. Young Gwydion wasn't hurt, was he?''

"He's fine," Alaira said when Kyellan did not speak. "We've been with him and Chela at Akesh. We came down here to get food and other winter supplies for them. They haven't dared send any of their own people."

"That was wise," Haval said. "Don't remind Garith that the Wizards' College still exists. The King is being pressured already by the Council of Royalty to send troops to clear the place out." He looked narrowly at Kyellan. "If you'll take my advice, you'll do what you'd planned. Buy your supplies and go back to Akesh. Keep quiet. Don't let word get to Arel where you are, or he'll convince King Marayn to send troops after you. There is nothing you can do."

"I can't believe that," he said softly. How could this have happened? He had placed spies close to Arel in Syryn when he had been working for Valahtia. Either his spies had been eliminated, or Arel's decision had been made the moment before he acted.

"Don't try anything," Haval said. "You'll only get your-self killed. Go back to Akesh and live quietly with your lady there."

"Do you command the ship that docked here?" Kyellan asked. Alaira looked at him, alarmed. "Could it make it to Cavernon City?"

"You're mad," Haval said furiously. "You're too good a soldier to waste your life in some dungeon."

"Tobas, Valahtia, Briana, the men I trained . . . I can't leave them to the mercy of Arel."

"No," said the older man wearily. "I don't suppose you can."

"Can your ship make it to Cavernon City?"

"With the best possible weather, not inside a week."

"When can you leave?"

"Damn it, Kyellan . . ."

"When?"

Haval sighed heavily. "We'd have to take on more sup-plies and more men. My men here would have to deliver my message, and I suppose they'll have to guide a supply caravan to Akesh if your wizard and his people are going to live out the winter." He paused, considering. "We could leave tonight."

"Then you'll help me?"

"I owe you something for Dallynd," Haval said. "Yes, I'll help you, you young fool. Help you seek your death, if that's what you want. Get your things and get aboard the *Seabird*."

Chapter Eighteen ──────────

"GODDESS protect me, Goddess defend me," Briana chanted in the old tongue she had learned at the Sanctuary. She would not attempt this journey without the strong backing of ritual and prayer. She had done great feats of magic without it in the wars, but this was different. She meant to interrupt one of the most powerful rituals of the Temple. "Wiolai, Maiden, guard me, stand with me. Cianya, Mother, give me your strength. Rahshaiya, Death-Bringer, grant me the Power to defeat my enemies. Three-Fold Goddess, I call you to help me, your servant Briana. Help me, Wiolai, Cianya, Rahshaiya. Goddess protect me, Goddess defend me . . ."

She built a wall of white flame around the small space in the bedroom where she sat. No one would endanger her here, but it was foolish to leave your body undefended during such a spell. Tapeth had sent for the S'tari priestesses of Laenar to watch her during her attempt. There were four of them. They sat one in each corner of the room, old women in veils and enveloping robes. They spoke no words of disapproval, but Briana knew they feared for her. They felt she was angry and acting without thought to strike back at those who had hurt her. It was true, but Briana knew if she did not act now she might as well concede to Ocasta the First Priestesshood and everything else. If she did not do something, Ocasta would have won.

She closed her eyes and reached deep within herself to loosen her soul from the countless tendrils of thought that held it in a deep part of her mind. It hurt. She had known that it would. But the histories said it was possible. If anyone could do it, she could. She was even more powerful than she had been before her pregnancy and her child's birth. Now the steel strength of the Mother aspect of the Goddess was a part of her, providing wells of Power she had not known were possible.

A thick silver cord that pulsed with life uncoiled as she slowly withdrew from the deep place. She was within her soul now as it rose weightless through her skin until it was free of her body, hovering over the flames that fenced her silent, seated form. She had never felt so aware or so alert before. She was seeing with her Power now. Everything was transformed into brilliant colors. The four S'tari priestesses glowed with a steady, reassuring green light. Briana's own Power was colorless white, as if the Goddess she had called was wreathed around her in pure light.

She could sense the growing mass of distant force that was the ceremony confirming Ocasta as First Priestess. It required little effort to drift in its direction. She wondered if she would pass over the meadows between Laenar and Cavernon, but it seemed not. She was drawn upward into a vortex of darkness, a clear, cold, timeless place where the pull of the Temple ritual was even stronger. This was the spirit road she had read about, a place that was always there, not created by each new spell. It was possible to create your own road, where only your spirit could travel, but it was easier to use the road that was already there.

Her silver tail uncoiled behind her. Briana began to see the whirling pattern of the First Dance coalesce in the darkness before her uncanny eyes of the soul. She pulled her Power in tightly and formed her insubstantial shape into a likeness of herself, a young, grave-looking woman clad in a robe of pitch black, with auburn hair caught in the back with a simple silver net. She could hear the atonal chanting now, as the Third and Fourth Rank priestesses in the Temple courtyard

joined to raise the first wall of Power around the quickening
pace of the dancers.

She drew nearer and saw that the ritual was ragged around
the edges. Without the strengthening knowledge of the old
First Priestess, and without any discipline or artistry in the
dance, the Power was less than half what it would have been
in the Sanctuary before the wizards came. Yet it was strong.

Ocasta was still underground in the Temple of the Altar
with the heart-stone of Cavernon City, deep within her meditation to prepare for the effort of calling the Goddess. Briana
could sense the old woman's doubt and her determination to
see this through. She almost felt sorry for Ocasta. Briana
would remind her this was a delusion. Ocasta would have to
face the Goddess honestly and demand to be made First
Priestess, knowing the true Candidate was still alive. If she
could carry it through under those conditions, she was stronger
than Briana guessed. Or more resistant to the Goddess's will.

The binding of the First Dance was complete. The sphere
of Power extended from the center of the circle of priestesses
to enclose them and bind them together. It was also intended
to keep out any forces from the outside that might be attracted
by the use of Power. Briana saw the holes in the fabric, the
unbound edges, and with a sudden effort she moved forward
and pierced the sphere.

She was blocked by a force that could not have been
created by this half-performed ritual. A force of fierce white
light like her own, which sprang between her and the priestesses and drove her back toward the sphere wall. Briana
reeled and called up a strong defense, a shield as powerful as
those she had used in battle. She managed to slow her
backward motion, then to stop just against the wall. What
was it? The white flame belonged to the Goddess. Had she
been wrong all this time? Was the Goddess against her now?

The light before her seemed invisible to the priestesses
below. No one looked up. The chants did not falter. The
dancers moved into the low, tortuous postures of the Second
Cycle. Briana stared as the white flame swirled and coa-
lesced into a form like her own. A slim young woman in a
blinding white robe, with a serious expression and narrowed
eyes.

"Gemon?" she whispered. The word traveled before her in the thick, Power-laden air.

"Briana." The novice smiled slightly. "You show more spirit than I would have guessed you had anymore. But you don't belong here, powerful as you are. My sisters and I have enough strength to send you back by force. Don't make us do it."

"I am the true Candidate," Briana said. "Does even the Hidden Temple oppose the Goddess's will?" Gemon's form was a sending like her own. The Goddess's Seat was not below, and the other women of the Hidden Temple were not among the ritual celebrants.

"You may have been chosen once," Gemon said. "I believe that you were. But you have ruined your chance, Briana, by your own actions. You have disobeyed the laws of the Order you were meant to lead." She seemed to lean forward, and her voice was knife-sharp. "I know you bore a child, and I know whose child it was."

Unable to deny it, Briana whispered, "Gemon, you know very little. You are powerful, but still you are only a novice. You can't know why I did what I did."

"I know why," the girl said scornfully. "Because you were weak enough to fall in love with Kyellan. And even after you knew he was the Shape-Changer, you were blinded by your love. You proved yourself unfit for your position long before Ocasta felt the call of the Goddess to be First Priestess."

"I can't tell you my reasons." Gemon was not a Candidate for First Priestess. She could not learn of the ritual of birth to serve Cianya. "But the Goddess led me then, and She still leads me. You cannot understand."

"I understand that you are weak." Gemon sounded almost sympathetic. "You betrayed your calling, betrayed your vows. It is blasphemy for you to pretend you are still a priestess. Sacrilege for you to use the white flame. I will overlook that. Go back to your body, Briana. Put off your priestess robes. Renounce your Power. We will not seek you out. Go back to your wizard child, if you wish. But do not try to interfere any more in the business of the Order, or claim to be favored of the Goddess."

"But I am," Briana said furiously. "And Ocasta is not. If

she survives this night, you may call her First Priestess. She may have the appearance of Power, the veneer of wisdom. But the Goddess will not be with her. I am the true Voice of the Goddess on the earth. That cannot be denied.'' She was suddenly certain of her words. The white flame around her warmed her, and she felt a hint of presence within it. Quicksilver brightness, an enfolding calm, fierce, angry heat. Only a hint, but it was enough.

Gemon surely had the Power to feel it too. Or perhaps the magnitude of the Seat's force blinded her to the gentle presence around Briana. She did not react as if she sensed the Goddess's Chosen before her. She lashed out with fury and malice, a hammerblow of pure, focused Power. It smashed Briana out of the protective sphere of the priestesses' ritual wall and sent her senseless, blinded, deafened, numb, into the clear cold of the spirit road.

Another bodiless spirit wandered into that dark place, drawn by the immense Power expended there, hoping to find its source and tap it for his own purposes. The Shape-Changer was not willing to accept his defeat. He had brooded for a long time in the timeless Otherworld, listening in on the demons' conferences, watching ribbon predators grow more and more bold in snatching small demons from within the city itself. At last he had made them an offer. He had built them a shield of his own Power, a network of golden flames that arched over their council city and repelled the color beings every time they approached.

In gratitude, they had helped him in his efforts to return to his world and his body. He was incredibly strong, incredibly powerful still. With their help he had made a door, and gone through it, to find himself trapped again. This time he was trapped on the spirit road. The dark limbo of loosed souls, the highway of wizards' travel. He had expended much of his Power in getting there, and he had no way to leave. He could not even return to the Otherworld.

The priestesses' ritual had been so ill-defended and badly closed that he had hoped to use some of its unfocused, excess force. He was not entirely sure what he meant to do with it. Kill some unsuspecting human, he supposed, and take the man's body. The thought did not please him. He did not want just any form. He wanted his own, the body Kyellan had so rudely appropriated.

He had been approaching the ritual sphere when he felt the shock that flung Briana out of it. The sphere was strengthened and completed by the force of the Goddess's Seat. It blocked the ragged places in the ritual where Briana had gotten through, leaving him no access either. A half-formed plan struck him, and he drew nearer to the place. The battered spirit of the Priestess Briana floated senseless from the attack. The white flame around her burned only dimly, and her silver soul-line was pale and thin. The Shape-Changer thought of severing her soul-line and taking her body for himself, but he could tell the body was guarded. It would mean a struggle, and he was already weary.

He hovered over her thoughtfully. There must be some way he could use her. Help her back to her body, win her gratitude, convince her to plead with Kyellan to call him back? There was no surety in the idea. Back in her body, the priestess would have no obligation to help him. Better to get Kyellan to call him back first, offering to help save Briana if he did so. He knew how strongly the young soldier felt for this injured priestess.

The Shape-Changer moved quickly, leaving behind the powerful ritual sphere and the high chanting of the priestesses as they called down their Goddess. He would go to Akesh, find Kyellan, use up most of his remaining Power to produce a sending to speak with Kyellan through the barrier of the spirit road. Surely Kyellan would agree to take him back. For Briana's sake, he would agree to do anything.

Gwydion was exhausted from his second futile attempt to destroy the lake monsters. They did not respond to any of the usual forms of control. He had tried the methods he used against the sea monster of Keor, but the beasts either were not summonings from the Otherworld, or someone was still controlling them. He had failed, and two of his most promising apprentices had died in the attempt. The monsters had taken them when they ventured too close, trying to touch the creatures physically with Power-laden staffs.

He was in no mood for hallucinations. He lay on his bed, under the canopy, as Chela prepared an herbal drink to put him to sleep, and the hangings over the bed seemed to form themselves into the features of the Shape-Changer. Gwydion blinked and tried to focus his bleary vision, but the hallucination remained. It even grew clearer. "Chela," he muttered. "Take a look up there. Does that look like the Shape-Changer to you?"

"Good . . ." a disembodied voice said from the image's lips. "It appears you had to say my name for me to speak. There must be rules that govern this sort of thing."

"Names of Power," Chela said, whirling around to stare with Gwydion at the speaking image. "It is him."

"Where is Kyellan?" the Shape-Changer asked. Each word was carefully formed, distinctly pronounced, and seemed to cost the face an immense effort.

"How did you manage this from the Otherworld?" Gwydion said, impressed. "That would take more Power than I could muster."

"I'm no longer in the Otherworld, where you left me to rot," the Shape-Changer said venomously. "I'm on the spirit road, as if I was traveling out-of-body. Where is Kyellan? I have to talk to him. I can't find him; he doesn't have any Power for me to see from here. Tell me where he is."

"What do you want from him?" Chela asked quietly, coming to sit on the bed beside Gwydion. She had not joined in the attempt on the monster. They had decided it would be foolish to risk both their lives.

"His beloved Briana is in danger," the Shape-Changer said after a moment. "Tell him that. I can help her, if he'll agree to have me back. She'll probably die without help. Tell him that."

Chela looked at Gwydion in concern, then back at the illusionary face. "He isn't here. We can't tell him anything. What happened to Briana?"

"Where is he?" the image demanded.

"He and Alaira had to leave here when a priestess of the Hidden Temple found us," Gwydion said weakly.

"He's with Alaira? Then I should be able to find him. She has a little Power, and I know her better than I know many people. I'll find them. You'll regret not helping me more," he said, and vanished.

Chela and Gwydion stared at the place where he had been for a moment. Chela shivered. "I don't trust him. If Briana is in danger, he's unlikely to help her no matter what Kyellan wants."

Gwydion tried to clear his fuzzy mind from the backlash that was rolling over him like a thundercloud. "He . . . said he could help her, and I think I believe he could. Whether he will or not. How can he help her from the spirit road? He can scarcely project a voice and features."

"Unless she's there too. On the spirit road, and hurt." Chela's voice was fierce. "I'll go, Gwydion. I'll find her if she's there."

He wanted to protest that it was too dangerous, that she might be hurt, but he said nothing. Chela was no longer his apprentice, and being her lover did not give him the right to command her. "Be careful," he whispered before the blackness overtook him.

There was a heavy rain off the coast of Ryasa as the *Seabird* made quick time toward the South. The courier ship was built to withstand rough seas since it was a Dallyndi vessel. It carried oars as well as sail, so it did not depend on the wind. Once Haval had decided to help Kyellan, he had been determined to get him to Cavernon City as quickly as possible.

It was not enough of a storm to endanger the ship, but it was enough to keep the two passengers off the deck. Haval had loaned them his cabin, the only one aboard, offering to bunk with his crew belowdecks. The *Seabird* was a much smaller ship than the *Jester* had been. The master's cabin was set under the slightly raised foredeck. Kyellan could hear the sounds of hurried footsteps above him as sailors adjusted bow lines and took readings with their instruments. The rain was cold, just short of being sleet, and the cloaks he and Alaira had worn earlier were hung above the smoking brazier in the corner of the cabin to dry.

If it had not been for the news from Caerlin, it would be a

pleasant journey, Kyellan thought. He and Alaira sat on the single bunk, watching the flames of the brazier, warmed by the easy camaraderie they had fallen into since the trip to Atolan. They could have been happy at Akesh, hunting and trapping for the students' food, making the journey south on occasion to bring back supplies, enjoying Gwydion and Chela's company. Kyellan was furious with Valahtia for losing her throne to subterfuge. He thought he had set up a better spy network than that. Tobas and Briana were apparently free, but Briana had lost her position, too, and Kyellan could not imagine how that could have happened.

"Look," Alaira said sleepily, leaning against him with one arm around his waist. "There are pictures in the flames."

A disembodied, flickering face, turning the fire to gold along the edges, with yellow eyes of dancing sparks. Kyellan stared. He knew the features. He had seen them in the mirror for the two months he had been trapped. "The Shape-Changer," he muttered.

"Kyellan," said the image in the flames, "I thought I'd find you with Alaira. I don't have the Power to speak long. Call me back into my body."

"Do you think I'm mad?" Kyellan shuddered. "I'll never do that."

"Look." The face dissolved and vanished, and was replaced by a dark scene of a woman lying crumpled on the floor of a bedroom. Thick auburn hair spread out from her upturned face, and her green eyes were open but lifeless.

"Briana," Kyellan said, leaning forward in fear. The picture disappeared, and the Shape-Changer's face came back to waver in the fire.

He told them what Briana had attempted and how she had failed. "Let me back into my body," he said. "Without my help, she may die." He provided a picture of the faintly glowing soul of the priestess, drifting aimlessly in a void of black with a pale silver cord trailing after her like a raveling thread.

Kyellan was not too frightened for Briana to think clearly. "Help her first. Then we'll talk about me calling you back. Help her from where you are. You don't need me to do that."

"Her soul-line is still intact," Alaira said quietly. "With that she can never be lost. I learned that much at Akesh."

"I will do it," the Shape-Changer said in a fading voice. "The priestess will tell you how I helped her, and you will call me back. You will find her in Laenar, in the palace of the Earl, and there I will come to you again."

Alaira leaped forward to throw one of the cloaks over the brazier. The fire was smothered, though the wet wool smoked for a moment. She whirled to face Kyellan, her legs braced against the roll of the ship. "You can't do this. You can't call him back, no matter what the reason."

"I haven't promised him anything."

"No, not in so many words. You know your honor will bind you if you let him save Briana. Say his name again! He'll hear you. Tell him he can help the priestess if he likes, but it will make no difference. You'll never take him back."

"There's a chance he can help her," he muttered. "I can't let her die."

"She can find her own way back." Alaira's voice broke. "Ky, do you still love her that much? Enough to throw your life away for her? She left you! She said she never wanted to see you again. Forget her. She isn't worth this. Nothing is worth this."

"I can't let her die," he repeated, meeting Alaira's fierce gaze.

Her breath caught in a half sob, and she sat down hard on the bunk beside him, staring ahead at the sooty wall of the small cabin. "You love her. Still, even after . . . after I called you back. . . ." Then her voice was steady and clear with fury. "I'm such a fool. I always have been, when it comes to you. You aren't worth it, Ky. He told me that. The Shape-Changer did. He said you weren't ever going to change. I should . . . should have known. . . ." She began to cry, sitting upright on the bed. Tears of anger and old frustration.

Kyellan watched her helplessly. "I always hurt you, don't I? I never mean to, Alaira." He rose from the bunk and lifted the cloak off the smothered fire, then turned back to her with sudden resolve. "Yes, I love Briana. That isn't going to change. But I . . . I love you too. I always have. I just never admitted it to myself. Alaira, please, I can't stand to see you hate me." He knelt down in front of her and took her hands between his.

"You love me?" she echoed, crying even harder.

"I think so. And no matter what I still feel for Briana, I know I can never have her. I was hoping at least I had you."

"At least!" She laughed harshly through her tears, but her hands gripped his tightly. "So I'll always be second to a cold and heartless little priestess . . . but you love me. I never had that much before." She tried to smile. "I guess it's more than I have any right to expect. Will you still go to your priestess to see if the Shape-Changer helps her?"

"I have to, Alaira," he said quietly.

"Then I'll go with you. I'll make sure you don't let him back into your body. I don't care about honor, Ky. I won't lose you again."

Briana regained consciousness very slowly. She drifted in a haze of pain, aware of the blasted state of her mental defenses, frightened that her enemies might attack her again. Her whole being throbbed with the shock of what had happened. She had never felt so helpless, so defeated. Even when she had been a captive of the wizard Belaric, she had still been strong. She had known then that she was the chosen one of the Goddess. Now she was no longer certain.

She drifted. When she felt the approach of another Power, a green entity that blazed with light that hurt, she lashed out with her remaining strength to ward it away. The half-familiar being checked its movement toward her and did not attack. Briana tried to curl herself up in a protective ball. The green Power did not go away. After a while she began to waken more fully. Something was giving her strength, only a little, but enough to enable her to feel the insistent tug from her soul-line. It was time to return to her waiting body.

She did not know how long she had been there. It seemed quiet, as if the confirmation ritual was over. Briana had been unable to prevent it, or interfere at all. Gemon had brought the Power of the Seat to guard Ocasta's confirmation. The Hidden Temple had shown itself to be Briana's enemy. Even Gemon, who had been a student in her dance classes at the Sanctuary. With the Power of the completed ritual and the strength of the Goddess's Seat ranged against her, how could Briana think to challenge Ocasta again?

She could not, she told herself. She had to concede defeat. She must have deluded herself all along to think the Goddess was with her. Utterly weary, Briana allowed herself to drift slowly along her soul-line. It tugged her back toward its anchorage in the palace in Laenar. The dark void seeped cold inside her through the holes in her defenses. Bits of Power fell behind her, a glimmering trail of her passage. She did not have the strength to hold herself together.

The green entity, which still seemed somehow familiar, would not leave her. It paced her, just out of reach, and once when Briana faltered she felt it give her a gentle push forward. At last she broke through the walls of the spirit road into the lamp-lit brightness of the Laenar bedroom. Briana hovered for a moment, exhausted. Her body lay as if in death, its limbs straightened, prone on the floor. The protective circle of white flame had vanished. She must have been gone a long time. The four S'tari women had left their corners, and sat wearily in chairs near her body. She could feel their resignation, their conviction that they watched over a corpse that would never waken.

Briana plummeted back into the chill of her stiffened body and wondered if she could revive it. The fire of her Power was almost out. She had no warmth to give her cold limbs. She searched through her body for any sign of life. She did not seem to be breathing, yet a slow, sluggish flow of blood still inched through her veins. There . . . a convulsive jerk of her heart, like a seizure, followed by stillness. She was alive, though her heart only beat once in ten minutes and her lungs were flat.

Her heart convulsed again, and she concentrated on speeding up its sluggish beat. A rattling sound came from her throat as she forced a breath into her deflated lungs. She heard a rustling as one of the S'tari women leaned forward. Briana guessed that the complete process would take a long time. She had been more than a day getting back, she judged. It would take three or four more before she was recovered enough to take any action. But she was not sure she wanted to do anything except seek out her child to protect him from

Gemon's seeking. If the Goddess wanted Ocasta as First Priestess, She could have her and welcome.

"She has returned," a low voice said. "Bring her over near the fire, and I'll get some blankets."

"Va'shindi preserve us from the priestesses and their strange ways," whispered a second voice. Briana thought that the woman had probably said the phrase before. It sounded like a litany. "I have never heard of such a thing before, a woman leaving her body to die soulless and empty. I hope I never see such a thing again."

"Va'shindi grant your wish," said the other woman impatiently. "Now we must get her warm, or she may die yet."

The dangerous sea channel that connected the great ocean to the Tarnsea between Parahn and Caerlin was known as the Claws, for the fingers of land that reached out for one another and interlocked against ships' passing. Few oceangoing vessels could negotiate the Claws. The *Seabird* was a small ship, and its oars provided maneuverability at very slow speeds, which was necessary to get through some of the tighter sections. The morning of the seventh day after they left Atolan, Kyellan and Alaira came out on deck to find the ship docked at anchor outside the harbor of Laenar. Haval was lowering the single ship's boat.

The Ryasan soldier looked up and saw them. "Get your things!" he called. "We'll row you ashore."

When they returned with their packs, Haval stood back. They climbed over the railing and down the ladder into the boat. Two of the Dallyndi sailors manned the oars. Kyellan saw Alaira safely seated, and already looking slightly ill, then glanced back up toward Haval. "Thanks again," he said inadequately.

"If you find there is nothing you can do, there will be a place for you in Dallynd." Haval unwound the boat's lines and tossed them into its bow. "The people are grateful to you for what you did to try to save it. When the city is rebuilt, they'll probably give you my old job." He paused. "Don't waste yourself if it's hopeless, Kyellan. Get out of Caerlin, and bring your lady here with you."

"It's a noble offer," Kyellan said with a troubled smile.

"But I hope I won't have to take it, Haval. Caerlin is my home."

"Not with Arel its King."

The boat floated away from the side of the ship. Kyellan sat down beside Alaira and turned his gaze toward the pastel city of Laenar.

Chapter Nineteen ━━━━━━━━

THE leader of the dock guards, a stocky old city militiaman, remembered Kyellan as his young Earl's old commander. "Aye, sir," he said. "Our lord is in his palace, but
he won't be much longer. The King knows he's there. He'll
be leaving tomorrow, and I don't know where he'll go."

"What about the Priestess Briana?" Kyellan asked, walking with the soldier toward the street where the pier began.
Alaira came behind them, and the boat that had rowed them
ashore was already headed back out toward the distant *Seabird*.
"Is she there too?"

"That I haven't heard, sir." The militiaman left them on
the street. "Can you find your own way from here? I have
my duty."

"Of course," Kyellan said quietly. "Come, Alaira. The
palace is that cluster of pink and grey buildings on the top of
the hill. Just a few miles."

They walked unnoticed through the streets of Laenar, a tall
young man with a soldier's stride and a graceful woman with
a scarred face. The city was too busy with its own unsettled
affairs to worry about strangers. And here, Kyellan realized,
they did not look like strangers. Everyone in Laenar had
black hair, brown eyes, olive skin or darker. Their wool
clothing was overwarm and shabby for city streets, but that
only made them less noticeable. Kyellan's rapier curving at

his right side was a weapon like every other man's. It was good Parahnese steel, but now he needed a right-handed blade again. Perhaps later he would have time to find a weapons shop.

Briana might not even be here. The Shape-Changer might have lied. Or she could well be dead. Her desperate attack on the Temple of Cavernon could have killed her. What if she was alive, but refused to see him? She had said long ago that it would be best if they never met again.

"Don't walk so fast," Alaira panted at his side. "I'm still trying to recover from seasickness, or had you forgotten?"

"Sorry." He tried to slow his pace as they climbed the steep, winding streets toward the palace. Houses in Laenar were invariably low, flat-roofed, no more than three stories, and painted light shades of pink and gold and green. It was a pretty place, and kept cleaner than most of the Kingdoms' cities. Kyellan preferred the noise and crowds of Cavernon City, though. As a young officer, when he had visited Laenar with Tobas, he had found it so peaceful it was boring.

The palace was not a fortress. Its twisted iron walls were decorative, not defensible. But it commanded a good view of the orchards and meadows and farmland of the fertile Laenar countryside. At least the Earls of Tobas's line could see their enemies coming. The morning sun was strong, even at midwinter. Kyellan was hot and sweaty by the time he and Alaira reached the gates.

S'tari warriors stood before them past the bars, scowling in the fierce way the S'tari seemed to learn as infants. "What's your business?" one of them demanded.

Kyellan recognized neither man. "We're good friends of the Earl, and we've come a long way. He'll want to see us immediately. My name is Kyellan, and this is Alaira."

"No one passes here without the Earl's approval. We've had no word of you," said the warrior who had spoken before.

"Take him our names."

The two young men looked at each other. If one of them left, it would mean only one remained to guard the gate. "Your sword first," the guard said at last. Kyellan handed it through the bars. The man trotted toward the sprawling main house with the sword in one hand. He was scarcely inside before he came out again, and shouted that it was all right, the Earl would see them.

Tobas met them at the front door of his parents' home. It was his now, Kyellan remembered, since his father had died, and his older brother. "I never thought you'd come back!" the Earl of Laenar shouted, grinning like a boy. He gripped Kyellan's wrists, then drew him into a fierce hug. "And your arm! You've gotten it healed. I guess you found what you were searching for after all."

"I came as soon as I heard the news," Kyellan said, not as cheerful as his younger friend. "How many escaped? And how in the nine hells did Arel do it, with spies reporting his every thought?"

"Valahtia sent Lord Foerad, the chamberlain, to Syryn with a message for Arel. It was apparently Foerad's idea that Arel come back in disguise with him. They acted on it the moment the chamberlain thought of it. We had no time to get a report. But my people are still with Arel, in Cavernon now, and we think they can help get us in to rescue Valahtia." Tobas took Alaira's arm with absentminded courtesy and led them into a front room where a varied group of S'tari guardsmen, city militiamen, and others Kyellan could not identify sat around a large table. A map of the Tiranon was spread out before them. "We leave tomorrow to attempt it. Will you go with us, Ky?"

He shrugged. "If you think you have a chance."

"The message Haval carried made it sound like Valahtia agreed to marry Werlinen freely," Alaira said. "I couldn't believe that."

"My spies tell me Arel is keeping her secluded," Tobas said, his face tight with frustration. "It's almost time for our baby to be born. I want her back before that happens. She can't have agreed to marry that Kerisian fool. She can't have. Arel must be lying."

"Tobas." Kyellan drew him aside into a corner of the room and asked in a low voice, "Is Briana here?" He was conscious of Alaira watching him, her face still and unreadable.

"How did you know that?" Tobas stared up at him. "No

one knows that. We couldn't risk any of the Temple hearing of it.''

"Never mind how I knew. Where is she? Is she all right?''

"She's been sick,'' Tobas whispered. "Some S'tari women are watching her. But they say she's better today. I want her to go with us tomorrow, but I don't know if she'll be able to. She's in the back bedroom on the second floor, where my older brother used to live. Do you remember where that is?''

"I can find it. I'll be back soon to hear your plans.''

Alaira met him at the doorway. "She's here, isn't she? And she's all right. What if the Shape-Changer brought her back? You aren't going to call him, Kyellan. Promise me you aren't.''

"I don't even know if he helped her.'' He looked down into her frightened eyes. "And I don't know what I'll do if he did. But I have to talk to her. If she'll see me at all.''

"I'll be waiting down here,'' she said dully.

"I'll be back.'' He leaned down to kiss her, to reassure himself as much as Alaira. He would not throw away what they had between them. Not for Briana, not for the Shape-Changer. He had almost convinced himself of that.

The back bedroom on the second floor. Kyellan had never known Tobas's brother Aven well. The old Earl's heir had been a typical young noble, looking down on soldiers in general and lowborn ones in particular. He and Kyellan had avoided each other when Tobas had brought his captain home with him. So Kyellan had rarely been in this part of the huge house, but he knew the way.

The wizards who had occupied the palace had left the ornate furnishings intact, no doubt enjoying them after the rustic towers of Akesh. Kyellan walked up carpeted stairs to a long corridor hung with tapestries and lined with arched windows that let in the morning sun. A veiled S'tari woman sat on a chair outside the last door of the hall. She was little and old, and looked up at him with bright, sharp eyes.

"Please tell your lady Kyellan would like to see her,'' he said.

"My lady sees no one,'' the old woman said in S'tari, glancing away from him indifferently.

"I've come a long way," he said. "Please tell her I'm here."

"My lady may be asleep. I would not like to disturb her. She needs her rest, poor thing."

"Tell her," he said very quietly.

Briana sat very still in the dark, upright on the soft noble's bed. Her Power had not yet fully healed, but it did not take much Power for her to sense Kyellan's presence. He had no shields to block her. There was no trace of wizard Power or the elaborate defenses in which he had bound the Shape-Changer. All that part of him had vanished completely. She could not imagine how. Kyellan was a part of the Shape-Changer, not the other way around. How could he be a separate being?

Her mind ranged on that question, whirling around the central realization that leaped within her. He had come. He had heard what had happened to her, and he had come. He could not still love her, she thought, not after what she had done to him. She could not imagine that he would solve her problems for her, offer her a new life to replace the one she had lost. Then why was he here? She did not want to face him. She could not face him. He must hate her.

"My lady?" Wiera's voice, giving in to Kyellan's persistence. "There is a man here who wants to see you. I will send him away."

"No," Briana said almost inaudibly.

"Briana?" Kyellan spoke loudly from the corridor. Whatever reason he had for coming, she owed him more than a brusque refusal.

"Send him in, Wiera," she said, raising her voice. Her hand went to her tangled hair, and she almost laughed. No doubt she looked terrible, pale and sickly and uncombed. It did not matter. The windows in the room were shuttered, and it was dark. She was supposed to still be asleep.

The door opened, and he walked inside hesitantly. He was as nervous as she was. Wiera peered in. "Shall I open the shutters, my lady?"

"Yes, please do," Briana said faintly. The old woman passed between them and thrust the hinged shutters back.

Morning sun lit the bedroom. Wiera looked suspiciously at Kyellan and went back into the corridor, closing the door.

He was dressed in dark, sea-stained woolen clothes, and he was unshaven. His brown eyes were no longer gold-flecked. They met hers briefly and looked down in confusion. Briana caught her breath at the rush of emotion she felt. She had forgotten how strong it was, this feeling, even when she had spoken of it to Yalna, even when she had said yes, she loved him still.

"Tobas said you were getting better," he said after a moment. "He thinks you were sick."

"I am getting better," she said weakly. "How . . . how did you find me? Even the new First Priestess hasn't been able to track me here."

"It was a sending," he said. "From the spirit road."

Briana looked down to keep from staring at him. "Did I call you? I don't remember it." She would not be surprised if she had. She had never needed him so much before.

"It was the Shape-Changer. He saw you there and promised to help you if I'd agree to take him back."

"Something helped me," she remembered. "But I don't think it was the Shape-Changer. It was green, and gentle."

"Chela, maybe," he said, surprised. "Then I don't have to worry about calling him back. I'm not sure I would have done it in any case."

"Then that's why you're here," she said, somehow relieved. "To see if the Shape-Changer helped me return to my body when I was hurt."

"I wanted to see if you were all right," he said. "I was afraid you'd be dead. And I wanted to know why you weren't First Priestess, after all we went through to get you there. And I wanted to see you again, Briana." He stepped forward to sit on the edge of her bed. "Why would you never see me in the Tiranon?"

"Because it was wiser not to," she said softly. "Because you could have convinced me to give it all up and go with you, if I'd been weak enough to listen. It seems silly now." Briana blinked away sudden tears and let her eyes raise to meet his again. "I'm not the First Priestess. The Goddess chose Ocasta. Maybe that's what She intended all along."

He looked troubled. "I can't believe that. When I fought with you in that last battle, you were so full of the Goddess's Power I could hardly look at you. You're supposed to be First Priestess." He paused. "Was it the child? Did someone find out about the child?"

"The Hidden Temple knows he exists," she said softly. "But I don't think they've told anyone else. No, it wasn't the child. He is safe. Our child . . . his name is Cian, for the Goddess. Erlin and Pima are caring for him, in a secret valley by the Tarnsea."

A memory jolted him. "I know. I'd forgotten I knew. When I was the Shape-Changer's prisoner . . . he traveled on the spirit road to find the baby. He found him in a stream, and you were there, too, I think. It was the last day before I regained control. He went to Barelin and asked the wizards there to find the child and bring him to Akesh." He got up from the bed. "Briana, if he's there still, you'd better move him. Those wizards will be looking for him."

"So that was the Shape-Changer." She shivered, remembering the way Cian had slipped from her hands in the cold water. "It should be all right, Kyellan. The valley is well guarded. Yalna has gone there to warn them about Arel and Ocasta. They'll be all right."

"It might be best for the baby to go to Akesh anyway," he said thoughtfully. "With Gwydion its Master, the College of Wizards could train him well. When this is over, maybe I'll go to that valley and guide them all north. It's the safest place I know."

"When this is over." She clasped her hands around her knees on the bed. "What are you going to do now?" She wanted to plead with him to let her go with him, whatever it was, but something stopped her. Despite his warmth and his concern, she sensed a reserve about him. Maybe she should expect it, after what she had done.

"Go with Tobas to Cavernon City, and try to rescue the Queen," he said. "Tobas wants you along. Your Power should be helpful in getting us into the palace."

"They're looking for me everywhere. I might as well be in Cavernon." She smiled. "I'll go. Maybe on the way you can tell me everything that happened in Akesh. What happened with the Shape-Changer, and how did Gwydion become Master of the College? And how did Alaira like it?''

His expression changed, tightened a little. "You can ask her. She's waiting downstairs for me, afraid I'm not coming back." His dark eyes were helpless. "Briana, I thought you'd always be a priestess. I never thought . . . there would be any chance for us."

"And you love Alaira," she said slowly, "and you can't hurt her again. You don't have any shields anymore, Ky. That was easy to read."

"I'm sorry."

"Don't be. I'm glad for you both." The intense disappointment she felt made Briana think. Had she been lying here all this time believing Kyellan would save her? Was that why she had given up so easily? She thought so. Somewhere deep inside her, she had expected him to be unchanged, to want her as strongly as he ever had. His decision was made. That forced her own. "You're right," she said. "I'll always be a priestess. And I should be First Priestess. The Goddess must be testing me. . . . I'll go to Cavernon with you and Tobas, and I'll do what I can to help you find the Queen. But after that . . ." She smiled, surprised at her sudden resolve. "After that I visit Ocasta. She won't be First Priestess for long."

"You're recovering," he said wryly.

"Tell Tobas I'll be down this afternoon to join his council."

Kyellan bent over to kiss her lightly on the lips. "Your Goddess knows I love you." He rose again and walked from the room.

She had gotten over this loss long ago, Briana told herself. Surely the Goddess's hand was in this. Kyellan was committed to Alaira. That left Briana no choice but to fight for what was hers. The Power and responsibility of the First Priestess.

Kyellan could see in Alaira's eyes that she had convinced herself she had lost him. Either to Briana or to the Shape-Changer. The S'tari and the city militiamen were having a heated argument over how far Tobas's spies could be trusted, and Tobas himself leaned over the diagram at the table, ignoring them. Alaira stood alone in a corner of the room, her thin shoulders slumped in defeat. She looked at him as if she was steeling herself against what he might say.

"Briana will be coming with us to Cavernon," he said, joining her. "To challenge the false First Priestess. The Shape-Changer never helped her. We think perhaps Chela may have."

Alaira whispered, "Did you learn what you came for? Does she still love you?"

"She loves her Goddess more." He had done the right thing, Kyellan thought. So why did it make him so unhappy? Briana would have gone with him if he had asked. He had realized that at the beginning of their conversation. She had lost confidence in her abilities, in her calling. But she would be as miserable without her rituals and her Order as Gwydion had been without his Power. Their love would not last long under the weight of her frustration and defeat. He had done the right thing. At least Alaira would come out of it unhurt.

"She'll stay a priestess, then." Alaira looked rueful. "But that didn't stop you before."

"Do I have to keep proving it to you?" he whispered. "Things have changed. I've changed."

"I wonder." She was still angry. He supposed he could not blame her.

"Kyellan." Tobas saw him at last. "Come here and look at this, will you?"

With Alaira at his side, Kyellan leaned over the heavily overdrawn map. There had apparently been many plans to rescue the Queen. The main problem, as he saw it, was that they could not guess where Valahtia would be kept. Tobas's spies had not been able to find out. Some of the diagrammed lines led to the dungeons, some to the royal suite, others to various towers of the Tiranon. "Briana can find that out for you," he said quietly. "It should be a small matter for her to find Valahtia, with her Power."

"Then she'll come with us?" Tobas grinned. "We can't fail now. Gentlemen!" He raised his voice and got the attention of the arguing soldiers. "I've just learned we're going to have help in this from a very powerful friend. Briana, the woman who was to be First Priestess under my Queen's rule."

"Call her the true First Priestess," Kyellan said. "That's what she intends to call herself. She'll be challenging Ocasta."

The young Earl winced. "She challenged her before, and barely survived. But that's her decision. Very well. With the First Priestess herself helping our enterprise, we must surely succeed," he concluded grandly.

"Religion?" muttered an older city man. "That's all we need. I say we send assassins after Arel! It should have been done while he was in exile, and it can still be done. With him dead, the Queen has the throne again. By legal inheritance."

"That may be possible later," Tobas said intently. "Right now we have to get Valahtia out of there. There is no time to seriously confront Arel. Once the Queen has her baby, they'll marry her to Prince Werlinen of Keris. I don't want to have to kill him too."

"Has Werlinen gone to Cavernon yet?" Kyellan asked.

"I've heard no word of it. He hosted the Council of Royalty where they declared Arel King in exile, and he was one of Arel's strongest supporters, naturally. He'll want the wedding to be soon. He's still calling himself Crown Prince, though his father is dead. In Keris an unmarried man can't succeed to the throne. He needs Valahtia." Tobas tried to control the frustration in his voice, but Kyellan had never seen him so nervous before.

To change the subject, Kyellan asked, "I know you have a plan for the palace. But how do we get into the city?" Access to Cavernon was likely to be tightly restricted, and S'tari especially would be immediately suspected.

"We'll be mercenaries, ready to join the new King's forces. One of the bands of brigand S'tari, throwing our lots in with the stronger side in preference to attacking caravans on the western edges of the desert." Tobas almost smiled. "No one's likely to look very closely at our faces. Arel still doesn't have a large enough army to defend himself against a concentrated attack, and he must think I'm organizing forces to besiege him. Laenar won't recognize his rule, and neither will Erinon, since he killed the Earl's son when he took power. The new S'tari Kingdom has been silent."

"So Arel thinks you're commanding them all?"

Tobas shrugged. "If I were he, that's what I'd think. Anyway, he'll be glad to buy more men."

"Seven of us escaped with the Earl," said one of the S'tari men. "With five of the Laenar men, you, and the Earl himself, we'll be enough. Some S'tari women from Laenar have offered to go with us. Then there will be your lady, and the priestess. The women are important, if we're to seem like a renegade tribe."

"What do you think, Captain?" a city man asked.

Kyellan shook his head. "It could work. Arel doesn't trust the S'tari, but he's unlikely to do his own hiring. If we accept an offer of low wages, we should get in. They might even billet us in the Tiranon itself." It seemed a long time since he had done anything like this. He felt a hint of his old excitement at the prospect of a fight. "I'm with you, Tobas, if you can find me a good right-handed sword."

Alaira lay awake that night long after Kyellan slept in the huge bed they shared. Tobas had given them the guest suite of the palace. It was beautiful, almost uncomfortably luxurious, heaven after the cramped cabin on the *Seabird*. She wished she could relax and enjoy it properly. She watched the moon shadows of tree branches wavering on the walls, marring a muted tapestry of grey and white that had been brilliantly colored in daylight.

Kyellan had made love to her fiercely, insistently, as if to prove everything was as he had said. The priestess was still a priestess, and had given up her love for her religion. He had made his choice, and he had chosen Alaira. She had no cause for worry. He had said he loved her. He would show her he loved her. Alaira smiled wanly as she watched the shadows. He forgot how well she knew him.

He was still miserable with love for Briana. He hid it better now than he had at the Tiranon, where the priestess's refusal even to reply to his messages had made him bitter and angry. But nothing had really changed. Alaira knew she was still second in his heart. She would never be first. It was not enough to know he would probably never leave her again. As long as the priestess stayed a priestess.

Alaira looked over at the sleeping form of Kyellan. He was

turned on his side, his broad back to her, his black hair curling to hide his face. He was all she wanted, but she could only have a part of him. She did not think she could ever make him forget Briana; yet she still could not leave him.

They rode out in the morning. The people of Laenar all knew they were leaving, and many of them climbed the hill to stand on either side of the palace road and shout support of their Earl as he clattered past. Tobas was one of a band of dangerous-looking S'tari brigands, heavily armed, unwashed, riding a scarred and ill-tempered horse. Kyellan rode beside him. The city men and real S'tari warriors followed, and the five volunteer women trailed with Alaira and Briana disguised to match them.

Kyellan was startled by the apparent loyalty of the city for their ruling family. He could not imagine such a spontaneous display happening in Cavernon. Many of these people had watched Tobas grow up, the carefree younger son of a sober and respected Earl. They had seen his advancement in the Royal Guard with pride. They had suffered through the wizards' occupation, and when it was over Tobas was Earl and the Queen's consort. He brought honor to the city, and they hoped he would favor them in the economic councils of the court. Now that he was defeated, Kyellan would have expected the people to turn on him, Instead, they cheered him.

"We'll make for the Caravan Road," Tobas said as they finally left the crowds behind and crossed into the meadows south of Laenar. "It will look better if we come into Cavernon that way."

"You're probably right," Kyellan said, guiding his restless horse around a cairn of rocks that marked the edge of one farmer's rich land.

Tobas glanced at him, his boyish face looking even younger under the S'tari headcloth that framed it. "I didn't dare hope you'd be with me in this. When you left, I never thought you'd come back. You said there was nothing for you here."

Kyellan did not speak for a moment. "When I learned what had happened, I felt I had to do something. And Alaira wanted to return to Cavernon City."

"I hope she doesn't expect to stay there long," Tobas said dryly. "If Arel ever hears you're back in Caerlin, you'll join me on his list of traitors. Once we steal the Queen, if we succeed, we'll have to leave the country fast. My old advisor Istam has been in hiding in the city, and he's arranged us a ship."

"Where do you plan to go?"

"One of the island Kingdoms. Venerin or Hoab, I suppose. Their rulers weren't present at the Council of Royalty, so they aren't bound to support Arel. They may grant us sanctuary. They won't turn away a desperate woman with a child. I hope."

"How much time do we have, Tobas?" Kyellan said quietly. "When is Valahtia's baby due?"

"Today. Next week. Two weeks from now. It could be any time."

Any hour, Valahtia thought. It could begin any hour now. She was so tired of waiting. The midwife gave her tea which she said was meant to calm her, but Valahtia would not drink. She had not accepted any of the medicines and herbs she had been offered, for fear they were meant to kill her baby. Arel had taken her familiar attendants from her, and given her a quiet, stern midwife from the city who brought two silent helpers. They sat in the straight-backed chairs Briana had left in the tower room, watching Valahtia as if she were a pot about to boil.

Valahtia sat in her usual place at the window seat, staring out over her lost gardens, though they told her she should lie down and rest. She did not want to close her eyes. She did not dare sleep. She was so afraid. Arel had stopped assuring her that Werlinen would agree to take her baby to raise as his own. That must mean her intended bridegroom had refused. Which meant they would want to kill the child. But if she backed out of the marriage now, Arel had promised her he would have Tobas killed immediately. Even if she refused to marry Werlinen and let Tobas die, they would probably kill the baby. Dear Goddess.

She wished she could keep it from being born. They wanted it dead, but they wanted her alive. She was valuable to the state. A tool for cementing alliances, whether with Keris or some other Kingdom. If her baby would just stay inside her, it would live, and they would not force her to marry while she was pregnant. Slow tears trickled down her cheeks as she pressed her forehead to the window pane.

"Your Highness is exhausted," said the midwife coaxingly. "Come lie down and let me rub your back. You'll feel better, my lady. I promise."

Valahtia thought of Tobas in a cold, dark cell below the palace, hating her, knowing she had betrayed him. He would stay there until her marriage. Then Arel would have him moved to Khymer, if her brother kept his word. Once she was safely allied to Keris, Arel could afford to be magnanimous. She prayed he would not kill Tobas out of spite. It would be like him, to mock her sacrifice thus.

"Your Highness must preserve your strength," the voice went on as it had all day. "It won't be long now, if I'm any judge. You'll wish you had gotten some rest beforehand."

"Then give me a rest from your endless tongue," Valahtia snapped. "You weary me." The woman took a breath to protest, but thought better of it. Even though she was a prisoner, Valahtia was of royal blood. For the moment, the midwife would obey her wishes.

Chapter Twenty ─────────

IT was midwinter day when Briana and the others stopped at the crest of a hill on the Caravan Road to see the first high towers and minarets of Cavernon City rising up from the dawn mist. They had been riding for most of the last three days, resting in short stretches. Though they had started the journey in high spirits, now a grim and uneasy resolve had set in. It would be tonight. The ship was waiting to take Tobas and Valahtia if the attempt succeeded. The rest of the company would scatter back to Laenar or into the desert. But for now they were united.

Midwinter day. Briana shivered. Ocasta and the rest of the Temple would be busy. There were three high days in the Order's year. The first day of spring was sacred to the Maiden, and its rites were hopeful, supplicating Wiolai for a favorable year. Midsummer belonged to the Mother, when Cianya was thanked for the harvest. Midwinter day was when the third aspect of the Goddess was most powerful.

Most believers in the Goddess tried to ignore the existence of Her third aspect, Rahshaiya, the Death-Bringer. The priestesses knew She could not be overlooked. The rites of midwinter were meant to placate Rahshaiya, so that She would not seek too many lives in the months to come. There was a ritual of symbolic mourning for all who had died in the past year; the Last Cycle dance would be performed, which was a dance of death; the First Priestess would spend the day alone in the underground Temple of the Altar with a long, exhausting spell of invocation and pleading. Briana wondered if Ocasta would be capable of it.

"I never thought I'd see the city again," Alaira said quietly from her horse at Briana's side. "If we succeed in stealing the Queen, then I can probably never go back." She looked the part of a renegade S'tari. Her black hair was loose under a half-veil that allowed part of her scar to show on her cheek. Like Briana and the volunteer S'tari women, she wore a long, unsheathed dagger hanging from the belt of her rough white robe.

"Will you and Kyellan go with Tobas on the ship?" Briana asked. She wore a full headcloth and veil to hide her obviously Garithian features and auburn hair, but still she thought anyone who looked closely would see through her disguise. She had no skill in riding. She would have to stay in the middle of the S'tari women and Alaira, while the men rode ahead of them looking fierce and dangerous.

"Maybe. We might go to Dallynd. Haval would give Kyellan a good place in the Ryasan army. I guess we could be happy there," she said doubtfully.

Briana could not help feeling jealous of Alaira's fortune. The girl had no grand destiny to get in her way, nothing to come between her and Kyellan. She could go with him wherever he went, with no regrets for something given up for him. It was not fair.

"Kyellan will be our spokesman," Tobas called back along the column. "Consider him in command. And from now on, no one speaks unless it's in S'tari. The game becomes real, my friends. I hope the Goddess is with us."

Briana did not know. She truly did not know.

There were few other travelers on the road that day. Kyellan remembered there was a superstition about midwinter day being inauspicious for starting any enterprise. He had never paid it any heed, and he was not going to let it unnerve him now. He needed complete confidence to pull this off, as much as any wizard had ever needed for a spell.

It was Tobas's plan, and his Queen they were going to

rescue, but the boyish Earl of Laenar could never convince anyone he was a ruthless S'tari brigand chief. Kyellan laughed quietly at himself. He was almost enjoying this. It had been a long time since he had used his old soldier skills, since the clumsy battle aboard the *Jester* in Chelm harbor. And no matter how much Briana disliked violence, sometimes it was necessary. Whether it was pleasant or not, Kyellan knew he was good at it. He always had been.

The Caravan Road threaded through the outlying inns and shops, then south along the walls toward the southeastern gate. The walls of the city were strongest on the eastern approach. There had been intermittent threats of S'tari invasions for centuries. It was a slow morning at the gate, however. Three mercenaries on duty within the high arch were taking their time inspecting a farmer's cargo of poultry. At last they waved the cart through, telling its driver how to get to the livestock bazaar. Then they turned, and their faces hardened as Kyellan led his mounted band to the gate. Their hands went as one to their sword hilts.

Their captain was a dark-skinned Parahnese. "What's your business?" he said in fluent S'tari. "His Majesty does not welcome armed brigands in his city."

"Unless he's paying them himself," Kyellan said sardonically. "Or so my men and I have heard." He raised an arm to halt the company behind him. One of the young S'tari urged his horse up a few paces and goaded it to rear just before the wary mercenaries.

"If he can't hire us, why waste our time here?" the youth said with elaborate contempt. "Do these three think to stop us at the gate?"

Kyellan made a show of ignoring him. He gestured at the arched battlement above him. "This will be your first line of defense, when the war comes, Parahni. Your new King will need more men than that on the walls."

"What war do you mean?" said the mercenary captain sharply.

"The war with the S'tari, once the King revokes the treaty. And they say the old Queen's consort is gathering troops." Kyellan shrugged. "There is sure to be a war. My men and I want to be on the winning side."

"Against your own people?"

"Our people won't have us." Kyellan laughed harshly. "We broke the peace of the new treaty too often."

The mercenary's narrowed eyes took in the heavily armed men and their fierce-looking women. "All right. You look like you won't be afraid to fight. The quartermaster may want to put you on retainer until this war of yours starts. You'll find him in the War Ministry building below the palace. But I warn you, you'll keep the peace while you're in this city. The new King's justice is hard on troublemakers."

Kyellan saluted him lazily and put heels to his horse. The well-trained S'tari animal leaped past the guards, and the company of thirteen men and seven women followed in a tight formation. The mercenaries had to leap out of the way, and Kyellan heard angry curses behind them as they swung into the city streets that led toward the Tiranon.

"Why can't you find Istam with your Power, Priestess?" Alaira whispered. "The way you've said you can find the Queen tonight?"

Kyellan turned on his tavern bench to glare at her. "Quiet, Alaira."

"There's no one here to take any notice," she said sullenly. It was true. The small Rahan Quarter inn was nearly empty at midday. Most of its patrons had gone to bed at dawn, and would wake at dusk. Tobas and his company were at scattered tables, and the women sat together near the cold hearth, but the only other person in the room was the innkeeper. He was currently explaining in bad S'tari that all he had at this time of day was bread and ale; since he was speaking to three of the Laenar men, they did not understand him at all.

Briana did not seem angered by Alaira's question. Through her thick veil, she said, "Istam was once a Nyesin priest. They have their own disciplines of the mind. It isn't a form of Power, but it has the effect of a shield."

"I'm just tired of waiting," Alaira said in near apology. "Why hasn't he come? He said he'd meet us here."

"Give him time," Kyellan said. He called in S'tari for more ale, and the sleepy-looking innkeeper hurried over to fill his mug.

Istam did not appear until the late afternoon, when the business of the inn began to improve. Kyellan watched the door as various cutpurses and chance artists, entertainers and street girls wandered in to break their fast. He knew a few of them, but no one recognized him, beyond glancing his way and realizing he did not look like an easy mark. The fat old man he wanted finally filled the doorway, squinted into the gloom, and saw him and Tobas sitting together near the fire the innkeeper had just laid.

"You've lost weight, my friend," Tobas said in a low voice as Istam came to sit beside him. "Only two chins now instead of three."

"It isn't that amusing," his erstwhile advisor said dryly. "Not now that the King has the priestesses of the Temple helping him search for the people on his traitor list. I've had to change my lodgings three times. If you manage to get out of this alive tonight, I'm coming with you on that ship."

"We'll be glad to have you," Tobas said, troubled. "The priestesses? Should we be worried about them?"

"Not tonight," Briana said from the corner where she had been listening. "The rituals of midwinter will last almost until dawn. They'll be preoccupied."

"What's the news from the palace?" Kyellan asked quietly. "Have you been in contact with our people in Arel's court?"

Istam looked at him wearily. "Spies can be bought, and I'm afraid the King has ours firmly in hand now. Don't worry. I never let them in on this plan. I didn't need to. Arel let Senomar out of his dungeons after a week, when he needed some work on a collapsed section of the wall. He's found him too useful to lock away again."

Kyellan had wondered what had happened to the old battle engineer. "Then Senomar is our contact inside the palace?"

The old priest nodded. "He set men to working on rebuilding a low part of the eastern palace wall. No one will think it strange to see him there inspecting the work after dark. You'll be able to climb across, and from then on it will be up to you."

"After full dark, then?" Tobas said eagerly. "Good. Most of my men will be stationed along our escape route to guard the retreat. Can you have horses ready in the park, Istam?"

"In the grove behind the Ministry of War," Istam said. "That's arranged, my lord."

Kyellan leaned back against the stones of the hearth and sipped his ale thoughtfully. Assuming Briana could find Valahtia, all that left them to do was elude the palace guards and get out of the city again. It seemed simple enough. He sighed. It would be so much easier if he had the Power of the Shape-Changer to use. But if the wizard spirit controlled him again, he would not be involving himself in a foolish mission to rescue a woman from the awful fate of becoming Queen of Keris.

"The gods go with you," Istam said, rising ponderously to his feet. "I'll see you aboard the ship. It's the third one docked at the fourteenth pier. The best mooring I could manage, I'm afraid." He left their table. At the doorway, he looked furtively in each direction before venturing out into the uncrowded afternoon streets.

Tobas rocked his empty mug back and forth with nervous fingers. "We'll have men at our backs going there and on the way back, but inside the Tiranon it will be just you and me. Two men have a better chance of going unnoticed."

"I have to go," Briana reminded them. "I can't find her from here." Kyellan wondered why she was risking it at all. If they failed, she might lose her chance to challenge Ocasta. But he was glad she was going along.

"And you're not going to leave me behind," Alaira said fiercely.

Tobas shook his head. "I'm sorry. No. You can wait with Istam aboard the ship."

"And if you don't come back I'll never know what happened. I'm going along." She looked at Kyellan for support. "It won't be the first time I've sneaked into a guarded place to steal its treasure."

"She goes," Kyellan said after a moment's pause.

Tobas spoke quietly. "Who commands here, you or I?"

"I never put myself under anyone's command," Alaira said coolly. "The risk is all mine. I'll do nothing to hinder you, I promise you that. And I might even be useful."

Left no choice, Tobas agreed to take her, but Kyellan could see that he was angry. Once, Tobas had been glad to relinquish command to Kyellan, to leave the final decisions to him. That had changed when he became the Royal Consort. New responsibility had been given him, and with it more power than a junior captain of the Guard had had. And perhaps Tobas had simply grown older, into a man who wanted to shape his own destiny. Kyellan did not blame him for his anger. But he could have told him that Alaira had never been easy to command.

Darkness was never complete in Cavernon City. Lamps glowed in windows and hung from doorways; torchbearers lit the way for groups of noblemen seeking amusement and danger; wealthy houses blazed with light from a hundred candles in ballrooms and banquet halls. Night was never overwhelming here, never the thick gathering of shadows that met in blackness on the desert or in the forests of Garith. Only the sharp edges of the city were blurred. The ugliness vanished. The night was full of the potential for beauty, in the grace of a stone arch or the passing of a veiled woman. Kyellan had forgotten how much he loved it.

It was as dark as it would get as he and Tobas, Briana and Alaira walked quietly through a grove of sheltering trees toward the Tiranon. The parkland sloped gently upward at the main road, but on the eastern approach to the palace it was steeper. The land here was terraced for gardens and orchards; some flowers still bloomed in Cavernon on midwinter day. Above the climbing levels, the palace spread out atop the rise like a jeweled headdress, its walls and towers faced in white marble and glowing with colored lights. Kyellan did not know how anyone could prefer the dark towers of Northern fortresses. These walls were as strong, and much more graceful.

"Can you seek out Valahtia now?" Kyellan asked Briana as they neared the top. He could see the collapsed section of wall ahead, and a man was walking slowly at its top with a swaying lantern in his hand. He hoped it was Senomar. "Once we're inside, we won't have time to stop for you."

They were at the edge of the grove of trees. Fifty feet of trimmed lawn stood between them and the wall, planned so that enemies would have no cover. Kyellan was very glad there was no moat. The builders of the Tiranon had thought one would spoil the beauty of their design.

"We're far enough out of the city," Briana said. "There aren't as many people's minds to interfere with my search. Though that palace is a small city in itself." With a quick movement, she tucked her S'tari robe beneath her and knelt on the dry grass of the slope. She seemed immediately at peace, her eyes closed, her breathing deep and regular. Kyellan marveled at how quickly she had gone into her seeking trance. While he had been imprisoned by the Shape-Changer, he had learned much about the ways of Power. He knew that such ready control was rare, the mark of the highest adept.

"Senomar is waiting for us," Tobas whispered. His hand clenched and unclenched on the hilt of his sword. Both he and Kyellan had discarded their costume S'tari scimitars for rapiers. The mercenary disguise had been necessary to get them into the city, but now they wanted to be absolutely familiar with their weapons. "How long will this take her?"

"Would you rather just go in and search the dungeons and the towers for Valahtia?" Alaira said caustically. She was still stung by his reluctance to allow her to come along.

"That's what we would have had to do if Briana hadn't agreed to help." Kyellan put his arm around Alaira's shoulders. He knew that part of the reason she had insisted on going was so that he and Briana would not have a chance to be alone. It annoyed him a little, but it was also flattering.

"I'm glad she's here," Tobas said. "I don't mean to sound ungrateful. But I had a hard enough time waiting for darkness. I want to get Valahtia and leave. And I'm afraid it won't be that easy. What if Briana can't find her? She may not even be here. Arel might have moved her."

Kyellan had a different fear. He was afraid Valahtia would not want to go with them. She might not look forward to a life in exile. She had had a taste of being Queen, and she could have that power again with Werlinen of Keris. She might well have accepted his offer of marriage on her own initiative, not forced by her brother. The spoiled princess who had briefly been his lover would not have given up any chance to retain her position, no matter who was hurt by it. Kyellan was deeply afraid of what might happen if Tobas found himself betrayed.

Briana's breath had become harsh and strained, and her

hands had closed into white-knuckled fists in her lap. The calm, smooth lines of her entranced face shifted into agitation, though her eyes remained closed. Her lips writhed back, and she uttered a soft cry of pain. Kyellan let go of Alaira and knelt down beside the young priestess. No simple seeking spell should affect her this way. He grasped her shoulders. The muscles in them were rigid. "Briana!" he said sharply, keeping his voice low so he would not be heard on the Tiranon walls. "Briana, come out of it."

"What's the matter?" Alaira leaned over his shoulder, as Tobas looked nervously on.

Then Briana's body relaxed a little, and her breathing slowed. The pained lines lessened. She opened her eyes and looked into Kyellan's in bewilderment. "What . . . I . . ." Her gaze sharpened and she got suddenly to her feet, brushing off Kyellan's proffered aid. "Oh, dear Goddess. Tobas, I found her, but she was so frightened and hurting, at first I didn't know what it was. She's in labor. It's been going on for hours already."

"In labor?" The young Earl looked as if someone had struck him. "With our child?"

"Surely that means we can't go in after her," Alaira said.

Briana shook her head fiercely. "We have to. We have to get her out of there. I only brushed the surface of her thoughts, but it was enough. Valahtia is convinced they'll kill the baby as soon as it's born. And I don't see any reason for Arel to let it live."

"Can you find her now?" Kyellan asked.

"They put her in my old rooms, on the top floor of one of the north towers." Briana pointed toward one of the smaller minarets.

Senomar, if it was he, signaled again with his lantern. The veiled light swayed back and forth twice, and stilled. He waited on top of the ruined section of wall. "Let's go," Kyellan said, gripping Tobas's shoulder for a moment.

They edged out of the trees and hesitated to scan the nearest lengths of the crooked wall. Most guards patrolled above the main road, far out of sight; perhaps Senomar had managed to distract the others. No moving lights showed but his. Alaira and Briana sprang out like two slim deer, in white

robes, graceful and swift across the lawn. Kyellan and Tobas
followed. There was no sound but their rapid breathing and
the soft thuds of their footfalls on the grass. No alarms were
shouted, no arrows fired. In a few heartbeats they were
scrambling up the piled rocks of the wall.

Senomar had had his workmen form a near-perfect stairway
of marble-faced slabs. Briana and Alaira had to stretch to
reach each step, but Kyellan and Tobas climbed easily behind
them. The spare figure of the old soldier bent down at the top,
and Senomar reached a hand to each woman to help her onto
the demolished battlements. The wall had been reduced in
height from twelve feet to eight. Kyellan could see that little
work would be needed to restore it to its original form.

"My lord Earl," the old man whispered as Tobas joined
him. "I wish I could do more. I cannot even tell you where
they have the Queen."

"We know where she is," Tobas said. "You could not
have served me better, my friend. Thank you. If I'm ever in a
position to reward you with more than my thanks . . ."

"Quickly now," Senomar said, herding them with spread
arms toward the rough workmen's ladder that was propped
against the stones.

Kyellan saw lanterns moving in their direction on the battlements of the undamaged walls on either side. "Will you be
able to time our escape with the guards' patterns?" he murmured as he waited for the others to descend.

"I'll be waiting for you below." Senomar indicated a tool
shed that had been erected against the wall on the inside.
"But I warn you, getting out will not be as easy as getting in
has been. Wherever they have the Queen, she'll be well
guarded. You'll have to kill to get to her. You have to expect
pursuit."

Kyellan followed him down the unsteady ladder. The others waited in the shadow of the wall. "If we're pursued, you
may have to plan to go with us, Senomar. You can't let
yourself be caught here."

The engineer nodded gravely. "Istam has a horse waiting
for me with yours. The Goddess be with us all."

They left him sitting quietly in the shed. The way to
Briana's tower led through the royal gardens, where once

Kyellan had stopped a group of young fools from baiting Gwydion. The spreading trees were leafless now, and the grass yellowed, but the clear ponds and fountains sparkled as beautifully in winter as any other time. In their S'tari dress, the four companions slipped through the gardens like ghosts.

There were no lanterns in the trees or along the pathways, and no sounds of merrymaking from the feast hall. "No party tonight," Alaira said to Briana as they trailed Kyellan. Tobas had moved ahead in his impatience, not as careful as the rest of them.

Briana's voice sounded tense and nervous, but Kyellan supposed that was natural when they could expect to be discovered and killed at any moment. "No. It's midwinter day until the next dawn." She paused and went on in a voice Kyellan could scarcely hear. "It's considered an unlucky day for many things."

"And parties are one of them," Alaira said.

"Childbirth is another. Midwives will try to bring labor on quicker or slow it if they can to avoid the child being born today." Her worry was evident, even in her whispered words; Kyellan wondered at her belief in what he had always considered a foolish superstition.

Tobas turned back in their direction and held his finger to his lips. He dropped down out of sight behind a large stone fountain. Kyellan, Briana, and Alaira crouched down beside an ornamental hedge that had kept its leaves in winter. A small patrol of guards in red and black livery turned into the garden and started down the main path. There were six of them, or Kyellan would have been tempted to ambush them and take two uniforms.

As it was, he waited with the others until the guards were long past. The night seemed less friendly as they rose and continued on.

Arel had dropped any pretense of sympathy. He entered through the curtains despite the protest of his three chosen midwives, and stood for a moment scowling in distaste at Valahtia. She lay beneath blankets to keep out the chill from the open window, her glossy black hair unbound and cascading thickly over her pillow, her olive-skinned face a pasty hue and filmed with sweat. She tried to concentrate on the deep breaths the midwives required of her, furious at Arel's presence, but more frightened than angry. Her birth canal had been widening, and she could feel the unrelenting pressure as the child began its downward journey. He would be born soon. There was nothing she could do to stop it.

"What . . . are you . . . doing here," she gasped; then another contraction hit, and she could not keep back a thin moan. Earlier she had screamed, but her cries had weakened as she grew more and more tired. She imagined she would scream again before it was over.

"You mustn't try to speak, Your Highness," said the elder midwife soothingly.

The King was dressed in black for midwinter day. He had attended parts of the solemn ceremonies at the Temple to mourn the year's dead. To Valahtia, it was as if Death had come into the room with him. Arel looked down at his gloved hands, and spoke quietly. "I'm here to be certain that the compassion of women does not provide me with an unsuspected rival in twenty years' time. There are so many old tales where the command is given to eliminate a child, but the servants fail to carry out the orders, giving the baby to an obscure peasant to raise. Such children always grow up, find out who they are, and return. I can't risk that."

"Monster!" Valahtia shrieked with another rising wave of pain. "You are my brother! How can you do this!"

"If I were not your brother, I wouldn't have to do this," he said. "I'm truly sorry, Valahtia. But it is necessary. Haven't we both been taught since we were children that our lives belong to the state? This baby will simply have to give his up sooner. For the good of the Kingdom."

"For the good of the Kingdom? If you kill this child, the Kingdom will be without an heir," Valahtia said weakly, hopelessly.

"You're young and strong," her brother said obliviously. "You'll have many more children. You may even get to keep this one, if it's a girl. I would be satisfied if you promised to give her to the Temple when she was old enough."

The outer door creaked open beyond the curtains, and a guard's voice called, "There is a disturbance at the bottom of the stairs, Your Majesty. I heard shouting."

"Damned mercenaries are impossible to control," Arel muttered. "Another argument. Go down and investigate!" he yelled. "But leave two men at the door here."

"Yes, sire." The door slammed and the bolt fell back into place. Briana's suite had locked from the inside, but Arel had ordered his men to change that soon after Valahtia had been put here. She did not know why. There was no way she could escape anyway.

Alaira had gone first into the tower, her veil removed and her hair free at her shoulders. She knew how to move so that a man would look at her. The guards challenged her halfheartedly, and Kyellan heard Alaira giggle, a high-pitched, affected sound. That was their signal. He and Tobas hurtled through the half-closed door to see Alaira turn on the nearest guard of the three mercenaries and shove her S'tari dagger up below his rib cage. A big man, he doubled over and fell to his knees.

The other two guards drew their swords as Kyellan and Tobas lunged to meet them with a flurry of steel. The man Kyellan faced was a brown-haired Kerisian who wore a cuirass of beaten metal beneath his Caer livery. Kyellan's first blow went under the man's guard, but the sword bent back against the armor and Kyellan had to roll beneath the blade that swept down at him.

The guard had the presence of mind to shout for help in a booming voice as Kyellan closed with him again. The first story of the tower held only palace storerooms, Kyellan knew, so he was unsure if the call would get any results. Tobas played his man furiously, at the top of his form, driving him around the small bare room at the base of the stairs. Kyellan was more cautious with his, looking for an opening to strike somewhere the guard was not protected.

It had been so long since he had fought right-handed that he found his rhythm and balance hard to regain. The guard's blade touched him on the left side, a thin hot line against his ribs. Kyellan twisted and brought his sword up under the man's raised arm. Cloth gave way, then flesh, and the artery began to spew blood. The Kerisian staggered backward, shocked, and Kyellan lunged from above to drive his sword in at the base of the man's throat. He pulled the weapon out and turned to help Tobas before the mercenary fell.

Mercenaries provided their own armor, and Tobas's opponent was not as well equipped as Kyellan's had been. He had fallen with a clean thrust into the heart. Briana came out of the shadowed doorway where she had been standing silently. Kyellan felt the glow of success fade as he saw her tight, pain-filled expression. Alaira took Briana's arm as the two men dragged the three bodies into the space beneath the stairs. Together, they started upward at a steady trot, Tobas again in the lead, as eager as a groom.

A guard who was running down the stairs toward the source of the yelling pulled up wide-eyed on the second landing, staring at Tobas. It was obvious that he recognized him. He did not have a chance to speak or draw his sword before Tobas took him with the same thrust he had used before. The body tumbled forward and down the stairs, falling past Keyllan and the two women.

"We honor Rahshaiya on Her day," Briana said under her breath. Kyellan shivered at her tone. Yet she did not say any more, and they climbed higher.

The door that had been Briana's was guarded by two more mercenaries, wearing the colors of the King's private bodyguard. They were big men. Both were Caer. No doubt Arel had thought to ensure their loyalty by filling the ranks of his bodyguards with his countrymen. But when the shorter, black-haired guard saw Tobas, his expression was one of wonder, not anger. He stepped back quickly and threw down his sword. "My lord Earl!"

The other turned and lunged, but Tobas was already past him, lifting the bolt on the door. Kyellan swept the sword out of the guard's unprepared grip and pinned him in the right shoulder with one swift movement. The Caer's face went pale, and he looked stupidly at his wound before dropping to his knees.

"I'll keep him quiet," said their unexpected ally, moving forward to stand over his partner, scowling. "Hurry, my lords. I can hear her screaming in there. And he's there too, the King. They say he means to kill the child. I was loyal to him until I learned that, but you must believe me, I am with you now."

Kyellan grinned at the mercenary, but his smile was interrupted by a full-throated scream from within. Tobas had the door open. Briana and Alaira pushed past Kyellan and ran inside. He followed them.

All the windows were open, and some foolish attendant had let the fire go out. The room was chill. Tobas sprang across the barren floor to thrust the curtains aside with his sword. A frozen tableau inside stared at him. Three poorly dressed women surrounded the bed, and the curly-haired young King stood with them. Only Valahtia, beneath the disheveled blankets, still writhed and twisted and screamed, a sound that did not stop.

"Get away from her!" Tobas roared, lunging toward Arel. The King's surprise changed to fear as he ducked under the swinging blade and ran back through the curtains. Tobas followed him closely, his face no longer handsome in its hatred. Kyellan stepped back to let them pass him.

Briana cried out, "Stop them! Tobas will kill him." She moved toward them. Kyellan reached a hand to halt her, and on her other side Alaira did the same.

Arel had a moment to draw his sword, and now he found enough courage to meet Tobas's blade, though each time they clashed he was driven backward toward the open door. "You were fools to come here," he gasped, out of breath with fear and exertion. "You'll never leave again. My guards . . . Guards!" he cried, stumbling back through the doorway. No one came to his call.

"Your Majesty!" one of the midwives shouted over Valahtia's screams. "The baby!"

"Go to the Queen," Kyellan said, giving Briana a rough shove in that direction. "There's nothing you can do for Arel."

Alaira took Briana's hand, and the priestess hurried with her into the back room. Kyellan heard Briana raise her voice in command. She would be all right. If any of them survived this night. He got a better grip on his sword and went to follow Tobas and Arel.

Neither of them could be seen on the landing. Kyellan went to the edge of the stairs, but he could not see far down its twisting length. The wounded guard sat against the wall, and the other man had torn cloth from his ceremonial cloak to make a bandage for the guard's shoulder. "What happened?" Kyellan demanded, scarcely able to get the words out. "Where are they?"

"The King fell," the soldier said grimly. "And the Earl went after him. Whether or not Arel survived the fall, he's dead now."

The screaming stopped from the tower room, and in the dark silence that followed, the baby's sudden angry cry was sweet. And unexpected, Kyellan thought. No doubt the midwives had orders to smother it as soon as it was free from Valahtia. Kyellan leaned on his sword at the top of the stairs and waited for Tobas to return. He was very tired, and blood was spattered across his white S'tari robe. The scratch along his ribs stung fiercely. Briana had called him a servant of Rahshaiya long ago, he remembered. It seemed he still was. He thought the killings had been necessary . . . he had to think that . . . but what if it was not true?

"The King is dead," Tobas said in a low, strained voice as he climbed back up the long flight to where Kyellan waited.

"Long live the Queen," said the wounded mercenary on the floor philosophically.

"Did the fall kill him?" Kyellan asked softly, looking at his young friend's half-bewildered face. It was over, then. There would be no need for the ship that waited in the harbor, the third one on the fourteenth pier.

"If he had not fallen . . ." Tobas shook his head, sheathing his stained sword. "I would have killed him. It's . . . it's really strange, Ky. All these years of being a soldier, but this was different. I've never killed in hatred before."

"You didn't kill him," Kyellan reminded him, knowing it would not help Tobas's mood.

"I saw the whole thing," said the cynical man Kyellan had wounded. "They were talking like civilized men, and the King slipped on a stone and fell, poor man." He grinned painfully. "I could be convinced to say that to anyone who asks."

Alaira walked hesitantly out the door, a cautious smile on her face. "Is it over? Then take a look at this."

Briana stood behind her, a tiny form in her arms wrapped

in a blanket. The baby had curly black hair. It would look
like Tobas. "His name is Duarnan," Briana said quietly,
"and I have given him the Goddess's blessing to rule Caerlin."

"The Goddess's blessing?" Kyellan repeated as Tobas
took the infant with a look of wonder. "Briana, does that
mean anything? You aren't First Priestess."

"Yes, I am." Her sea-green eyes met his gaze challengingly. "I'm certain of it now. Ocasta has failed in the ritual to
placate Rahshaiya. I felt it happen, a moment ago. That
means she is not First Priestess, no matter whether she was
confirmed. She is not." She ran a hand up through her
tangled auburn hair, pushing back her S'tari headcloth, and
her voice became grim. "It also means that the next year may
be a time of death and burning, with Rahshaiya unsatisfied.
What you and Tobas have done here tonight will be only the
beginning." She turned back wearily into the tower rooms to
tend to Valahtia.

Tobas seemed not to have listened to her words. "My
son," he was saying in a whisper. "My son."

"It's over, isn't it?" Alaira said. Kyellan nodded. More
things than one were finished now. Arel was dead, though
they had not come here tonight meaning to kill him. And
Kyellan thought he had seen the death of Briana's love for
him in her cold green eyes when she spoke of Rahshaiya. She
would find a way to be acknowledged First Priestess. He
would help her if he could. There was no reason why he
should be unhappy, he thought, looking at the lovely young
woman whose face was turned up toward him. He held out
his arms, and Alaira laughed softly and pressed herself against
him. He held her tightly as Tobas cradled his son, and the
muted darkness of the midwinter night seeped in the open
windows.

THE BEST IN FANTASY

ANDRÉ NORTON

- [ ] 54738-1 THE CRYSTAL GRYPHON $2.95
  54739-X Canada $3.50

- [ ] 48558-1 FORERUNNER $2.75

- [ ] 54747-0 FORERUNNER: THE SECOND $2.95
  54748-9 VENTURE Canada $3.50

- [ ] 54736-5 GRYPHON'S EYRIE $2.95
  54737-3 (with A. C. Crispin) Canada $3.50

- [ ] 54732-2 HERE ABIDE MONSTERS $2.95
  54733-0 Canada $3.50

- [ ] 54743-8 HOUSE OF SHADOWS $2.95
  54744-6 (with Phyllis Miller) Canada $3.50

- [ ] 54740-3 MAGIC IN ITHKAR (edited by
  Andre Norton and Robert Adams) Trade $6.95
  54741-1 Canada $7.95

- [ ] 54745-4 MAGIC IN ITHKAR 2 (edited by
  Norton and Adams) Trade $6.95
  54746-2 Canada $7.95

- [ ] 54734-9 MAGIC IN ITHKAR 3 (edited by
  Norton and Adams) Trade $6.95
  54735-7 Canada $8.95

- [ ] 54727-6 MOON CALLED $2.95
  54728-4 Canada $3.50

- [ ] 54725-X WHEEL OF STARS $2.95
  54726-8 Canada $3.50

Buy them at your local bookstore or use this handy coupon:
Clip and mail this page with your order

TOR BOOKS—Reader Service Dept.
49 W. 24 Street, 9th Floor, New York, NY 10010

Please send me the book(s) I have checked above. I am enclosing
$_____ (please add $1.00 to cover postage and handling).
Send check or money order only—no cash or C.O.D.'s.

Mr./Mrs./Miss _____
Address _____
City _____ State/Zip _____
Please allow six weeks for delivery. Prices subject to change without notice.